KU-339-295

About the author

Christine Marion Fraser is one of Scotland's top selling authors with world-wide readership and translations into many foreign languages. Second youngest of a large family, she soon learned independence during childhood years spent in the post-war Govan district of Glasgow. At the age of ten she contracted a rare illness which landed her in a wheelchair and virtually ended her formal education. From early years, Christine had been an avid storyteller; her first novel *Rhanna* was published in 1978.

Christine Marion Fraser lives with her husband in an old Scottish manse on the shores of the Kyles of Bute, Argyllshire.

Praise for Christine Marion Fraser

'Christine Marion Fraser weaves an intriguing story in which the characters are alive against a spellbinding background'

Yorkshire Herald

'Fraser writes with a great depth of feeling and has the knack of making her characters come alive. She paints beautiful pictures of the countryside and their changing seasons'

Aberdeen Express

'Full-blooded romance, a strong, authentic setting'

Scotsman

'An author who has won a huge audience for her warm, absorbing tales of ordinary folk'

Annabel

'Christine Marion Fraser writes characters so real they almost leap out of the pages . . . you would swear she must have grown up with them'

Sun

Song of
Rhanna

Christine Marion Fraser

CORONET BOOKS
Hodder & Stoughton

First published in Great Britain in 1985 by Fontana
A division of HarperCollins *Publishers*

This edition published in 2001 by Hodder & Stoughton
A division of Hodder Headline
A Coronet Paperback

10 9 8 7 6 5 4 3 2 1

A CIP catalogue record for this title is available from the
British Library

ISBN 0 340 73392 6

Typeset by Palimpsest Book Production Limited,
Polmont, Stirlingshire
Printed and bound in Great Britain by
Mackays of Chatham plc, Chatham, Kent

Hodder & Stoughton
A division of Hodder Headline
338 Euston Road
London NW1 3BH

To Doreen, Ian and Karen. Lang May Yer Lum Reek

With grateful thanks to Doctor Bill Wilkie, Strone, for all
his friendly help and advice, and Doctor David Walker,
Kilmun, a real old country GP and a 'gentleman chust'

Abbey ruins

Dunuaigh

Cave

Croynach

Sgurr na Gill

Burnbreddie House

Sgurr nan Gabhar

Biddy's Cottage

Sgurr nan Ruadh

NIGG

Slochmhor

Dodie's House

R of RHANNA

Murdy's House

Kirkyard

Loch Tenee

Todd the Shod

Schoolhouse

PORTCULL

Sgor Creags

Cave

Port Rum Point

Ranald's Boats

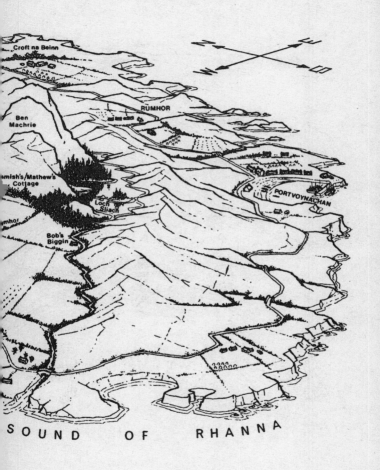

Croft na Beinn

RÙMHOR

Ben
Machrie

Hamish's/Mathew's
Cottage

Loch
Sliach

PORTVOYNACHAN

Rùmhor

Bob's
Biggin

SOUND   OF   RHANNA

Part One

Late Winter 1964

Chapter One

Ruth pegged the last of her washing on to the line and paused for a moment to listen to the wind keening low over the moor, whining eerily as it buffeted the amber grasses and whipped the gnarled heather stalks to a frenzy. Through a gap in the trees she could see the tiny basin of Loch Sliach lying huddled under the lower slopes of Ben Machrie, a splash of blue contrasting with the green of the pines, its surface slashed to white where it was caught by the capricious elements. The trees were swaying madly, their branches creaking as they bowed submissively to the whims of the Rhanna weather. The smoke from the sturdy stone cottage sitting in the lee of a grassy knoll, spiralled briefly against the blue sky before it was snatched off unceremoniously in the clutches of the breeze.

The wildness of the day made the interior of the house known as Fàilte, the Gaelic for Welcome, seem all the cosier, and Ruth looked round appreciatively as she went indoors. It was all so different from the clinical confines of the house in Portcull where she had lived with her parents before her marriage to Lorn McKenzie. Referred to as 'the Temple' by herself and her father it hadn't been so much a home as a carbolic-smelling prison, and she hadn't felt a single qualm on the day she turned her back on it. Her religious fanatic of a mother had made the Temple a hell instead of the haven Ruth had always longed for. It was different now, now that her mother was dead. Her father had painted and papered all the sterile-looking rooms, little by little erasing the coldness that had ruled his life, stamping it with his own personality which had been crushed for so long. Now he wrote and painted to his heart's content, cluttering the rooms with homeliness, with warmth.

As a young girl, Ruth had vowed to have a home of her own one day, a place that would be comfortable and warm: clean, but never too clean; an abode where it wasn't a crime to dream by the fire, to put your feet up on the range if you so desired. The Temple had always been a bustle of senseless activity, a useless wasting of energy that Ruth had always felt could be spent on better things.

Fàilte had always been an easy-going sort of house. In the day of Hamish, the big, good-natured Highlander who had been grieve at Laigmhor, it had bulged at the seams with homeliness, with dogs and cats lounging by the fire, with hens poking in the scullery. Matthew and his wife Tina had succeeded Hamish and they had carried on the easygoing tradition so that it seemed the house in some way attracted people of a certain type. Generations of cats had come and gone, now a new generation were arranged decoratively by the polished range, and a retired sheepdog with one eye good-naturedly allowed itself to be dressed as a baby, much to the delight of three-year-old Lorna Morag who was making full use of the pile of baby clothes her mother had given her for her dolls. The little girl played contentedly on the rug, her hair shining in the light from the window, her smooth cheeks fire-flushed, her whole being absorbed in the task of fastening the ties of a woolly bonnet under Ben's thick white ruff.

In the playpen in a corner of the room, eighteen-month-old Douglas Lorn McKenzie had rolled up his vest and with great interest was contemplating his little mound of a belly, chuckling with fiendish glee as he dug a fat, exploratory finger into the whorls of his navel. Distracted by a full bladder he sat back and frowned at the empty chamber pot placed invitingly by his side. Throwing his mother a wide-eyed cherubic glance he spat bubbles, crowed with the sly knowledge that he was master of his own small domain, and filled his nappy. With a screech of wicked triumph he seized the pot and jammed it firmly over his mop of curly hair, trying to see how much of his nose and mouth he could fit into the handle.

Ruth glanced at the clock which told her it was almost midday. Lorn would be in soon for his dinner and a small stab of pleasure went through her at the thought. Much as she enjoyed the quiet morning routine of her home, she always looked forward to the dinner-time break with Lorn, enjoying hearing him talk about his work at Laigmhor, most of all enjoying his reassuring presence in her life. She set the pan of potatoes on the fire then went through to the pantry to fetch the bacon. Soon it was sputtering in the pan, the edges crisping to a deep golden brown. A frazzle of smoky fat bubbles exploded to release a tantalizing aroma which filled the kitchen and made Douglas forget about the chamber pot, his attention turning to the table and the activities around it. Lorna had risen from her corner and had fetched knives and forks from the sideboard which she clattered on to the table without ceremony. Clambering up on a chair she set about making an attempt to lay the table, a little task she had lately taken upon herself, growing quite annoyed if her mother intervened, even if only to show her how to properly position the utensils.

Left alone, Ben took the opportunity to slither under the couch where he sighed deeply and set about worrying the buttons of the yellow cardigan fastened over his hairy chest. Lorna's tongue was sticking out from the corner of her mouth in utmost concentration and Ruth had to hide a smile. At almost three years old the child was adorable, an entrancing mixture of baby habits and a small girl's awareness of the bigger, more intriguing world which awaited her.

'One, two, free,' solemnly she counted the places, making sure her father got his own special fork, a big one which Ruth laughingly told him would be better suited for use in the garden. Douglas let out a bored wail from his playpen, a strength in his voice that promised greater things to come. Ruth turned from the fire and made to go to him but Lorna had beaten her to it, with a patient, elderly sigh abandoning the table to go to her baby brother and punch a furry toy dog at his nose. He squealed in delight, a row of pearly teeth showing between his laughing rosy lips. Looking to the window for a sign of Lorn, Ruth saw instead the red post van hurtling along the bumpy road to the cottage. A few minutes later, Erchy popped his balding, sandy head round the door and sniffed the air appreciatively.

'My, my, that is indeed a smell to tempt the appetite of a hungry man. It will be a whily before I get my own dinner,' he hinted gently.

'Sit you down and I'll get you a cuppy,' Ruth invited hospitably. Within a short space of time a steaming cup of tea reposed at Erchy's elbow together with a plate bearing thick doorsteps of buttery bread filled with piping hot, crispy bacon.

Erchy bit into it with relish, wiping away the rivulet of melted butter on his chin with a stubby finger. 'You're a grand wee cook, Ruth,' he said with conviction. 'Lorn is a lucky mannie indeed. I could have done fine wi' a wife like you when I was younger. Now I wouldny know what to do wi' one, a man gets gey set in his ways after the age of sixty.'

Ruth held on to her patience. Erchy was renowned for his enjoyment of a nice cosy gossip at each of the houses he had reason to visit, and took his time in handing over the mail. She eyed his satchel, wondering what was in it for her, but Erchy was too busy blethering to notice her look. Lorna was perched comfortably on his knee, her eyes following every bite he took while she played with the buttons of his jacket, Douglas screeched from his corner, demanding a share of the attention.

Ruth busied herself at the fire, saying over her shoulder, 'Didn't you ever think about getting yourself wed, Erchy? Surely you must have had a favourite girl in your day.'

Erchy's face took on a bemused look. 'Oh ay, and no' just one, I might no' be much to look at now but there was a time when I was a fine figure o' a lad.' He puffed out his chest. 'I will never know how I managed to escape all those women who were aye chasin' me but now I'm thinkin' I managed it maybe a mite too successfully. There was one lass I had my eye on for years but . . .' He stopped, abashed, and Ruth turned a quizzical gaze on him.

'And who was that, Erchy McKay?'

Erchy wriggled uncomfortably, an unusual flush spreading over his smooth-skinned face. 'Ach, it was a long time ago, I forget her very name now.'

Ruth's dimples deepened. 'Get away wi' you, fine I know you're lying. Tell me this minute. I won't let you out of the house till you do.'

Erchy's face was now bright red with embarrassment. 'Ach, women! You are all alike. Prying into the very corners of a man's heart. If you must know, it was Morag Ruadh – your mother – ay, she was a bonny, bonny lass in her day and could have got any man if she had played her cards right. But that tongue o' hers was sharper than a kitten's claws, she just scared the breeks off all the men so that in time none o' them would ask her out for fear she would hack them to ribbons wi' a few choice words.'

Ruth's eyes grew dark. Could it really be her mother that Erchy spoke of with such fondness, Morag of the red hair and the fiery temper to match? To Ruth, her mother had always seemed middle-aged and entirely set in her ways. She couldn't imagine a young Morag, fresh faced, attractive to men, yet when she had smiled in a certain way Ruth had glimpsed an echo of the girl she had once been, a girl who had been bonny enough to make men like Erchy remember her with blushing affection.

'Strange,' murmured Ruth almost to herself. 'I never thought of what she must have been like as a young girl.'

'Oh, she had looks all right,' Erchy hastened to assure her. 'No' bonny in the usual way but a sparkle about her if you know what I mean. Those green eyes o' hers, big and bright, and that red hair – like a beacon it was, shining in the light o' day. I could aye tell Morag, even from a distance – ay – she was an attractive one – pity she went queer in the head but I don't mind tellin' you I shed a wee tear to myself on the day she died. She was part o' the old days you see, lass,' he ended apologetically, fearing he had said too much.

But Ruth smiled at him, an expression of gratitude showing in her eyes. 'I'm glad you told me, Erchy. It's nice to know there were some who wept when she died. I often used to feel sad thinking no one ever really liked Mam. She brought it on herself but it was sad just the same.'

Erchy ran his fingers through his sparse locks and pushed back his chair. 'Ay, it was that, too much religion makes some folks go daft altogether.' He threw Ruth a sly smile. 'At least she brought a daughter into the world she could be proud of. God, lassie, little did I know when you used to sit beside me in my post van you would grow up to be a famous writer.'

'Ach, not that famous,' protested Ruth, flushing. 'Only the folks round here know that I have some stories published.'

'Indeed, that's where you are wrong, mo ghaoil. Some English towrists who were on the island last summer asked me where the writer lassie lived. They had read all your stuff and wanted to have a wee peep at you. I didny tell them though for I know fine you like to be private but it lets you see you are more famous than you think. Shona was telling me some whily back that you were writing one o' they big novel books. Are you after finishing it at all?'

Ruth made a dive to rescue Douglas who was in the act of slithering down the sides of his playpen, head first. 'With these two at my apron strings! No, Erchy, it will be a whily yet before I get to finish my book.'

Erchy swung his satchel over his shoulder. 'Ach well, it will be something for us all to look forward to.' He opened the door and the March wind whistled in through his legs. 'God! Would you listen to the sough in that breeze!' he exclaimed. 'Shona was just after saying that the roof o' her hen hoosie was blown off last night.'

'Erchy,' Ruth began anxiously. He came back into the room, closing the door behind him.

'Talking of Shona,' he grinned. 'I maybe shouldny tell you this for she'll want to be tellin' it herself . . .' He paused cryptically and Ruth, curiosity getting the better of her, cried in exasperation, 'Tell me what, Erchy?'

'Well, I took a letter to her – I couldny help seein' it was from one o' they foreign places, it had a real fancy stamp on it. She was gey excited by the look o' it and tore it open there and then, and I couldny very well go away till I found out what it was all about. I'm no' a nosy body as a rule but I canny help but be excited by letters from other countries – even though they might no' be addressed to me . . .'

'Erchy!' Ruth cried in desperation and with a chuckle Erchy relented.

'Well, as I was sayin', she tore it open and began laughing in that way she has and then she grabbed me and whirled me round till my head was birlin'. She might even have kissed me she was that happy but I slithered out o' her reach in the nick o' time – no' that I wouldny mind a kiss off Shona, she has lips on her to tempt any man but I was feart Niall might get to know about it and think – ay, all right, all right. My, you're an impatient wee wittrock – and just remember, I haveny told you anything for I wouldny like her to think . . .'

'You *haven't* told me anything!' yelled Ruth, all her reserve dissipating in sheer frustration.

Erchy threw back his head and laughed. 'Ach, don't foul

your breeks and listen to this. The letter was from Grant telling his sister there is going to be a wee one. Shona was as excited as if it was herself going to have it.'

'And to think Fiona always vowed never to have bairns,' laughed Ruth.

Erchy shook his head wisely. 'There's many a slip between the boat and the jetty if you see what I mean. No doubt Shona will tell you all the facts herself for I know only too well how women enjoy a good blether.'

'Women enjoy blethering! Erchy McKay, your tongue clacks faster than any woman I know,' Ruth scolded, though her face was wreathed in smiles. 'And though Shona might confide the facts to me I have no doubt you will have found out every single one before the week is out.'

Erchy's grin was unrepentant. 'Oh ay, I admit I make it my business to find out about other folks – after all – a lonely mannie like myself has to have something to keep him going.'

The wind rushed in as once more he opened the door. Ruth let him get halfway down the path and was about to shout on him when he turned abruptly and came back to push two letters into her hand. 'One of them is for Lorn – from his brother – I recognize the stamp,' he said without a blush. 'The other is for you – from Rachel. I can aye tell her letters, usually the fancy postmark, though this one is from Glasgow, I know her writing well enough by now. You see the way she strokes her t's? So high up it just about flies off the paper? Behag was after tellin' me that is the sign o' a very ambitious person. She read an article about handwriting in one o' they wimmen's papers she aye pretends no' to read.'

He went on his way on a somewhat breathless but tuneful whistle leaving Ruth to wander back into the kitchen clutching her mail. Propping Lorn's on the mantelpiece, she turned her attention to her own, savouring all that was on the envelope, the postmark, the date of posting, the tiny R which Rachel used to personalize mail to her and which had always eluded even Erchy's eagle eyes. She wondered if she would have time to read it and really savour the contents before Lorn arrived home, then with an unusually impatient gesture she slit the envelope and sank down on a chair by the fire. Rachel's name as a solo violinist was becoming widely known, though the very island from which she had sprung was the last place to hear much about her successes with everyone tending to rely on what was passed by word of mouth.

Through regular correspondence Ruth had followed her friend's career, a pride glowing in her as she read accounts of concerts all over Britain and Europe, a wonder in her when Rachel had written to tell her that she had signed contracts with recording companies, the resulting records selling worldwide. She had made recordings with the London Symphony Orchestra, played the Beethoven Violin Concerto with the Radio Frankfurt Symphony Orchestra, recorded with the Orchestre National in Paris, and had also done concerts with them. Her husband, Jon, had given up his musical teaching to be her manager, travelling everywhere with his young wife. To Ruth it was like a fairy tale and she never tired of hearing about her friend's exciting life. Yet, though Jon and Rachel had a fine house in Salzburg in Austria, Ruth could always detect a hint of homesickness in almost every letter Rachel wrote. At the moment she was in Glasgow recording a concert for the BBC. Her name had recently been in all the papers, hailing her as a young Scottish virtuoso. Yet her letter gave hardly a mention of these latest happenings. It lacked sparkle. The big, sprawling, untidy writing filled the pages, yet said little of importance. Towards the end Rachel mentioned how exhausted she was. Jon had flown home to Germany to be with his aged and ailing mother.

'I have almost finished my commitments here,' Rachel wrote. 'Before Jon left he urged me to go home to Rhanna for a long holiday. You've no idea how I long to get home, Ruth, so I am taking Jon's advice. He will join me as soon as his mother is able to be left. I will be arriving about Easter and wondered if you could book me in at the hotel. I know there isn't enough room to swing a cat but I will put up with anything so long as I am home. It's a quiet enough place – except when the bar opens and my Grandpa Tam and his cronies come in to prop it up. Kate, my gran, would let me stay with her, I know; but now that she has old Joe to look after she has enough to contend with. Forbye that, she never stops talking and I think I would end up deaf as well as dumb! I want to be really quiet for a while with only the sound of the sea in my lugs so the hotel it is. When Jon comes we'll go and stay with Babbie and Anton for a while. I don't want to go there on my own because they are both out all day and, while I want to be quiet I don't want to be exactly buried. I'll have to be here for a week or two yet and then I'm free! Free! Free! I'll drop you a note nearer the time to let you know the time of my boat. It's funny, but I don't think I would feel right coming back to Rhanna and your bonny face not at the harbour to greet me. My love to Lorna and Douglas and my regards to Lorn.

Yours as ever, Rachel.'

Ruth folded the letter and put it into her apron pocket, a frown creasing her smooth brow. It seemed wrong somehow for Rachel to be staying in the Portcull Hotel when she had her mother's house to go to. Yet Ruth knew only too well that Rachel's mother had never gone out of her way to make her daughter feel welcome at home. Oh, she was proud enough of her talented eldest child, but she had never understood her or gone out of her way to even try, and things hadn't been made easier since her marriage to big, strapping Torquill Andrew. Rachel had made it quite plain that he would never take her adored father's place. Both Annie and Torquill were well aware of the fact with the result that relations between the three were always somewhat strained.

Ruth gazed thoughtfully into the fire, her curtain of fine flaxen hair falling over her face. A surge of excitement grew inside her. Supposing – supposing she were to ask Rachel to stay with her? It would be lovely to have someone her own age about the place and there was a spare room at Fàilte, a tiny room to be sure, situated off the parlour to the front of the house, but Rachel would have plenty of privacy there and all the peace and quiet she could ever want.

The idea grew in her, making her heart beat a little faster as her mind went racing ahead, forming joyous plans. She saw herself, walking with Rachel over the moors or down by the sea, talking in that uninhibited way she had always talked with Rachel, confiding in her as she had confided in no other, with the exception of Lorn and her father. In her mind she became a child again, the years rolled away and she saw herself with her friend, her fair head against the other's raven curls, whispering, laughing, the wind tossing their cheeks to roses, wrapping their skirts about their legs. In her mind picture she wasn't wearing a caliper because somehow the exhilaration of Rachel's company had always made her forget the ugly leg brace she'd had to wear from infancy, made her forget too that her friend couldn't communicate with words.

With her there was freedom too, the kind of wild, glorious abandoned freedom that went hand in hand with a girl who looked like an untamed gypsy, whose long brown, graceful limbs had never been fettered by stockings or shoes when she was a child. Always, whenever Ruth thought of her, she saw her as she had been, running barefoot over the moors, splashing in the warm, sunlit summer seas . . .

'Favver!'

Lorna's joyful cry broke rudely into her thoughts. With a start she came back to reality to hear the harsh puttering of the tractor as it trundled up the track.

'The tatties!' She jumped up to remove the heavy pan from the fire, scalding her fingers on the lid which slipped from her grasp to clatter on to the hearth. 'Oh – bugger it!' she muttered under her breath but was relieved to find that she had rescued the potatoes before the water boiled away.

'Swearing in front o' the bairns.' Lorn came in, striding over to kiss her hot cheek and squeeze her round the waist.

'Lorn, be careful,' she protested. 'This pan is heavy and if you go on like that I'll drop it on your toes.'

He took the pan from her and set it firmly on the range. 'Is that any way to greet a hard-working husband? All morning I've been looking forward to coming home to my bonny sweet-tempered wife and my angelic bairns – and what do I find? A wife with a de'il in her eye and a son who's filled his breeks from the look of the bulge at his backside – even poor old Ben canny make up his mind whether to come and welcome me or stay where he is for fear of being molested again.' He bent to pick up Lorna and swing her high in the air. 'This is the only decent human being in sight – aren't you, my bonny wee lamb? Have you got a kiss for your tired and hungry daddy?'

Ruth pushed back her hair and looked at him silhouetted against the window, Lorna's rosy delighted face just inches from his. His powerful body seemed to fill the kitchen; the masculine aura of him filled her senses. Sometimes she couldn't believe that Lorn McKenzie was hers: strong, silent Lorn who had filled her life with love and happiness for four years now. He had matured a lot since those early days as her husband, yet at heart he was still the boy who had almost drowned in his own shyness the night he took her to her first dance at Burnbreddie House. Nowadays though, he was more able to hide his feelings, so that very often she didn't know what was going on behind those deep dark eyes of his. His head was thrown back, the light caught the auburn glints in his hair, played on the boyish planes of his deeply tanned face, lingered tantalizingly on the wide, sensual contours of his mouth.

Douglas bounced on chubby legs and gnawed the rail of his playpen; Ben peeped out from under the couch, the frilly bonnet tilted rakishly over one eye; Bramble, a big black and white tom, sat on one of the chairs at the table, his huge green orbs gently panning over the jug of milk set temptingly close to his whiskers.

Ruth gave a peal of delighted laughter. Oh, it was good, so very good to be Mrs Lorn McKenzie, to have children that drove her to distraction one minute and to pinnacles of joy the next; to live in this cosy homely cottage with a man who often infuriated her, but more often delighted her.

He threw her a responsive grin and went to the sink to wash, Lorna dancing attendance at his side, passing him the soap, toddling to fetch a dry towel.

A few minutes later Douglas was changed and sitting in the little baby chair his father had first made for Lorna. The seat was closed in on all sides with a fitted tray at the front and castors screwed at the bottom so that it could be pushed where it would. The little boy banged his spoon on the tray and Lorn ruffled his hair, so fair it was almost white. Lorn leaned his elbows on the table and looked at his wife. 'Nice family we have here, Mrs McKenzie.'

'Ay,' she agreed softly, 'very nice, Mr McKenzie.' She fingered the letter in her pocket. Lorn would never agree to have Rachel stay with them. He had resented her since her rejection of Lewis, the twin brother who had meant the world to him and who had died tragically when he was just eighteen. Lorna was Lewis' daughter, conceived in those troubled days when he hadn't had long to live and had turned to Ruth for comfort. In the beginning he had loved Rachel, but she had had her career to think about and had gone away from the island, not knowing how desperately ill Lewis was. Ruth had been there when he had needed love so badly and little Lorna had been the result of that strange, unreal, tempestuous affair. Lorn had married Ruth, had given his brother's child a name and a secure start in life – yet Ruth knew that he blamed Rachel for all that had happened. Ruth sighed softly to herself. She realized that he had good reason to feel as he did – yet – it was all in the past now – it was time to forgive and forget, life was too short, too sweet for such bitterness.

'I got a letter from Rachel this morning,' she hazarded somewhat defensively.

He looked up, his blue eyes smouldering with a strange resentment as he said heavily, 'She never lets go, does she? Yet she was quick enough to ditch Lewis when it suited her. And how is our brilliant prodigy? Still hopping around Europe with poor old Jon tagging at her heels?'

'No, she's in Glasgow,' Ruth answered quietly. 'She wants to come home to Rhanna for a rest.'

He lowered his head and went on eating. 'The wanderer returns, eh?' His lilting voice was heavy with sarcasm. 'Well, I'm sure Annie and Torquill will put out the flags – after all it must be – how many years since her last visit?'

Ruth kept her voice level. 'The year Mam died and Shona lost wee Ellie.'

'Oh well, easy come, easy go.' His tones were flippant. 'I canny understand why she bothers to come back at all. After all, she has the world at her feet: why make the effort to come back here when she has made her life elsewhere?'

'Because she was born here, that's why,' Ruth couldn't keep a note of anger out of her voice. 'Rhanna is in her blood and no doubt it will be till the day she dies.'

He glanced up and she saw that he was smiling. 'Ay, of course it is,' he said quietly. 'I was only teasing you: you never could stand me saying a word against Rachel, could you? For your sake I'm pleased she's coming back. There was always something between you and her that was good and strong. You were always able to see the best in her and always quick to forgive her for anything she did – even though you knew that her ambitions took first place to everything – even people. She has a hard streak in her, Rachel, while you're as soft as butter. Maybe it's a good mixture, it saw the pair o' you over a few hurdles. I hope it will always be like that.'

'Oh, it will,' she said with assurance. 'And Rachel isn't hard, not in the way you think, she cares about things far more than you'll ever know. Mostly folks only see what they call her hard side, but I've seen the other and it's truly good and beautiful.' She subsided, content enough for the moment to know that she had broken the ice and had got him talking about Rachel. Her eye alighted on the letter propped on the mantelpiece. 'Oh, I nearly forgot, Erchy brought you a letter as well. It's from Grant and I know what's in it, but will let you read the news for yourself.'

Lorn took the proffered envelope and tore it open eagerly, his face lighting as he devoured the hastily written scrawl. 'Bugger me! He's done it at last – and Fiona vowed she would never have bairnies. Well, they'll have to settle on dry land now. Much as Grant would like it they won't be able to bring up a family on the high seas.'

'Shona got a letter too – no doubt so did your father and Lachlan and Phebie.'

Lorn put the letter on the table and sat back. 'Father was going over to Shona's at dinner time so he'll know he's to be a grandfather again. Wait till I see Mother, she'll be over the moon, I know fine she's hankered for years to have her eldest son about her skirts. If they decide to come back here to settle she'll go daft with happiness.'

In the excitement over family discussions Rachel was forgotten, but after Lorn had driven away in the tractor Ruth read her letter again and when she had cleared the table and washed the dishes, she bundled the children into outdoor clothes and walked with them over the shorn winter fields to Mo Dhachaidh, Rachel's letter tucked into the pocket of her coat.

Chapter Two

A blue banner of smoke was pouring from the chimney of the sturdy stone house in Glen Fallan, tossing hither and thither in the wind sweeping down through the narrow funnel of Downie's Pass. In the neat garden a few early daffodils were swaying, their yellow trumpets rising above clumps of snowdrops and crocus; in a walled-off enclosure at the side of the house a tiny girl with fluffy fair hair was playing with a spaniel puppy, her shrieks of laughter ringing merrily in the air. She was Ellie Dawn McLachlan, all of nineteen months old, small, neat, her rosy face aglow with health and happiness.

Ruth looked at her daughter. 'Are you coming in with me or would you rather stay out here and play with wee Ellie?'

'Stay with Ellie,' Lorna's tones were decided. 'I'll look after her and Douglas.' Seizing her little brother by the hand, she led him through the gate where they were both received ecstatically by Ellie and the puppy.

The smell inside Mo Dhachaidh was a concoction of disinfectant and medication from the surgery where Niall saw to the ails of the island pets, and a mingling of new-baked bread from the kitchen. Shona was in the surgery, wiping it down energetically with carbolic, a smell which evoked a certain revulsion in Ruth as it reminded her so much of the antiseptic confines of the Temple during her mother's day. An assortment of brushes and other cleaning utensils were arrayed round the cheerful little waiting room at the back of the house, proof that Shona had been busy there too. She was oblivious to Ruth's arrival, immersed as she was in scrubbing the table, a gay tune tumbling from her lips. Every so often she paused in her task and bent to speak soothingly to a cat and two dogs who, ensconced in wire cages, were recovering from recent surgery. Some time ago she had thrown years of caution to the winds and had taken to 'wearing the trowser', her abandon due in part to her sister-in-law Fiona who had used every opportunity to press her into 'going modern'. On her last visit home Fiona had brought back two pairs of smart slacks which she had presented to Shona.

'They cost me a small fortune,' she had said severely, 'and if I find you've shoved them to the back of a drawer I'll – I'll choke you with them.'

'Ach to hell,' Shona had giggled with devilment. 'Of course I'll wear them and make all the purple-legged cailleachs so green with envy they'll be red in the face talking about me to prove they're not jealous, if you see what I mean.'

'Very colourful people,' Fiona had commented dryly and they had both erupted into gales of laughter.

Thanks to years of restriction imposed on her by her mother, Ruth wouldn't entertain the idea of wearing trousers, though she often looked at Shona with envy and wished she had the courage to throw off her conventions. Most of the younger women on the island were 'covering their legs' as the menfolk mournfully put it, and Ruth studied Shona for the umpteenth time and wondered if she would look as good as the older woman if she could pluck up the courage to dress like her. Slender in her dark slacks and yellow jersey, a wisp of yellow scarf holding back her tumble of auburn hair, Shona could have passed for thirty instead of the forty-one she was. Ruth watched her, struck by her abundant energy, by her exuberance, her enthusiasm. Yet she had suffered a lot of tragedy in her life. Little more than two and a half years had passed since the death of her beloved daughter, Ellie, just thirteen years old with all her life in front of her. Shona had suffered a nervous breakdown and in the trauma of that dreadful time she and Niall had been on the verge of drifting apart. Then, to everyone's joy, Ellie Dawn had arrived on the scene, giving back to her parents so much that they had lost.

Ruth smiled with affection at Shona's oblivious back and coming forward into the room she said severely, 'Shona McLachlan! Are you deaf? I've been standing here for ages watching you steaming ahead like an express train.'

Shona turned a sparkling face. 'Ruth! I didn't hear you come in. Did you hear about Grant and Fiona? Ach, of course you did! No doubt that gossiping Erchy will have told half the island by now. It's lovely, isn't it, to think there's going to be another bairn in the family? I can hardly wait to see that pair to tease them about it. After all the talk about careers coming before everything.'

During this discourse she had swept Ruth into the kitchen where she flopped herself down on a battered but comfortable rocking chair which she had inherited from Biddy, the old nurse who had previously owned the house. 'Will you take a strupak with me?' she inquired rather breathlessly. 'I could be doing with a good hot brew. I started in the surgery this morning and I had to try and finish it before Niall gets back from Kintyre tonight. My throat is parched with all those antiseptic fumes so I'll make a good big pot and then spend the rest of the day running to the wee hoosie. Is Ellie all right out there? She girned all morning to get out to play with Sporran and in the end I gave in if only to get them from under my feet for a whily.'

'Oh, she's as happy as a wee lintie out there and has lungs on her as good as your own. She shrieked louder than the wind itself when she saw my two so I popped them in beside her and now they're all shrieking together – even the puppy.'

Shona lay back and groaned. 'That dog! I mind fine when Hamish gave me Tot and poor Nancy seemed to do nothing but slide about the kitchen in platters and piddles. At the time I never gave it much thought but now I've to clean up after Sporran I feel as Nancy must have felt – like packing her up and sending her back from whence she came.'

'Burnbreddie wouldny thank you for that. If I mind right he let Niall have the pick of the litter.'

'Only because he saved the bitch's life when she was in labour.' Shona's blue eyes grew dreamy. 'Ach, I wouldny part with the wee rascal. She's so like dear old Tot as a pup. Sometimes I look at her lying with her nose up the lum and I imagine I'm a wee lass again in the kitchen at Laigmhor, Tot snoring on the rug, Mirabelle rocking herself by the fire knitting, her old hands never still.' She sighed and looked at Ruth. 'They were such happy days – the days of childhood – don't you feel that?'

Ruth looked pensive and didn't answer. Shona groaned. 'They weren't for you. I'm sorry, Ruth, I always did put my foot in it. Father aye said my blethers carried me away.'

'It wasn't all bad,' Ruth said hastily, her fingers curling absently into Woody's thick fur as he lay purring on her knee. 'I had some good times with Father and Rachel was always there to make me forget Mam and the Temple – even my limp, it never seemed as bad when we were out walking over the moors.' She took the letter from her pocket. 'I got this from Rachel this morning – Erchy brought it together with some juicy bits of gossip concerning the McKenzies.'

Shona laughed. 'Good, you can tell me what it says over a cuppy.' She made to jump up but Ruth pushed her back.

'Sit you down, I'll make it, you've done enough for one day.'

'Ach, Ruth.' Shona pushed her fingers through her hair, in the process removing the scarf and allowing the mass of rich tresses to cascade about her glowing face. 'I know you're just a bairn compared to me, but it doesn't give you the right to treat me like an ancient cailleach.'

Ruth held the kettle under the tap and raised her voice above the sound of the running water. 'Hardly that! No wonder men look at you — I've even seen the minister at it, though he doesny do it in an obvious way like the others.'

She turned and was surprised to see that Shona's face had flamed to red. 'You're blushing!' she accused teasingly. 'Don't tell me you admire Mr James as much as he seems to admire you?'

But Shona did not discount what Ruth had thought was an amusing question, instead she said in a low voice, 'He's a very attractive man, Ruth. When I was so strange and horrible after Ellie died, Mark James was the only one who was able to reach through the ugly shell I'd built round myself and touch the real me I was keeping buried. I had always felt warmth for him but at that time I felt something more. I've never told this to anyone else and I don't know why I've just told you — it just seemed to come out.'

'But — but — you love Niall!' Ruth burst out, shock showing on her young face.

Shona nodded. 'It's because I love Niall so deeply that

nothing happened to spoil our love – yet – for a long time afterwards I felt guilty because for one weak moment in my life I actually had feelings for another man. But remember this, Ruth; temptation often comes to us when we're least strong and that's about the only excuse I have for feeling as I did.'

Ruth sat down heavily on the nearest chair. 'But – you and Niall have always been together – like – like me and Lorn – there was never anyone else for you.'

Shona sighed, wishing that she hadn't spoken about the thing she had kept locked in her heart for so long. In many ways Ruth was immature for her age and entirely unworldly. She had so many young ideals firmly fixed in her mind and Shona searched for the right things to say, even when all she wanted to do was close the subject and try to forget about it.

'Och, I don't know, Ruth, maybe that was why it happened. I'd no experience of any other man but Niall – perhaps in all of us there's a small craving to know what it would have been like with – with another.'

Suddenly she remembered Lewis – Lewis and Ruth, Ruth who had loved Lorn, but had been intimate enough with his brother to actually bear his child, although it was perfectly obvious to Shona in those moments of truth, that that was an episode in Ruth's life which she had managed to shut away so effectively it just didn't occur to her even then.

'Ach, don't look like that!' Shona chided with a forced laugh. 'Nothing happened. I like Mark James, I'll always like him, but it's Niall I love and always will. I love him so much I often cry to myself thinking how I almost drove him away from me. It's Niall's daughter out there now and – and that's proof enough of our feelings for one another.' Even then it didn't strike Ruth that while it was Niall's child they were discussing it wasn't Lorn's daughter who ran outside now, her laughter drifting to them in carefree abandon. So successfully had Lorn accepted the little girl as his own it was as if the past had never been. He had never cast it up, not even during times of domestic argument, and gradually Ruth had allowed herself to slip into a relaxed state of mind and was quite content to let her affair with Lewis McKenzie drift into the obscure corners of her mind.

Shona found herself feeling annoyed at Ruth's self-satisfied righteousness and to stop herself from saying something she might later regret, she got quickly to her feet to take up where Ruth had left off abruptly, putting the kettle on to the fire, spooning tea into the warmed pot. 'You haveny told me what was in Rachel's letter yet,' she said, her voice level as she handed Ruth her tea and set a plate of biscuits at her elbow.

Ruth, still reeling under the shock of Shona's disclosures, plunged into a rather reserved account of her friend's correspondence. 'She wants to come back for a long holiday,' Ruth finished slowly, 'and has asked me to book her into the hotel – only I don't feel that's right somehow – not when she has a home here, though I know she never feels really at ease there. I was wondering if I ought to ask her to stay at Fàilte with me. Och, it would be lovely to have her – like old times again – only I don't think Lorn would be too pleased at the idea.'

Shona said nothing for a few moments. She was remembering a certain look on Rachel's face every time she saw Lorn. Shona had never been able to decide if the expression in the girl's great luminous eyes was engendered by unease in his company or because the very sight of him reminded her of his twin brother, Lewis. Shona sensed a certain danger in a situation that would throw Lorn and Rachel together. Oh, he had always maintained a dislike for her, but that didn't mean he would always feel like that. Rachel was too attractive, too magnetic, for any man to entertain ill feelings towards her for long.

'I wonder if Annie knows that her daughter plans to come home for a whily,' mused Shona. 'I think we should finish our strupak and go over there to find out. Annie can be gey high-handed at times and she might not like the idea of Rachel coming back to the island and her not having a say in where she is to stay.'

'Ay, that might be best,' agreed Ruth slightly unwillingly. She set down her cup and went outside to fetch the children indoors.

Sporran romped along beside them as they made their way outside, for Shona didn't dare leave him in the house on his own, knowing only too well the havoc he could create in a surprisingly short time. Glen Fallan was a picture with snow on the hill peaks and the red of the winter bracken furring the lower slopes. The wind was keening low over the moors, making a strange, almost musical sound as it whistled through the heather.

'Listen to it.' Shona stopped suddenly, her blue eyes intent as she cocked her head in the direction of the moor. 'It minds me of that lovely piece of music we've been hearing a lot on the wireless this whily back. I canny get it out of my head and I've heard some of the islanders humming it in the village.'

'Rachel composed it.' Ruth's voice was warm with pride. 'The mannie on the wireless talked about her this morning just before he played it. It's called *Song of Rhanna*.'

Shona repeated the name, rolling it round her tongue as she savoured the sound of it. '*Song of Rhanna*,' she murmured appreciatively. 'And it is just that. Listen to the sounds around us, the burnie purling over the stones, the wind moaning in from the sea, the gulls crying. Rachel has captured the very soul of the island.'

She bent to pick up Ellie Dawn and swing her high against the patchy blue sky, laughter and love lighting her eyes. 'Wee Ellie, Wee Ellie,' she chanted. 'How do you like the idea of our island becoming famous and folks singing about it all over the world?' The child gurgled and pointed a chubby finger at the clouds racing over the hills. Shona caught her breath. Never, never, could anyone take the place of the darling little daughter she and Niall had loved and lost. She had been a happy, sweet-tempered soul, so in love with life she had made others see the wonder in it too. There could never be another like her – and yet how could Shona help but see her in her baby sister's enchanting small face with its upturned button of a nose and big golden-brown orbs in which the hectic March sky was reflected? They were sisters after all, and if the elder Ellie had lived she would surely have adored her tiny sister as she had adored all babies she had ever set eyes on.

Ruth looked at the entrancing picture made by mother and child and something of Shona's joyous mood transferred itself to her. Sweeping her little son off his unsteady feet she hugged him and grabbing Lorna's ready hand she swung it to and fro and began to hum the *Song of Rhanna*. Shona also took up the refrain and they arrived at Annie's cottage in a carefree mood.

Annie's face hovered at the window and, seeing the visitors, she lifted her hand and beckoned them inside. The cottage was warm after the cold and smelled strongly, due no doubt to a tiny mongrel pup who had just crept out guiltily from behind a chair. It greeted Sporran ecstatically and Shona lifted up both puppies and put them out to romp in the grassy yard at the back, well away from the carefully dug furrows in the garden. By the fire, her brown-mottled legs spread to the heat, was Annie's older sister, Nancy, her good-natured face wreathing into smiles as the children clambered up beside her, Lorna to monopolize her knee, the others to squeeze themselves in at her ample sides.

'Ach my, I just love bairnies,' Nancy said through a mouthful of Lorna's hair. 'And fine they know it too for they aye make a beeline for my knee. If I was young enough I'd have more, that I would, but . . .' she glanced down at the flatness of her chest where a double mastectomy had robbed her of the big breasts that had once been her pride, 'the poor wee sowels would have nothin' to sook and I was aye a believer in feedin' my bairns myself – Archie used to enjoy them too, the sowel,' she finished rather sadly.

'Ach, never mind,' comforted Shona. 'I'm sure you have plenty of other things left to compensate him.'

'Ay indeed,' Nancy agreed in delight. 'He was aye a one for bums too and he can still coorie into that. The Lord provided well when he created me.'

'You will take a strupak?' Annie asked the visitors, giggling at her sister's frank self-assessment. She studied Shona's face. 'You are lookin' well, Shona, mo ghaoil, no, more than that, you look as if you are burstin' to tell us something and canny wait a minute longer.'

Shona told them about Fiona's expected baby and instead of putting the kettle on, Annie went to the cupboard and poured everyone a generous amount of whisky.

'Here's to the new bairnie,' Nancy held up her glass. 'As long as it comes into the world wi' all its parts in workin' order Fiona will no' be carin' if it's a boy or a wee lass. The pair o' them took long enough to start a family but sometimes, once the first one comes, they just keep on arriving like wee rabbits.'

'Well, that certainly wasn't the case with me,' said Shona rather sadly. 'I wouldny mind if it did.'

Nancy's expression grew serious. 'Well, Shona, mo ghaoil, you are no' exactly a spring chicken and if you get pregnant again you will have to ca' canny if you are to come through it safe.'

Shona turned an indignant face. 'Havers! I'm only forty-one! Some of the cailleachs on the island don't start a family till they're forty, and go on to have a fair brood by the time they're fifty. It's their way of providing for their old age though that certainly wouldn't be my reason for having more. If it just happens, the way Ellie Dawn did, and if I'm lucky enough for it to go on happening then so be it.'

'Ay indeed,' said Annie placatingly. 'But what would Niall have to say about it? With the house full o' bairns and ailing animals he would have no room left to swing a cat.'

Shona had recovered her temper and laughed. 'Ach, if it happens he will feel the same as I do. Wait till I tell him about his sister. He's been away at Kintyre for a few days helping his old partner during a busy spell. It's an arrangement they have during the winter when the beasts on Rhanna seem to go into hibernation. I was going to phone him but decided to wait and see his face.'

Nancy sighed. 'My, you and that bonny Niall are still as romantic as the moon. Archie and me are at the stage of comparing all our wee aches and pains and are so busy wi' our corns and bunions we have no time for lookin' into each other's eyes.'

Ruth had said little till then. Annie wasn't the most methodical of housekeepers and the cottage was so untidy you could have stirred it with a spurtle as Kate told her youngest daughter often enough. The children's clothes were draped by the fire, toys, books and cats littered the floor; a dejected-looking tortoise in a box by Nancy's feet was stretching its neck tentatively towards a dirty, snail-pocked cabbage leaf watched over by a mangy-looking mongrel dog whose left ear was in tatters; the tea-stained table held the remains of breakfast and dinner; a pet hen was clucking round the floor looking for crumbs, its ample droppings trodden into the dusty carpet by many uncaring feet.

Ruth shuddered slightly. She liked a house to be homely, but Annie's was positively filthy and Ruth simply couldn't imagine Rachel in such surroundings. It had been different when she was a small girl but the grown-up Rachel had travelled the world, lived in luxurious surroundings. It was no surprise that she didn't like coming home to be faced with all this as well as her mother's uncaring attitude.

'Have you heard from Rachel at all, Annie?' Ruth asked conversationally.

Annie screwed her face. 'Indeed no. The last time I had word was at Christmas when she sent all the bairnies wee gifts and myself a bottle of scent.' She omitted to mention that her daughter had also sent her a generous sum of money, a sense of guilt making her feel that she had done nothing to deserve such generosity. 'Rachel is too busy to be writing letters to the likes o' me – even though I am her mother. Ach, my poor dumb lassie, she will be growing too big for her boots now and we will likely never see her back on the island again.'

'She has no' forgotten Rhanna,' Nancy defended her niece somewhat indignantly. 'Only this very mornin' I heard a bit o' music she had written played on the wireless. *Song o' Rhanna* it was called and by God! That lass put all her memories into it as well as her heart. It was beautiful just. I had a wee greet to myself it was that nice. You should be proud o' your bonny daughter, Annie, she's brought nothing but good to the family name and fame to this island.' A thought struck her making her chuckle. 'If we are no' careful we will be gettin' overrun wi' people wantin' to see the place where all the famous people were born – Rachel wi' her music, Ruth wi' her poems and stories . . .'

'Ranald wi' his fart studio,' Annie couldn't resist putting in, her dimples deepening in her attractive face.

Nancy threw up her hands. 'Ach God! Do you mind that time? My, was it no' the talk o' the town for weeks afterwards! Ranald was black affronted, but Barra just laughed. She's a sporty wee soul is Barra. How is she and Robbie gettin' on by the way? It's a whily since I saw them. Barra is no' about so much since she married Robbie.'

'I hear tell she's been helping Mairi to set herself up in this hairdressing business,' supplied Annie eagerly. 'Mairi has applied for permission to turn one o' the rooms in her house into one o' they fancy saloons.'

'Oh here, that will be just the job,' said Nancy, patting her unruly grey-black curls. 'It will be fine to have somewhere to go for a hairdo, and a hairdresser is a good place to hear all the gossip.'

'I had a letter from Rachel this morning,' put in Ruth persistently, determined to get the talk back to her friend.

Annie's lips pursed. 'Did you indeed? Ay well, you are her friend after all, and I am only her mother.' She glanced round the untidy room and shrugged. 'It is just as well my lassie has made her life away from the island. There would be no room here for her now. As it is, Torquill and me are havin' trouble wi' Jeannie and Iain sharing a room – and forbye, we wouldny be grand enough now for the likes o' Rachel. She'll be used to all thon fancy modern places – a house in Austria indeed! Hmph – she is hardly ever near the place. It will just be a piece o' swank, somewhere to spend her money on.'

Ruth's lips tightened. 'She is very tired and badly needing a rest. Jon's mother is ill and he has gone to Germany to be with her, so Rachel is coming home to Rhanna – I have asked her to stay with me as I knew fine you didn't have the room.'

'Well now, that is kind o' you, Ruth,' Annie's tones were cold. 'If she had written to ask me I would no doubt have found a corner for her, but you are solving all our problems.'

'That's settled then.' Ruth stood up, avoiding the questions in Shona's eyes. 'She'll be here in a week or two and will likely be along to see you when she's settled.'

'Tell her to come and see me as well,' directed Nancy good-naturedly. 'I like fine when Rachel comes home. It's exciting to hear all about the furrin parts she's visited. If I'd known I could have had her stay wi' me though she would have had to share a room wi' Janet. I'm sure Janet wouldny have minded, she loves to know what's going on in the world.'

The door burst open and Kate came breezing in, skirling with pleasure when she saw the roomful of people, sweeping the children into her strong capable arms. Her two daughters obviously had much to tell her. They both started talking at once and the babble of voices, mingling with a high-pitched, pitiful wailing from the dog whose tail had been trodden on, was deafening.

Close on Kate's heels came Dodie, the island's old eccentric, whom Kate had invited in for his afternoon strupak. When he saw the roomful of womenfolk he was temporarily nonplussed and stood nervously in the middle of the floor, stretching his lips and fiddling with the frayed edges of his greasy cuffs.

'Here, Dodie, drink this,' Ruth pushed her untouched whisky into his cold hands. 'It will warm you up. Go and sit on that wee stool by the fire and toast your feet. You could be doing with a good heat I'm sure.'

In making for the indicated spot Dodie did not melt unobtrusively into the background. He lunged for the fireplace, by some miracle missing the cats and the tortoise, but tripping over the hen so that he arrived on the lumpy contours of a fireside chair much sooner than intended. Clucking with indignation the hen rose up in the air; the children shrieked; the tortoise withdrew into its shell; the hen came back down to earth with ruffled feathers and took refuge under the table where it went to sleep roosting on a cross-spar; the dog moaned quietly under its breath then went to plant its muzzle on Dodie's knee, sensing that there was sympathy to be had there. Closing his eyes, Dodie stretched his wellington-clad feet to the fire while his big hands gently fondled the mongrel's remaining ear. Within minutes the heat had coaxed the trapped smells from the old man's boots but he sat on happily, oblivious to both the odour and the innuendoes cast at him by all three McKinnon women.

Shona and Ruth smothered their giggles and seizing their respective offspring made good their escape. A roomful of McKinnons was an overpowering and often a rather frustrating experience, since they all tended to talk at once making it difficult for anyone else to get in a word, 'no' even edgeways' as Torquill was wont to complain to his companions.

Once on the glen road the smiles left Shona however and turning to Ruth she demanded, 'What did you mean back there when you said you had invited Rachel? It's the first I knew of it.'

The wind whipped Ruth's hair over her eyes and she pushed it away with an impatient hand. 'Och, I had to say that, Shona. You heard Annie, going on about Rachel as if she was a stranger. She never could thole her and now Rachel's made a name for herself things are even worse. I know she's proud of her in her own way but she never understood her and with Rachel away so often they've grown further apart than ever.'

'*Are* you going to ask her to stay with you?' Shona asked bluntly.

Ruth hesitated, thinking of Lorn, what he would have to say on the matter. Casting him out of her thoughts she squared her shoulders and looked Shona straight in the eye. 'Ay, Shona, I am. It will be lovely to have her, I could be doing with the company and Rachel could be doing with a break. She won't get that at the hotel or at her mother's, and Nancy's place is just as bad – so is Kate's.'

'Lorn won't like it,' Shona warned, her blue eyes full of an unusual disapproval.

Ruth lifted Douglas up and put out her hand to Lorna, trying to appear nonchalant as she said, 'He'll just have to, won't he?'

'I'm sure Babbie and Anton would be pleased to have her.' Shona wasn't going to let the matter rest so easily. 'You said they had asked both Rachel and Jon to stay.'

'Only when Jon comes back from Germany. Rachel doesn't want to go to Croft na Ard without him. Babbie and Anton are out a lot and she would be left on her own. She'll enjoy it better with me.'

'With you, ay, but not with Lorn. He throws daggers at her every time they meet.'

Ruth tilted her chin while her violet eyes grew dark with determination. 'It's high time he got over all that, he's behaving like a baby and I'm not going to give in to his sulks this time.'

Shona had to smile. 'You know, you grow more like a McKenzie every day, Ruth. I thought I was the only stubborn female in the clan.'

Ruth smiled back. 'I *am* a McKenzie in case you didn't know. I have learned that to survive living with one you have to become one and not just in name either. McKenzie o' the Glen fathered a fine brood of dour-tempered, pigheaded bairns but they are no' the only ones to stand in front o' the wind and dare it to stop blowing.'

Shona gave vent to a shriek of merriment. 'You know, Ruth, there was a time when you would hardly say boo to a goose, but you've changed, mo ghaoil, that you have. 'Tis proud I am to have you for a sister-in-law.'

The wind was whipping the roses into Ruth's pale cheeks, but at Shona's words they bloomed to a fiery red. Shona had always been her friend, her ally in times of trouble, her comforter in times of stress – yet she had always stood slightly in awe of the beautiful, wilful daughter of the McKenzie household, had always felt that she was too shy and serious to ever be on a par with such a vibrant personality.

But now she lost some of that awe and the knowledge grew within her that one day she would walk as tall as any McKenzie – she had to if she was to survive as the wife of

Lorn McKenzie whose pride and stubbornness sometimes worried her. When he was in one of his blacker moods, he refused to see anybody's point of view but his own and she was always the first to back down and say she was sorry. But this was one time she was going to stand firm – she wouldn't let him come between her and Rachel – too many people had tried to do that – first her mother – now Lorn.

They had reached the track that led to Fàilte and she paused. 'I'll get along now, Shona.'

'Ay, let me know how you get on with Lorn.' Shona waved and walked away, her steps light, a good warm feeling in her breast as she hugged Ellie Dawn close to it. She was looking forward to Niall coming home that evening and she forgot about Ruth as she made her way homeward. Ruth watched her go and a sigh escaped her. Shona was lucky having a husband like Niall, a very understanding and sensible sort of man, rarely prone to rages or unreasonable behaviour, good-naturedly letting Shona have her way in the things that meant a lot to her.

Ruth thought of her tall, handsome husband and a tiny smile hovered at her mouth. Would she change him if she could? No, she decided, she loved him just as he was – if only he wasn't so strong-minded. She might be able to handle him better if he hadn't inherited so much of his father's difficult ways.

Chapter Three

The cottage was warm and welcoming as Ruth let herself in. The fire slumbered in the hearth; the clock on the mantelpiece tick-tocked the lazy minutes away; Bramble sat atop the oven washing his face; Ben thumped his tail in welcome but didn't open his eyes; Mallow, the dainty little white female cat, rolled on her back and opening her pink mouth squeaked out a half-hearted miaow.

But the tranquillity of the house failed to find an echo in Ruth's heart. On the walk up the track some of her earlier resolution had dissolved and a glance at the clock further weakened what was left. Lorn would be home in an hour and she knew if she still felt as she did when he appeared she would have no courage left to face him with her decision about Rachel.

Peeling off her coat she settled the children and spent a busy hour, filling it with numerous domestic tasks in order to keep herself occupied and keep her mind off the confrontation with Lorn. He came home in a cheery mood, ravenously hungry, complimenting her on her cooking, in fact doing and saying all the right things to make her even more reluctant to shatter what she knew would have been a happy evening.

But her mind was made up and when the children were in bed and she and Lorn settled cosily by the fire, she cleared her throat and said as firmly as her fast-beating heart would allow, 'I went over to see Annie this afternoon and one look at that boorach of a house made me realize why Rachel would rather stay anywhere but there.'

Mallow was stretched comfortably on Lorn's knee, her great purrs of contentment filling the room as his fingers raked the silky fur at her neck. Lorn appeared to be engrossed with the cat and merely grunted at Ruth's words. She looked at him, at his lithe body stretched out on the chair, at the fire-shadowed hollows of his darkly handsome face, at the firm, rebellious set of his mouth – and she fancied she saw a hint of mockery in the glance he threw at her from under his brows. Oh, he was like his father all right! No, more than that, the image of him, not just in looks but in nature – and she had heard many stories of what Fergus had been like at Lorn's age. A flicker of anger kindled inside her, giving her the spur she needed for what she had to say.

'I'm asking Rachel to come here to stay. It will only be for a wee whily – till Jon comes over, and it will be company for me. I could often be doing with someone to blether with when you're out all day.' The words came tumbling out breathlessly and she was angry at herself because she had wanted to sound firm, sure of herself.

'*No!*' Lorn's hand came crashing down on the arm of the chair, startling Mallow, who fled from his knee to crouch under the table. Ruth's head jerked up to stare at her husband in disbelief. She had expected opposition, but nothing quite so violent as this. He was glaring at her, his eyes glittering beneath lowered brows, his body tensed as if ready to spring.

'Why? Och, why are you saying that? Without giving me a chance to explain?' The protest was torn from her, her voice high and agitated in her throat.

'You don't have to explain!' He threw the words at her, black fury in his icy tones. 'I canny bide Rachel and fine you know it. I will not have her in my house!'

'It's my house too!' she tossed back at him. 'And I don't see what makes you think you have the right to order me about. I will not be browbeaten, by you or anyone else. Rachel's my friend. Oh, I will admit I was angry at her too after what happened between herself and Lewis, but it was all a long time ago and I've forgiven her. It's high time you did too. You're behaving like a spoilt baby and I won't stand for it. I am going to ask Rachel to stay here whether you like it or not.'

Slowly he uncoiled his lean frame and got up to stand over her. 'Do that, Ruthie, and you'll only have yourself to blame for the consequences. I will not bide under the same roof as Rachel McKinnon – or Jodl – whatever she calls herself. You and she can have a nice cosy time on your own, for I won't be around to share it; there's plenty of places I can go to get out of the road.'

She drew in her breath painfully, hearing only the dull thudding of her heart in her ears, seeing only his black menacing shadow dancing on the wall opposite the fire – for she didn't dare look up at him, the very power of his presence being enough to turn her insides to jelly. She twisted her shaking fingers together and, getting up, pushed past him to place another lump of peat on the fire, her legs so strange beneath her she felt as if they didn't belong to her body. Leaning against the mantelpiece she laid her head on her arm and spoke slowly and deliberately, knowing if she didn't she might never get the words out.

'Very well, Lorn, if that's what you want . . .'

'It isn't what I want . . .' Seizing her roughly by the arm he spun her round to face him. 'It's what you want, isn't it, Ruthie, to have Rachel here regardless of my feelings on the matter?'

She pulled her arm away and turned her face away from him. 'You're talking nonsense, Lorn, and you know it,' she whispered. 'There's absolutely no need for you to behave like this. Why don't you give Rachel a chance? Please, Lorn, for my sake if not hers.'

'No, Ruthie.' His lips were very close to her ear and she shivered. 'I don't want Rachel here upsetting everything . . .' She jerked her head round to voice her disbelief in his words, but before she could open her mouth he went on forcibly, 'That's right, Ruthie, upsetting everything. We're fine as we are, we don't need Rachel here, she – she's a strange lass, she rubs people up the wrong way . . .'

'Ay, rubs you up the wrong way, you mean,' she accused him bitterly. 'If I didny know better, I'd say you were jealous of her, ay, that's right, Lorn, jealous. You want it all your own way; your house, your bairns running to welcome you, your dear obedient little wife always here at your beck and call, always ready and willing to please. You're jealous of anyone who might come and disrupt the nice cosy wee routine of the Lord and Master – and most of all you're jealous of Rachel because with a few exceptions she's the only other living person I care truly for.'

Catching her arms he pinioned them to her sides, rendering her powerless to move. His jaw was tense, his eyes black with anger. 'Ruthie, you're a fool,' he rasped harshly. 'Sometimes I honestly believe you still see yourself and Rachel as bairns, giggling your wee secrets into her ears, whispering your fairy tales at her. You're not a bairnie anymore, Ruthie, and neither is Rachel. You're both grown women now and it's high time you, at any rate, started to behave like one. I'm asking you for the last time to get this nonsense about Rachel out of your head.'

But she wasn't listening. She was laughing, an incredulous, mocking laugh that rang eerily round the firelit room. He was telling her to grow up, when all the time he was the one who was behaving like an unreasoning infant.

She struggled to free her arms. 'Let go of me this minute, Lorn, I'm going to bed. I won't stay here another second and listen to your childish nonsense. Let go of me, Lorn!'

Yet the more she struggled the tighter he held her and she saw from the fiery gleam in his eye that he was enjoying his feeling of power over her. Ruth seldom got into the kind of rages that were commonplace in the McKenzie clan, but now a burst of fury seized her, giving her the strength to wrench her arm away from his vice-like grip. Blinded by anger and frustration she lashed out at him, her nails digging into the flesh of his face to leave a trail of bloody ragged furrows along the length of one cheek. He let her go, so abruptly she almost fell backwards into the grate. He was breathing heavily, the corner of his mouth stained with gathering blood, a depth in his anger she had never seen before.

'Away you go then,' he spoke roughly and contemptuously. 'When this is all over and done with, we'll find out who the child is among us. Go on then, go and hide yourself in the bedroom: women are all the same when it comes to the bit – they simply run away when the truth is staring them in the face and they canny see it for looking.'

She went hurriedly out of the room, her limp pronounced as it always was when her mind was in a turmoil. She half thought of going to sleep in the little spare room but decided no – she wouldn't give him the satisfaction of seeing how much he had upset her. She stood for a moment in the hall, forcing herself into a state of calm before going through to take a last look at the children.

'Mam,' Lorna's voice came sleepily. 'I fink Douglas did it on himself. He's smelly.' Ruth went into the bedroom with its bright walls and polished wooden floor. Lorna was sitting up in bed, cherubic-looking in her fluffy pink nightdress, her big eyes questioning as she said, 'Why were you and Favver shouting?'

Ruth tucked her up and planted a kiss on her rosy cheek. 'Go to sleep, my babby, you and Douglas get angry at each other sometimes and your father and I have our wee rows too. It's nothing for you to worry your wee head about.'

Douglas was gurgling contentedly in his cot, his long silken lashes caressing his plump baby cheeks like twin fans. Ruth changed him with as little fuss as possible, knowing only too well that once properly wakened he was quite capable of keeping the rest of the household in the same state till the early hours.

Ruth was dismayed to find that Lorn had beaten her into bed as she had hoped to be under the blankets and pretending to be asleep by the time he came in. She got undressed quickly, shivering as she shrugged herself into her night things. In the cold nights of winter it was lovely to snuggle into her husband, to feel the heat of his body beating into her, his strong arms holding her close. But there would be none of that tonight. As soon as she slid under the big fluffy quilt, Lorn heaved himself round so that the rigid column of his back was to her. They lay as far from one another as possible, thinking their separate thoughts, each acutely aware of the other but neither making the move that would begin the process of making up.

Ruth felt utterly miserable, telling herself over and over that nothing was worth this. But after a few minutes of tense, wakeful silence her anger returned and she told herself fiercely that this was one time she wasn't going to make the first move. The silence of the dark room enshrouded her, emphasizing her feelings of desolation and she couldn't suppress a little shiver.

Lorn moved, seemed closer than before, she could feel his heat radiating over her back, he made a small sighing sound, then came a tiny snore and she realized with horror that he was asleep. Tears of frustration squeezed between her tense eyelids. Oh God! Were all men like Lorn? Able to sleep and be utterly and boorishly normal under any circumstances?

Outside the wind soughed through the trees and she lay listening to it for a long time before drifting into an uneasy sleep beset by strange dreams. She was running, running looking for Lorn but never quite finding him. Always he was just out of reach and no matter how hard she tried she couldn't catch up with him – to touch him, to tell him she loved him, no matter what happened she loved him, but then the dream reversed itself and now it was Lorn who was chasing her – yet – strangely – no matter how fast his long stride carried him he never could reach her – even though her limp was forcing her to go much slower than him he couldn't touch her – because – she was out of his reach and she couldn't understand why.

Lorn rose early, pausing for a minute to gaze down at Ruth's tousled head on the pillow. She looked like a little girl in her repose, her strangely innocent face framed in its halo of flaxen hair already bringing the first tug of remorse to his heart. Her translucent milky skin was sleep-flushed, her lids delicately purpled by fine veins; her soft, pale mouth deceptively childlike for he knew its secrets, how it responded to his during times of lovemaking. In the years of marriage to her he had discovered her strengths and weaknesses and that shy reserve of hers that made her oddly elusive, sometimes even to him. Sometimes he wished she would take life less seriously, learn to laugh more, but he knew that the restrictions imposed on her by her mother during her formative years had a lot to do with the way she was now. Her strict upbringing had left its mark and even though she would have refuted that fiercely there was no escaping the truth of it. She tried so hard to achieve all the things in her marriage her mother had neglected in hers – too hard – often Lorn wished that she would relax and allow their lives to run a more natural course. She was also oddly unworldly for her age, her views on sex and marriage were definitely old-fashioned and ran on strict lines. She was also delightfully romantic, an idealist who didn't care to plumb the harsher aspects of life too deeply. Lorn put it down to her imaginative talents in the writing world, for writers wrote things that other people could escape into and who could blame Ruthie, as the creator of such stuff, for wanting to evade life's mundanities by the romance of words. Lorn understood all this to a certain degree, though often he wanted to shake her out of the self-satisfied shell she had built round herself and make her stare the real world in its face.

But he could never hurt her by doing any such thing – oh no – he could never hurt his darling Ruthie. His hand went to his face to tentatively touch the scratches she had planted there with such uncharacteristic ferocity. Well, she had hurt him all right – more his feelings than anything, though deep down he knew he had deserved everything she had given him. A rueful smile lifted the corners of his mouth. Little vixen, a spitfire if ever there was one. The thought of her rage last night excited him now, and as he stood looking at her she half turned so that the soft roundness of her breasts thrust out enticingly towards him. A surge of desire stirred the slumbering heat in the pit of his belly to fire and he was angry to know that a gentle little thing like Ruth could stir him to such an arousal, making it impossible for him to maintain any sort of cool detachment towards her. He wanted to crush her in his arms, to witness her surprised awakening, her softening, her yielding – but he was still too angry with her to permit himself to give in to his desires. His hands clenched into fists at his sides, his jaw tightened, and he went from the room, shrugging himself into his his working jacket and letting himself quietly out of the house. The morning was bright and cold the early sky star littered, illuminated by the pale disc of the moon slipping towards the glittering horizon of the Sound of Rhanna which lay silver and serene in the distance. The fields rolled away to the south, the wide well-kept fields of Laigmhor, white with hoar frost except where the trees cast their dark mysterious shadows.

From where he stood, high on the windswept knoll above the house, it was possible to see the west gable and the chimneys of Laigmhor. A soft glimmer of light shone from an upstairs window – his father's window. The perfume of peat smoke drifted on the clean air of morning and he knew that his mother would be in the kitchen, stirring the fire to life, setting the porridge pan over the flames. In all the years that Lorn had lived at Laigmhor, his father had never started his day without his bowl of thick creamy porridge. Lorn could almost smell it cooking, a subtle tempting aroma, mixing with the tang of glowing turf, the evocative smell of hot crusty toast piled high on the range to keep warm, generous knobs of butter lying in melting pockets over its golden coloured texture. A picture came to him of the morning kitchen, himself crouched by the fire holding bread on the end of a twisty steel fork, his face smarting with the heat, his hand unbearably hot even though his mother had wound a towel round it. And he saw Lewis perched on a tiny raffia stool beside him, swishing butter over the toasted bread, popping big crunchy pieces into his mouth while he giggled at his own audacity, his blue eyes alive with devilment.

Lorn stared ahead, seeing nothing as his inward-turning thoughts took him back over the years he had spent with his brother. Even though he had so often been ill they had been good years. If only he'd had the strength then that he had now, what times he and Lewis could have had. Lewis had frequently bemoaned the fact that his brother had been so often ill. Lorn could hear his voice as plainly as if he was standing beside him now, talking about all the things they might have done – 'if only . . .'

He threw back his head and sighed. God, how he missed his brother. Though it was years since his death, Lorn still felt as if part of himself was missing, like an arm or a leg that had been severed – no – it was more than that – it was a spiritual loss, they had been so close, never a day passed but he felt that Lewis was by his side, walking beside him – an ever-present shadow that wouldn't go away. It was an odd feeling with an uncanniness about it that often made him shiver and wish sometimes he could feel entirely alone – free. The thought struck him with unexpected suddenness and he frowned. What had made him think it? He didn't ever want to forget – to be free of the twin who had been so much a part of him. And there was another reason that made him very aware of Lewis' closeness; a much more tangible force than a spiritual awareness. He was reminded of it every day when he looked at little Lorna, his brother's child, the daughter whom Lewis had never lived to see and who was the delight of Lorn's life. Before Douglas' birth he had wondered if perhaps a child of his own would make him feel less for Lorna — but it hadn't been so. After all she was the flesh of his flesh, and because she was part of Lewis there was a special place in his heart for her. He was proud of his baby son, but little Lorna was his joy and he adored her to such an extent he had to force himself not to give her more attention than her brother.

'You're there, Lewis, aren't you, you fly bugger?' he whispered softly into the wind. 'Always you're there. You made damned sure of that when you left behind a living legacy through whom you can weave your magic spells.'

He laughed softly and bracing his shoulders breathed deeply before leaving the knoll to stride over the fields to Laigmhor. As he drew near, the morning sounds of the farm came to him; the rattling of the churns in the dairy; a young cockerel exercising its voice; the hens clucking sleepily; the short, delighted barking of the sheepdogs frisking by Donald's side, as together, he and Old Bob strode away towards the fields, the old man leaning a little heavier on his crook but otherwise showing few signs of his eighty-five years. Occasionally Bob took a morning off, especially in winter, but he scorned any suggestion that he should retire. Fergus didn't press the matter knowing that the day the old shepherd admitted to age would be the day that would see the start of his decline.

The kitchen was warm with that atmosphere of morning peace about it that was so peculiarly Laigmhor. Though streaks of dawn were silvering the eastern sky, night still draped the island in a dark cold blanket, and the curtains were pulled over the windows, shutting out the cold, giving the room an air of a self-contained little world which nothing unpleasant could penetrate. Lorn had always loved this special dreaming hour, seeing it as a time of leisurely re-acquaintance with familiar things and people, before dawn stirred the rambling old house to life. His affection for his boyhood home had never dimmed and he knew it never would. He had his own home, his own life to lead, but Laigmhor was where his heart lay. Often he had teased Shona for voicing the selfsame sentiments but she had just smiled and given him her 'blue-eyed, knowing look' which told him that he didn't fool her for one minute.

His mother was at the range stirring the porridge, her hair silvered by the soft lamplight shining from the mantelpiece; her sweet face as smooth as a girl's in the kindly shadows flitting round the fireplace. She looked round at his entry, a smile breaking the composure of her features.

'You're early,' she observed in some surprise. 'Did Ruth make you rise too soon? If I mind right you were aye the sleepyhead in the morning and never got up before you had to. Lewis was different, he was the lark, trilling away at the top of his voice the minute he opened his eyes.'

Lorn sat down at the table and smiled at her ruefully. 'Ay, and fine I knew it too. He used to punch me awake with a pillow and I hated it.'

'What do you think of your eldest brother then?' A sparkle kindled in her eyes. 'He'll have to set his feet on dry land with a bairn on the way.'

'Just what I said, though knowing him he'll likely leave it till the last minute. It would suit Grant fine if his firstborn was launched on the high seas.'

'Ach you,' she scolded mildly. 'Don't say things like that. If I know Fiona she'll make sure she's home in plenty of time to have her baby here.' She ladled porridge into two plates and was about to share out the remainder amongst the cats when she caught the hungry look on her son's face. 'Would you like some? You have the look of a starving man about you this morning.'

Lorn got up and fetching a bowl held it out to be filled. Kirsteen laughed. 'You daft big gowk of a laddie! You mind me of that story by Dickens – Oliver Twist in the workhouse holding out his bowl to be filled with gruel. Your eyes are bigger than your belly, for I know fine Ruth never lets you out the house without a decent cooked breakfast inside you – and what on earth have you done to your face? It's a bonny sight I must say.'

Lorn poured cream over his porridge and chose to ignore the reference to his scratches. 'I left Ruth in bed. I was wakened before the alarm and thought not to disturb her. It's no' often she gets the chance of a long lie.'

Fergus came in, his rugged face glowing after a brisk wash in icy cold water from the bowl in his bedroom. Sitting down he drew his plate towards him. 'How are the bairns?' he asked, a question which he put to his son every morning and which in anyone else might have been asked out of a sense of duty, but Lorn knew different.

'They're fine.' Lorn tried to cover his scratched cheek with his hand and hunched over his plate awkwardly.

'And Ruth? I heard you saying she was still in bed when you left.'

'She's fine.' Lorn was angry that the words came out more offhanded than he had intended and he expected the inevitable keen scrutiny in the black eyes across from him.

'She isn't ill, is she?' Fergus asked tersely. His family had become more and more important to him with the passing years. He tried never to interfere in their lives if he could help it, always having scorned the interfering busybodies he had encountered all too often in his own youth. He could never abide prying for prying's sake; his interest in the lives of his offspring was motivated purely by caring and though he knew that his concern had intensified with the years he could no more ignore it than he could ignore the fact that he had been born a McKenzie.

'Ach, Father, of course she isn't ill,' Lorn sounded unusually impatient. 'She's been a bitty tired this whily back, she has a busy time looking after me and the bairns. I thought a long lie would do her good.'

Fergus studied his son for a few moments, his attention riveted on the red weals on his face, then he turned his attention back to his breakfast, saying no more on the subject till they were walking side by side over the fields to fetch down a cow who was due to have her first calf at any time.

'You've been in the wars,' Fergus observed shortly as he opened the gate to the top field.

Lorn's hand shot self-consciously to his cheek and he reddened as he lied quickly. 'It was one of the cats. They get carried away sometimes.'

'Some cat,' said Fergus dryly. 'More like a buggering tiger – or a woman in a fit of rage. You and Ruth have had a row.' There was no hint that it might be a question, it was a blunt statement and Lorn glowered at his father, annoyed at the way he had of burrowing straight to the truth of a matter.

'Ay, we have.' His normally soft voice was harsh. 'It's natural for a man and wife to disagree now and then. No doubt you and Mother did it in your time, and like as no' still do.'

'We're discussing you and Ruth at the moment, your mother and me don't come into it.'

'*You're* discussing it,' Lorn threw out sulkily. 'I didn't bring up the subject and have no wish to make an issue out of nothing.'

He strode away, his pace quickening so that he was well ahead of Fergus and for the rest of the morning he was careful to keep his distance for fear of being asked more of those straightforward questions that were so awkward to answer. He had no difficulty keeping himself busy. His role at Laigmhor had become bigger over the years with his father allowing him more and more say in the running of things. He enjoyed the challenge of his work, the hours never dragged by, rather they were often too quick in passing so that there was always some task that had to be left for another day. Working in the silence of the frosty fields he thought over the events of the previous night. It was the first really serious row he had had with Ruthie, and now that he had time to see it all in retrospect he wondered why he had been so violently opposed to having Rachel at Fàilte. That temper of his, that buggering curse of the McKenzies had blinded him with fury but now he was puzzled as to why he had flared up like a bull with a sore head – and yet – he knew – all the time he knew and it was the knowing what he did that had made him oppose Ruthie's suggestion.

'Damn you, Rachel!' He spoke the words aloud, his breath clouding in the frosty air. Pulling his hand into a fist he banged it hard against a gatepost. 'Damn, damn, damn you!' His mouth tightened, his eyes grew dark as he remembered Rachel – that last time she had been on the island – those great expressive eyes of hers watching him, always watching him, as if she was trying to tell him something, yet in an odd sort of way not wanting him to know what it was. But he knew all right and Rachel was aware that he knew – and he hated her for picking on him – even though he understood why, she and he shared similar feelings.

In her case she could look at him and relive her time with Lewis, in his case he could look at her and understand the excitement Lewis must have felt in her company. Ruth thought that his resentment of Rachel was born of her rejection of his brother – oh, for a long time he had hated her for that but somewhere along the way his hatred for her had died, leaving space in his heart for other feelings – feelings that he wouldn't admit even to himself – and so he had had to protect himself some way and the only way he knew was to keep up the pretence of anger against her. It had proved a successful compromise, so successful he had fooled Ruth, had even managed to convince himself that his dislike of Rachel was genuine. So far it had worked; for as long as she was just an elusive figure outside of his own world, it worked, but now his self-deception was under threat. Ruth wanted to bring Rachel into his world, to rob him of his contentment and make him feel discontent in all the safe, secure trappings that marriage had brought him. Ruth didn't know – she couldn't know – of the dangers that existed outside their own cosy little domestic world.

A movement caught his eye in one of the lower fields and he walked slowly down to stand watching his father examine a sickly ewe who was in lamb, the muscles of that powerful right arm of his standing out like rope as he flipped the creature expertly back on to her feet.

'Father, can I ask you something?' Lorn said gruffly.

'Ay, what is it?' Fergus didn't look up.

'If Mother wanted to have a friend to stay and you couldny stand the sight of her – because of some very personal reason – would you – still let Mother have her way?'

Fergus' dark head jerked up and his black eyes snapped with amusement. 'Let her! God, lad, can you really see

63

your mother bowing meekly to *my* will? She has a pretty determined one of her own in case you haveny noticed. Oh ay, she would have her way all right but if the body was such a thorn in my side I'd make pretty buggering sure I made myself scarce at every opportunity. Does that answer your question?'

Lorn nodded. 'Ay, thanks, Father,' he said seriously then added cheekily, 'Does wisdom like that always come with great age?'

'Well, of all the . . .' Fergus, eyes glinting, let go of the ewe and took hold of his son as if he was about to spank him. There in the fields father and son tussled, emerging from the fray laughing and panting, Lorn's arm thrown over the older man's broad shoulders.

'Your old man can still spar with the best of them,' smiled Fergus. 'One arm or no.'

'Ay, it never did keep you back!' Lorn's laughing face became serious. 'I wish I'd known you when you – when . . .'

'When I was all in one piece,' Fergus' rugged face also became serious. 'You wouldny have liked the man I was then – too buggering proud and stubborn for my own or anyone else's good. You mustny let the McKenzie thrawn pride ever stand in the way of your good sense, Lorn. You all inherited it in varying degrees, but you – you, my lad, are your old man all over again, though I think you're too sensible to ever let it rule your head.'

'I don't know about that,' Lorn's voice was low. 'Ruthie

and I argued last night and she got the brunt of my temper. For a long time now I haven't been able to thole Rachel because of what she did to Lewis, and last night, when Ruthie asked me if she could have Rachel to stay, my damt pride wouldny let me say yes, even though I can thole Rachel better now and can understand in a way why she turned her back on my brother.'

Fergus slapped his son on the back. 'Ruth must have her friends, Lorn, and if you really canny abide Rachel the way you say, then just do as I suggest and stay out the road – without being too boorish about it. Once Rachel's here you might feel differently. If I'm minding right there was a time when you and she got on fine together. When you and Lewis were bairns you couldny keep away from Rachel. I mind fine the lot of you going off together on the back of old Myrtle and you were always down guddling by the shore with Squint splashing about beside you.'

Lorn nodded, not really hearing what his father was saying. He glanced away over the fields to the chimneys of Fàilte peeping over the knoll. Poor Ruthie! How bewildered she must have been last night – and he had been a swine, shouting at her, pulling her about, not giving her a chance to speak. And she had looked so weary too, weary and hurt and apprehensive. No wonder she had flared up at him . . . His fingers went unconsciously to his face to rub the ragged scratches. He deserved these. Ruthie seldom got really riled, but when she did she was like an enraged wildcat freed from bonds of imprisonment. Remorse, deep and raw, flooded his being and suddenly he couldn't wait to get home to tell her everything was all right. She could have Rachel to stay for as long as she liked – forever if it would please her – it wouldn't matter to him one way or another how long Rachel remained at Fàilte. He would make damned sure he would give her no opportunity to be alone with him – to watch him with that indefinable expression in her eyes that made him feel as if he was being swallowed up in a void of unknown passion . . .

'Rachel canny eat you, you know,' Fergus' deep voice startled Lorn out of his reverie.

Annoyed to feel his face growing hot he said with feigned lightheartedness, 'Oh ay, she can, she can swallow me up, spit out the pieces, and then go back to living her life as if nothing had happened.'

Again Fergus frowned, but said nothing, turning instead once more to the ewe to take her by the horns and lead her down to the paddock where he could keep a close eye on her.

Chapter Four

Ruth was hurt when she awoke to discover that Lorn had risen and left the house without even bidding her goodbye. But as she dressed and fed the children her hurt turned to fresh anger. Spoilt McKenzie baby! That's what he was! Sneaking away out of the house because he wasn't man enough to face her after his behaviour last night. Slowly and automatically she bundled Douglas into a woolly playsuit, her long, nimble fingers doing up the buttons which the little boy immediately began to undo. Lorn, not a man! Hardly that, Ruth McKenzie, she told herself derisively. He was a man all right, that was part of the trouble, she never could resist the manliness of the silent, laughing McKenzie who was her husband. She loved him so much it often hurt – as it did now, knowing that he was angry with her and wouldn't speak to her. That was why she was always the one to make the first move, she just couldn't bear those moody silences. She was weak while he was strong and so she always swallowed her pride first and apologized, even while she hated herself for saying she was sorry for things that weren't always her fault.

Viciously she tugged on Douglas' socks. Well, she

wouldn't say she was sorry this time, she had nothing to be sorry about. She had almost hated him last night, the way he had shouted at her – and she hated him now for instilling such a foreign and bitter emotion in her heart.

Rising abruptly, she plunked the baby unceremoniously into his playpen and, finding a writing pad and envelopes, she sat down by the fire to invite Rachel to stay with her. She dashed through the letter, a demon of determination driving her on, and when it was finished she signed it with a triumphant flourish of her pen. But something prevented her from making the final move of sealing and stamping the envelope. Instead she contented herself by tucking in the flap and propping it on the mantelpiece so that Lorn would have to see it when he came in.

She glanced at the clock, amazed to see that almost an hour had passed and she hadn't yet fed the hens. Douglas was growing restless. He had loosened his cardigan, removed his socks and was now engaged in gnawing the rails of his prison, a monotonous girn flowing in a ceaseless drone from between his busily engaged teeth. With a sigh, Ruth lifted him up and tucking him under her arm she went across the hall with the intention of fetching the hens' pot from the larder. She was in time to see Lorna toddling away outside, the heavy pot held shakily in her small grasp. The little girl enjoyed going about with her mother to see to the hundred and one small tasks about the place and Ruth had always encouraged this helpful streak. Lately however she had decided that she was now old enough to do things for herself and was growing more independent with each passing day, often to Ruth's amusement, occasionally to her chagrin as very often the child got under her feet in her eagerness to help.

Ruth held her breath as the tiny figure wobbled its way over the grass, the pot held stiffly in front, the rosy little face set into lines of grim concentration. But as she neared the burn she tripped on a stone and the pot and its contents went flying into the gurgling water.

'Lorna!' Ruth's voice was frayed with unreasoning anger. She put Douglas down on the grass and in a few strides she reached her daughter, yanked her to her feet, examined her swiftly to make sure she wasn't hurt, then brought her hand down to smack the child's quivering little bottom. It wasn't a hard smack and only the child's pride had been hurt. She stood, dry-eyed, gazing up at her mother, her gentian eyes filled with dark reproach, her soft baby mouth tightened into lines of defiance.

'Serves you right, madam,' Ruth lashed out. 'You take far too much upon yourself! Don't you ever creep behind my back like that again. Do you hear, Lorna?'

The child made no response, except for a silent jutting of her lower lip. Ruth smacked her again, over and over, knowing as she did so that she was taking out her feelings on an innocent child. 'You're a McKenzie all right,' she panted harshly, straightening up to gaze down upon the trembling little girl whose eyes were still dry but whose expression was one of hurt bewilderment. 'Just like your father, your grandfather and all the other pig-headed McKenzies who ever lived and breathed. Why can't you cry like a normal wee lass, why can't you, Lorna?'

The child bowed her head and her voice came out low, 'Favver says it's only babies who cry – and – I'm – I'm a big girl now.'

Ruth looked at her, at the small, dimpled fingers twisting nervously together, the proud, trembling little chin, the big troubled eyes speaking volumes, mutely wanting to know what she had done that had been so terrible. Ruth looked at the sturdy small arms with the baby fat still at the wrists, arms that were always ready to lift and lay, to show affection. How often they had wound themselves round her neck while the satin-smooth face was pressed close to hers in a gesture of pure little girl love. She knew when to be silent, this dear, intelligent small creature and when she sensed unhappiness in the grown-up world around her she would sit in grave, unspeaking sympathy, her hands folded patiently in her lap till she knew things were better.

With a muffled sob Ruth dropped on her knees and folded her daughter to her breast. No wonder Lorn adored this tiny scrap of humanity. She was just three, yet her character and personality were so highly developed it was difficult at times to remember that she was still, after all, just a baby.

'I'm sorry, I'm sorry, my dear wee babby,' Ruth crooned huskily. 'I was in a bad mood and was a bad mother to take it out on you. These greedy hens can do without their pot for once. You can be a really big girl and go into the hen hoosie to fetch some grain to scatter, then you can come into the kitchen and help me make some nice wee cakes. Later on we'll put some into a poke and take them down to Grandpa Donaldson at Portcull. You can tell him you baked them all by yourself.'

Lorna's face sparkled. 'Can I push Douglas in his pram?'

Ruth smiled. 'Ay, even though the last time you pushed him into a ditch. I'll trust you to do better – now that you're such a big girl.'

Lorna's fingers curled forgivingly into Ruth's, then she withdrew her hand and went away to the hen run where she was immediately surrounded by a hungry mob of chickens. Ruth watched, a mist in her eyes, but all at once she found herself giggling. Lorna was scattering the grain in a most businesslike manner, then seemed to forget that she was such a 'big girl now'. Putting down the meal basin she dropped on all fours to crawl among the hens, her realistic clucks ringing through the frosty air with exuberant childish enthusiasm.

When Lorn came in at dinner time the house was empty except for the animals heaped by the fire. He gazed round the empty room, surprised at the sense of disappointment that welled up in his breast. He had come home, full of remorse, eager and anxious to make up. He had visualized taking Ruth in his arms, holding her soft body close to his, hearing her musical voice telling him not to worry, that everything was going to be all right.

A scrap of paper under the butter dish caught his eye and snatching it up he read the short note left by Ruth informing him that she was taking the children to see her father and would most likely have dinner with him. Lorn's was in the oven keeping warm. He crushed the paper into a ball and threw it into the fire, feeling strangely deflated. Ruth was seldom out of the house at mealtimes – in fact she was always here to welcome him, to set his meal on the table, to talk to him – or rather to listen while he talked. She was a very good listener was Ruthie, a trait he had come to accept, even to enjoy. She had a knack of making him feel that his work in the fields was of the utmost interest to her. He ran his fingers through his thick thatch of hair, a frown on his brow as he thought of going over to Dugald's house himself. Old Isabel would see that there was enough left in the pot to fill a plate for him. Dugald would welcome him surely – but would Ruthie?

No, dammit! Not after last night. She would be cold towards him and he was damned if he could stand that sort of thing – not in front of other people.

Taking the dish from the oven he clattered it on to the table and scraped in his chair. The silence of the house enveloped him, magnifying the very sound of his own chewing inside his head. He stared ahead, his young face set into lines of brooding as he pondered on how empty his life would be without Ruthie and the bairns – empty and dead. Last night she had told him he took her too much for granted, he could see her now, her face white, her eyes big and purple, anger a strange visitor on her gentle features. He thought back to the days when he was so in love with her, but was so shy and awkward he didn't know how to go about winning her over – and then he had discovered that she loved him too and had done for a long time. And hers was a generous love, it filled his life with a rare and precious light and made him feel contented and good. Every day of their lives together Ruthie showed her love for him – but his frown deepened, furrowing his brow – did he reciprocate that love? Was Ruth as sure of him as he was of her? Sometimes she chided him, told him that she kept his affections solely for the bedroom – but he couldn't help the way he was made. He just wasn't the sort to throw his feelings around so easily – not like Lewis – he had never cared who knew how he felt. Women had loved Lewis, he had always seemed to know instinctively how to treat them, to give them what they wanted.

'Girls love to get presents.' Lorn heard his brother's voice so plainly he might have been standing beside his chair. 'And I don't mean things like woolly bonnets and knitted scarves either.'

Lorn glanced at the clock. If he hurried he would catch Merry Mary before she closed the shop for dinner. She might not have what he wanted but anything was better than facing Ruth with stuttered words of apology and empty hands.

*   *   *

Dugald was coming out of the shop as Ruth approached the village. At sight of her his steps quickened and the smile that she knew and loved so well was on his face long before he reached her.

'Ruthie,' his greeting was full of pleasure. 'Are you just going to the shops or have you time to take a strupak with your old man first?'

Ruth appraised him silently. He looked better than he had ever done and had regained a lot of the sparkle that had departed from his life for so long. Ruth was delighted to see the happiness that took away the gauntness of his thin ascetic face. His mop of hair had grown whiter during Morag Ruadh's last, tortured illness but it only added to the distinguished air that had settled about him over the years.

'I hope I'll get more than just a strupak. Father,' she smiled at him. 'I thought we might have our dinner together.'

He swept Douglas out of his pram and took Lorna's ready hand in his firm clasp. 'Do you hear that, bairnies? I am to have the pleasure of having my dinner with my grandchildren just as I was beginning to think you had all forgotten me.'

'Ach, Father, it hasn't been as long as all that,' Ruth laughed. 'I meant to drop in last time I was in the village but got waylaid by Mairi wanting me to go and look at the new hairdryer she had just had installed.'

Old Isabel was puffing up the brae to her cottage which

adjoined that of her son-in-law, an arrangement made years ago by Morag, which had been the cause of much consternation for Isabel and Jim Jim. Now, however, they were only too glad to have Dugald next door to them as he made it his business to carry out all the little tasks which had become so irksome to them.

Old Isabel's rosy face lit up at sight of her great-grandchildren. Jim Jim, peeping from behind his curtain, saw the visitors approaching and he too made haste to welcome them. Ruth laughed at their obvious pleasure and gave up the idea of a cosy strupak and a chat with her father. A noisy and cheerful hour followed during which everyone drank tea and ate buttered scones and vied with each other to relate all the latest local gossip. The children were never short of attention from one or other of their elders and the Temple rang with sounds of childish laughter and grown-up chatter.

'How different it all is now,' thought Ruth looking around at the bright walls hung with dozens of her father's little watercolours. Barra McLean, herself a keen artist, was a regular visitor to the house and it wasn't unusual to see her and Dugald sitting companionably close in the garden with their easels propped strategically in front of them as they painted views of the Sound of Rhanna to the west and the hills of Glen Fallan to the north. It had struck Ruth on several occasions how well Barra and her father got on in their arty world and how well suited they were in other ways. But Barra was now married to round-faced, blue-eyed

Robbie Beag and anyway, a liaison had existed between Dugald and Totie for a long time. Totie had certainly been a great comfort to him all through the difficult and trying years of his marriage to Morag Ruadh. Ruth had been very young when she had discovered that Dugald and Totie had not only been friends, but lovers too, and at first she had been shocked and horrified though never once had she given away her feelings to her father.

'Did you want to see me, Father?' she began, once Isabel and Jim Jim had departed, taking the children 'for a whily'.

'Ay, that's right, Ruthie,' Dugald said quietly. 'I wanted you to know that Totie and I have decided to get married.'

Ruth stiffened slightly. 'Oh – have you now?' Her tones were anything but enthusiastic. 'I'm delighted to hear it. I know that you and she have been friends for years.'

'Are you, Ruthie?' He was looking at her quizzically, his expressive grey eyes full of a gentle amusement.

She kept her eyes averted from him. 'Ay – well, och yes, you know I am – it's just . . .'

'Och, c'mon now, Ruthie, will you stop clattering those dishes about, sit down where I can see you and tell me what you really think.'

She sat down opposite him and looked him straight in the eye. 'Father, I only want what's best for you. You've already suffered years of unhappiness because you married the wrong sort of woman. Totie's such a strong character. You've said to me more than once you canny abide the way she goes into your den and tidies away all the things you don't want tidied away and that was a trait Mam had and which you just couldny stand. It's maybe only a wee thing, but you've got this place so nice and homely now I – I'd hate to think of you going back to where you started and living in a place that isn't so much a home but a – a sort of filing cabinet.'

She stopped, her father was smiling at her, a smile full of tenderness, for he knew what she was trying to say and could understand her concern.

'Ruthie, I know what Totie is like. I should, having known her for more years than I care to remember. She has her wee foibles – just like the rest o' us, but over and above all that she is a bonny, warm, caring woman and I know she cares enough for me to come and go with me a wee bit. She's waited for me a long time has Totie, and that has meant a great deal to me forbye letting me know that she thinks I was worth waiting for. I am by no means a perfect person myself but if two people care enough for each other then they have to learn to live with the other's faults and failings and make the best of them. Sometimes to have what we want from this life we have to put up with a few annoyances and I am quite willing to take a chance with Totie just as she is with me. When two people live together they are bound to fight each other in an effort to retain their own identity; it's what marriage is all about really – the good with the bad. You must have found that in your own marriage.'

'Ay, I have,' she admitted slowly. 'It isn't always easy living with someone you know is stronger than yourself in every way.'

'But is it no' lovely to have a marriage like that, Ruthie? It canny be dull and to make up for all the bad things you have all the other good things to make it worthwhile. Lorn's a good man, he's been a good husband to you, he's closed his eyes to a lot o' things that any other man might rake up just for the sake o' an argument. Ay, Ruthie, he's a good man and Totie's a good woman and if she's stronger than I am, then so be it. Sometimes people like you and me, Ruthie, need a stronger shoulder to lean on. We're very alike, you and I, and maybe that's why we've both chosen partners the complete opposite of ourselves. I canny see you married to a meek and mild mannie, just as I canny see myself living with a colourless gentle wee body creeping about the house for fear she'll disturb me at my work. Och no – Totie's my kind o' woman; a good strong character with no nonsense in her head and a heart as big as a house when it comes to caring and sharing.'

Ruth's dimples showed. 'You've convinced me, I'm delighted for you and pleased at myself for having got a whole lot off my chest. When is the wedding?'

'The week after Easter. Mr James is going to marry us here in Rhanna and afterwards Totie and me are going away for a whole month together. I haveny had a holiday in years and neither has she, so we're going off to Cornwall where Totie has a married brother.'

He got up and went through to the larder to see what was to be had there for dinner, leaving Ruth gazing absently from the window, wondering how Lorn was enjoying his lonely dinner hour at the cottage. Looking down the brae she saw Lorn emerging from the shop with a parcel tucked under his arm. Her heart accelerated and she half-rose from her seat with the intention of going to the door to call on him. Then she decided no, she would be making the first move if she did and she wasn't going to give in so lightly over the question of Rachel. She watched him walking back in the direction of the glen and as his tall figure was lost to sight she was unable to suppress a sigh.

'Have you and Lorn fallen out?' Her father's voice at her elbow made her start. She regarded him silently for a few moments then she began to tell him about Rachel and Lorn's reaction to the proposed visit.

'Maybe Lorn has good reason for wanting to keep Rachel at arm's length,' Dugald said thoughtfully.

'Oh, he has reason all right, but it isn't good. He canny forgive her for that affair over Lewis and it's high time he did.'

'Ay, you're right, Ruthie,' conceded Dugald. 'But just the same, I've never known Lorn yet to stand firm without a justifiable reason. It might be he has more on his mind than something that happened years ago. Rachel is a very tempestuous lass and maybe Lorn canny bear the idea of her coming into his home and disrupting the nice peaceful life you and he have together.'

Ruth stared at him. 'Disrupting our lives! Och, Father, that doesn't sound like you at all – you sound more like Lorn saying daft things like that! How on earth could Rachel disrupt our lives? You make her sound like some sort of ogre. She's only coming for a rest and will want all the peace and quiet she can get.'

Dugald's smile was apologetic. 'Ay, you're right, Ruthie, it was a daft thing to say and I canny think what brought it out. It's just – well, she's a strange lass is Rachel. Will any o' us ever know what goes on behind those great black eyes o' hers?'

'I know well enough,' cried Ruth in bewilderment. 'Rachel always let me know what she was thinking.'

'Mostly – ay,' he tried to choose his words carefully. 'But was she so frank when it came to her affair wi' Lewis?'

'No,' admitted Ruth reluctantly. 'She was pretty secretive about that – and about Jon too, now that you mention it . . .' She frowned. 'But what has all that got to do with her coming to stay with me?'

'Ach, nothing at all, she is the sort o' lass who likes to keep the affairs o' her heart to herself but there's a few people like that. You're right, Ruthie, it has nothing at all to do wi' any o' this. Wait you, when you go home you and Lorn will make up your differences and I can safely guess he'll be only too ready to let you have your way over Rachel.'

Ruth lifted her head high in an unconscious gesture of assertion. 'He'd better, Father, for I have already written a letter to Rachel inviting her to stay.'

'So be it,' said Dugald quietly but his words were lost in a noisy invasion of Isabel, Jim Jim and the children into the room.

Ruth wasn't in the kitchen when Lorn came home at teatime but the children surrounded him eagerly, Douglas to totter over and grab his leg, Lorna to throw her arms round his waist and breathlessly tell him that she had baked cakes that morning and he was to have some for his tea.

Lorn reached inside his pocket and presented them each with a bag of sweets which they accepted eagerly though not without surprise on Lorna's part, for as a rule it was forbidden to eat anything before a meal. Ruth came through from the larder. She looked pale and tired and kept her eyes averted from Lorn, her gaze going instead to the children sitting quietly on the rug in blissful concentration on the colourful assorted sweets Merry Mary had stuffed into the bags.

'Lorn,' began Ruth in annoyance, 'you know fine the bairns are not allowed . . .'

He covered the distance that separated them in two quick strides. 'Leave them be, Ruthie, just this once.' Somewhat sheepishly and brusquely he pushed an enormous box of chocolates into her hands. 'Merry Mary had to hunt for these. She's likely had them in the shop for ages so I hope to hell they areny fusty—' He paused, remembering the beaming winks and smiles on Merry Mary's happy, ruddy face as she wrapped the chocolates up, and the teasing and banter from Kate who was in the shop buying tobacco for Old Joe.

'And what has Ruth done to deserve these?' Kate had demanded in her usual boisterous way. 'Has she maybe locked you out the bedroom, eh, my lad, and you're huggin' yourself wi' excitement thinkin' these will maybe unlock it for you?' She had peered closer at his face. 'By God! You'll be telling us a cat did these! Well, well, she is no' Morag Ruadh's daughter for nothing and that's a fact! I mind fine Morag doing the selfsame thing to Colin Watson when he tried to take down her breeks in a hayshed. That was a long time ago of course but some things never change, no indeed, men are all the same when they want something. They think they only have to give us one sniff o' a sweetie and we will allow them to get a leg over as if nothing had ever happened. Fine I know it too for my Tam has done it often enough wi' me only I was never as lucky as Ruth – oh no – the stupid bugger buys his way into my affections wi' bars o' toffee and I'm kept so busy pickin' the damt stuff off my teeths I have no time to spare for him and his desires.'

Merry Mary had choked into her hanky at this and Lorn had thrown back his head and roared with laughter for it was difficult to keep a straight face in Kate's outrageous company. But he didn't feel like laughing now, not with Ruth so close beside him, her fair face flushing to pink, her big violet eyes regarding him steadily. She saw the misery in his own eyes, mingling with a deep intense gleam of guilt that touched her heart and made it suddenly lighter. The sight of the red weals over the smooth tan of his cheek brought guilt flooding into her own heart and she had to hold herself on a tight rein in order to stop herself reaching out to him.

'Ruthie, I'm sorry,' his lilting voice was low. 'You were right in what you said, I am a stubborn, buggering pig-headed McKenzie who deserves a good thrashing! Of course ask Rachel to come; you must get lonely here sometimes with only the bairns for company. It will do you good to have another female around. Rachel might no' be able to speak but I know that's never bothered you. Lorna will get a chance to get to know her godmother – she was only a babe in arms last time Rachel was here—' He stopped suddenly, knowing he was saying too much, almost as if he was trying to convince himself that Rachel's presence could bring nothing but good to them all. He wound his arms around Ruth and pulling her close kissed her so deeply she gave a soft cry of unwilling protest.

'Lorn, the bairns,' she warned, though there was a look on her face that Lorn knew well and never failed to excite him.

'Forget the bairns.' His voice was deep and intimate. 'Why do you think I gave them sweeties before their tea

– they won't be getting any for a whily yet – you and me have something to settle first.'

A dimple of mischief dispersed the weariness on Ruth's face. 'I knew you would give in once you had swallowed that thrawn pride of yours – that's why I've already written to Rachel inviting her to stay – I left the letter on the mantelpiece thinking you would see it when you came in at dinner time.'

'No, I didn't see it, I was too busy feeling sorry for myself to notice anything much.' Lorn's jaw had tensed. He said nothing more but his arms tightened instinctively round Ruth. Her soft hair tickled his face but he was barely aware of it. All at once his thoughts were overwhelmed by Rachel. He thought of her power, her passion – and a small niggle of unease worried its way into his heart.

Part Two

Spring 1964

Chapter Five

Mollie McDonald pushed open the door of Kate's cottage, letting in a blast of salt-laden sea breezes which stirred the muslin curtains at the deeply recessed windows and ruffled the petals of a jar of daffodils sitting on the ledge. Mollie wrinkled her nose as the heat of the cottage and its assorted smells enfolded her in an almost tangible embrace, the most prevalent of these owing itself to the row of kippers pegged on to a wire above the smoky peat fire which old Joe claimed gave the fish a delicious and distinctive flavour. The cloud of smoke from his pipe mingled with the pleasant smell of baking and the pungent reek of onions which Kate was cutting with vigour on a board at the table before sloshing them into a pan of mutton stock.

Old Joe, who had come to live with Kate when he could no longer look after himself, was comfortably ensconced in a big easy chair close by the fire, a towel draped round his shoulders in readiness for his monthly haircut which was always presided over by the able Kate. The soup prepared and set on the fire to cook, Kate seized upon a large pair of kitchen shears and began to snip away industriously at the old man's snowy locks.

'It is yourself, Mollie,' greeted Kate affably. 'Come you in and sit yourself down. I will no' be long wi' the bodach. We are waiting for Rachel to come off the boat and then we will all have a nice strupak together. I made some nice wee scones this morning, they are Tam's favourite though he doesny know I made them or there wouldny be a crumb left for anybody else.'

Baking wasn't one of Kate's strong points and Mollie privately thought that Tam must have been born with an iron-clad stomach. She politely refrained from making comment however and took a chair opposite Old Joe. But the old man, annoyed at being referred to as a bodach, though he had reached the grand old age of a hundred and three, was more blunt about such matters.

'Scones is what you call them,' he sniggered wheezily, making a well-aimed spit in the fire. 'I have found softer rocks on the beaches. I canny get my teeths into the damty things and am aye feart I break my jaw.'

Kate hooted indignantly while Mollie permitted herself a strangled chuckle. 'Maybe that is why I have heard Tam callin' them rock cakes,' she hazarded daringly.

Old Joe's shoulders shook, sending a cascade of jagged white hairs to the floor. 'Ay, it is a good name for them right enough. I wish I had thought about it myself.' Kate prodded the shears vigorously into the skin at his neck making him wince.

'Weesht, you ungrateful old bugger!' she scolded sternly. 'Or I'll slice the top o' your head off wi' these. My scones is all right, it's your damty teeths that are all wrong. You must have had them since the year one and could be doing wi' changin' them.'

'At my age there is no' much point,' Joe asserted fearlessly, adding thoughtfully, 'Mind you, thon dentist mannie is due on the island this year. At least I will go to my rest lookin' respectful.'

Mollie had removed her headscarf and was self-consciously patting her hair, trying hard not to look as if there was anything new about her that day. Kate paused with the open shears dangerously close to one of Joe's ears and treated her friend to an amazed scrutiny. 'Your hair, Mollie McDonald, what have you done wi' it? It's purple!'

Mollie blushed red and wondered whether to put her scarf back on. Kate's tones were anything but complimentary and Mollie's plump face set firmly so that she wouldn't give her embarrassment away. 'It wasny me, it was our Mairi,' she explained defensively.

'Ach yes, of course, this is the opening day o' her hair shop,' nodded Kate. 'If I mind right she had a notice up sayin' she was givin' hairdos at half price the first day. I didny rush wi' the rest, for I like to think I am one o' these who will no' get something done that isn't needin' just for the sake o' gettin' it cheap.'

Mollie grew redder still and said tightly, 'Well, Kate, that is a matter of opinion. A blind man could see that you are the sort o' woman who has just taken shears to your hair all your days – just like the sheeps.'

Kate looked at her friend's indignant face framed in its elegant coiffure, and burst out laughing. 'Ach, Mollie, your hair is lovely just! Mairi has made a fine job o' it. It's all the thing now that purple dye and makes a nice change from salt and pepper.'

'It is not a dye, it is a rinse,' Mollie corrected with dignity and with a slight sniff of disdain.

Kate nodded cheerfully. 'It's the same thing wi' a fancy name, but I wasny criticizing, in fact, now that I see how good Mairi is I'll make that mean bugger Tam treat me to a hairdo for Doug and Totie's wedding.' She blew over Joe's neck vigorously and whipping the towel away handed him a mirror. 'There now, isn't that a lovely job just? I've a good mind to start chargin' you for my services. If Mairi can do it so can I.'

Old Joe peered at his shorn locks and gave an ungrateful snort. 'Would you look at me, woman! I am as baldy as the erse o' a moultin' hen! A man o' my age needs all the hair he can get to keep his lugs warm.'

'Havers,' laughed Kate unconcernedly. 'You're an ungrateful bodach and next time you can just get along to Mairi's wi' your damt hair and let her put curls over your ears – see how you like that forbye havin' to pay a mint to get it crimped all fancy like.'

The two women erupted into gales of merriment and the old man, thoroughly disgruntled, got up muttering and stomped away outside to smoke his pipe, his rheumatism temporarily forgotten in his haste to escape further ridicule.

Left to their own devices, the two women set about an eager exchange of gossip, triggered off by Mollie who had just come from the Post Office, an establishment now run by Totie Little, who had for years been Postmistress at Portvoynachan, but who had managed to get transferred to Portcull in order to be nearer Dugald.

'You will never guess who was there behind the counter wi' Totie, tellin' her what to do as if she was a simple bairn,' began Mollie energetically.

Kate's lips folded grimly. 'It doesny need much brains to know who you are talking about. It will have been Behag, I haveny a doubt.'

'As large as life and twice as vindictive,' agreed Mollie, shaking her head. 'As you know yourself Totie has had years of experience behind a Post Office counter and doesn't need anybody to tell her what to do.'

'She will have put Behag in her place,' said Kate with conviction. 'Totie was never a body to take snash from any livin' cratur' far less old Behag.'

'Indeed you are right,' nodded Mollie eagerly, her eyes gleaming at the memory of Totie and Behag warring at each other. 'She went for Behag hammer and tongs and the old bitch gave as good as she got though in the end she stalked away wi' her nose in the air muttering something about the ingratitude of some folk.'

Kate filled the teapot and set it to keep warm on the range. 'Wait you, we will all be gettin' a taste o' Behag before very long. She has lain low since her retirement but knowing her she will no' be likin' being away from the centre o' the village gossip. It used to go to her but now she will have to go lookin' for it and will soon be puttin' her nose into everybody's affairs. She'll be hauntin' Mairi's place, mark my words. A hair shop is just the place to hear all that's goin' on. I can just imagine her sittin' under the dryer, thon big lugs o' hers cocked as high as a dog liftin' its leg to pee.'

'Ach, she'll no' go spendin' her money at Mairi's, and from what I have seen o' her hair sproutin' from under her headscarf there is precious little there for curling.'

'As much as would cover a gull's egg,' sniggered Kate wickedly. 'But she'll go along to Mairi's just the same for if I'm mindin' right the good kind sowel is lettin' anybody over the age o' sixty-five have their hair done at half price.'

'Well, that will no' be me for a whily,' averred Mollie hastily and set about busying herself helping Kate to lay out cups and saucers. 'I was hearin' a wee thing myself while I was at Mairi's.' She threw out the hint cryptically making Kate pause with a saucer suspended in mid-air.

'Oh, and what would that be – or are you no' in the mood for telling?' Kate's knowing tones were dry for Mollie was renowned for her enjoyment of suspense, particularly when she was the one to dangle the carrot. It gave her a great deal of satisfaction to be first with some juicy item of gossip, as it was mostly Kate who brought first hand pieces of information.

'Well, I don't know if I should.' Mollie's face had taken

on a familiar closed look and she wore the air of someone who rarely divulged the 'secrets' passed on to her from someone who had already heard them from another. 'It was Elspeth who let it out and she was whispering as if she didny want to be heard even though your Nancy was on the other side of me.'

'Ach well, I will get it from her,' rejoined Kate rather huffily. 'She will be along in a wee while to see Rachel when she comes.'

'Well, seein' it's you I don't see the harm in it,' said Mollie hastily, having no wish to let another steal her thunder. 'It is about the doctor. He has decided to take an early retirement and it seems as if we will be havin' a new mannie whenever one can be found.'

'Lachlan, retiring!' Kate's pleasant face was dismayed. 'I thought we would be havin' him for a couple o' years yet. Ach my, it will no' be the same wi' another doctor, Lachlan is just one o' us and though he is a man I have never felt shy about showin' him my personal parts. I mind I had an awful itch once – down below,' she had lowered her voice to a loud whisper. 'Lachlan told me to take off my breeks and the damty things got caught on my toenail. I weeched my leg high in the air and off came my breeks wi' a flourish – right into Lachlan's face. They were clean mind for I had just put them on before seeing him but just the same a woman's knickers is no' the sort o' thing a man gets thrown in his face every day o' the week. Well, I was so flabbergasted that for a minute I couldny speak then

Lachlan began laughing and couldny stop and there the pair o' us were, me wi' my bare bum and Lachlan wi' my breeks decorating his shoulders, shriekin' the place down wi' such force Phebie came runnin' to see if he was maybe murderin' one o' his patients. Phebie sat down on a chair and began laughing too, fanning herself wi' my breeks of all things, and just about peein' her own. The three o' us near died wi' exhaustion it was that funny.' Kate paused for breath and shook her head. 'I canny see the same sort o' thing happening wi' a new doctor, it will be terrible just,' she ended somewhat dismally.

'Ach, it might no' be all that bad,' consoled Mollie. 'He might turn out to be like auld McLure and he was never a mannie to turn up his nose at a pair o' breeks if I'm mindin' right.'

'Auld McLure! He was a dirty old bugger, that he was, he couldny wait to get the breeks off his women patients – forbye that he was so busy drinkin' and gossiping he had no time to spare to see to the ails o' the island. We don't want his likes here again.'

'It will be a young mannie maybe,' said Mollie soothingly. 'But whatever he is we will just have to put up wi' it or do without. Now, we had better get this table set, the boat will be coming in soon.'

Ruth waited rather nervously on the pier watching the crowd streaming down the gangplank. She scanned the faces anxiously, wishing for the umpteenth time that day that she was possessed of more confidence to handle situations like this. She had so looked forward to Rachel coming but now that the moment was actually here she found a slight panic rising within her.

'Ach, stop it!' she scolded herself impatiently. 'It's Rachel you've come to meet, someone you've known and loved all your life . . .'

Rachel's tall figure was making its way down the gangplank. She was more beautiful than Ruth had ever remembered, a figure of elegance in a stunning red suit that enhanced every curve of her shapely body and was a perfect foil for the masses of shining black hair that tumbled about her shoulders. She was poised and confident, so perfectly groomed she seemed to Ruth during those first swift impressions to be entirely out of keeping with her surroundings. Then she looked up, spotted Ruth among the crowd and a warm smile of pleasure lit her face. All her sophistication left her as she rushed forward and threw her arms round her friend.

They stood back to survey one another. Ruth's fair skin was glowing, her hair against the sun was dazzling, the soft folds of her simple print dress sat well on her dainty figure, so that altogether she was a picture of natural prettiness. 'It's lovely to see you again, Rachel,' she said softly, rather shyly. Rachel smiled and nodded. She gazed around at the hills and breathed a deep sigh of appreciation then she and Ruth gathered up the cases and walked together along the harbour to Kate's cottage.

Old Joe was so wrapped up in his thoughts he didn't see the figures of the two girls approaching the cottage till their shadows blotted out the sun and Ruth's light musical voice came to him as softly as the whisper of the breeze over the waves.

'Dreaming of the mermaids again I see. You were that still we thought for a minute you were one of these wee gnomes folks put in their gardens till we saw the smoke from your pipe floating upwards.'

'Ach, havers, lass,' Joe's sea-green eyes twinkled. 'Can you imagine Tam wi' a fairy in his garden? Thon great feet o' his would have stamped it to powder long ago.'

Rising stiffly he paused to take stock of the raven-haired girl standing beside Ruth. Joe had to remind himself that this sophisticated-looking creature was still, after all, a relative of his, a distant one to be sure but one nevertheless in whose veins the McKinnon blood flowed. She was looking at him, an anxious little frown marring her brow. She couldn't bear to come back to her birthplace and not be treated as the child he had once rocked on his knee while he whispered his wondrous tales of the sea into her delighted ears.

He held out his big, strong old arms and she threw her own around him with such enthusiasm he wheezed and chuckled and held her back to beam at her. 'My, you're a bonny, bonny lassie, and we are all so proud o' you we could burst. I see though you have come back to us in the nick o' time. You're too skinny, mo ghaoil, we'll have to feed you up.'

Over her head he winked at Ruth standing a little way back. Ruth had wanted to take Rachel straight back to Fàilte, but Kate had been most adamant that they stop off at her cottage first so that they could all get a chance to see Rachel as soon as she came off the boat. And now Ruth was glad that they had, for her first sight of her friend had woken a shyness in her that had been totally unexpected. She was so poised, so different from the Rachel she knew and after the first greetings a mild panic had sprung into Ruth's breast as she wondered if she had done the right thing asking Rachel to stay at her humble little house. She was glad of people like Joe who she felt wouldn't have batted one eyelid if the Queen herself had come to visit and she nodded in agreement as he went on, 'We will take her inside and feed her some o' her grannie's rock cakes. By God!' He shook his head emphatically. 'A few o' them will put you on your feets all right for they will sink there like stones and make you feel you are on a pedestal – and don't be surprised if you never get off the damty island again for wi' Kate's bakin' inside you the boat would just sink to the bottom wi' you and everybody else in it.'

'Joe McKinnon!' Kate's lusty voice lashed out. 'What are you haverin' about out there?'

The door was thrown open and Kate appeared, her face wreathed in smiles at sight of her granddaughter. 'Rachel, it is yourself! And the bodach never bringing you inside. The kettle has been on the boil ever since I saw the boat comin' in. Ruth, away you go ben the larder and bring out the sandwiches. Where are the bairns, by the way? I made them some special wee cakes wi' coloured icing on top.'

'I left them with Kirsteen,' explained Ruth, ignoring Joe's nudges and winks and his whispered, 'It's as well you didny bring them. They would never have survived Kate's baking.'

Tam arrived on the scene, puffing and out of breath, for he had been well warned by Kate to be home in time to welcome Rachel or suffer the consequences.

In the noisy happy hour that followed Rachel threw off her cloak of convention and became once again the Rachel that everyone remembered. Some of her happiest memories were of Kate's cluttered, homely cottage with its stunning views over the white sands of the bay and the great bulk of Sgurr nan Ruadh prodding its sullen peak into the clouds. She sat by the window, drinking tea, listening in delight to the lilting voices around her, glad, oh so glad to be home again, feeling as if she had never been away from an island where time drifted so pleasantly and people lived such natural lives. The noise, the stress of city life seemed very very far away. Here she wasn't Rachel Jodl, a rising star to be worshipped and applauded. Here she was plain Rachel McKinnon, an island girl – one of *them*. She gazed with sparkling eyes round the little room, at the people with their laughing faces and musical voices, she looked from the window with its pattern of cobwebs in the corners to the great peaceful tracts of moor, sea, and sky, and her heart sang. Her eloquent hands spoke all the volumes her lips would never speak and though Tam and Kate only understood some of the things she tried to convey it was enough that they smiled and nodded and occasionally looked awed as she rhymed off all the places in the world she had visited.

During a lull she sat back and gave her attention to Ruth. They smiled at one another, smiles that brought the past into the present. Each recalled their own particular memories of one another and it was all there in their eyes as gradually the last three years of separation slipped away along with all the little politenesses they had displayed towards each other since meeting at the harbour.

The clocks ticked, the fire crackled, Old Joe slept, Tam poked the depths of his pipe with a piece of bent wire, Mollie and Kate muttered sympathetically over their respective bunions, and all the while Rachel and Ruth longed to be alone so that they could catch up on three missed years. Ruth was bonny and glowing that day, her hair was a sheaf of pure flax in the sunlight, her cheeks were sun-flushed roses, her eyes the purple of pansies, dark and velvety. Rachel felt an affinity with her as she felt with no other. As a child she had been shy, plain and skinny, as a young girl Ruth had blossomed painfully into a being of grace and loveliness. Now she had grown into a more assured young woman, quiet and restful looking on the surface but exuding an oddly sensual quality which contrasted strangely with her look of shyness and air of vulnerability. Yet, despite it she had found her love, found it so completely – with Lorn, that dour, handsome young McKenzie who seemed to grow more and more like Lewis every time she saw him . . .

Rachel turned her thoughts away and wondered if Jon was missing her. But of course he was! He always missed her when they had to be apart – too much sometimes. Often she felt she wasn't strong enough or good enough to deserve such an unselfish devoted love as Jon's. She could never give him such an unstinting love in return. Oh, he had her undying affection, her caring, but never never could she give to him that wild, abandoned, carefree love she had given for the first and last time to Lewis McKenzie – and Jon deserved so much more than Lewis had ever done – yet, much as she worshipped the dear steadfast man who had given her so much, she couldn't give him her heart and sometimes she hated herself for it . . .

A movement outside the window caught her eye. The next minute the door opened to admit her Aunt Nancy and Annie, her mother; rosy, windblown, slightly embarrassed looking as she stood hesitating on the threshold.

'Come you in and have a cuppy,' Kate invited her daughters, eyeing Annie with some annoyance. Exuberant and outgoing herself, with a heart amply brimming with affection for her offspring, she couldn't understand a child of hers who couldn't exhibit similar feelings towards her own daughter. Somewhere in Kate's happy-go-lucky nature she knew it was because Annie was bemused by her beautiful daughter's successes and wasn't possessed of the sophistication to know how best to conduct herself in the girl's company.

Rachel had half risen, unfolding her long legs slowly, till she stood, a striking figure in the homely kitchen, a defensive look about her which clashed with the glint of expectancy in her dark eyes. Annie patted her dark hair nervously and cleared her throat. 'You're lookin' well, Rachel, a mite thin but I suppose it is to be expected in the kind o' life you lead.'

The fire in Rachel's eyes died quickly away and she turned her head to hide her disappointment. Her mother always welcomed her in this formal, rather critical way but Rachel hoped, always she hoped, that one day things might be different.

Tam looked at his daughter, his homely face creased into a frown. 'Annie, Annie, is that any way to welcome back a lassie you have no' set eyes on for years? Look you, I am only her grandfather but by God! I'm proud o' her, that I am! I have just come from the hotel and Rachel's song was playin' there on the wireless. Some o' the lads picked it up on their fiddles and I was that happy I nearly choked in my beer!' He turned to Rachel, his eyes shining. 'I tell you, mo ghaoil, you have brought honour to the good family name, ay, you have that. Wait you till Jon comes back, we'll have a real grand ceilidh to celebrate all your successes.'

Nancy nodded eagerly at this. 'Ay, and I will put on my best pair o' bosoms and get Mairi to do my hair.' She hoisted up the left side of her chest with a giggle. 'These buggers are aye slipping, it wouldny do to wear them to a ceilidh in honour o' a famous violinist.'

Everyone laughed. It was impossible not to laugh in Nancy's company. She was so amusingly frank about her mastectomy operation that nobody ever felt embarrassed when she spoke about it and indeed, she did a great deal to allay the fears a lot of the womenfolk felt about the dread disease that had cost Nancy both her breasts. She made no secret of the fact that she had different artificial breasts for different occasions and it was commonplace to hear her discussing which set to wear the way other women might ponder over what dress they ought to wear for this or that outing. At home she had a set hanging above the dressing table in her bedroom, 'to keep them in shape and to mind Archie of the joys of a woman's body'. She was not at all dismayed should anyone happen to see them there, explaining the reasons with perfect frankness. She lay back in her chair and began to hum the *Song of Rhanna* and old Joe, wakened from his sleep, tapped his feet on the hearth. The tune really getting into his blood he took up his fiddle and began to play. Tam slipped over to the sideboard to pour drinks for everyone and in minutes a good-going impromptu ceilidh was in full swing. Rachel didn't take up her own violin, content just then to leave the musical side to the others, but she clapped her hands and laughed as Mollie and Kate held the floor in a jig and Tam grabbed Ruth to whirl her round till the cups on the table rattled and the floorboards creaked under the dusty carpet.

Annie tossed back her whisky and slipped over to sit beside her daughter. Rachel stopped clapping and looked at her mother, wondering if she was going to say something critical again. But Annie's hand came out to clasp Rachel's tightly and she said in a husky voice, 'I *am* proud o' you, my lassie, I – I just don't know how best to tell you these things. It was nice o' you to write at Christmas – and to send me – what you did. You're a good, good daughter and I'm glad to see you back on the island.'

It was a gruff welcome home but it was more than enough for Rachel. Visibly she relaxed and returned her mother's clasp, her long fingers trembling very slightly. Ruth threw herself down beside them, her hair mussed attractively about her sparkling face, her breath coming quickly.

'Tam McKinnon, you don't dance, you clod-hop,' she panted and Annie laughed.

'Father aye had two left feet! That's why Mother has such bonny bunions on her today. He nearly kicked her to death when they were courtin'.'

Rachel's hands moved, asking her mother if she minded her staying with Ruth. To Annie's credit she had taken the trouble to learn a certain amount of her daughter's sign language and was able to interpret the message. She shook her head, too readily, 'Indeed no, mo ghaoil, you go and enjoy yourself wi' Ruth. I haveny the room for grand young ladies such as you, even if you are my own daughter.'

Rachel nodded slowly. She had no desire to be thought of as a grand young lady and never had, despite the glamour of her busy life. Now that she was home her only desire was to be treated like everyone else and not to be looked upon as different in any way.

The ceilidh was really warming up when she and Ruth took their leave. Several neighbours, having heard the wild skirls and hoochs, arrived to join in the fun and the house was so full Rachel gave up trying to reach Kate to thank her for the strupak and turned instead to the door to see that Dugald had just arrived with his van, an arrangement made previously by Ruth. Into the battered old van he piled Rachel's cases, smiling warmly at her as he commented, 'You must be planning to stay for a whily, lass. You have enough here to last a year.'

Rachel smiled back, glad to see that he had regained a lot of his sparkle. The last time she had seen him had been at Morag's deathbed and then he had looked gaunt and ill and near to death himself.

On the short drive to Laigmhor, where they were to look in to say hello, Ruth spoke about her father's forthcoming marriage to Totie. 'You've come at a good time, Rachel. Maybe Jon will be back in time for the wedding and we can let him see what a real island wedding is like. It was a pity you never had your own here, I was sorry to have missed it.'

She wondered if she had said the wrong thing because Rachel made little response, seemingly too engrossed in the scenery to be bothered with much else. Her wedding to Jon had taken place in Germany, far away from island tradition, far too from painful memories which she often wondered if she would ever be allowed to forget. She saw that it was going to be difficult to even try, folks on the island had long memories and enjoyed dwelling on the more momentous happenings of the past, raking them up with nostalgia and a certain amount of malice if they had been events that had shocked at the time. But Rachel knew nothing like that existed in Ruth's mind and that her mention of weddings was only an attempt to make pleasant conversation. Squeezing her friend's hand to show she understood she turned once more to the window and Ruth said nothing more till they reached Laigmhor. Kirsteen insisted that they all come in 'for a whily' and it was almost an hour later and well after teatime when they finally took their leave. The children had exhausted themselves playing with all the animals in and around the farm and they sat quietly with their mother in the makeshift seat Dugald had installed in the back of the vehicle.

Rachel sat in the front, watching the glen road unwind as the rickety old van bounced and rattled its way along. The hills reared up on either side, serene and blue except where the sinking sun splashed on the bracken, turning it a fiery red. The peace of the island lay all around, Rachel could feel it seeping into her very marrow and a little shiver went through her. This was her home, where she belonged, she felt steeped in the very rocks of the hills. The strange, sweet, poignant mystery of the Hebridean evening brought a thousand memories flooding back. The scent of peat smoke was so evocative she felt the tears springing to her eyes. The whiteness of the little cottage slumbering in the gloaming near Downie's Pass, leapt out at her like a ghost in the night. But it was a friendly ghost, invoking memories of auld Biddy; standing by the gate waving her hanky to passers-by; dozing in her rocking chair by the fire. Rachel knew that Shona and Niall lived there now, but to her, in that moment it was Biddy's house. The gurgling of the River Fallan caressed her ears like notes of music; the fluted piping of the curlew's call mingled with the heron's sharp cry as it glided on silent wings along the river's course. These were the sounds she had remembered on her journeyings to foreign lands. They had filled her head, constantly tormenting her till order emerged from tumult and each one took its place as a note of music. The final composition had been written frantically as the sounds of the island poured into her head, pounding seas beating the shores, echoing into vast caverns, crashing over rocks; the wind moaning low over the heather; the purling of the burns; birdsong over the summer moors; soft breezes stirring the fields of golden corn. Might and majesty, peace and serenity, all had come together to produce the piece of music which had haunted her for so long. Now her song was echoing over all the land, the *Song of Rhanna* which the private part of her had wanted to keep to herself but which the extrovert in her had not allowed . . . Dugald was turning the van into the track which led to Fàilte. Rachel's fingers tightened in her lap.

Moors and fields sped away, the spruce hedge loomed, shutting out space, enclosing them all in a narrow dark tunnel. It fell away and once more there was light and emptiness all around except where the slopes of Ben Machrie spread down gently to meet them. Dugald breasted a rise and the chimneys of Fàilte appeared below, then they were descending the brae, slowly because of the bumps in the track. The children sensed home and stirred on Ruth's knee. Ruth's heart beat a little faster as she hoped that Lorn would keep his word and be pleasant to Rachel. The van swerved to avoid Ben cocking his leg on a tuft of grass, halted at last. The engine died and there was a momentary silence. The trees on the knoll rustled in the wind, the whinny of a horse came plaintively from the fields. The windows of the house were softly lit, welcoming. The door opened, spreading a larger oblong of light over the grass. Rachel's heart beat faster than Ruth's. Lorn stood motionless for a moment, silhouetted, a tall, powerful figure.

'Favver!' Lorna stirred and struggled to get up. Everyone seemed to move at once and all things intangible, fleeting, gave way to warmth, light, voices, laughter.

Chapter Six

'You look – well, Rachel.' Lorn knew that the greeting was pitifully inadequate but they were the only words he could think of in those first hectic moments of Rachel's arrival. The children were clamouring in the background, Dugald's deep pleasant voice was droning on, telling Ruth about some incident that had happened in the shop that afternoon, Ruth was laughing, a nervous little laugh that told of her inner anxieties, the animals had risen, going from one new arrival to the next, sniffing and snuffling.

Rachel and Lorn were left looking at one another, their eyes guarded, uneasy. Ruth had spent the whole of yesterday and most of that morning making the house as welcoming as possible. They had taken the visitor into the parlour, seldom used but now gleaming like a new pin. The brasses winked in the cheery grate, the fire leapt up the chimney, the chintz-covered sofa and chairs looked stolidly inviting, arranged as they were around the hearth, several of Dugald's watercolours decorated the wall together with some of Ruth's pastels of animals.

Rachel glanced round at it all and felt a momentary sensation of panic. It was lovely, so lovely to be here on

Rhanna, so good to be here at last in Ruth's house with its air of homeliness and its old-fashioned furnishings – but it was Lorn's house also and the realization came to her fully as she stood there looking at him, her heart beating so fast she couldn't stop the quick rising and falling of her breasts. She had expected that he would have looked much the same as the last time she saw him but he had changed.

He was taller, his shoulders strained against the white shirt he wore, his chest was deep and powerful, his shadowed eyes were darker, more intense than she ever remembered; so too was his hair, dark and crisp, a little tendril of it falling over his brow. He was as Lewis had been but he was something else, he had overtaken the twin who had died on the brink of manhood, he had left behind the boy and he was a man now, supremely virile and masculine, so self-contained she felt overpowered by him. His words, cool and clipped, fell on her ears. He didn't raise his voice above the general din but she heard distinctly each clean-cut note, saw his black gaze sweeping over her so assessively she felt most uncomfortable. All her sophistication floated away like a mist before the wind leaving her feeling unsure and embarrassed. A stab of anger pierced her being. She had travelled the world, been the centrepiece for a million eyes, had been applauded, adored, fussed over wherever she went – and with just the flick of an eye Lorn McKenzie had robbed her of all the confidence she had thought was hers for all time.

Lorn saw the anger in her dark vibrant eyes and it

made him feel uncomfortable. She was more beautiful than he ever remembered, poised and confident, so perfectly groomed she seemed to him entirely out of keeping with her surroundings. Then he noticed her hands, the long sensitive fingers moving restlessly at her sides, the well-manicured nails nervously gathering little tucks in the expensive material of her skirt. It struck him that she was more than slender, she was thin, too thin, her wrists were delicate looking, the bones of her face so finely honed they endowed her with a sharpness that made her look too mature for her twenty-two years. He tried to pull his gaze away from her, but was too mesmerized by her beauty to do so. Her great dark orbs were on him, watching him, exerting a magnetism over him that was uncanny. Yet her eyes too lacked something that had been so essentially Rachel; the inner glow was extinguished, leaving them dull and rather tired looking.

'You came back just in time.' His voice was so low only she caught the words. 'You look as though you could be doing wi' a rest. You'll have all you want of that here. No one will disturb you, you can be sure of that.'

She knew quite well what he meant. He wouldn't disturb her. He was telling her quite plainly that while she remained in the house he would make it his business to get out of it whenever possible. 'So, nothing has really changed,' she thought a little wearily. Lorn still resented her, had never forgiven her for what she did to his brother – 'Well damn you, Lorn McKenzie, I'll enjoy this precious holiday on Rhanna, despite you and your pig-headed attitude – you're determined not to like me. Two can play at that game though I won't even give you the satisfaction of letting you see that. It will sink in, slowly, and by then you will realize that I am the winner – in every respect.'

'I can't persuade Father to stay for his tea.' Ruth broke into her musings. 'It seems he has arranged to have it with Totie,' she smiled in some bemusement. 'Now that he has another woman in his life I will have to learn to take a back seat for a whily.'

Dugald grinned. 'Havers, lassie, you will always be my best girl and fine you know it.'

Lorn couldn't help comparing Ruth with Rachel. She looked so young, with her fair skin stained pink and her fine hair framing her small face in a silken cloud. She was slight and fragile looking, so utterly lacking in sophistication she seemed immature for her years, certainly too young looking to be a wife, let alone the mother of two sturdy infants. On impulse he caught her and kissed the tip of her freckled nose. Her face flushed and she looked at him askance for he was never demonstrative in company. 'Will you behave yourself, Lorn McKenzie,' she hissed in some embarrassment, although she felt warm and good, and there was a spring in her step when she escorted her father out into the fresh, windy night.

'I'll bring Rachel over to visit you, Father,' she said as he folded his long frame in behind the steering wheel.

'Ay, do that, Ruthie,' he said warmly. 'Better still, bring her over to have dinner with me and Totie. I know the pair o'you will have a lot planned and won't want to waste time on an old fogey like myself but I'd like fine for you to get to know Totie better.'

Ruth bent over to kiss the top of his silvery head. 'Ach, I know her well enough as it is, certainly enough to know that she won't turn out to be one o' thon awful wicked stepmothers you hear so much about. As for you, you might be a fogey but you're anything but an old one – you just said that because you wanted me to say otherwise.'

Dugald ruffled her hair and banging the door shut was off with a cheery wave, the van groaning on its springs as it hurtled away down the steep track.

When Ruth went back into the house it was to find Lorn in the kitchen getting the children into their night things on the rug by the fire. 'Rachel wanted a wash,' he explained briefly. 'I showed her her room and left her to it.'

Ruth looked worried. There was no proper bathroom in the cottage. On bathnights the zinc tub was brought before the fire and at other times the family just washed at the kitchen sink. Ruth had placed a china jug and basin in the spare room but now she wondered if such basic amenities would be adequate for such a sophisticated guest.

Lorn saw her look and shook his head. 'Ach, don't fash. I put hot water in her room and filled the jug with cold. If she wants a bath at any time I'll lug the tub into the parlour where she can have a bit of privacy. You mustny fret, I'm no' going to sit back like an ornament and let you fetch and carry . . .'

'Oh, Lorn, I haven't . . .' she began, but he put his finger to her lips and whispered, 'Weesht, you've been dancing about like a scalded hen and fine you know it. Just relax; she might be a grand lady to look at, but deep down she's still the wild wee lassie who roamed the island barefoot, washing her face in the burn and paddling her feet in the sea. And when you think what it was like for her at Annie's – the wee hoosie in the bushes – the zinc tub at the fire on a Saturday night – and sometimes no' even that. I mind fine Rachel and her brothers being scrubbed in the sink at the kitchen window for all the world to see.'

Ruth giggled. 'Ay, you're right, it's easy sometimes to forget these things.' She hesitated. 'Lorn – it will be all right, won't it? She's so pleased to be here. On the road up from Kate's she was so eager to take it all in – and – I want her to enjoy her wee holiday so much.'

'Ay, it will be all right,' he assured gruffly.

'She's beautiful, isn't she, Lorn? Such bonny clothes, I've never seen the likes in all my life.'

There was a wistfulness in her voice that made Lorn look at her with deep tenderness.

'I canny deny it, she is a bonny young woman – as for her clothes – I'd rather have my Ruthie any day in her simple frock and peeny. Can you imagine cleaning out the fire and looking after the bairns done up in all that finery? You would look like a tinker in no time.'

'Daftie,' she smiled but couldn't suppress a little sigh as she went to put the finishing touches, to the table which she had set in the parlour earlier that day.

The meal was a simple one, requested by Rachel herself in her last letter when final arrangements were being made. Ruth felt nervous as she brought the dishes to the table, wondering if her friend was just being polite asking for a traditional island dish to be served. But Rachel, her face shining from its recent wash, looked positively delighted and clasped her hands as if in anticipation of a big treat. She had changed out of her red suit into a simple white polo-necked jersey and fawn slacks and she had tied back her raven curls with a red scarf. All at once she wasn't a sophisticated town girl anymore but the Rachel that Ruth remembered and felt at ease with. With shining eyes she removed the lids from the dishes and gazed with joy at mounds of fluffy mashed potatoes and at the piping hot rolls of herring sprinkled with toasted oatmeal. Closing her eyes she sniffed and sniffed the tempting aroma as if she could never get enough of it and the children, who until then had been gazing at her in silent, round-eyed appraisal, began to laugh, their peals of childish merriment ringing out to break the rather formal silence which had filled the house since Rachel's arrival. Lorn looked at Ruth. Simultaneously they both let go of their breath in unconscious relief and Ruth felt the little knot of nerves which had lain in her belly all day slowly dissipating.

The rest of the meal passed in lighthearted mood,

though little Lorna could hardly take her eyes off her godmother, a frown on her brow as she watched the lively exchanges between Rachel and her mother. Only Ruth could understand such rapid sign language and Lorn kept his attention on his plate, annoyed to find himself embarrassed and at a disadvantage. A lot of unexpected emotions were besetting him. He had been surprised at how utterly peaceful it could be in the presence of a person without speech. He had expected an awkwardness in the atmosphere but watching Rachel's expressive eyes speaking the volumes her lips would never utter, seeing the grace of her slender hands flashing out word after word, he knew that his embarrassment came strictly from his own inability to understand the girl's mute conversation. There had been a time when he could follow her sign language, but that had been long ago and now he had forgotten most of what he had ever learnt. He noticed that Ruth's face was animated as she followed each rapid move and spoke eagerly in return, for though Rachel couldn't speak she could hear perfectly, and it was an easy matter to hold a conversation with her – as long as you understood what her hands were saying.

Glancing at his daughter he couldn't suppress a smile. Frowning in concentration, she was following Rachel's every move whilst trying to copy them with her chubby little fingers. Douglas was too engrossed with the contents of his plate to take much notice of anything else but Lorna had almost forgotten her food in the new challenge before her. Rachel turned and saw the little girl's actions and her face broke into a smile of radiance which swept away all its weariness.

'We must all learn your language, Rachel.' Lorn spoke for the first time since the start of the meal. 'If not, I can see night after night stretching ahead with me being forced to sit watching you two women gossiping.'

'Oh, Lorn, would you?' Ruth's skin was pink with the excitement of that first evening at Fàilte in the company of Rachel. 'It's really very easy – look – start with the simple words first.'

Lorn's tanned skin flushed. He felt a surge of annoyance at Ruth for pinning him down like this, and rather moodily he watched as she took him through some of the basics. The children too were entranced by this new and unusual 'game' and an oddly peaceful silence pervaded the room. Ben sneaked through from the kitchen and proceeded to mop up the crumbs that were always to be had near Douglas' little chair; Bracken sat in rapt attention on one of the spare chairs by the table, large green orbs gently panning the remainder of the herring in the dish; Mallow rolled on the rug by the fire, her purrs filling the silence; a shower of sparks crackled in the chimney breast; the clock ticked lazily.

Rachel sat back in her chair watching all the fingers working furiously and a smile lit her face at the sight of Lorn's big masculine hands trying gamely to keep up with Ruth's. Rachel's gaze travelled to her god-daughter and she caught the child's eyes on her in wide-eyed assessment. All at once, and to Lorna's utter astonishment, Rachel pulled a truly hideous face, pushing the tip of her nose back with her middle finger, with the others slanting her eyes till the whole effect was totally horrific in one who had only moments before been a picture of loveliness. A slow smile spread over the child's rosy features, she began to chuckle heartily, attracting her baby brother's attention to Rachel's face. The little boy showed his pearly white teeth and then he began to laugh, a fat, deep, hearty laugh that made Ruth and Lorn look at him in anticipation. From an early age Douglas had shown himself to have a well-developed sense of humour, matched by a laugh so infectious it was a joy to hear.

Rachel pulled one funny face after another and the child's throaty chuckle, so deep it might have come from his tiny boots, continued to grow in volume till he shook, wobbled and rolled in his seat. He paused for breath, while everyone else held theirs and then he was off again, gurgling, giggling, chuckling, his little pot belly wobbling, his crinkled eyes fixed on Rachel's face in unending fascination. In the end he laughed so much he lost control of everything. He began hiccuping uncontrollably and at the same time a great surge of wind broke from his layers of pants with such gusto he was momentarily stunned. For a few seconds it looked as if he didn't know whether to laugh or cry then the sprite came back to his eyes and he was off again, looking like a jolly little friar with the baldy patch on top of his fair head and his chubby fists tucked into his sleeves.

Rachel got up from the table to go through to her room, emerging with her arms filled with presents for everyone, toys for the children, a neat little portable typewriter for Ruth, and a new fiddle for Lorn. Ruth was speechless with delight, Lorn once more swamped by an embarrassment that made him awkward and brusque in his thanks. The children were in raptures over the new toys, but Lorn went over to take his son in his arms. 'Come on, young man, bed for you, you've had enough excitement for one night – you too, Lorna. You can take the toys through and play for a wee whily in bed. I'll tuck you both up and tell you the story about the fairy folk that live in the caves by Burg Bay.'

But for once Lorna was not swayed by such temptations. She hovered shyly by Rachel's side and holding up her hands made little gestures that were recognizable as letters in the sign language. A strange, indefinable expression touched Rachel's face. She gazed down at the tiny girl and her hand came out to touch the mop of curly hair, fair in babyhood but now turning a rich, glowing brown. A smile took away the strangeness of Rachel's look and standing up she plucked Douglas from Lorn's arms, held out her hand to Lorna and went with them out of the room. Like lambs they allowed her to take them, not even a murmur of protest from Douglas who normally liked his father to take him to bed.

Ruth and Lorn were left to stare at one another. 'The bairns like her,' Ruth sounded surprised.

Lorn nodded and said slowly, 'Ay, it would seem so – though fascinated might be a better word.'

'And I always thought she wasny keen on wee ones.'

'They're certainly keen enough on her. It was aye said that Rachel had the power. Maybe she has it over the wee folk and can spirit them away as easily as she once spirited Squint away from Lewis and me.'

Ruth shivered. 'Ach, don't say things like that. I had enough of folk spiriting Lorna away when she was a baby – first Mam thinking she was me, then Shona thinking she was Ellie – I couldn't bear anyone else to take my family away from me – I think if that happened I would leave Rhanna and never want to come back.'

Lorn put his arm round her and drew her close. 'Daft wee thing,' he murmured against the delicate shell of her ear. 'It's no wonder you're a writer – you let your imagination run away with you at every turn. No one is going to take anyone away from you – not while I'm around.'

Ruth snuggled against him. 'Oh, Lorn, I'm glad you're my husband, you're so strong and sensible – when you're not being pig-headed that is.' She sighed with deep contentment. 'Och, I'm that happy. I wanted Rachel here – yet I was a wee bit worried about how it would all turn out. But it's been a bonny evening, I'm glad the bairns have taken to her so quickly and – and that you were so good tempered about everything. Now I won't worry about anything and will have a fine time while she's here.'

Lorn nuzzled her hair. 'Ay, you will that — and don't you fret yourself about me. I — I canny promise that there won't be times I'll look at Rachel and remember what she did to Lewis, but I promise you I won't go all moody and dour and take my temper out on her.'

She chuckled. 'If you feel a temper coming on, Lorn McKenzie, just you go right out of this house and take a long walk by yourself.'

'If you promise not to leave Rhanna and never come back.'

She moved against him. He squeezed her arms. She felt soft and warm and reassuring. 'I promise,' she murmured.

The drumming of the horses' hooves beat an insistent but pleasant tattoo inside Lorn's head as he galloped with Rachel over the wide white sands of Mara Oran Bay, Bay of the Seasong. It was a clean fresh windswept day with a soft mackerel sky embracing the sparkling blue waters of the Sound of Rhanna, softening the sombre grandeur of the great cliffs which sheered up from the shoreline, the grey basalt columns scarred by the Atlantic winds, pitted with vast caverns that gulped in the swirling sea then spat it out again in a disdainful flood to send it leaping and foaming against the stark pinnacles of rock which gashed the coastline.

The wind tore through Lorn's hair, sculpting it into rich brown waves against his head; his ears tingled; his skin felt icy cold yet glowing. The blood in his veins coursed quickly, making him feel very aware of the great panoramas of sea and sky unfolding in ever-changing patterns in front of his eager vision. The horse felt powerful beneath him, its strong muscles rippled under its sable hair; the veins stood out on the arch of its neck, its ears were laid back, its coffee-coloured mane streamed backwards so that all was movement and speed and grace.

Lorn was aware that the blackness of the mood which had beset him since morning was rapidly dispersing in the exhilaration of the ride over the bay. It had been a long time since he'd sat on the back of a horse, a long time since he'd felt such freedom. With each powerful thrust of his horse's hooves he felt himself to be unfettered, free of the responsibilities of the farm, free even of the duties of being a husband and father. All the little cosy domesticities which he had clung to as being safe and secure now faded into insignificance, and he wondered why he hadn't sought such times of freedom more often, why he had craved dull routine and the monotony of day-to-day living with such fierce and jealous possession. Yet little more than an hour ago he had rebelled at the very idea of taking a couple of hours off to go riding with Rachel.

Ruth hadn't felt well that morning. She had looked white and strained and when he had asked anxiously if she was ill she had been unusually irritable, had snapped at him and told him she would be a lot better if he didn't ask such silly questions all the time. But a few minutes later she had been apologetic and had admitted to feeling squeamish and out of sorts.

'You're not pregnant again?' he had asked rather sharply and she had sighed and told him no, it was just a pain in the stomach. All she wanted was a quiet seat by the fire and she would be fine. 'Except – I won't be much company for Rachel,' she had said slowly then almost pleadingly, 'Lorn, why don't you take an hour or two off and go riding with her? She would love that. Do you remember how you and Lewis and Rachel used to go riding together? She was as much at home on a horse's back as she was on the ground.'

Lorn remembered all right – he remembered that Ruth had always been wary of horses, unlike her daredevil friend who had often gone riding bareback, simply borrowing any horse she found grazing in the fields or wandering on the machair near the shore. But Lorn had had no intention of taking Rachel riding. He had quite successfully managed to evade her since her arrival, always having some excuse to get out of the house as quickly as he could. She had done nothing to antagonize him or annoy him in any way, in fact, she herself was inclined to slip away whenever she could, sometimes to take solitary walks over the hills, at others to go to her room and quietly compose little tunes that came into her head. She indeed appeared to have come home with the sole intention of having a well-earned rest and Lorn was gradually allowing himself to relax, to even chide himself for having read something in Rachel's eyes that had no existence outside his imagination. She gave him as much attention as he gave her, which was next to none. She had proved a help to Ruth, never shirking mundanities like washing up or tidying the house. She had lavished a great deal of her time on the children so that they had come to trust and like her; she hung out washing; baked mouthwatering apple pies, and seemed positively to be revelling in a way of life long gone for her.

She and Ruth shared so many common interests that often he watched them laughing together and was annoyed at himself for feeling shut out. It was what he had wanted, yet he was beginning to suspect that Rachel was going out of her way to avoid him so that he could find no fault with her. That morning the realization came to him that he wasn't avoiding Rachel, she was avoiding him, to such a degree that almost a week had slipped by and he had hardly taken in the fact that she was staying at his house at all. When he came in at mealtimes she had either packed a picnic lunch and gone off on one of her solitary wanders or else she was away visiting her numerous relatives scattered all over the island. She was playing him at his own game and while he appreciated her quick wits he wasn't taking kindly to the idea of being almost ignored by her for a whole week and he was damned if he was going to climb down now to go meekly seeking her company. So he had rejected Ruth's suggestion fiercely, using the excuse of being too busy with the lambing to have any time to spare.

'Och, Lorn, you're still behaving like a big baby,' Ruth

had retorted wearily. 'Bob and Donald can manage fine without you for an hour or two and anyway – I was talking to your father yesterday and he said it was high time you had a day off. I thought we might take the bairns for a picnic this afternoon, they hardly know what it's like to have an outing with their father. If I could have the house to myself for a whily this morning I could catch up on myself a bit. Kirsteen is coming over to take the bairns over to Burnbreddie, she and the laird's wife are going to Oban in a day or two and I thought it would be a good chance to get them to get some new things for Lorna and Douglas. They will need to be measured and so Kirsteen thought . . .'

'You have it all worked out, haven't you?' Lorn had begun bitterly, but the look of tiredness on Ruth's face had stilled his tongue though it was with bad grace that he had gone to Rachel and suggested that they go riding. She had conceded without enthusiasm which had not improved his mood, though the vitality that he knew so well came into her eyes at sight of the horses in Laigmhor's fields, running to meet them, blowing down their noses with pleasure as they were led to the stable to be saddled. Lorn had given her Lewis' horse, a sturdy fourteen-year-old black stallion who had once been frisky enough for Lewis' taste but who was now quiet and respectful in his prime. Lorn had Dusk, the shaggy hill pony he had known and loved since its arrival at Laigmhor as a sweet-tempered four-year-old. When Lorn's brother had been alive they had gone riding as often as they could, glorying in the vast, empty spaces of Rhanna, the thunder of horses' hooves in their ears. Lewis had always ridden faster, harder, than his brother, tempting danger at every turn, shouting with abandon as he hung over his horse's neck, urging it on, faster, and faster, leaving Lorn far behind in his seeking after excitement.

Now Lorn felt as his brother must have felt, a heady intoxication pounding through his veins as he urged Dusk to go faster so that the sand flew up under his hooves and his nostrils worked furiously like twin valves.

Yet Lorn was aware that a greater part of his exhilaration owed itself to Rachel, the sight of her astride her horse, her long, graceful limbs exuding an earthy sensuality, her raven-black hair streaming back against the wind, her face alive, aglow with life. It had filled out in the last week, had lost its look of maturity, she was abloom with youth and vigour and the same sort of excitement that was in him ran swift and mercurial through her. A huge bubble of joy swelled deep in her breast, exploded out to every fibre of her being so that she wanted to cry out with the exuberance she felt. She opened her lips as if to shout her delight to the skies, but only the sounds of her own swift breathing escaped so that frustration and joy mingled as she arched her neck and lifted her face to the clouds which roamed free and clear above.

Lorn saw the swan-like grace of the slender column of her neck, saw her breasts, silhouetted against the racing mosaic of sea and sky. Sweat broke out on his brow. He wanted to leap off his horse, pull her down from hers, remove the flimsy garments from her body so that her breasts fell full and free against his chest. Desire, strong and treacherous poured through him. Combined with his exaltation it was a heady concoction. All the fetters that he had allowed to ensnare him fell away so that he felt unsafe and defenceless without those familiar bonds. All at once Lewis seemed very near, goading him on, making him very aware of his new sense of freedom and to his own surprise his voice rang out.

'Lewis! Lewis! This is how you felt! I can understand now – and I'm not afraid of life anymore!'

Rachel heard his wild cries, but the wind distorted the words so that she couldn't understand what he was saying. But she understood the rapture that had made him call out in such abandon. She had never seen Lorn McKenzie like this – the Lorn that she knew was back there at the cottage, his dark, brooding gaze turned away from her, his body hunched as if against any eventuality that might force him out of the self-contained world he had created for himself. Since her arrival, since her sensing of his decision to ignore her as much as possible, she had thrown herself into anything that might exclude him from her world. She would let him see that her strength of will could outmatch any McKenzie's any day and she was perfectly aware of the fact that she had succeeded. After just one short week she had beaten him at his own game and she had smiled to herself because he hadn't been able to hide his annoyance at her.

It had given her a good deal of satisfaction to have thwarted him and she felt that in some small measure she had managed to pay him back for all the dark looks, the innuendoes he had cast at her ever since the death of Lewis. Nevertheless she was intensely aware of the thrill she experienced at the sight of the unleashing of his hitherto hidden carefree spirit. Perhaps he himself had never been conscious that such feelings existed within himself. He had never been abandoned like his brother, Lewis, he had been shy and awkward, too concerned about what the world thought of him. His natural reserve had often been a stumbling block in his life – until now, these moments of sheer escapism astride his horse. The sight of his powerful, leaping body, his handsome, animated face, his dark curls tossing in the wind, excited Rachel more than she could have believed possible. It was an excitement she hadn't known for a long time – not since Lewis. She had thought she could never feel like that again but it was here now, throbbing deep within her, accelerating her heartbeats, tingling her skin. The great tracts of beach and ocean seemed to have been created for their pleasure alone that day. She could have gone on and on, riding forever, riding to the end of the rainbow which was slowly disappearing over the misted seas far far to the east, but the horses were tiring and Lorn brought the wild chase to an abrupt halt, reining in Dusk, leaping off his broad back to send him with a slap on his rump towards a patch of machair above the beach. Rachel followed his example. Her horse, trailing his reins, wandered to join Dusk and soon the two were munching contentedly at the sweet shoots of new grass.

Now that she was no longer divorced from Lorn by speed and distance, Rachel felt strangely awkward and she turned away quickly to seat herself on a rock. Clasping her hands round her knees she gazed with dark, restless eyes far out over the sparkling sea. The sun was breaking through the clouds, beating warmly on her back, making her roll up her sleeves and shut her eyes in blissful concentration on the warming rays. She didn't look to see what Lorn was doing – she didn't want to know – the very idea of being out here alone with him on the wide empty shore was almost too much for her to bear.

She knew she would have to maintain a cool front, never give Lorn one inkling of the emotions his presence wrought in her. It was better that way – it was the only way to keep things safe between them. She thought of Jon; dear Jon. He was so far away from her. She had written of course to let him know her plans, had explained that she was staying with Lorn and Ruth – Ruth . . . She lowered her chin to her knees and thought about her friend. She loved Ruth, for her innocence and her trust, for the unwavering loyalty she had always given to her so freely – yet, she wished sometimes that Ruth was less naïve. She was all but throwing Rachel and Lorn together, the thought never entering her head that her husband and best friend could possibly betray her . . . Rachel shuddered. Nothing like that must ever happen, there was too much at stake, too many people that could be hurt . . .

The sea lapped the shore at her feet. It was soothing and peaceful with the sun warm and delicious on her bare arms . . . The light was suddenly obliterated and she looked up startled to see Lorn standing over her, a look on his flushed face that she had never seen before – but yes, she *had* seen that look before – only it hadn't been on Lorn, it had been on Lewis – many, many times had she seen it on Lewis, a look of dazed desire, of need and want that wouldn't be quenched until . . . Her heart pounded and she got up quickly to run from the danger that Lorn McKenzie all at once presented. But he was too quick for her. One bronzed arm flashed out to pull her so swiftly against the hard wall of his chest she was powerless to prevent it. Momentarily she glimpsed his eyes, hard and black with desire – with wanting.

She tried to turn her head to ward off that which was inevitable, but his hand on the back of her head was a vicious clamp that forced her mouth ever closer to his. He made no sound, said no word, his breath was quick and sharp in her ears. His mouth came down, hard, firm, seeking, his lips cool but in seconds charged with fire. It was a kiss of fierce and burning passion and the flame of it curled into her, unleashing fires she had thought could never be wakened again. The kiss went deeper and deeper, she opened her mouth as if to voice a protest and immediately his tongue probed the warm moist recesses. One imprisoning hand on the small of her back forced her in closer against the hard bones of his pelvis, the other explored the soft curves of her hips and all the time he moulded her body ever further into his. Her limbs weakened as a shaft of response seared deep inside her belly.

She was tempted to return his passion but a spasm of anger seized her with an intensity that matched her trembling of desire. Who did he think he was? To ignore her, then to think he had the right to take possession of her whenever the mood took him? She struggled against him, the palms of her hands braced against the solid, unyielding wall of his chest. But he was beyond all resistance and her struggles only served to make him hold her tighter. His lips were doing things to her that almost made her relinquish her hold on her temper. It would be easy, so easy to give in to the demands of that warm, persuasive mouth . . . She concentrated on her anger – the reasons for it – she concentrated too on reality, on the dark, deep knowledge that if she was to let this thing between them get out of hand there would be no turning back for either of them . . . Raising her knee she pulled it up under him with all her strength and as he staggered back in pain her hand shot out to slap him resoundingly on the face.

She ran from him then, her long legs swiftly covering the space that separated her from her horse. Mounting she rode back the way they had come, her breath heaving rapidly. She didn't look back to see if he was following, something told her he wouldn't ever again. He would need time, time to calm down, to come to his senses, time also to consider the folly that could have grown from the interlude if she had allowed it. Yet she knew she would be lying to herself if she pretended she hadn't wanted it to happen. She had wanted Lorn McKenzie every bit as much as he had wanted her. The heat of passion still burned deep within her and she knew it would never be assuaged, not now, not after she had rejected and humiliated him. He was a proud one, this McKenzie and her one great surprise over the whole episode was that he had behaved so uncharacteristically. She tossed the hair back from her eyes and lifted her head. He might never look her way again, but at least she could face Ruth with a clear mind. Ruth's friendship was one that she cherished and she never wanted anything to jeopardize it – not any man – particularly Lorn McKenzie who, for years, had made it plain she was someone to be despised. Yet, despite herself, she couldn't stop the niggling feeling of regret that tugged at her heart nor could she help the fillip to her spirits at the realization that Lorn had wanted her badly enough to completely lose his head and make a fool of himself over her. It had been there all along of course, simmering under the surface, just waiting for an opportunity like today to bring it all to the boil.

She rode on, part of her lost in thought, the other revelling in the freedom that was all around her. Her ambitions and all that they meant seemed to belong to another self, someone outside of this green and blue jewel that was her home. Despite what had happened she was having the time of her life. She wished the holiday would last forever, but it wouldn't, it would pass very swiftly, she would have to savour each precious minute of every hour of every day.

Lorn watched her thundering away over the beach, riding her horse into the shallows where his hooves threw spray against the sun so that millions of droplets cascaded like diamonds all around, and Rachel was almost lost in the dazzling display. The madness that had seized him for the last hour had dispersed rapidly in that humiliating scene, leaving him starkly and miserably aware of the foolishness of his actions.

'Bitch! Bitch! Bitch!' He spat the blasphemy savagely through gritted teeth, too angry in the aftermath of the episode to admit to himself that the blame for it lay firmly with him. Sinking down on the cool sand he dug in his elbows and leaning back, closed his eyes while he drew air greedily into his lungs. After a few minutes his breathing grew steadier and with the returning of normality his irrationality left him, cold reason taking its place. Sitting up, he buried his face in his hands and whispered harshly, 'What have I done? God Almighty, what have I done?' He realized then that, thanks to Rachel, he hadn't done anything, certainly not the drastic and ill-fated step he had almost taken without thought or consideration for anyone else. Something had possessed him, something outside his understanding. If he'd had his way there would have been no peace of mind for him for the rest of his days.

Thoughts of Ruth crowded his mind and his face turned whiter than it already was. 'Oh, God, Ruthie, I'm sorry,' he murmured brokenly, then in a rush of anger, 'I knew something like this might happen, I warned you, Ruthie, but you wouldn't listen – it's happened; Rachel has already disrupted our lives – I knew she would – I knew . . .' He stopped and beat his fist into the soft, yielding sand. It hadn't been Rachel who had lost control just now, it had been he, himself – but it was because of her that it had happened. If she hadn't intruded, none of this would have happened and he would still be living in that cosy, safe world he had built for himself and Ruthie.

He got up slowly, all the fire gone out of him. He felt leaden, tired and miserable. Mounting Dusk he made his way slowly back, lost in thought. Nothing like this would ever happen again, he would make damned sure of that. He vowed he would give himself no opportunity to be alone with Rachel again – he daren't ever allow that to happen for he knew, deep in himself, that he couldn't trust himself with her, that if a like opportunity presented itself he wouldn't be strong enough to withstand the lovely, exciting creature whose voluptuous body promised undreamed-of pleasures which he had tasted but briefly in the soft, burning promise of her lips.

*　　*　　*

High on the cliffs above Mara Oran Bay, Anton Büttger slowly laid his binoculars on the close-cropped turf at his side. He loved this spot, the scent of the emerald green machair which stretched way back to the vault of the heavens; the limitless panorama of sea and sky; the majesty of the great cliffs plummeting to meet the might of the sea; the wind tearing at his body, shrieking angrily up from the sea to lift the seabirds aloft and bear them effortlessly along. Often he came to this place to take a few minutes' respite from his labours in the fields around Croft na Ard.

The sweep of his glasses over the terrain below had been swift and careless and the advent of Lorn and Rachel into his line of vision had been as unexpected as it had been fleeting. Feeling like an intruder he had brought the glasses round to focus on them with more attention. Whatever he had expected, he hadn't expected to see them embracing and after the first rapid impression he had felt suddenly guilty of spying and now the glasses reposed at his side while he tried to dismiss Rachel and Lorn from his mind. Drawing his knees up to his chin he gazed contemplatively into the distance and was quite unprepared for the sudden burst of apprehension that flooded his mind as the full import of what he had just seen struck him. What the hell was Rachel playing at? he wondered. Surely it couldn't be that she and Lorn McKenzie were – lovers? Quickly he rejected the idea. She was devoted to Jon, her husband, she couldn't be so foolish as to start playing around the minute Jon's back was turned!

Jon was a personal friend of Anton's. They had been in the Luftwaffe together, Anton as a bomber pilot, Jon as a flight engineer. He had always liked the gentle, insecure young man with his hatred of war and his love of music. Jon had been a brilliant musician, could have made a notable career for himself, but on that fateful crash landing on Rhanna his heart had been captured forever by the untamed little dumb girl, Rachel. After many years he had come back to Rhanna to fall in love and finally marry her. For her he had given up his own career to allow her to pursue hers for he had recognized in her a far greater talent than his own. And it had worked; despite their age difference it had worked – and they had been happy – or so it had seemed. Anton's handsome face puckered into a frown. Had he after all been deceived by the outward success of Rachel and Jon's marriage? Perhaps a girl as beautiful and vibrant as Rachel needed something more than Jon could give her . . . Wild ideas surged through Anton's head. Ought he to phone Jon, tell him to come as quickly as he could – he could say Rachel was missing him – needing him? Anton shook himself and smiled wryly. What a fool he was. He was making mountains out of molehills. It was quite possible that the incident he had witnessed was just an isolated one with some perfectly reasonable explanation – his gaze travelled downward and he saw a horse fleeing back along the sands. Picking up his binoculars he saw that the rider was Rachel – and way back among the rocks she had left Lorn behind. Anton put down the glasses and let out a little sigh of relief. He was getting as bad as Behag Beag with her ability to turn small incidents into monumental scandals. Whatever had happened down there, Rachel was having none of it. He had been wrong to jump to conclusions about her. It was obvious she was as devoted to Jon as he was to her. Anton stood up and walked back to his tractor, deciding that what he had seen was so trivial it wasn't even worth mentioning to Babbie.

Rachel was hanging out the washing in the little green below the knoll when Lorn finally arrived home. He didn't look at her but went straight into the house, half of him cold at the thought of facing Ruth, the other half longing to see her, to reassure himself that everything was as it had been. She was in the bedroom, going through her wardrobe, sighing as she skimmed past each item in turn. He stood hesitating, looking at her and she half turned in fright.

'Lorn, I didn't hear you come in – what kept you? Dinner has been ready for ages.'

'Dusk turned his hoof. I had to walk back part of the way.' The lie came readily to his lips and he hated himself for the deceit. He went to her and nuzzled her hair. 'What are you doing? Looking out things for the ragman?'

She giggled. 'Ach, I might as well for it seems the only things I've got left are rags. I was wondering what to wear for Father's wedding – nothing I've got looks decent enough.'

'Why don't you go over to Oban with Mother and get yourself something?' he suggested, glad to be talking of everyday affairs.

She shook her head. 'Och no, we canny afford it, I'll make do with what I have, the bairns need new things more than me.'

He pulled her to him and cupping her face in his hands kissed her tenderly on the lips.

She gazed up at him in some surprise. 'What's wrong, Lorn? It's not often you do things like that in the middle of the day.'

'I felt like it – can I not kiss my own wee wife when the mood takes me?'

She snuggled against him. 'I wish it would take you more often, I wish it wasn't dinner time . . .'

'And I wish we had the place to ourselves!' he interposed bitterly, spying Rachel coming towards the house.

Ruth's brow furrowed. 'Lorn, don't start that again – I thought you had settled your feelings about Rachel.'

'I'm putting up with her for your sake.' He knew he sounded too vehement and added, 'Och, Rachel's all right – it's just – I'll be glad when it's just you and me and the wee ones again.' He held her away and studied her face. 'You're looking better. How's the bellyache?'

'Gone. I had a quiet time to myself and even managed to get a bit of writing done. I'm looking forward to the picnic this afternoon. Kirsteen is keeping Lorna and Douglas for the afternoon so it will be just you and me. Rachel isn't coming, she thought she ought to go and see her mother.'

A wave of relief washed over him, mingling with a strange sense of regret that wouldn't be denied. It would be lovely to go away with Ruth, to be alone with her such as he hadn't been in a long time – yet – how much more exhilarating it would have been had Rachel been there with them. Then he thought about his resolve never to think of her in that way again. But it wasn't as simple as that. Just knowing that he would see her in a minute or two drove all reason out of his mind. He couldn't stop the thoughts that crowded in on him and he was afraid – afraid for the lovely life he and Ruthie had built together. Sharply he pulled in his breath. Ruth looked at him in bemusement.

'Lorn, are you deaf? I said it would be just you and me this afternoon.'

He crushed her to him and stroked her hair. 'I heard, Ruthie, I heard, and I'm glad. It's high time we got away on our own. We've had precious little time to ourselves since we got married.'

His hands moved over her arms. She felt young and soft – and somehow rather fragile.

Chapter Seven

The first thing that struck the Reverend Mark James as he stood before Dugald and Totie preparatory to taking the marriage ceremony, was the quantity of blue and purple heads which bobbed into the sweep of his vision. Without exception, all the ladies in question wore hats, jammed so far down over their eyes that it was a wonder their owners had managed to see their way to kirk, yet even so enough of the hair escaped to cause immediate and startling effect. It was obvious that Mairi had had a busy and profitable start to her new hairdressing venture, though it was equally obvious that zeal had got the better of her normally cautious nature and had allowed her to 'go daft wi' the dye' as Elspeth Morrison, herself having fallen foul of Mairi's enthusiasm, so eloquently put it.

'You look just like a bunch o' fallen wimmen,' Tam McKinnon had told a red-faced coterie who were gathered in Merry Mary's shop the day before the wedding to air their horrified grievances. 'I am glad my Kate had the good sense no' to allow anybody to tamper wi' the natural colours God gave her. I wouldny be seen dead wi' a woman wi' hair that colour. I have no notion at all to be havin' a wife lookin' like a Jezebel.'

But Tam had crowed too loudly and too soon because Kate, having left her hairdressing appointment till the last possible moment, had emerged from her daughter-in-law's premises just after nine that morning sporting a head just a shade bluer than the Sound of Rhanna itself.

'My God, it canny be Kate!' Tam had cried aghast, stopping dead in the middle of the street to stare in disbelief at the apparition approaching him with beaming smiles.

'And what is wrong wi' you, my man?' Kate had demanded severely while self-consciously surveying the windows in the nearby harbour cottages for signs of twitching net curtains. 'Have you no sense o' culture at all, Tam McKinnon?' she said haughtily patting her coiffure in an affected manner which was totally out of keeping with her straightforward ways.

'Culture! Is that what you call it?' Tam had spluttered. 'A waste o' good money more like. What is this island comin' to I'd like to know!'

'Into the twentieth century that's what!' Kate told him venomously. 'It's all the thing now, this colour o' hair. The ladies in Oban have had it long ago and it's high time we caught up wi' them. The bodachs o' this island have had it easy for too long. You are just annoyed because for once in your mean life you actually dug into your pouch to pay for a hairdo for your very own wife.' With belligerence she had eyed the untidy strands escaping his cap. 'While we are on the subject, just you get along to Mairi's and get her to give you a decent haircut. And go this minute, Tam McKinnon, I don't want you givin' me a showing up at Doug's wedding this morning.'

Tam had almost had apoplexy and had gaped at her in open-mouthed horror. 'Ach, will you stop haverin', Kate,' he said beseechingly. 'You know fine you always do my hair wi' the shears — they have always been good enough for me.'

Kate's lips had set grimly. 'Well, this time it's goin' to be different. I am no' liftin' one finger to you for I'm that mad I just might cut off your lugs wi' the shears. The first hairdo I've had in my life and all you have done is moan. Any other man would have said they liked it fine, even if it was only to keep the peace, but no' you, my silly mannie, oh no! You have nothing between your lugs but fresh air! I have felt the draught of it often enough, so mind you tell Mairi to leave a few strands round about your head or the bairns will be queuein' up for a free peep show.'

Gathering herself up to her full height she had stuck out her ample bosom, glared round defiantly at the now furiously twitching curtains, and had stomped off with the parting shot, 'Go you along to Mairi's now. I'm away home to see to Old Joe's hair. The bodach would go to kirk lookin' like a forsaken scarecrow if it wasny for me. Hmph. Men! They are all alike, dirty buggers the lot o' them!'

Now Old Joe sat beside a thoroughly crestfallen Tam, his snowy locks cropped to the bone, a grimace on his pink-skinned face as the residue of jagged hair caught in his vest made him twitch restlessly in his seat. Kate had not been in the best of moods when she had taken the shears to his head and he hadn't dared to utter one protest as she snipped energetically 'right down to the bones of his skull'. Nor had he dared to make any comment about her new hairdo, though he had been so startled at sight of it he had choked over his breakfast egg which had given Kate a good excuse to take her irate feelings out on his back, thumping it so heartily she had knocked out his false teeth, though fortunately they had landed on the rug and so had escaped drastic damage. Old Joe sighed as he sat on the hard pew of the kirk, and thought longingly of the house by the harbour that his advancing years had forced him to give up. Kate had insisted that he come and live with her. He was a McKinnon after all and she would allow no relative of hers to spend their last days in some home away from family and friends. For that he had been extremely grateful but it wasn't easy living with the forceful Kate and trying to adjust himself to ways that were so different from his own. She was always making him wash himself and change into clean underwear when he had only just 'broken in' the last set. He shifted in his seat and glanced malevolently at Kate's primly held blue coiffure. Nudging Tam in the ribs he whispered with a certain amount of grim humour. 'She is sittin' there lookin' like the stiff end o' a peacock's erse. I'm thinkin', Tam, that this will be a blue do, a very blue do indeed.'

Tam squirmed as the old man's wheezy chuckle broke the rather stunned silence which had fallen over the males in the gathering ever since the 'blue and lavender brigade' had filed into their pews. Without exception the women looked exceedingly self-conscious and uncomfortably aware of the astounded glances thrown at them askance from all quarters. Indeed, it was a wonder that any of them had dared to put in an appearance at all and one or two of the more sober minded had opted to stay at home rather than face the critical public eye.

Mairi gazed round with admirable calm for she was somewhat shocked to see the results of her work gathered in a relatively confined space. She determined that next time she would have to aim for a more subtle effect, though when her husband Wullie nudged her and sniggered, 'God, woman! Are you colour blind?' her rather vacant brown eyes grew troubled and she swallowed hard as she wondered if there would be a next time.

The minister's lips twitched as his eye fell on Behag Beag sitting in her pew, a black cloche hat pulled down so far over her forehead it was difficult to see her eyes. As eager as a sniffing bloodhound, Behag had gone to Mairi's to claim her right to a half price hairdo with 'a nice wee rinse' thrown in to the bargain. Shocked beyond measure at the results she had gone home and had tried to lather away the offending dye to no avail. Afterwards she had swithered mightily about appearing outside till the colour had worn off, but a glance at her BEM medal in its frame above the fireplace had reminded her anew just how important a personage she was and pulling her hat over her long ears she had marched off determinedly to the kirk, ignoring the remark Erchy made in her hearing about her looking like a 'chanty wi' legs'.

The minister's eye caught that of Shona sitting beside Niall in the middle of the church, and as always, the sight of her brought a warm glow to his heart. He could see plainly her dimples, the convulsive twitching of her lips in her laughter-bright face. Almost imperceptibly he lowered one of his eyelids and her hand flew up to her mouth to stifle the merriment that threatened to engulf her. Niall, fair head bowed, eyes glued to a sweet wrapping on the floor by Captain Mac's big, stout black shoes, sidled up closer to her and hissed from the side of his mouth, 'For God's sake don't! I'm in agony keeping my own back.' A glint of devilment shone in his eyes. 'Look at Merry Mary. The dye has stained one of her ears.'

Sure enough one of Merry Mary's generous ears had escaped her Sunday best hat and stood out in all its orange-tinged glory for the world to see. Merry Mary, having naturally ginger hair of her own, had decided to enhance it with an auburn rinse but the results were not quite what she had expected and the wispy hair lurking under her hat was more ginger than it had ever been, with a sheen of bright orange to add to the shocking effect.

Shona clutched Niall. 'Don't! If I see another orange ear or strand of purple hair I'll burst.'

Fortunately, just then the deep, pleasant voice of the minister rang out and the marriage ceremony began. Dugald had heard the words twice before, the first time when he was just nineteen, his young bride seventeen, full of tender innocence that had remained with her till her early death three years later. It had taken him a long time to get over the blow of such a premature parting and he had given no thought to marriage till the advent of Morag Ruadh into his life. All through those long unhappy years spent with Morag it seemed Totie had always been there, strong, handsome Totie with her bright green eyes and her mass of thick hair, once dark, now a steely grey but as wavy and attractive as it had always been.

She was wearing a dress of forest green that day with a single pink rose fixed above the swell of her sturdy breasts, another nestling in the band of her big floppy ridiculous hat. Memories swamped Dugald, joys and sorrows all mingling together, making him feel slightly apprehensive of what the future held in store for him. But it was too late now to turn back even if he had wanted to. 'Third time lucky.' The rather cynical prediction of the islanders seemed to ring in his ears. He straightened his shoulders, cleared his throat nervously and turned to see Ruth watching him, her fair face as serious as his but a smile lighting it as she caught his eye. He smiled back, saw Totie's green, unwavering gaze fixed on him and he relaxed. She was a mountain this woman, a solid reliable presence who gave him the same sort of reassurance that he got from the hills each morning he looked upon them from his window. Mark James was handing him the ring, his fingers shook, for a moment he thought he was going to drop it.

Ruth held her breath while her own fingers tightened convulsively over Lorn's hand. She had never loved her father more than in these moments. He was so distinguished looking in his dark suit, his mop of silvery hair standing out like a halo against the crimson light from the stained glass window. She had come to kirk early to sit in the quietness and say a prayer for his future happiness. She wasn't feeling too well that morning. The pain in her stomach had grown more constant of late, and she knew she ought to go to Doctor Lachlan's to see about it – she would – just as soon as her father was safely married and away on his honeymoon. She didn't want him to be upset or anxious in any way at a time like this and she certainly didn't want him going away with an uneasy mind, for she knew he worried if there was anything at all wrong with her.

The minister was nodding at Dugald, giving him mute encouragement and now the ring was on Totie's finger and the kirk let go its breath.

Ruth moved closer to Lorn and his hand closed over hers even tighter. He had surprised and delighted her that morning by presenting her with a parcel which contained a new outfit for the wedding, together with some very feminine underwear.

'Lorn,' she had gasped. 'How on earth . . . ?'

'Easy.' His strong dark face had relaxed into the happiest smile she had seen for days, for there had been a constraint in his manner of late that made him moody and silent. 'I got Mother to get them in Oban when she was over with Burnbreddie's wife. She knew your size but wasn't so sure about the style—' Anxiously he had looked at her, eager to allay the guilt that had lain black and heavy on his conscience for days.

With shining eyes she had picked up the pink linen suit and held it against her. 'Oh, Lorn, it's perfect! Kirsteen aye did have good taste – and – the underclothes – what on earth did you say to her? I canny imagine you describing frillies to your very own mother, you won't even do it with me.'

His bronzed face lit. Catching her and kissing her he laughed. 'I just told her to get you some new breeks and things but Mother aye did have a romantic nature – these are what she came back with.' He had moved closer against her. 'I didn't tell her you won't get to put them on – I thought I might have a go at that.'

'Ach, you would just take them right off again,' she had murmured shyly, a flush high on her cheekbones as his hands had brushed her breasts and his dark head came down to nuzzle her ears till she tingled. He hadn't made love to her for more than a week and there had been an urgency in the arms that enclosed her – then Rachel had come into the room and he had sprung away, a dark flush of anger staining his tanned skin, the dourness back in his manner. But now, with his hand warm and firm in hers she sensed a warmness back in him once more and she whispered, 'I love you, Lorn McKenzie.'

'Me too, Ruthie.' He squeezed her hand and felt a lump in his throat because her fingers were so slender, so trusting lying in his. He was very conscious of Rachel close by, utterly and strikingly beautiful in the sombre setting of the kirk, and he hated himself for even thinking of her when Ruth's hand lay so confidingly in his.

Rachel saw the exchange between the two. She closed her eyes and tried to think of Jon from whom she had just received a letter, telling her he would be away a while yet and he was missing her more and more every day. But he seemed very far away and out of reach, out even of the recall of memory for no matter how hard she tried she couldn't bring to mind his dear honest face. The only face she saw, in dreams, in reality, was the face of Lorn McKenzie and she kept her eyes squeezed tight shut and forced herself to concentrate on the notes of a skylark's song, now near, now far away, trilling in ecstasy over the moors. The *Song of Rhanna* came sighing into her head, growing, swelling. A smile hovered at her lips and quite unconsciously her fingers strummed on her Bible, beating time, beat beating, faster and faster – like her heart every time she looked at Lorn and remembered the feel of his muscular arms around her, his lips burning into hers . . .

She opened her eyes. The ceremony was over. Dugald and Totie were coming down the aisle, smiling, relieved.

The triumphal strains of Mendelssohn's Wedding March reverberated through the time-worn cloisters, coaxed from the ancient harmonium by Barra McLean's persuasive hands and feet. Once upon a time the cantankerous old instrument had been Morag Ruadh's jealously guarded possession. After her death it had lain silent and neglected and Sunday worship had not seemed the same without its wheezy strains filling the kirk. In the end Mark James had appealed to Barra and though she had protested that she only knew how to play the piano she had finally capitulated. Now she perspired, grew beetroot-red, her two small feet thumped the pedals with vigour, her fingers flew unerringly over the keyboard. Undeterred by a pigeon's droppings which rained down from the lofty rafters to land with military precision on the music sheets, she wheezed, thumped and played the newlyweds out of the kirk and on to the Hillock where Todd the Shod was ready to take over with the pipes. Everybody streamed outside, the party mood already on them as stirring tunes reeled through the air. Dugald and Totie were surrounded, congratulated, bombarded with rice and confetti.

Dodie arrived on the scene, his lips stretching into the familiar 'He breeah', his big calloused hands holding tightly to a large piece of driftwood shaped like a dolphin. He had smoothed and polished it, lavishing many nights of care upon it, for it was his habit to present all newlyweds with a simple gift. And even though he was bemused by Dugald's third marriage he handed over his gift graciously though couldn't refrain from saying, 'Are you no' feart Morag Ruadh will maybe come down and haunt you? She might no' take kindly to another lady in her house.'

Dugald's eyes twinkled though he tried to look serious for Dodie's sake. 'Ach no, Dodie, Morag will be far too busy up yonder to be bothered haunting the likes o' me. She aye liked to keep busy you see, and she will have more and enough to do making sure everything gets kept nice and clean and that none of the cratur's up there try to shirk their work.'

Dodie's dreamy eyes had grown round. 'Do you really think that, Dugald? My, it would be grand if it was the case, for I'm aye feart she takes it into her head to come down and haunt the kirkyard the way she used to when she was alive.'

'You can rest easy, Dodie,' interposed Totie firmly. 'Morag is at peace now and is no' likely to come back down here – to haunt you or anybody else for that matter.'

'Are you coming to the reception later, Dodie?' Dugald expected a negative reply because the old eccentric rarely appeared at social gatherings and he was taken aback therefore when Dodie nodded his head violently and burst out, 'I am that – Hector the Boat is bringing over a creel o' fresh lobsters and there is nothing I like better than a lobster straight from the pot—' He gulped and rushed on, 'I dinna like dances and things as a rule, but I haveny anything for my tea and Hector says I will no' get a taste o' one lobster unless I show my face so I'm away home now to see will I have something to wear grand enough to come to your party.'

He galloped off, almost knocking down Kate who, skirts held high, was already jigging in time to the pipes.

Mark James was at the kirk door, talking to Rachel, telling her how much he had enjoyed hearing the *Song of Rhanna* on the wireless. He had first met Rachel when he had come to the island three years before and he had never forgotten the girl with the lovely face and the restless eyes which gave away so much of what she was feeling. He had also been impressed by her bravery and by the strange gift of healing which she had displayed at Morag Ruadh's deathbed. She hadn't been able to avert Morag's death, nobody could have done that because it was what she had wanted, but she had almost miraculously calmed Morag's troubled soul so that she had departed life peacefully and without any of the fears which had beset her for years.

The minister's smoky grey gaze held Rachel's as he said, 'I was wondering if you would mind me having a go at putting words to your tune? I've always been interested in music and quite often while away my spare time composing little verses that I think might go with some tune I've heard. I know I could never do your melody justice, but could you – would you allow me to try?'

Rachel thought to herself that it was little wonder this man had earned the trust and love of the islanders. His lack of ego was one of his most endearing traits and gave him the ability to understand others whose self-confidence was low. Rachel showed her eager approval of his suggestion and they parted after making an arrangement for her to come to the Manse any evening she felt like it.

Mark James turned his attention to the scene on the Hillock. The grass here was a bright emerald green against the blue of the sky. Everyone was wearing their best clothes and the colourful mosaic they made as they stood about talking, or in Kate and Nancy's case dancing with arms entwined, was not a usual sight, as normally the sombre Sabbath clothing and the reserved demeanour of the islanders on this high, windblown hill made it a place of hushed voices and sober chatter. Captain Mac bustled up, a splendid sight to behold. He had allowed his whiskers to grow and grow and now the bushy white beard fairly bristled with its own importance. He had always been an eyecatching sight but now, with his big, bulbous red nose shining in the sun, his luxuriant silvery hair and whiskers gleaming, his kilt flying in the breezes, he was the kind of man to stand out in a crowd and not be dismayed by the fact.

'You'll be coming to the reception, Minister?' he greeted Mark James. 'It wouldny be the same without you and that's a fact. Nellie was just sayin' it is a pity a fine figure o' a man like yourself hasny a woman to enjoy these things with.' One bushy eyebrow descended as he winked knowingly. 'Nellie might be my sister but she is just the same as the rest. Women seem to think that men like you and me canny content ourselves unless we have a woman to look to us. I tell you, much as I miss my cailleach, I would think twice before taking on another woman: they can be buggering pests betimes, ay, even Nellie herself gets me down wi' her continual nagging at me to keep off the rum, no' to smoke my pipe, no' to put my feet up on the hearth.' He shook his head sadly. 'Ay, we're better off without them, ay indeed.'

'They make the world a brighter place, Mac. I for one wouldn't like to live in a world without them.' Mark James' face was perfectly serious and Captain Mac's big smile beamed out.

'Ach, you're right there, son. I only said all that for I have been feeling a kind of restlessness comin' over me this whily and I didny like to admit it might be because I have a hankering to be takin' another woman to myself – mind – she would have to be special. I was fond o' my cailleach and know I will never get her likes again but somebody near enough – ay, somebody near enough as perfect as my Mary!' He was gazing into the distance as he spoke and quite suddenly he strode away, making for a grassy knoll on which was ensconced the hunched-up figure of Aunt Grace, Dugald's sister who had hitherto lived in Coll but who was now comfortably installed in a little cottage by Portcull harbour. She was crying her eyes out into a sodden scrap of lace hanky, sniffing loudly as if hoping she would be heard. She reposed on the knoll in all her Sabbath splendour, her green felt hat held in place by a fearsome hat pin decorated by a glazed china cherry, her brown tweed coat hugging her ankles. The cherries in her hat matched that on the end of the pin and strummed a gay little tattoo in time to her sobs; her sturdy black-booted feet, as if divorced from the rest of her, were contrarily tapping in time to the tunes from Todd's pipes, though as Mac approached her feet became still and she buried her face further into her hanky.

'What ails you, Grace?' asked Mac kindly, admiring the coy turn of her head away from him. 'I had thought you would be happy to be at Doug's weddin'.'

'I am, I am,' she waved her hanky at him with vigour. 'It was beautiful just, but it minded me o' Jeemie on our weddin' day and I just had to have a wee greet. He wasny sober you see, Jeemie aye had the nerves and before the cermony he had a dram too many and had to be held up by his brothers till he took his vows. Ach, it was lovely just and today in kirk minded me on it.'

'Ach, you're havering, lass,' blustered Mac, his eyes twinkling as he noted that her feet were going again. 'Doug only had the one dram before he came out. He was perfectly sober.'

Aunt Grace waved her hanky again and wailed. 'I know, I know, that's why I'm greetin'. You see, I aye told Jeemie he shouldny have been drunk at the altar o' God but by God! He took his vows as bravely and as sincerely as Doug did today and I just wish Jeemie was here so that I could tell him I'm sorry for all those years o' nagging the poor good mannie. I get lonely betimes and just wish I had my man back again to keep me company.'

Her feet were gaining momentum as she spoke and quite suddenly and with great agility she sprachled up and told Mac, 'I'll be fine when I've had a good hot cuppy. Will you be comin' wi' me? You can tell me about your own poor, dear departed wife while I'm makin' the tea and changin' out these awful drab clothes – I treated myself to an awful bonny frock for the reception and you can be havin' the first peep at it – if it pleases you that is,' she added with a sidelong glance.

Mac crooked his arm and away they went down the brae, Mac's kilt swinging in the breeze, Aunt Grace's cherries waggling merrily. Halfway down she executed a kind of shuffling jig, her black boots twinkling in the sunshine, and Mac put back his head and gave vent to the deep hearty bellow for which he was famed.

Old Joe, thoroughly disgruntled because Kate had told him sternly that he didn't have time to go to his beloved harbour before the reception began, looked after Aunt Grace's quaint figure thoughtfully. 'She is an able wee woman, that sister o' yours, Dugald,' he observed with studied indifference.

'Ay, she is that, Joe,' agreed Dugald, watching his sister's cherries bobbing in the distance.

'She'll be a youngster compared wi' myself, I'm thinkin',' hazarded the old man carefully.

'If I'm minding right she'll be seventy on her next birthday – a mite older than myself.'

Old Joe couldn't keep a gleam of interest from his eyes.

'As young as that, eh? And she'll be owning the house at the harbour I haveny a doubt? I mind you sayin' the house in Coll was hers so she will have had enough and plenty to buy the new place?'

'Oh, she's comfortably off is Grace,' nodded Dugald, surprised at Joe's interest and at the unusual garrulity with which he spoke of everyday affairs since he had been a dreamer all his days and always avoided the harsher realities if he could help it.

Joe rubbed his chin absently and his sea-green eyes positively sparkled, for an idea had come into his head, one so astounding that he was taken aback at himself for even thinking it. 'A fine wee body,' he murmured almost to himself. 'And she'll be at the reception I haveny a doubt?'

'Oh ay, she will that,' assured Dugald. 'She'll be away home now to change into her best bib and tucker.'

Old Joe turned away, forgetting the harbour in the new diversions which crowded into his mind. So engrossed was he in thought, he made no objection to Kate ushering him away down the hill with the intention of making him change from his boots into the despised dressy shoes she had told him to wear to kirk but which he had conveniently forgotten.

Everyone else dispersed to go home and change, leaving Erchy and Todd stamping their sturdy feet on the turf and blowing into their pipes with such vigour the sound carried for miles, tingling the blood of all who heard and making them tap their feet in anticipation of the night of fun which lay ahead. Dugald had hired the village hall for the reception and the villagers had seen to it that it was decorated appropriately for the occasion. Streamers and balloons hung from the ceiling, a banner across the stage yelled out congratulations to the newlyweds in large red letters, while a small message underneath said cryptically, 'If at first you don't succeed, try, try and try again. Well done, Dugald Ban.'

Niall who had directed the proceedings had not thought this to be in the best of taste but Tam, the instigator, had told him seriously, 'Och, get away wi' you, son, everyone is knowing this is Doug's third time, you canny hide the truth o' that. If Robert the Bruce can do it wi' a spider then Doug can do it wi' a woman. It gives the other lads a wee bit o' hope into the bargain. When our cailleachs see the likes o' that they will maybe treat us wi' more appreciation in case we might take a fancy to have a wee taste somewhere else.'

The hall filled up in no time with everyone flocking to help themselves from the cold buffet which had been set near the door. Plates rattled, piles of cold chicken, ham and tongue disappeared rapidly. Hector the Boat had set up a copper washtub just inside the door, connected to a gas cylinder. Into the tub of boiling hot water he was dropping live lobsters with relish and was doing an altogether roaring trade. As wily as he was simple he was quick to seize opportunity when it chanced along and despite a storm of protest that this was a wedding feast free to all comers, he was charging five shillings for an admittedly generous portion of lobster with most people paying up since few could resist the savoury aroma which assailed their nostrils as they approached the hall.

Dodie arrived on the scene, hungry and gaunt looking though he had spruced himself up, having changed into a smart, if thin, blue jacket and fawn trousers so well pressed the men told him they could cut ham on the crease.

'What way did you get it so sharp?' Jim Jim asked curiously. 'You haveny the electricity to use wi' an iron and you never got a crease like that from putting your breeks under the mattress.'

But Dodie was not going to tell him that, under great duress to himself and at the cost of one of his beautiful painted stones, he had persuaded the crotchety old kitchen maid at Burnbreddie House to undertake to do his laundry for him though she had insisted 'outer layers only and these had better be clean or I'll rub your nose in them – though mind—' she had paused and wrinkled her sharp nose thoughtfully – 'they couldny be any worse than some o' the things this household presents me with – especially Scott Balfour the Younger. Over the moors he goes whenever he is at home and I'm thinkin' he must go crawling about in peat bogs for the knees o' his breeks are aye coated wi' mud and other unpleasant stuff that I have no wish to mention.'

Despite her sour nature she was an excellent laundress

and Dodie was well pleased with her handiwork, so much so he had spent ten minutes staring at himself in his grimy mirror before venturing outside. The tempting smell of boiled lobster set his mouth watering but he was dismayed when Hector, his beguiling, one-toothed smile never faltering, stuck out a leathery palm and demanded payment for his wares.

'You are a buggering cheat, just!' wailed Dodie, his belly rumbling so loudly those in the vicinity commented on it. 'You only brought those lobsters here because Colin Mor said they wereny fit to take over to the fish market. Forbye, you promised me one whole one for nothing! I didny go to all the bother o' dressing up just to come to this dance thing! I want my tea and I want it now.'

Hector's smile had fallen away like a veil and with a quick look round he hastily shoved a generous portion of lobster at Dodie and told him he could have as much as he liked free, though he wasn't to broadcast the fact to another living soul. Dodie, delighted at his success, went off with a brimming plate, leaving Hector muttering darkly that the old eccentric wasn't as green as he was cabbage looking.

After the cake had been cut and all the usual pleasantries dispensed with, the hall was cleared of unnecessary furnishings, the bar was officially opened by Angus who had been imbibing freely for the last hour, and the band struck up with vigour. The dancing was soon in full progress and Ruth, who had come down early in case her help was needed, looked round for a sign of Lorn who hadn't been keen to come, telling her that he would rather stay home and look after the children. But Kirsteen had committed herself to looking after all the wee ones in the family so Lorn had no excuse, though he had grumbled at the idea of going to all the fuss of donning his best suit to go out. He came through the door, shining and brushed, looking so different from the farmer husband she knew that Ruth could do nothing but admire him for a few silent minutes. He hovered near the door, red faced, looking as though he would like to run back through it the way he had come for he had never been keen on dancing, though he occasionally took Ruth to the informal affairs in the village.

The floor was filling as one by one the men, helped by a few drams of the uisge beatha, plucked up the courage to lead their partners into a waltz. Shona and Niall were dancing close together, Shona graceful and lovely in a long turquoise dress, Niall handsome and striking in his lovat jacket and McLachlan kilt.

'Get that Lorn to dance with you, Ruth,' Shona hissed on the way past and Niall winked and with his eyes indicated a knot of young men who were eyeing Ruth with admiration for she was exceedingly attractive and feminine in a long rose-pink dress which showed her fair skin and flaxen hair to advantage.

Between the heads of the dancers Lorn caught Ruth's eye and despite his flush of embarrassment he winked at her and smiled. Of a sudden she was transported back to the night of the Burnbreddie dance, the music, the laughter, the love in her heart for Lorn McKenzie. It had been for her an evening of vividly conflicting emotions, of joy and unhappiness, for Lorn had started off the night in a highly confident mood though the minute he stepped over the threshold of Burnbreddie House his confidence had dropped away like a mantle, leaving him so nervous and unsure of himself he had ended up getting drunk and she, thinking he hadn't wanted to be seen dancing with her because of her limp, had fled the scene to return home in a deep state of unhappiness and doubt over his feelings for her.

A smile touched the corners of her mouth. How foolish they had been in those early, searching days of their young love. He had changed in so many ways though at times he was still unsure of himself and, winding her way through the crowd, she went up to him, smiled, said coyly, 'Will you do the honour of dancing with me, my man?'

He let go of his breath and giggled suddenly. 'If you're sure you don't mind me stamping on your toes?'

'My dear chap,' she assumed the 'Burnbreddie drawl' as it was known locally, 'I wouldn't give a damn if you put your feet on mine and let me dance you round the entire hall.'

She could be exceedingly funny when the mood took her and he stood looking down at her admiring the dainty sprinkling of freckles on her small, straight nose. 'Daft wee thing,' he smiled affectionately. 'Come on, let's get it over with or I'll never pluck up the courage.'

The dance came to an end, everyone was walking back

to the benches set along the walls when the door opened to admit Rachel. A hush fell over the young males at the sight of her. She was wearing a simple, white, off-the-shoulder dress which intimately hugged every exciting contour of her body. Her dark hair was piled on top of her head, showing the symmetrical grace of her long smooth neck. Long diamanté drops hung from her delicately shaped ears, a red rosebud nestled in the luxuriant coils of her shining hair, another was pinned to her shoulder, the red against the pure white looking like a blob of blood. When she walked across the hall all eyes turned to watch her tall statuesque figure and Ruth, going forward to meet her, suddenly felt pale and insignificant beside her.

'Hmph, would you look at the lass!' Elspeth Morrison's gaunt immobile face was disapproving. 'She is out to have a good time and no mistake. She hasny got her man to keep an eye on her so she'll be huntin' down any other foolish enough to take her on.'

'Just you mind your tongue, my woman,' Kate leapt to the defence of her granddaughter. 'Rachel might be a beautiful lass to look at but her heart is wi' one man and that is Jon. She canny help lookin' the way she does. If there's any huntin' to be done it will be yourself stalkin' them down like a jungle tigress – I've seen you watching our very own Isaac McIntosh wi' a hungry glint in your eye and he's no' the first one by a long shot.'

Elspeth's face flamed and she was about to make an angry retort when old Sorcha jumped readily into the argument, her lips folded tightly in disapproval of Rachel who was being swept on to the floor by Mark James, anxious to talk to her about music.

'Mistress Morrison is right,' she nodded grimly. 'That Rachel has even got our minister under her spell. Men are all alike when it comes to girls like her – flaunting everything she's got without even a blush to cover her bosoms.'

With chagrin, Kate eyed the strands of dyed wispy hair lurking about Sorcha's long ears. 'At least she didny have to get her hair dyed to force folks into gawping at her. Ay, Sorcha, you must be gettin' desperate for attention to make such a spectacle of yourself and I was always under the impression that you were such a respectable body.'

Sorcha treated Kate to a contemptuous glare. 'Folks in glasshouses shouldny talk. What is that covering your own head I'd like to know? It's no' a blue powder puff, that I can vouch for.'

'Ach, I did it to make cratur's like you sit up and take notice,' answered Kate with asperity. 'I have my man which is more than can be said for the likes o' you, though I would have thought you would be past it at your age.'

'Here comes Behag,' Elspeth forgot her enmity in the heat of the moment. 'Mercy on us! Would you look at her! I'm thinkin' she's taken the shears to her head.' Kate forgot her argument with both Sorcha and Elspeth. For a few moments at least they became bosom friends as they discussed the haughty-looking Behag's latest escapade.

'I doubt you're right, Elspeth,' verified Kate eagerly. 'I think she's lopped off every one o' they purple hairs she was flaunting in kirk this morning. There is a nary a single one roamin' out from under that chanty hat o' hers. And would you look at the besom – her nose stuck in the air like she was the bee's knees and pryin' into other folks' affairs as if she was already behind the counter o' the Post Office. It is just a pity Totie asked her to look after it while she is away on her honeymoon. We will hear nothing else but boasting for the next few weeks, for her head is bigger than ever since she got that damty tin medal she keeps stuck on her wall. Look you, Elspeth, away and get Mollie and Merry Mary. We will all go and have a wee talk wi' auld Behag – we could maybe ask her advice about hair dye. Before the night is over we will have her dancing all right – wi' pure rage!'

The hall was really livening up now. The bar was doing a roaring trade and was well supported by Tam and his cronies downing beer and whisky as if they were afraid the glasses were going to be whipped away from under their noses at any moment. Old Joe, having seized his chance the minute Captain Mac vacated his seat, was cosily ensconced in a corner beside a fetchingly attired Aunt Grace, her pink face enthralled as she listened to his stories about his seafaring days. The old sea dog made good use of his considerable charm. Into his tales he wove enchanting anecdotes of beautiful mermaids and Aunt Grace's face grew from pink to red as the descriptions of these fabled creatures unfolded. To her astonishment each one sounded exactly like herself except for the long fish tail. She forgot all about Captain Mac and his more mundane stories of the sea and gave herself up to the enchantment of hearing about eyes as green as emeralds and tresses o' hair so fine the fairies themselves might have spun it on their magic spinning wheels.

At one point when Old Joe's attention was diverted, she surreptitiously took out her mirror to gaze at herself and sure enough eyes as green as emeralds looked back at her and she saw a cloud of silvery hair so fine the fairies might indeed have had a hand in creating it. A little sigh escaped her. Oh, how nice it would be to share her fireside with a man like Joe, even if it was only for a year or two. At his age he would demand nothing more than a warm bed and good cooked meals and in return her reward would be cosy fireside nights in his company. He was an old romantic, indeed he was, though nowadays any notions he had were channelled into his magical tales of the sea and all she would have to do would be to listen.

Captain Mac on the other hand was a younger, full-blooded man, he would want more than just a full belly and a warm bed – he would want her in that bed beside him, so perhaps it might be safer not to encourage his attentions too much. Pity – he was a fine figure of a man but suited to a much younger woman than herself . . . With a coy little giggle Aunt Grace turned once more to Joe and asked him to tell her another of his tales. The old man stretched his neck and his eyes roved round the room. He didn't want

Kate interrupting him at this vital stage in his plans but she was with a crowd of her cronies and with a satisfied smile he turned the full battery of his sea-green gaze on Aunt Grace, put his big, hairy hand over her dainty little one, and plunged into another fishy tale.

Chapter Eight

Lachlan, sitting quietly by Phebie having a drink, was suddenly seized upon by one or two nearby villagers, anxious to know if the rumour about his retirement was genuine. Brown eyes twinkling mischievously, he put his arm round Phebie's shoulders and said to her with mock seriousness, 'Well, what do you think, my bonny plump rose? Will we tell them or is it too early in the day for that?'

Phebie puckered her brow and pondered the matter heavily while all around impatience grew. 'Well now, Doctor,' she said at last, 'I would say the time is not yet ripe to be saying a word to anyone.' With a carefully composed face she added, 'After all you haveny yet told me if you are giving up the practice or not and as your wife I think I ought to be the first to know.'

'Oh you will, never fear,' nodded Lachlan, his thin face alight with mischief.

Niall and Shona threw themselves down on the bench and the former, immediately sizing up the situation, spoke severely. 'Father, you don't mean to tell me you have been keeping the identity of the new doctor a secret? That isn't fair – is it, Shona?'

Shona's blue eyes sparkled and she said, aghast, 'And to think we always believed you to be the most honest of men. That nice Indian doctor will be expecting you to pave the way for him and all the time you haven't said one word for him.'

Kate came over in time to hear Shona's words and her shout of outrage soared above the general din. 'An Indian doctor you say! Mercy on us! It canny be! It will be bad enough having a new doctor at all but an Indian mannie! He will no' understand a word we're saying and we'll no' be knowing what he's yabblin' about either.'

A chorus of agreement rose at her words. Everybody looked at everybody else in dismay before they all began to talk among themselves at the one time. Lachlan could hold back his mirth no longer and throwing back his head gave vent to his laughter.

'Doctor! This is no time for jokes!' scolded a red-faced Elspeth, her prim face puckered with worry. As housekeeper at Slochmhor she was of the opinion that she should have, in common with the family, the privilege of knowing all there was to know about the affairs of the household. At the back of her mind too were the niggling anxieties for her future. She knew only too well that the doctor had only kept her on as housekeeper because she was not only good at the job but because he recognized her need to have something to do to fill her empty life. She was long past retirement age and she dreaded the idea of having to give up her job and all that it meant to her. She knew of course that he and Phebie would likely continue to live on at Slochmhor and because the duties of the house would be less she was perfectly willing to stay on at a much reduced salary. She wanted to say all this, but the village hall was not the place for such personal discussions so instead she contented herself by emphasizing her disapproval of his flippant attitude. 'This is no laughing matter, Doctor. You know fine well you haveny made your mind up one way or another about retiring.'

Lachlan recovered his breath. '*I* know fine well, Elspeth, but neither you nor anyone else will be knowing until I decide the time is right – and you more than anyone should know better than to talk to me about my work when I am here to enjoy myself like any other body.'

Kate sniggered and Elspeth's mouth folded into a tight line. 'If that's how you feel, Doctor. I had thought that after all these years o' being part o' the household I would have had my place in it respected but it just shows how wrong a body can be.' Huffily she walked away and looking rather shamefaced everyone else disappeared, albeit unwillingly, in the circumstances.

Phebie squeezed her husband's arm. 'When are you going to tell them that you have definitely decided to retire, Lachy?'

'In my own good time and not before. I'm enjoying keeping the Kates and the Elspeths in suspense for a whily.'

Shona shook back her hair and eyed him with deep affection. 'They think the world of you, that's why they're so anxious to know if they are going to have you for a whily longer or thole the idea of a stranger taking over.'

Lachlan looked slightly apologetic. 'Ay, you're right, lass, I'm not being fair.' His slow, pleasant smile crinkled his eyes. 'To tell the truth I never thought of it that way. I'll be just as sorry to lose them – though it will be pleasant to have them as friends rather than patients. I'll tell Elspeth in the morning,' he decided with a rueful shake of his head. 'By dinner time the whole of Rhanna should know that old Doc Lachlan's retiring.'

Niall looked at his father, an expression of love and sadness showing in the depth of eyes so like those of the man he sat beside. 'It seems – strange – after all these years to think of you – retired.'

Phebie held her husband's hand tightly as she thought of his long years of devotion and self-denial that at times had almost amounted to self-neglect. These years had taken their toll, had drained him to such a degree of physical exhaustion that often he couldn't find rest in sleep. These had been the nights he had tossed and turned in bed beside her, sometimes rising in the early hours to walk among the sleeping bens. Just recently he had been quite ill and unable to hold her counsel any longer she broached the subject of his retirement. At first he had resisted the suggestion fiercely but gradually he had listened more and more to her arguments until finally he had admitted to his own doubts of being able to carry on for another two years. In triumph she had hugged him and they had sat well into the night talking about all the things they would do when work was no longer his master.

At his son's words he nodded thoughtfully, 'Ay, Niall, it will be strange. I haveny a doubt there will be times when I will sorely miss my work – but a doctor never really retires – more than likely I'll be called upon to do my locum and I'll come in handy whenever I'm needed – but—' he squeezed Phebie's shoulder, 'this bonny mother of yours has worked as hard as me all these years and it's time she put her feet up. We'll not fade out of things, you can be sure, just be a wee bit more conspicuous by our absence.'

Till that moment there had been a fairly lengthy lull in the proceedings, but now Old Bob took up his fiddle and began softly to play the *Song of Rhanna*. Erchy also took up the tune and one by one the other fiddlers followed suit. A silence descended on the gathering and all eyes turned to Rachel sitting quietly by her mother. As Rachel heard the music swelling and growing, her eyes grew big and luminous and she sat still and very erect, then all at once her composure broke and a flush spread over her lovely face. Todd began softly to play the tune on his pipes and as the notes rose, evocative, haunting, oddly and poignantly beautiful, the hush in the hall deepened to a rapture that was almost tangible.

Annie's eyes grew misty. Furtively she hunted for her hanky and surreptitiously wiped her eyes. 'Rachel, Rachel,' she said huskily, 'if your thoughts are as clean and bonny as your music you are indeed a child blessed by God. I never really listened to your song until tonight – and by God, it's beautiful just!'

Rachel barely heard her mother's words. She didn't know where to look and wanted to get up and run. Yet even so a pride swelled in her heart as the notes of her song rose higher and higher. The crowd in the hall faded before her vision. It was as if she was all alone in a drifting world of music and only a small part of her could focus on reality – and suddenly, in that small narrow part of her vision she saw only one face – the face of Lorn McKenzie. It was as if she was looking down a long narrow tunnel which excluded everything but the image at the end and although he was just across the hall from her he seemed very far away and out of reach. He wasn't looking at her, yet she knew every part of him, every nerve in his body was so painfully aware of her he was afraid to meet her eyes, though the space that divided them ensured safety for them both. Only one reason could make him keep his eyes averted like that. She knew and he knew what that reason was. Her senses reeled with the awareness of him in her heart. All her life she had known that she possessed a strange power that endowed her with the ability to know what people were feeling – thinking. Often she had cursed that power, had rebelled against the claims it made on her mind, but never had she wanted it less than she wanted it tonight. She didn't want to see inside Lorn McKenzie's mind – to know what he was thinking – wanting.

People were taking the floor, looking as if they were

mesmerized by the music. Dugald drifted by with Totie, Niall with Shona, Babbie with Anton. A feeling of such loneliness engulfed Rachel she felt afraid. Often she felt like this even whilst in company, sometimes even in the arms of Jon. She felt herself to be divided from the crowd and often wondered if perhaps she would have been happier, more content, if she hadn't had such driving ambitions in her life. Yet, she couldn't help herself, her music drove her to such a degree she felt herself to be possessed by it and occasionally resented the hold it had on her. But it had been born into her, just as surely as the colour of her eyes, her hair.

She thought of little Lorna and Douglas and a sigh escaped her. At one time she had had no desire for children but just lately a longing had seized her though she hadn't recognized what it was, until coming back to Rhanna and getting to know Ruth's children.

Ruth watched the dancers gliding over the floor though in the case of Tam and a few others tripping would be a more accurate description.

He and his cronies had hidden a few bottles of malt whisky in the bushes and after frequent trips outside to fortify themselves they were in various stages of inebriation and it was quite hilarious to observe them and to hear the comments from their thoroughly disgusted spouses. Ruth had to laugh too, even though the pain in her stomach had worsened and she was feeling sick. She didn't say anything to Lorn. She wasn't going to spoil her father's wedding day if she could help it, so she made a pretence of lightheartedness and forced herself to smile as Lorn reminisced about the night of the Burnbreddie dance.

'Ay, that was the night I knew I really loved you, Lorn,' she told him seriously. 'But when you got drunk I thought it was because you were too ashamed to dance with me and I flew away home to cry my eyes out in my room.'

His dark eyes were full of tenderness as he looked at her. 'Let me dance with you again, Ruthie. I'm not very good I know, I never could get the hang of it the way Lewis did but I'm willing to learn – if you don't mind me treading on your toes occasionally.'

But she shook her head, her eyes going to Rachel on the other side of the room. 'Ach no, I don't feel like it, Lorn. Why don't you ask Rachel instead? She hasn't got Jon and looks a wee bit out of things tonight.'

In reply he drew down his brows and was silent for a time before he said peevishly, 'You never feel like anything these days, Ruthie. I want to dance with you – not Rachel.'

Ruth flushed. 'Oh, go on, Lorn, it's been a long day and – I – I didn't sleep too well last night. It would do no harm to ask Rachel, you've kept out of her way all evening.'

Lorn's jaw tightened. Ruth's words rang mockingly in his head. Do no harm to dance with Rachel! Oh, God, Ruthie, he thought, if only you knew the harm it might do to all of us!

He was conscious that Rachel had looked up and was watching him – almost as if she had heard what Ruth had said. But she couldn't – she was too far away – there was too much noise. She hadn't heard, she had sensed, that uncanny insight she had into other people's minds was directing its full force on him. An imperceptible shiver went through him. Against his will he heard himself say, 'All right, Ruthie, if it will please you.' He seemed to glide towards Rachel, she towards him. Before he could speak she was in his arms and they were floating away in a world of their own.

Sights and sounds faded from his awareness. Rachel was the only living creature in his world. Her slender young body was thistledown in his arms, her dark eyes seared his soul, her lips, slightly parted, provoked in him a yearning that was almost beyond bearing. Through the flimsy material of her dress her flesh burned into him. His heart was beating so swiftly he felt as if he was suffocating. Her perfume wafted to him, rocked his reason. It was a light yet heady fragrance that mingled with a feminine scent which was wholly hers. He had the sensation of drowning in it.

Rachel tried to focus her attention on the music but failed. Her thoughts carried her back, back to the night of the Burnbreddie dance. She had danced, in the arms of Lewis McKenzie, a dance that was simply a prelude to undreamed-of pleasures yet to come. Now she was dancing again, not with Lewis but with Lorn – but this time there was something more – something much more. This time she was a fully grown woman, this time she danced with a man not a boy, and all the feelings she ever had for Lewis were magnified a thousandfold for Lorn. He was looking at her, directly into her eyes, as if trying to see inside her to her very soul. He hadn't uttered a single word but he didn't have to – it was all there, in the burning depths of his eyes, in the big strong hands that held her so lightly yet with a possessiveness that suggested complete mastery over her. She drew in a little shuddering breath and forced herself not to move any closer to him – after all, this man wasn't hers, he was Ruth's, and she had to do everything in her power never to jeopardize the friendship that had always meant so much to her . . .

'Doug and Totie are going away!' The cry went up and in minutes the hall was empty. The men had decorated Dugald's old van with all the usual paraphernalia but the ingenious Ranald had added something extra, a huge cardboard cutout of a bride and groom floating together on a big fluffy cloud, fixed to the back bumper in all its ridiculous splendour.

'Here, they are no' going to heaven,' Tam had objected when first he saw Ranald's handiwork.

'Ach, you have no imagination, Tam McKinnon,' Ranald had said with dignity. 'It is to signify what they'll be feelin' like on their honeymoon, makin' love and floating on a cloud o' happiness.'

'Well it never happened that way wi' me and Kate,' Tam had grinned. 'We had hardly left the kirk as man and wife when we were back again wi' Angus having him christened.

It was a case of getting the ring on fast before the bairnie beat us all to it.'

At the bottom of the steps Dugald turned to his daughter and took her hands. 'Well, Ruthie, it's all over bar the shouting. It's been a grand day, one I will no' forget in a hurry.' He studied her face anxiously. 'You're looking pale, mo ghaoil. Are you sure you're all right? I've noticed this whily back that you have lost all that bonny colour you had in your cheeks.'

Ruth shrugged. 'Och, I'm right enough, Father. It's been a busy time but now it's over and I can put my feet up for a whily. You go away and enjoy yourself – and don't worry about a thing. Behag will see to the Post Office and Merry Mary has the shop well in hand. I'll look in from time to time and make sure the pair o' them are behaving – especially old Behag – she is positively gloating at the idea of getting back behind the counter and will no doubt get a few backs up before she's through.'

Totie came up and without ado took Ruth in her strong arms to embrace her thoroughly. Ruth wondered if her new stepmother had been imbibing too freely. She certainly didn't smell of drink yet it wasn't in her nature to be demonstrative. Totie laughed at the look on her stepdaughter's face.

'Don't worry, Ruth, I'm no' drunk, no' yet anyway. I'll keep all that for the honeymoon and might even get your father to let his hair down a bitty. I'm just pleased to be part of the family now, I will do everything in my power to make your father a happy man. I know you wondered if I was the right woman for him but I have known him long enough to believe I am.'

Ruth blushed with embarrassment and eyed Totie's strong, lively face hesitantly. 'I was just being careful. He never did have much happiness with Mam and I want him to have as much as he can get in the years that are left to him.'

'He will, Ruth, he will.' Totie straightened her hat and slid Ruth a sidelong glance. 'As for you and me, lassie, we will be honest with each other from the start. I will make no pretence of being a mother to you. I wouldny know where to begin for a start and for another I know fine no other woman can ever take a mother's place. Ach, Morag Ruadh wasny all a mother might have been but she was the only one you had and the only one you're ever likely to get for I'm no' cast in the mother mould, never was. It will be better if we try just to be good friends. I'll be here if you ever feel you need someone to talk to – just remember that, Ruth.'

Relief washed over Ruth. Totie had voiced everything that she herself felt and she took the older woman's hand to squeeze it tightly before turning away, her heart too full suddenly for words.

Everyone was clamouring, waiting to give the newlyweds a right rousing send-off. The steamer was in the harbour, ready to cast off in a few minutes. Dugald and Totie could easily have walked to the pier but that didn't seem right somehow and anyway, Dugald knew that everyone would be disappointed if they couldn't watch the decorated van driving away so into it he climbed after first seeing Totie settled in her seat. A cheer went up, the pennies rained from the windows, sending the children scattering in all directions. The van hurtled away, the tin cans rattling, Ranald's cardboard cutout flapping so much in the breeze it broke loose and went sailing along on a gust of wind, over the sea wall to land face upwards in the waves.

Tam smirked. 'Maybe it will sail away to the mainland to be found by a body thinking it was an epitaph for some newlywed couple who died in their honeymoon bed.'

Ranald glowered and stomped away back into the deserted hall to help himself to a generous whisky from the bar. Ruth too wandered inside. The place was deserted, even the band having left their post to see the newlyweds on their way. Ruth paused in the doorway, utterly dumbfounded at the sight which met her eyes. There, in the middle of the floor, Lorn and Rachel were still dancing in each other's arms, seemingly entirely unaware that the music had long ago stopped and they were the only couple left on the floor.

Lorn's face was flushed, Rachel's eyes were closed, both appeared to be oblivious to all but each other.

Ruth was about to make some laughing remark but some instinct stayed her. The hall was filling once more. Pipes, accordions and fiddles were soon in full swing. It was the start of a night of ceilidhing which would go on to the small hours. Lorn and Rachel drew apart, dazed looking, both of them glancing round as if they had travelled back from a long distance.

'I'd watch that Rachel wi' your man,' Behag's voice grated in Ruth's ear but she barely heard. For the first time she wondered if something more than mere antagonism existed between her husband and her best friend. All week they had avoided one another but Ruth had expected that, Lorn had warned her of his feelings, yet even so she hadn't been prepared for the resentment he had displayed towards Rachel, it had built up to a point where Ruth felt they truly hated the sight of each other. But there had been no sign of that in the scene she had just witnessed. They had looked – rapturous, as if the opportunity to be so close was something for which they had both waited for a long time.

Ruth tried to push the thoughts away but they needled persistently into her consciousness and wouldn't be ignored. The laughter, the music, the banter, faded into insignificance as terrifying suspicions filled her head. Lorn was coming towards her, excited looking, his hair mussed, his eyes showing some inner emotion which she could only just guess at. He was smiling at her, his lips forming a greeting as he came nearer, but there was an unnatural flush on his face and she looked away, not wanting to see what lay in the deep blue fathoms of his eyes.

'You dance well for somebody who claims to be useless at it,' she greeted him sarcastically.

He had been about to take her hand but drew away quickly to search her face. 'I wasn't dancing, I was just hanging about till you came back.'

'You could have come too, it's no' every day my father goes away on a honeymoon – he was looking for you – to wish him luck, I suppose.'

'Are they – he's away then,' he faltered, surprise in his tones.

'I should have thought everyone knew that,' she said bitterly. 'There was enough noise outside to waken the dead.'

A frown creased his brow and she saw that he was obviously trying to recall anything that might have pierced his consciousness while he had Rachel in his arms.

'I – I think I'd like to go home, Lorn.' She sounded breathless and quickly she added, 'I'm a wee bitty tired, it's been a long day.'

He seemed about to voice a protest but instead said quietly, 'All right, Ruthie, though I had thought you would have stayed to enjoy the ceilidh.'

'No, I can't. You go and tell Rachel to stay as long as she likes. She can lie as long as she wants in the morning – I have to be up to see to Lorna and Douglas.'

Without another word she turned away, not looking back once at the merry gathering in the hall – or at Rachel.

Chapter Nine

It had been a day of warm spring sunshine, of sights and sounds and a fleeting, intangible happiness. Her father's wedding was three days in the past, and during those days an almost unbelievable peace had descended on the little cottage by Sliach. Ruth couldn't quite put her finger on it but she knew it mostly owed itself to Lorn's vastly changed attitude to Rachel. He had stopped avoiding her, his attitude was no longer one of dour forbearance but one of cheerful acceptance of the situation. At first this had only served to make Ruth feel that her suspicions about him and Rachel had been right but as the atmosphere inside Fàilte lightened she felt she had been wrong about everything, that she had imagined it all, that it had been the culmination of nights without sleep and the days of continued weariness, coupled with all the extra little tasks she'd had to undertake in the time leading up to the wedding. The dull, throbbing pain in her stomach was worsening, keeping her off her sleep so that she had to force herself to rise in the morning. Each day she promised herself that she would go and see Lachlan, but always the children demanded her attention together with the hundred and one tasks which claimed her time.

Rising that morning she had vowed she would pay Lachlan a call but Lorn, enthusiastic and shining-eyed, had announced his intention of taking them all out for the day. She had been swept along by his keenness and had pushed the thought of Lachlan away. And she was glad that she had for it had been a wonderful day. They had packed a picnic and had gone to Mara Oran Bay. It had started off dull but by mid-morning the sun had broken through the clouds; the sea had been a smoky, lazy blue stretching away to a pearly horizon. It had become so warm the children had splashed in delight at the edge of the ocean, led there by Rachel who in bare feet looked like the tanned gypsy of bygone days with her black curls shining in the sun and her long limbs flashing as she ran with the wee ones. Lorn had sat on the sands beside Ruth, hugging his knees, chuckling as he watched his sturdy son crawling among the rock pools, his bonny face filled with the joy of sun-kissed seas, of warm golden sand on which he could emboss his tiny footprints and watch in wonder as the laughing waves sneaked up behind him to snatch the marks away in their frothy clutches.

Lorn's arm had tightened on Ruth's shoulder, his dark head had touched her dazzling hair and some of the buoyancy had transferred itself to her. They had giggled together at Lorna standing in the creamy shallows, her dress tucked into her knickers, her face alight as she threw handfuls of water into the air and stood transfixed while the sparkling sea-diamonds cascaded above, below and all around her. And then she had found a huge pink conch shell which she held to the perfect shell that was her own little ear and her violet eyes had grown big with wonder for these were the homes of the sea fairies, whose rushing laughter you heard if you stayed very still and listened. Her Grandpa Donaldson had told her many stories concerning fairies and mermaids. She knew every cave where the wee folk lived and the safe calm bays where the mermaids came to sit on the rocks in the sunshine to comb their long silken locks while they sang their songs of the oceans in their clear, bell-like voices. Yes, Lorna knew all this and much much more and so she listened intently to the fairies singing inside the shell, her breath firmly held, one chubby hand held to her mouth in ecstasy.

Lorn had suddenly, and almost sadly, buried his face in Ruth's neck to whisper fiercely, 'Oh, Ruthie, we're so lucky – to have each other – to have been blessed with such bonny and enchanting bairns.'

Her heart filled with so much love for him she had wanted to cry and laugh at the same time and in these moments she knew that he loved her too, that a man who so adored his wife and children could never be guilty of the thing that she had suspected him of.

After the picnic they had gone out in one of Ranald's boats and though she had felt sick she had hung on to her happiness, unwilling to relinquish the joys of such a rare and precious interlude. Rachel had enjoyed herself too, talking to Ruth with her animated hands, pulling faces for the benefit of the children, being amiable and friendly towards Lorn. Ruth had allowed herself to relax, to enjoy Rachel's company, even to look forward to other happy days like it. After all, when Jon came back his wife would go with him to Croft na Ard and it wouldn't be such an easy matter to see her every day, so Ruth determined to enjoy her friend's vital and stimulating companionship while she could.

And now Ruth sat in her kitchen, trying to ignore the dull throb of pain which had moved from her middle to her right side, to concentrate instead on the little watercolour she was painting of the caves by Mara Oran Bay. The children, having exhausted themselves, were having a nap and the house was quiet and peaceful. Outside the sun still shone and the bright, clear light that belonged peculiarly to the Hebrides, embraced the island. Mark James had arrived just after three o'clock, bearing sheafs of paper on which he had written the words for Rachel's song. He and Rachel had gone over the music at the Manse the previous evening, she playing it over and over on the fine old Cremonese violin gifted to her by old Mo, the tinker who had come every year to Rhanna until his death.

Lorn, Rachel, and the minister had taken chairs outside and now they were playing the tune on their fiddles while Mark James sang the words in his rich baritone voice. Ruth had opted to stay indoors. It was cooler there away from the sun, she was already too warm and uncomfortable, her brow was hot and moist to touch. She sat listening, looking up every so often from her painting to the open door through which she could see the others grouped together, beyond them the green foliage of the trees surrounding Sliach, the blue backdrop of the sky. The beat of the music was pleasant, soothing; the words echoed inside her head, instilling in her such a sense of sadness she felt transported into another dimension. It was as if she was far, far away, an outsider looking in on the friendly scene outwith the walls of Fàilte. Everything was strangely mixed up, yet she saw plainly enough Rachel's black curls touching the minister's equally dark hair as she leaned over to study the words he had written. Lorn's face lay against the polished wood of his new fiddle, serious, intent, the expression in his blue eyes faraway, as if the music had carried him also into another world. Ruth stared in fascination at his hands moving so sensitively on the strings. They weren't typical farmer's hands; though strong, they were finely shaped, the fingers long and supple. The gleam of sunlight lay over his earth-brown hair, his tanned skin was warm looking, his mouth in repose looked so boyishly innocent she wanted to get up and go outside to touch his lips with her finger. The haunting sounds he was extracting from his fiddle blended with the more professional ones made by Rachel. It was lovely to hear such instruments being played in the open air, echoing the sounds which Rachel had captured in music.

Mark James' rugged, good-looking face was solemn as he sang. He was wearing only a shirt and light trousers that day and didn't look in the least bit like the Mark James of the Sabbath in his flowing cloth.

The words spilled out, rhythmically, poignantly:

Take me back where I belong,
Where the skylark sings his song,
And the peace of island life is all around.
Where the people raise a hand,
And there's a welcome in the land,
And honest, friendly faces can be found . . .

Take me home, oh take me home,
For I no longer want to roam,
My heart is yearning for the hills, the glens,
For the sea's tumultuous roar,
For the spume upon the shore,
For the mist that veils the corries on the bens.

The song went on, pounding into Ruth's head in an oddly distorted fashion. Pain and sadness mingled and merged. Her eyes went out of focus, filled with tears, though she didn't know if she was crying for the beauty of Rachel's song or for the insistent notion that in a very short while all things dear and wonderful were about to be lost to her. Nausea swept over her, pain bit into her side, she couldn't stop a little gasp escaping her lips. The music ebbed and throbbed, closing in on her, stifling her, bringing a trembling feeling to her limbs. She felt so weak she could no longer hold her brush. Carefully and deliberately she laid it down, lay back, closed her eyes and clutched her side.

'Lorn, Lorn, I think you'll have to call Lachlan.' The words came out on a sigh. Lorn couldn't hear them, but glancing through the door he saw in the dimness Ruth stretched out on her chair, her hands over her stomach. Jumping up he went inside to gaze down at her and demand anxiously, 'Ruthie! Are you ill? You look terrible.'

A ghost of a smile hovered at her lips. 'Ay, as terrible as I feel. I – I think you'll have to call Lachlan. That pain in my belly is much worse.'

The minister had stopped singing, Rachel laid down her violin, both came into the house to look with concern at Ruth. Lorn was already struggling into his jacket, without hesitation running quickly outside to Dugald's old van parked at the back of the cottage. The vehicle now belonged to Lorn. Dugald was buying a new one while on the mainland and having it shipped over in time for his return. Lorn drove recklessly along the rutted track, for once ignoring the potholes in his anxiety to get over to Slochmhor as speedily as possible.

Inside the cottage, Mark James was scooping Ruth into his arms, laying her on the big soft chintz sofa while Rachel fetched blankets and pillows from the bedroom. Leaving the minister to tuck Ruth in, Rachel went to the scullery to fill a bowl with cold water which she carried back to the kitchen. Settling herself by Ruth's side she smoothed the hair from her brow and proceeded to bathe her face gently, and all the while her eyes held Ruth's, eyes which showed no trace of anxiety but which were instead great black, languorous pools full of tranquillity and peace. Willingly, Ruth allowed herself to drown in waves of calm. She felt as if she had left behind a troubled shore and was floating in safe waters. Even the pain had lessened and with its departure she was lulled into a state of such utter relaxation all she wanted to do was close her eyes and sleep.

'I'd better stay,' Mark James decided, 'just in case my help might be needed,'

He made himself busy, re-fuelling the fire, placing on the resultant glow a big black kettle should Lachlan need hot water. The animals watched, waited, eyes and ears alert, as if they sensed that all was not as it should be. Time stretched, slowly, lazily, yet Lachlan was back with Lorn in a surprisingly short time, arriving in his own car because he had met Lorn on the road. He came striding in, his gentle eyes full of the reassurance that had stilled the fears of countless of his patients. His examination of Ruth was swift and sure. Folding away his stethoscope he sat down on the couch beside her and took her hand. 'Appendicitis, my lassie! We'll have to get you into hospital quickly. Has this pain been going on for a time?'

Ruth looked shamefaced. 'On and off, but more recently it's been there most of the time – today it just seemed to come to a head.'

'That's exactly what's happened. A grumbling appendix can go on for long enough and never come to anything much. In your case an operation will soon get rid of it, don't worry, you'll be up on your feet in no time.'

While he spoke his mind was racing. Ruth was worse than he had allowed her to believe and he knew if he didn't get her to hospital within an hour or two the inflamed appendix could rupture. In his time he had performed quite a few kitchen table appendectomies, though more recently he had been able to carry out minor surgery in the little room at Slochmhor which he had equipped for the purpose. If at all possible he liked to get his patients to hospital as quickly as possible, yet, that wasn't always such an easy matter on an island like Rhanna. The nearest air ambulance strip was at Barra, and to get there meant a good two hours by boat. He thought about a helicopter but quickly rejected the idea. They would do a lift-off service in an extreme emergency, but even then the whole procedure of getting one would take too long. A frown creased his brow. He looked again at Ruth. She was lying back on her pillows, her respiration rapid, little moans of pain escaping through her clenched teeth.

Lorn stroked her hair and gazed anxiously at Lachlan. 'What will we do, Doctor? Should I phone the laird and ask him to bring his boat round to Portcull?'

Mention of the laird seemed to trigger off something in Mark James' head. He stood up, so tall his head almost touched the low-beamed ceiling. 'I was round seeing Burnbreddie yesterday and was introduced to that flying friend of his – Charlie. I believe he came over to the island in that small plane you often see buzzing about. The laird simply clears the cows off the machair on the estate so that Charlie can use it as a runway . . .'

'That's right,' interrupted Lachlan eagerly. 'By God! That would be the answer to our problems! Lorn, you go over to Mo Dhachaidh and phone the laird from there. Find out if the flying chappie is still there and if so would he be willing to take Ruth to Barra. Tell him it's an emergency – oh, and while you're about it phone Babbie and ask her to come over here and also contact the airstrip at Barra and ask them to have an air ambulance standing by . . .'

Before he had finished speaking Lorn was off again, arriving at Mo Dhachaidh in the middle of afternoon surgery. The place seemed to be full of ailing cats and dogs whose owners were exchanging gory details about their own particular pet's symptoms. Shona appeared. She often assisted Niall in surgery and looked most attractive in a white overall with her hair pinned round her head in rich gleaming coils. She intercepted her brother in the hall and after hearing his rapid explanation ushered him into the parlour where sat the phone.

'Let me know if you need any help,' she offered warmly then withdrew, closing the door softly behind her. Lorn got quickly through to the laird who heard him out in silence.

'I'd love to say I could help, old chap,' the laird's somewhat nasal drawl floated over the line. 'Old Charlie is still here all right but I'm afraid he's too drunk to fly. Hits the bottle a bit does Charlie, though if we'd known this was going to happen . . .' He let his words tail off and Lorn stood nonplussed, almost beside himself with anxiety, his mind unable to work beyond this obstacle in the path of Ruth's deliverance. He felt helpless, detached, his brain annoyingly and frighteningly refusing to concentrate on the problems to hand, dwelling instead on the sounds within the house – Ellie Dawn's laughter – the yelping of a puppy – the long drawn-out wail of a frightened cat . . .

'Got it, old chap!' The laird's voice recalled him to earth with nerveshattering suddenness. 'See if you can get a hold of Anton Büttger. Charlie has had him up several times so he should know what to do. Anton was a bomber pilot with the Luftwaffe – last war . . .'

'Ay, I know all that,' Lorn interrupted impatiently, having listened enthralled to the many accounts of the German bomber's crash landing on Rhanna and Anton's subsequent accident on the cruel slopes of Ben Machrie, 'I'll get on to Anton right away.' Forgetting to thank the laird, he crashed the phone down on the receiver, his hands shaking so much he wondered how he was going to pick the instrument up again to make all his imperative calls. Shona solved the situation. Calm and wonderfully composed, she came into the room bearing a glass of brandy, stood over him while he spluttered it down, waited till he was steadier before asking him what had transpired.

Shakily he explained, and she nodded decidedly. 'Right, leave all the phoning to me, you get along home to Ruth – she'll be needing you.'

He gripped her hands briefly then made haste back to Fàilte, expecting at least to find Ruth in some distress. Instead she was calmly and peacefully lying with eyes closed, her small, delicate hands tranquilly in repose at her sides. Rachel was beside her, smoothing back her hair from her forehead, stroking her brow with a touch so sure and gentle Lorn was mesmerized just watching.

Lachlan and Mark James were at the fire, each nursing a glass of whisky, both of them looking more anxious than the patient herself. At Lorn's entry, Lachlan rose from his chair, his face full of inquiry but holding on to his questions till Lorn had a chance to explain what had happened.

'All we can do now is wait,' Lorn tried to sound calm. His gaze travelled once more to Ruth. 'How is she?'

The minister's slow and pleasant smile broke over his face. 'Thanks to Rachel, your wife is calmer than any of us. We might as well not be here for all the good we've done.'

Lorn saw that Rachel had efficiently attended to Ruth's needs. She had packed a small bag with night things and all the necessary toilet accoutrements and had thoughtfully, added some magazines and books. Painfully Lorn met Rachel's dark gaze. Her expression was dreamy, almost as if all her perceptions were turned inward and she wasn't really seeing him.

It had taken every shred of his willpower to behave normally in her presence over the last few days. He had been aware of every look, every move she made. The effort to behave as usual had been supreme, but for Ruth's sake he had made it, if only to prove to her that it was she he loved and always would, for on the night of her father's wedding he had known that she was beginning to suspect that there was something between himself and Rachel. And it was true that he loved his darling young wife. What he felt for Rachel was purely a physical attraction. He knew it and so did she, and he thanked God now that they had both managed to maintain a façade of nonchalance, for in some strange way the delusion had succeeded in making him feel that there *was* normality in a situation so utterly foreign to his nature. A cold sweat seized him at the very idea of what could have happened that day of dizzy euphoria on the ride over the sands of Mara Òran Bay. It was too impossible to even think about it now – now that his Ruthie needed him . . .

'Lorn.' Ruth's hand came out and he strode over to take it gently, struck anew by its daintiness, by her overall fragility which had captured him from the start. Yet he knew that behind her air of vulnerability there lay a core of strength and determination which in many ways was even greater than his own. She opened her eyes to look at him and he felt himself pulled into the purpled depths of her gaze. He smiled, a nervous, half-shy smile, and despite her feelings of unreality she felt a renewal of that sense of wonder that this tall young giant was her husband. The outline of his face was slightly blurred. Rachel's wonderful hands had transported her into a state of such tranquillity she seemed to belong to another world. She had allowed herself to relax, to drift – no wonder her mother had died with contentment in her soul. Rachel was possessed of a power that was uncanny and Ruth was thankful that she should be there at this time, smoothing away the fears that had plagued her from the minute she knew that she had to leave Fàilte – her children . . .

'Lorn.' Her fingers curled over his. 'Rachel is going to look after the children – here in their own home. It will be best for them – but you, Lorn, what about you?'

'Ach, Ruthie,' he smiled at her and touched her cheek with his finger. 'Don't worry your head about me. I'll get all the attention I need over at Laigmhor, Mother will see to that. We'll all be fine, it's you we're thinking about at the moment – I wonder if I ought to let your father know.'

'No, Lorn,' her voice was adamant. 'There's nothing he can do for me that isn't already being done. He hasny had a break in years and I don't want him running back here because of me . . .'

'I think I hear a car.' Mark James was already at the door to usher in Babbie and Anton. The latter had come straight from the fields, his fair hair was wind-tossed, his boots caked with earth, sweat glistened on his tanned skin.

'Anton, can you fly Charlie's plane?' Lachlan's greeting was imperative and Anton smiled ruefully.

'I would be lying if I said I was completely at home in her, I've only taken the controls once or twice – also I do not have a current pilot's licence which makes this a bit complicated.'

There was a short silence in which everybody looked deflated. Babbie glanced at her husband. On the journey to the cottage he had expressed his doubts over the venture, yet she knew he wouldn't have put in an appearance unless ... The determined jut of his jaw which she knew so well expelled her remaining fears.

'Of course I will fly the plane. It's an emergency after all and no one is likely to ask to see my licence on a windswept tidal runway such as they have on Barra.' He turned to Ruth. 'Will you trust me to deliver you safely, liebling?'

A smile lit her pale face. 'Ay, Anton, I couldny ask for a nicer pilot.'

'Then it is settled. We will get you into the back of your father's old van. Bumpy I know, but at least you can stretch out. You will have to take it very easy, Lorn.'

'Babbie will have to go in the plane with her,' said Lachlan. 'I don't know if there will be room for you, Lorn.'

Lorn's disappointment showed in his eyes. He swallowed hard and didn't look at Ruth. Instead he rushed away to put pillows and blankets in the van, glad of the chance to do something useful.

The laird and his inebriated friend were waiting on the stretch of machair which began at the Burnbreddie boundary and ended up at the cliffs beyond Nigg. It was a belt of sweet green turf, stretching acre upon acre inland of the marram grass of the sandy shores. In summer, before the cattle were allowed to graze it, the green became covered in heartsease, clover, and great balls of bird's foot trefoil, so that the whole effect was like a giant counterpane of sweet wildflowers over the land. Over by a grove of silver birch was parked a small, shining plane with a red flash on either side. When Anton saw it his face registered dismay and the watchful Lachlan wondered if there would be another unforeseen delay. Lorn had driven the van over the machair to draw up near the plane, followed closely by Babbie in the little Mini. She too had noted the look on her husband's face and her green eyes were filled with apprehension as she got out of the car to follow his tall sturdy figure.

'Burnbreddie – Charlie,' Anton greeted them in some abstraction. 'You have been up to your tricks again, Charlie,' he scolded the moon-faced, glazed-eyed big man who was twirling his handlebar moustaches in some enjoyment, not the least perturbed by the severity in the younger man's voice. 'She isn't the same plane I went up in the last time you were here.'

Charlie staggered and treated Anton to what the islanders would have described as 'a glaikit grin'.

'A beauty, isn't she, old chap?' Charlie eyed his new plaything with dazed fondness. 'Felt like a change so I got rid of the Piper – couldn't resist my silver beauty from the minute I clapped eyes on her.'

Anton went over to the Beagle and an exclamation

escaped him. 'Gott in Himmel! She is just like the Storch I did my training in. Single engine – unlike the Piper with its twin . . .'

Charlie gave him a hearty slap on the shoulder blades. 'In that case you will have no trouble flying her. I'll give you the lowdown before you set off – show you how the radio works—'

'It wasn't yesterday I flew the Storch,' Anton reminded the inebriated Charlie grimly. 'My main memories are of the Heinkel – no comparison to the likes of this.'

Lachlan was beginning to stamp impatiently, a sign Babbie knew well. It meant anxiety was getting the better of him and he wanted action – fast. She took her husband by the arm and said in an aside, 'Anton, Ruth is getting worse. We must get her to hospital right away.'

Anton squared his shoulders. 'Hush, liebling, I'm just playing for a bit of time.' He raised his voice. 'Right, Charlie, let's get into the cockpit so that you can show me what's what. There is no time to be wasted.'

With some difficulty Charlie wriggled in beside Anton. They were enclosed for some minutes, but at last Charlie slithered out and Anton called, 'Right, everyone, action stations!' Charlie looked back over his shoulder. 'You will take care of her, old chap?'

Anton's blue eyes twinkled. 'The patient or the plane?'

Charlie grinned appreciatively. 'Both – give as much to one as you give to the other and I will personally present you with a flask of my best malt when you get back.'

The laird climbed up beside Anton. 'I took the liberty of phoning the airstrip at Barra and explained to them the pilot would be unfamiliar with this type of plane. They're clearing the runway in readiness.'

Anton nodded his appreciation while his keen gaze swept over the instrument panel.

'Wind direction – did you get that, Burnbreddie?'

The pair went into a huddle. 'Sorry about old Charlie.' The laird's thin face with its aquiline nose and slightly receding chin, took on a fatherly look as he gazed out at his friend who was engaged in a loud, but earnest conversation with Lachlan. 'He's a good chap really – didn't bat an eye at the idea of letting someone else fly his new baby – he must have a lot of faith in you, old boy.'

Anton was anxious to be off. Lachlan was organizing Ruth's transfer from the van to the plane. The minister went forward to help, but Lorn had already swung her gently into his strong arms. She clung to him, feeling unreal and afraid now that the time for parting had come. 'I wish you were coming with me, Lorn.' She couldn't keep a tear from her eye or a wobble from her voice.

Bending his dark head he kissed her eyelids. 'Weesht, weesht, my babby,' he murmured soothingly, fighting down the lump that had arisen in his throat. 'There's only room for three, but I'll phone the hospital every chance I get and I'll be over to see you on the next boat.'

She gripped his arm. 'Rachel's been wonderful, hasn't

she? She seemed only too pleased to take the responsibility of looking after Lorna and Douglas.'

'Ay, she's got a good heart under that glamorous surface. The wee ones like her.'

'Do you – do you still love me, Lorn?'

The question caught him unawares. He stopped in his tracks to gaze down at her. She looked exactly like a little girl with her flaxen hair tumbling over the pink blanket which enclosed her. '*Still* love you? I've always loved you and always will. God, Ruthie, don't you know how much I'm going to miss coorieing into you in bed tonight? I never dreamed anything like this was going to happen . . .'

'Come on, Lorn, for God's sake!' Lachlan was waiting impatiently by the plane. 'Get her over here quickly.'

Between them the men soon had Ruth settled across the two back seats, tucking blankets round her to make her as comfortable as possible. Anton climbed back into the pilot's seat, the engine roared, revved. Babbie got in beside her husband, her red hair gleaming in a ray of sunshine. Twisting round she made a last check of her patient before take-off, her warm, reassuring smile flashed across her freckled face, comforting Ruth, making her feel a deep appreciation for the capable beings who surrounded her. Lorn's hand was in hers. He smiled, a boyish, crooked smile. She smiled but winced as a vice-like pain gripped her innards. Anton revved the engine again, Lachlan shouted something Ruth couldn't hear. Slowly Lorn withdrew his hand, reluctantly letting go of her slender fingers. 'I love you, Ruthie.' His lilting voice had never sounded dearer, sweeter. The music of it beat into her swiftly beating heart. He began to back away, his smile faltering a little.

Lachlan's face hovered in the door aperture before it was blotted out by Lorn's hard-muscled frame. He gave her one last, lingering look, then he was gone. The door shut, panic invaded her. She struggled to raise her head. Anton was taxi-ing, swinging the Beagle round. They passed the men in the field. Each face was just a blur, each one the same as the other. The aircraft gathered speed. Babbie turned again smiling reassurance, the plane lifted, gained height. Anton had made a perfect take-off, but even so Ruth's stomach lurched sickeningly. She wanted only to lie back, to allow things to come as they would, but she had to have one last glimpse of Lorn. Pulling herself up on her elbow she looked down. Anton was circling, bringing the Beagle round so that her nose was pointing south-east. Five figures dotted the machair below. Ruth bit her lip. It was impossible to tell which one was Lorn. One of the figures broke away, began to run, a tiny white blob of a face was turned skywards. Ruth's heart lifted. That was Lorn down there, looking up, watching the plane flying away. She raised her hand and waved though she knew he couldn't possibly see it.

'Are you all right, Ruth?' Babbie spoke from the front.

Ruth tried to keep her voice steady. 'Ay, Babbie, I'm fine.'

Lorn was running, like a young buck, as if trying to

keep up with the plane. Anton took her higher. The figure below was now a tiny dot. It halted abruptly and she knew he would be standing alone on the machair watching the Beagle growing smaller in the sky.

She watched Rhanna slipping away. The fields and moors were a green and brown patchwork, the blue-green fringes of the sea lapped the miles of dazzling white sand. Ruth stared and stared at the scene, hardly able to believe that just as recently as that very morning she had sat with Lorn on those selfsame sands, had laughed with him as they watched the antics of the children. Love for her son and daughter swamped her heart. They would have wakened by now, would be wondering where she was, what had happened to her. Lying back on her pillows she turned her head to the side and hoped and prayed that Rachel would manage them, would be patient with them, especially Douglas who was such a baby still. She started, remembering that she hadn't told Rachel what to give them for tea – her brow creased – had there been anything in the house for the evening meal? She relaxed. Lorn had told her that Shona had said she would bring something over that first night till Rachel got the hang of things.

'Oh, Shona,' Ruth thought, 'you're so good, you always seem to be there when you're needed, maybe someday I'll be able to pay you back for all you've ever done for me.' She propped herself up again and gazed below. The sea heaved, blue, endless, studded with tiny green islands that looked like emeralds scattered at random over the vast reaches of the Atlantic. Mostly they were deserted, inhabited only by sheep – Ruth turned her head – Rhanna had disappeared – swallowed up by the misted distance of sea and sky. She looked to where she knew it to be till her eyes grew hot and sore. She lay down again. Anton and Babbie were talking softly in the front – yet even so Ruth felt alone and somehow – desolate.

Lorn watched the black speck of the Beagle till it grew fainter and fainter and finally disappeared over the sea. Taking his hand away from his eyes he was surprised to find that he was trembling. He stood alone on the machair, trying to steady himself. Everything had happened so quickly he hadn't yet taken in the full import of events. The wind blew his hair, tossing it over his brow, the sweet perfume of blown wildflowers sifted into his senses; the lapwings called; from somewhere in the tumbled sky a stonechat was pouring out its beautiful song. Lorn heard and saw it all, but didn't take any of it in. To him it seemed impossible that Ruth was gone from the island when they had so recently shared the beauty of it. The thought struck him that this was the first time in their marriage they had been separated. It made him feel terribly alone and brought it home to him how much he depended on her for companionship – how much perhaps he took her for granted.

The other men were dispersing, the laird leading the

unsteady Charlie over to his Land-Rover, Lachlan and Mark James walking to Lachlan's ancient old Austin with its peculiar air of ageless dignity. Lorn started to wander towards Dugald's old van feeling unreasonably deserted, but he had got no more than halfway when Lachlan drew up alongside him. His tranquil brown eyes searched Lorn's face.

'She'll be fine, lad. We'll hear from Babbie the minute she gets back and you can phone the hospital tonight.'

Lorn nodded. 'Ay, I'll do that.'

Mark James looked past Lachlan. 'If you don't mind, Lorn, I'll come with you when you go over to Glasgow to see Ruth. I have some business to see to and I could pop into the hospital with you.'

Lorn felt immensely cheered. The undemanding company of the minister made the trip to Glasgow sound bearable, for it had been a long time since he had visited the city and he was never at ease in the hustle and bustle of such busy places. He began to move away. 'I'd better go and let my folks know what's happening – though I haveny a doubt Shona's already done that for me. I'll have to stay with them until Ruth comes home. I can't stay under my own roof alone with Rachel,' he added with a wry smile. 'The cailleachs will have me on a second wife before you can blink an eye.'

That evening he walked over the fields to Fàilte to collect some of his things. He would have made do with what he was wearing and with what Fergus could lend him, but

Kirsteen had caught him mooning about the house, and told him he ought to go and let Rachel know the news about Ruth and to find out how she was coping with the children. He hadn't dared voice a protest, knowing how suspicious it would seem, so he went unwillingly to Fàilte, his hands dug deep into his pockets, his head bent low. It was a soft, gentle evening, the sky to the west was a sheet of flame with the black velvet of the hills silhouetted like sturdy sentinels; the liquid song of the linnet rang sweetly over the hushed fields, the music of it contrasting with the grating of the corncrakes among the flags at the edges of the meadows. Lorn breathed deeply of the clean perfumed air. He felt better than he did that afternoon. He had phoned the hospital and the news about Ruth was good, she had come through the operation well and was resting comfortably. He knew of course that she might feel less than well when she wakened from the anaesthetic but Lachlan had assured him that an appendectomy was a routine enough operation and that she would soon be feeling fit enough to be up and about.

Cresting a rise he saw the chimneys of the cottage nestling beneath the knoll. Smoke was spiralling lazily from them. The hens were preparing to retire for the night and were crooning to one another as they made their unhurried way homeward, pausing occasionally to snatch at the insects in the undergrowth. Ben was lying at the back door, his nose in his paws, one eye open, the feathers of his tail beginning to fan the ground as he sniffed his master's scent; the cats were stalking mice in the long grasses, their tails waving as they pounced.

It was as it had always been, a picturesque scene of calm domesticity and for a moment Lorn was annoyed that it should be so, as if it didn't matter whether he and Ruth lived there or not. Even the washing on the line was pegged out neatly, the way Ruthie did it, yet it hadn't been there when she was taken ill – and the blue satin scraps of underwear certainly weren't Ruth's; she would never have been bold enough to purchase anything so – sensual. Quickly he switched his gaze, concentrating on the rising, stretching form of Ben by the door. The old dog trotted unhurriedly to meet him, quickening his pace as his master drew nearer and he could bury his greying muzzle in the outstretched caressing hand. After a short hesitation, Lorn went decisively indoors, bracing himself for any eventuality. The kitchen was clean and peaceful with a bright fire burning in the grate. It was obvious that Rachel had bathed the children. A tubful of soapy water reposed by the fire; a bottle of bath oil stood on the hearth, together with talcum powder and a hairbrush. On the couch where Ruth had so recently lain, the blankets had been neatly folded and were stacked at one end. The silence in the house bordered on the oppressive, then, from along the hall, he heard Lorna's sleepy murmur of goodnight. A door closed softly, footsteps came across the passage. His first instinct was to turn and go but his feet were frozen into immobility.

Rachel appeared in the dark oblong of the door. He saw instantly that it was she who had used the tub – she was wearing a pure white bathrobe tied lightly at the waist. Her tanned skin glowed against it; her hair was damp and looked as if it had just been towelled; jet-black tendrils clung to her brow, caressed her ears, hung loosely about the white collar of the robe. Unable to help himself he stared at her. The realization struck him – he could easily have walked in whilst she was having her bath – anybody could have walked in.

Anger seized him. What was she trying to do to him? Had she perhaps hoped that he would catch her out in a compromising situation? His rage subsided as quickly as it had come. Of course she hadn't known he was coming. He had left the visit late enough – she probably hadn't expected anyone at this time of night. With everyone out of the house, the children in bed, she had seized the chance to bathe – privacy wasn't such a common commodity in the house – and he remembered that he hadn't offered once to remove himself from the kitchen in order that she could bathe before the fire . . . it was different with Ruthie and the children, but hardly the same for Rachel. He saw by the look in her eyes that she was startled at the sight of him and knew his surmise had been correct.

She came further into the room and in clipped tones he told her the news about Ruth. He knew that his only defence lay in a cool front, but he hadn't meant to sound quite so cold. She was looking directly at him, mutely willing him to meet her eyes and he was reminded that the only way for her to be able to communicate was by a direct approach. Unwillingly he faced her, saw her hands signalling her gladness that everything was going to be all right for Ruth. She frowned slightly. She had had her hands full that day and was in no mood to cope with his sullenness. Douglas had managed to get into every sort of mischief and though Lorna had been co-operative, she had constantly asked when her mother was coming home. The arrival of Shona with a basket of foodstuffs had made things easier. Once the children had been pacified with fruit and buttered scones they had settled down better. Lorna loved her aunt and chattered happily while Douglas tired himself out playing with Ellie and the puppy on the drying green outside.

Shona had been able to report that she had phoned the hospital to learn that Ruth was being prepared for surgery and was bearing up well. Rachel had been glad of Shona's relaxed attitude to the whole situation. She had offered to take Douglas over to Mo Dhachaidh to relieve things, but Rachel had declined the offer. Ruth had entrusted her to look after the children and she was determined to keep her promise. Besides – she had smiled her radiant smile at Shona – she didn't mind and was actually quite looking forward to the experience.

With Shona's departure she felt less confident. Supper had been a sloppy, disorganized affair. There had been all the dishes to do as well as the washing, the children to bathe and get ready for bed. Once in his room Douglas had wailed fretfully for his parents and though Lorna's lips had puckered and she looked as if she might join forces with her brother, she seemed to think better of it, deciding instead to be a big girl and help Rachel pacify her brother. The little boy had finally fallen asleep, leaving Rachel free to slip back into the kitchen to replenish the hot water in the tub and finally to sink into its blissful warmth, content in the knowledge that the children were safely in bed and she could soak in peace for as long as she liked.

Now here was Lorn to disrupt her relaxed frame of mind, dark, exciting Lorn whose unexpected presence was making her heart beat uncomfortably fast . . . The thought came to her – he could easily have walked in while she was bathing – in all the bustle of the evening she had forgotten to lock the back door. Flushing, she turned away to retrieve a blue ribbon from the mantelpiece with which to tie back her hair. As she stretched upwards the hem of her robe ascended an inch, showing her bare feet, her ankles, her toes curling into the pile of the hearthrug, and he sensed that she wore nothing under the robe.

'I'll empty this.' Abruptly he bent and lifted the zinc tub away from the fire to take it outside and pour the contents into the burn. Taking it back to the house he hung it on its hook in the little wash house by the back door. Rachel came out of the house still in her bare feet, going to the drying green to collect the washing from the line. Leaning back against the inside wall of the shed he allowed himself the luxury of observing her at his leisure, unseen by her, but able to see every move she made. She walked like a cat, he noticed, lithe and graceful, each step carefully considered and surely taken. Her round, firm hips had a distinctly provocative sway to them; her unfettered breasts rose and fell under the fine material of the garment she wore. She looked excitingly sensual – desirable. With deliberate enjoyment he watched her removing the washing from the line. There was no one to observe his enjoyment, no one to be shocked by it, there was only himself, cool, fully aware of what he was doing. Why shouldn't he savour the sight of her, stretching, bending? He had no one to answer to, only himself ... Before she came back, he went indoors with the intention of saying goodnight to Lorna. Ruth's unfinished painting on the little table by the window caught his eye. Her hanky, half hidden by the cushions on the couch, seemed to leap out at him. Fool that he was! A stupid buggering fool! Of course he had someone other than himself to answer to. Ruthie was all around him. She might be far away in a hospital bed but her presence was here in this room – this home – the home in which he had dared to allow himself to look with pleasure at another woman when his own darling wife lay ill and alone in some strange place.

Rachel had come in at his back. She was sorting out clothes, hanging them on a wooden clothes horse over by the fire. She bent over to retrieve a fallen garment, the lapels of her robe drew apart, the full, creamy channel of her cleavage was revealed. The firelight was playing on her hair, throwing one side of her face into shadow, brushing the other with gold. Lorn licked his dry lips. It would be the easiest thing in the world to rip the flimsy garment from her, to push her voluptuous body down on the warm rug, to . . .

Abruptly he turned and strode to the door, forgetting his intention to go and look in on the children. 'I'll let you know how things are.' The words came out harshly. 'If you need anything – let me know.'

Thankfully he walked away from the house, glad of the cool night air which washed against his burning face and gradually allowed the heat to go out of his loins. He wouldn't go back to the house again if he could help it – not till Ruthie came home. He paused at the edge of the fields, realizing suddenly that he hadn't collected any of his things, he hadn't done any of the things he had gone to the house with the intention of doing. He didn't turn back again – he daren't think of Rachel in there, looking like a goddess in her robe of purest white – in fact he daren't think of Rachel in any way if he was to keep his sanity. The lights of Laigmhor beckoned – like a safe anchorage in a stormy sea. His steps quickened and he all but ran to the safety of the haven of his old home.

Chapter Ten

Three days later, Erchy the Post came whistling through the door and into the kitchen where Kirsteen was making a batch of soda scones. 'Letter for you, Mistress McKenzie – it will be from young Grant – it's his postmark.'

Kirsteen wiped her brow with the back of a floury hand and smiled at him in fond exasperation. 'Oh, so Grant has his own postmark now, has he? Well, seeing you are so clever and obviously know just what goes on in the world, you could maybe tell me what's inside the envelope. It would save me the trouble of opening it.'

Erchy scratched his head and grinned. 'Ach, I'm no' that clever – no, I was hoping to hear the laddie's news from your own bonny lips.'

He ignored her look of outrage and made a few exaggerated puffing sounds. 'My, it's hot, more like summer than spring. I've seen April worse than December, but this is no' natural, no' natural at all. The towrists are all out in summer frocks and the men are wearin' thon awful shorts – more like short longs if you ask me – I wouldny be seen dead in them. Have you seen some o' their knees?

God, I've better myself but wouldny show them off like that even if you paid me.'

'You show them when you're wearing the kilt,' Kirsteen pointed out, glancing anxiously at his sack to see if he had any intention of producing her letter.

'Ach, that's different,' he asserted smugly. 'The kilt has a dignity to it that lends itself to folk's knees, besides, it's worn in a way that allows only a wee bit o' them to show. These shorts hide nothing – and some o' they folk have big bellies on them as well – they pop out over the rim at the top. One o' the cratur's I saw had his shirt tails hangin' loose but even so I couldny help seein' his belly button.' He paused, made a few more exaggerated thirsty noises and Kirsteen, taking the hint as always, bade him sit down for a strupak.

'And how is our Ruth?' he asked between mouthfuls of tea and scone. 'I hear tell she'll be home in a few days.'

'Ay, she will though she almost left the whole thing too late, for it would seem that she was suffering for quite a while before the appendix came to a head. Lachlan says she could easily have done herself a lot of harm but thankfully it's turned out fine.'

'Ach well, she had her bairns and her man to see to,' Erchy said indulgently for he had always been extremely fond of Ruth. 'Forbye that, she had Rachel staying – though you would have thought the lass could have gone to bide wi' her own people.'

'Oh, hardly, Erchy, you know what Annie's like.' She

wiped her hands on her apron and fixed him with a blue, accusing stare. 'Am I to get this letter you know so much about – or do you want me to beg for it?'

'Och, here, I forgot all about it.' He delved into his satchel and handed over the letter which Kirsteen immediately tore open, her face wreathing into smiles. 'They're coming home in September – Fiona wants to have the baby on the island—' She looked up frowning. 'September! That's leaving it a bit late. She'll be dropping the bairn in the middle of the ocean if she's not careful.'

'Ach, Grant will see she gets here in time,' Erchy assured her placidly. 'Where will they stay when they arrive?'

'Oh, here.' Kirsteen's reply came quickly to her lips. 'It's years since I had a chance to have my son to myself and I'm not going to miss the opportunity.'

Erchy slid her a sly look. 'No doubt Mistress McLachlan will feel exactly the same about her daughter – she'll be wantin' her at Slochmhor wi' her. I know fine she's looking forward to it and is beginning to talk of little else.'

Kirsteen lifted her chin. 'There's plenty of time yet to decide – we'll see what happens nearer the time.'

Fergus came in with Lorn and a horrified Kirsteen jumped up to rush to the stove and peer into the various pots simmering there. 'I had no idea it was so near dinner time. This man aye keeps me back with his blethers!'

'Well, that's a fine thing to say to a guest!' Erchy hooted indignantly. 'If I mind you were the one doing all the blethering – I only listened.'

'Oh, get away with you.' Kirsteen shooed him out of the door just as Old Bob arrived to bang his boots against the outside wall, blow his nose on the cobbles, and yell at his dogs to lie down, his usual preliminaries before entering the house for his midday meal.

'If you have any letters for me I'll take them now,' the old man said imperiously to the good-natured Erchy. 'It will save you a journey up to my cottage.'

'Ach, you know fine I always leave your mail down here,' Erchy remonstrated gently. 'I'm not daft enough to go hiking up to that Godforsaken house o' yours.'

Old Bob looked wistful. 'Fine I know it. It would be nice, just once, to have a letter poppin' through my door. Never once, in all my years o' livin' up yonder has the likes ever happened.' He stretched out a hairy hand for the brown envelope Erchy was extracting from his bag. 'It will be a bill,' Erchy predicted with suave assurance. 'They always come in these shitty brown envelopes.'

'It will no' be a bill,' grunted Bob dourly. 'I have no electrics and no tellyphone and no other buggering thing to rob me o' my hard-earned money. I never incurred debt in the whole of my life and I am no' likely to start now.'

His hands were trembling a little as he took the envelope and stuffed it into his pocket. When, over the dinner table, the family were engrossed in chatter over Fiona and Grant, he carefully perched his specs on the end of his nose, slit open the envelope with a horny thumbnail, and proceeded to read, his lips moving as his eyes slowly absorbed the words. Laying the letter carefully by his plate, he removed his specs with slow deliberation, slipped them into their case, returned them to the inside pocket of his ancient tweed jacket, and sat back to stare at the wall, his gaze transfixed as one in a trance.

Fergus looked up from his plate and saw that the old shepherd hadn't touched his food. 'What ails you, Bob? You're not eating – it's your favourite mince and doughballs too.'

'You're not ill, are you?' Kirsteen eyed Bob's somewhat pallid face anxiously. 'It's not bad news, is it?'

Bob swivelled his head towards her and came back to earth. 'I wonder if I could impose upon you to get me a good big glass o' whisky?' he asked courteously but with an effort.

Lorn was first up, going through to the cupboard in the parlour, returning shortly with a bottle of spirits and a large glass, which he set up at the old man's elbow. Into it he poured a generous amount of liquor and all three watched as Bob downed it in two noisy gulps.

'I am feeling more like myself now,' he announced with dignity and a loud hiccup.

'Good, that's good, man—' Fergus eyed Bob's face doubtfully. 'You're sure it isn't bad news?'

Bob raised his hand to his face, his thumb rasped over the grey stubble on his chin. A twinkle appeared in his rheumy blue eyes. He seemed bemused, bewildered, and amused all at the same time. He looked as if he was about to blurt something out but instead played for time, his mottled hand roving over the cutlery, replacing each item carefully on the white linen cloth. He looked at the wall again and appeared to address it as he announced without a tremor, 'I have won ten thousand pounds on the football pools.'

There was a stunned silence. Bob lapsed once more into a trance-like state – as if the utterance of the words had brought home the reality of the news contained in the brown envelope.

'Ten thousand!' Fergus stammered out at last. 'Are you having us on, man?'

'Indeed no,' Bob replied haughtily. 'I wouldny joke about a thing like that – here – read it for yourself.' He shoved the envelope across the table and everyone crowded beside Fergus to stare in disbelief at the typed words. Kirsteen raised wide, astounded eyes. 'It's true enough, well I'm blessed.' She sat down with a thump and stared at the now smug countenance of the old shepherd and one by one everyone followed her example. Fergus ran his hand through his hair. 'I – I don't know what to say. I had no idea you even did the pools.'

Bob fumbled for his hanky and wiped his nose as nonchalantly as he could. 'Ach well, it is something I have always done to occupy my evenings. It can get gey lonesome living alone and the pools was just a wee pastime o' mine . . .' He paused and his voice lifted in awe. 'I never gave one thought to ever winning the damty things. By jove! I canny believe it.' He sat back and relapsed once more into a stunned silence as the full import of the news seeped more thoroughly into his head.

'This calls for a celebration dram.' Fergus' hand slid over the table to seize the whisky bottle. 'Go you through and fetch more glasses, Lorn. I'm thinking I'll have a good stiff few to steady my nerves. It's not every day I get to sit beside a rich man—' He eyed Bob's shocked countenance. 'No doubt you will be retiring now and taking life easy for a bit?'

Bob glared at him. 'Indeed I will no'. I'll work till I drop!' he scolded indignantly. 'What good would it do me to sit up yonder, counting my money like a miser? Ach no, I'm happy as I am—' He thought for a moment then added slowly, 'Mind you, I have a fancy for a wee place o' my own, somewhere nearer the village wi' a good plot o' land in which I can grow vegetables – that's for the future mind,' he stressed hastily. 'Just now I am quite content wi' my cottage up on the ben and my dogs for company – later on I'll maybe think about taking a wife to myself.'

This last utterance was even more earthshattering than his news of a win on the football pools. Everyone stared at him in renewed astonishment and, as one, burst out laughing.

'You romantic old rogue,' Fergus chuckled. 'You always swore blind you wouldn't have a woman in your home! I wouldn't be surprised if you had one in your mind all along.'

Bob was unperturbed though his eyes were twinkling as

he nodded. 'Ay, you might be right at that. I could never ask a woman to stay wi' me up yonder, forbye the fact I wasny ready to settle down. Now I have this wee bitty money I can afford a wife and anyway – it's high time I settled down and took a good woman to look to me – I'm no' gettin' any younger.'

It was the understatement of the year. Bob would be eighty-six on his next birthday though he had stopped counting at eighty, insisting that someone had been spreading lies about his age. Fergus hid a smile as a thought struck him. 'When news of this gets around the women will be flocking for your attentions, you'll have to be on your guard, Bob. There will be a few gold diggers after you.'

Bob looked down his rather aquiline nose at this. 'Ach well, I can afford to be fussy wi' a good herd to pick from – you needny worry about me, son. I wasny born yesterday and I'm no' a daft wee laddie any longer, I know fine what I'm doing – besides – I have a nice wee body already in mind, I can court her in the manner which I have dreamed of all my life.'

At this the kitchen erupted into gales of merriment which had not diminished an hour later. Fergus looked at the clock and reluctantly scraped back his chair, saying he was not one of the idle rich and it was high time he got back to work. Bob too stood up only to stagger and fall back in his seat with a surprised hiccup and decided thump. He had always been able to hold a good dram but this time he had gone beyond his limits and for the firs time in his life was drunk and incapable. Kirsteen winked merrily at Fergus and helping the old shepherd to his feet she assisted him through to the parlour where he collapsed on the couch to sink into a dreamless stupor.

Fergus and Lorn went laughing outside. 'I'll manage by myself for an hour or two,' said the former. 'You had better get along home and see how Rachel is coping.'

Lorn was feeling lightheaded and very relaxed after consuming a fair amount of alcohol. His father's words caught him unawares and he answered flippantly, 'Och, she'll be fine. Shona has been going over a lot to make sure the bairns are behaving.'

Fergus' black eyes glittered. 'They aren't Shona's bairns – they're yours, Lorn, and you must take the responsibility of them. Rachel was good enough to say she'd look after them but that doesn't mean to say you've to neglect them. You get along there and let her know the latest news about Ruth.'

Lorn knew it was useless to argue further. Abruptly he left his father and made his way over the fields. The sun beat down warmly on his back, making him remove his jacket and throw it over his shoulder, his fingers hooked into the collar. He thought of Ruth. Yesterday he had gone to Glasgow to see her, glad of the company of Mark James who went to the city several times a year to visit old haunts and former parishioners. Ruth had been delighted to see them both. Now that her ordeal was behind her she had been relaxed and happy, eager to hear all the news from home. Lorn didn't tell her that he had only been once to the cottage since her departure. The little anecdotes he passed on about the children had been second hand, gleaned from Shona on her visits to Laigmhor. But Ruth had suspected nothing and had chattered eagerly about getting home as soon as she was able. Though she had only been gone a few days, he missed her in his life though perhaps not as much as he might have done if he had continued to spend his days and nights at Fàilte.

Climbing up to the highest point of the warm, fragrant field he could see the winding glen road far below. On it was the unmistakable figure of Shona going in the direction of Portcull. She was pushing a pram and hanging on to her hand was the tiny doll-like figure of Lorna. He realized that his sister must recently have come from his house after collecting the children in order to relieve Rachel for an hour or two. He hesitated, shading his eyes as he watched his sister's progress along the road. There was really no need for him to carry on, Shona had the children, it would be pointless for him to go home now – yet he knew that his father wouldn't take kindly to this careless attitude. He would expect a complete report – how the children were faring without their mother – how Rachel was managing. It wouldn't do to just tell him that Shona was seeing to things. He would expect his son to at least have the manners to see how a guest of his was faring. He walked on feeling slightly unreal. The whisky lay like a fire in his belly, making him unsteady on his feet, dulling his wits slightly. His thoughts turned to Bob and the hilarious banter they had all shared for the last hour. The old man had been on top mettle, and, unconscious comedian that he was, had come away with one funny revelation after another so that they had all exhausted themselves laughing. He smiled to himself. It was a good feeling that, to laugh in such sheer abandon over the small trivialities of life, though ten thousand pounds was certainly not to be taken so lightly. Every so often Bob had stopped in the middle of a sentence to say in a dazed voice, 'I'm buggered, I really am buggered. I canny yet take in the fact that I've won all that money. By jove! Pour me another drink, Fergus, till I get the facts right in my head.'

It was a wide, blue, glorious day with light and life all around. The lambs were gambolling in the fields; peewits were tossing and tumbling in the sky in their nuptial flight; big fat bumblebees were prodding busily into the wildflowers growing along the banks of the burn, and all along the way the first spikes of the bluebells were poking their heads through the green tangle of uncurling ferns. He was distracted by the delights of the bursting hedgerows, by the beauty of the island lit by sunlight, by the sensing of Lewis' presence which came to him as if borne on the breeze wafting up from the sea. He had the notion that his brother was walking right beside him, marking his own pathway through the sweet grasses of the field. His defences were down and he wasn't prepared for the sight that met his eyes as he topped the knoll. His heart, so peaceful and relaxed only moments before, began to beat a familiar, rapid tattoo inside his breast. Rachel was lying in a sun-drenched hollow almost directly below him and although she was half-hidden by tender young ferns, from his vantage point he was able to see her as clearly as day. She lay spreadeagled in the warm suntrap, her eyes closed, her face to the sky, her body naked from the waist up. Lorn's heartbeat pounded in his ears, the world spun, his entire being was consumed by a fire that he knew could never be extinguished . . .

Almost stealthily he made his way downwards. Rachel didn't stir at his approach and he saw she was fast asleep. He stood there in the hot sun staring at her, drinking in every aspect of her face in repose, the dark lashes fanning the smooth cheeks, her glorious hair tumbled about her naked shoulders. Her breasts were rising and falling rhythmically, full and white against the surrounding flesh of shoulders and arms which were a smooth golden brown; her waist was diminutive plunging down to secrets hidden from him by the cotton material of her skirt. Sweat broke on his brow. Every one of his senses was alert now and he knew he had to flee from this spot, get right away from her before it was too late. He moved clumsily, his foot clattered against a stone, the sound of it like thunder in his ears, competing with the rushing of his heart. She awoke, her black eyes momentarily dazed, but in seconds growing big with shock as she took in the sight of him looming upwards against the sky.

Abruptly she sat up and as she did so her breasts stood

out, firm, perfect, yet fragile in all their in all their feminine vulnerability. Anger and desire tore him apart. He wanted to reach down, grab her clothes and throw them disdainfully at her before turning on his heel and walking away. But every shred of his will had dissipated like smoke before the wind. He was powerless to do anything that commanded strength and sanity. The sight of her lying innocently asleep had already robbed him of self-command, now the sight of her warm, flushed limbs, moving, struggling to make sense of the little bundle that was her blouse and cardigan, drove him to the brink of madness.

'Rachel.' Her name came out in a husky sigh. She looked up, frozen into immobility by the passion in his voice. The shreds of her own reason fell away. She wanted nothing else but to feel his arms around her, his lips on hers . . . His figure filled her being with its tense sensuality. Jon, Ruth, everyone she cared for, slipped off into obscurity. Lorn, and only Lorn, was in her world that warm, breathless spring day. He took a step nearer, a step that was to lead him to his undoing. His eyes burned into her face. They stared at one another for eternal moments – and then he was beside her, falling hungrily into her waiting arms. He tore off his shirt, trembled with excitement as he pressed his hard chest against her soft breasts. His mouth came down to meet hers, hard and demanding. She opened her lips to the bruising, crushing pressure, willingly, wantonly. He was awash with passion and could think of nothing but her silken body beneath him – no wonder Lewis had lost his head over her – she was the epitome of warm, desirable young womanhood. He had to know what it was like with her – he – had to – possess her – Lewis was all at once overpoweringly near – goading him on, making him taste what he had tasted – Ruth – Ruth was a million miles away – the world was here – in the clinging passionate circle of Rachel's arms . . . The sun beat down hotly on their naked bodies; the insects buzzed among the flowers; the linnet sang, higher and higher, reached a crescendo that went on and on . . . And down below the little house known as Fàilte slumbered peacefully in the afternoon sun – as if nothing had changed – as if the two young people who had loved within its walls still reposed within, happy and contented in their lives together – and in the lives of their children.

Jon walked briskly along the winding Glen Fallan road towards the cottage by Sliach. He had come on a late boat and had gone at once to Croft na Ard to let Babbie and Anton know that he had arrived. They had been surprised to see him and he had smiled at the look on their faces. He had explained that his mother was much better and rather than waste time contacting everyone he had decided to come to Rhanna as quickly as he could.

'Rachel will be surprised to see you,' Babbie told him warmly, smiling at the eagerness in his eyes at mention of his wife's name. She had told him how Ruth had been taken ill six days ago and how Rachel had volunteered to look after the children. Jon had looked slightly puzzled. 'She didn't write to tell me this.'

'Oh, it only happened recently, Jon, my friend,' Anton said. 'Everything was rushed. No doubt she hasn't had the time to spare to pick up a pen. Two young children can be quite a handful, you know – well of course you don't, like my Babbie and I, we have no real idea what it is to cope with babies.'

He had gone on to tell Jon how he had flown the Beagle to Barra because the laird's friend had been too drunk to take the controls, and they had laughed together over Anton's description of his feelings inside the strange cockpit. But Jon had been impatient to get over the glen though he had refused Babbie's offer of the car, preferring to walk on such a perfect evening.

He braced his shoulders and breathed deeply of the clean hill air. The sounds of the open places were music in his ears after the rush of city life. Corncrakes were muttering in the long grasses; the bleating of lambs floated downward; a dog barked; a cow lowed. The hills were a hazy purple, merging into the deep dark blue of the evening sky. He smiled, a little smile of pleasure. How good it was to be back on Rhanna. No matter how far he travelled he remembered this island with affection and gratitude. For him life had truly begun here, begun with the meeting of a raven-haired child who had fascinated him from the start and whom he had never forgotten. Now she was his wife and often he couldn't believe his good luck. She could have had anyone she chose but she had married him. The thought of her kindled anew his anticipation at seeing her again. He was lost in happy thought as he traversed the hilly track and there was a spring in his step as he approached the house sitting so peacefully in the lee of the knoll. On soundless feet he drew nearer, his heart beating a little faster as he pictured Rachel's surprise at seeing him.

Closer to hand the house was deserted looking though the door at the back lay open. Tiptoeing inside he went into each room but no one was there, only the children fast asleep in the small bedroom opposite the kitchen. Going down the passageway he peered into the parlour but it too was empty and he stood at the window, nonplussed and somewhat deflated. A movement in the woods caught his eye. He saw two indistinct figures walking very close, disappearing among the trees. Letting himself out of the front door he crossed the green and opened the wooden gate into rougher pastures. Treading carefully, for the ground was pitted with rabbit burrows and splattered with cow dung, he reached the belt of trees and plunged into them. A thick canopy of green blotted out the sky. It was very still, dim and mysterious. Something warned him to tread carefully, his footsteps were hushed as he wound his way over a thickly carpeted path of pine needles till finally he stopped in the shadows that fringed the wild shores of Sliach. The sight that met his eyes was as unexpected as it was earthshattering. He drew back a little, the cold fingers of horror clutching at his heart. Lorn and Rachel were sitting on the sandy shore of the loch and they were talking, at least Lorn was talking, telling her that something had to stop before it was too late. His voice, harsh with misery, floated quite clearly to Jon in the still air. And they were kissing, passionately, over and over, and Jon put a hand over his eyes as if he couldn't bear to see any more.

Down by the loch Lorn and Rachel were oblivious to everything but the poignancy of this last time they had together. They had both known it would be a brief affair but now that the time had come to say goodbye they recognized only too plainly the pain of such a bittersweet parting. They had had such a short time together yet at the time each day had seemed endless, each kiss only the one preceding the next, each fiery, secretive laughing glance a breathless prelude to the next burning touch, the next ecstasy – and the next ... They had never thought that anything so intense, so deep, could end so soon – but it had to – they both knew that, and when Lorn had come to the cottage that evening looking solemn and serious she had known that he was going to tell her it was over. And so they had come to this their favourite place, their haunt for the last few unreal, glorious days. The shapes of their bodies were imprinted into the hollow of sand under the high tussocky bank.

He was talking again, telling her that it was Ruth that he loved and that what had happened between them had been brought about by sheer infatuation. His eyes were black with shame and misery. Her hands were on his arms, he could feel the heat of them burning through his thin shirt. He could feel her pain as he spoke to her. Her head was thrown slightly back, he could see the pulse of her life beating in the creamy skin of her neck. He had discovered why his brother had been so fascinated with her. She was exciting to be with, so vibrant and alive he could imagine her life to be like a fountain, continually being replenished from within, bubbling up and out to meet life force with life force. No wonder her eyes were like turbulent, liquid pools – she had so much life in her, this beautiful creature – it was as well, perhaps, that she was able to channel her energies into the demanding career she had set herself – life like that had to have an outlet, like a volcano erupting when inside pressures became too much. Yet she could be as peaceful as the waters of the loch on a summer's day, there had been something divine in the silence of her presence. Very often he had had no need to communicate with her verbally, a kind of telepathy had taken the place of words. Looking into her eyes now he saw his own misery reflected – but there was something deeper than that and for the first time he wondered if she had felt something more for him than purely physical attraction.

If he could have looked into her heart he would have seen this to be true. For Rachel the affair had been charged with all the emotions she had felt for Lewis and much much more. She had always known that Lewis' feelings for her weren't born of love, but of need, but she had accepted that selfish part that was in him. Lorn was different. He had wanted her, certainly, but through it all there had been a tenderness, a regard for how she was feeling, thinking.

He didn't love her. She knew that. Ruth was his first and only love, but she knew her feelings for him would always remain with her. It hurt her to hear him dismissing her so easily, but then she saw how unhappy he was and tears filled her eyes.

He had never seen her cry before and a great surge of remorse tore him apart. 'Rachel, Rachel,' he murmured brokenly, 'I'm sorry, if I've hurt you I don't think I can bear it. I didn't mean it to happen that way – oh God!' He buried his face in his hands. 'I didn't want any of it to happen but it has, Rachel, and I can only pray that we are the only ones ever to be hurt by what we have done!'

Jon leaned against the bole of a tree, utterly stricken. He felt as if his world had been turned upside down and didn't know which way to turn. With a shaking hand he removed his glasses to wipe his eyes. The glasses fell from his nerveless fingers and in a panic he moved his foot only to hear an ominous crunching under his shoe. With a cry of anguish he turned and stumbled away, unable to see where he was going for the tears that blinded his already shortsighted eyes.

At the sound of snapping twigs Rachel jerked up her

head to look rather fearfully at the pines standing like sentinels over the loch. She saw a blurred shape moving through the trees – a shape that was somehow familiar to her . . . But it couldn't be! Oh, God, it mustn't be . . . Her face was ashen beneath its tan, a strong sense of unease niggled at her. Getting up she ran to the path between the trees and almost at once saw the pitiful little pile of crushed glass and metal that had been Jon's specs. Slowly she retrieved the fragments and laid them on the palm of her hand.

'Jon, oh no, not Jon,' she thought in horror. Lorn came up at her back and saw what she held in her hand.

'They – could be anybody's,' he tried to sound reassuring. 'Maybe they've been lying there for ages.'

Vehemently she shook her dark head and he put a comforting arm across her shoulders. 'Come on, we'll get your things. I'll take you over to Croft na Ard to find out if he is home – though surely he would have warned you.'

She smiled, a half smile as she thought about her husband, how he enjoyed doing things to please her, how he loved surprising her when she least expected it. Swiftly she conveyed to Lorn that he must stay with the children. She would walk to the croft and didn't know if she would be back that night. He watched her walk away and turned to make his way back to the house, a cold finger of dread clutching at his heart as he thought about the enormity of the thing he and Rachel had started – and where it would all end.

*   *   *

Babbie was wrapped in a green dressing gown that matched her odd, amber-flecked eyes. They had a bemused expression in them as she ushered Rachel into the house. 'Isn't Jon with you?' she asked puzzled. 'He came home unexpectedly and went over to Fàilte to surprise you. I wonder why you didn't see him.'

Rachel turned white. So – it had, after all, been Jon she had heard in the woods. He must have seen – heard everything that had passed between her and Lorn. She pulled herself together. It would never do to let anyone see how upset she was – she must wait for Jon – to face what she had to when the dreadful moment of truth came to pass. Raising her head she smiled at Babbie who wasn't taken in for a moment. She had had too much experience of people to be in the least taken in by the girl's forced brightness and she sighed a little as she wondered just what had happened over at Fàilte to make Rachel appear without Jon at her side.

Jon walked unseeingly over the cliffs, his thoughts in a turmoil. Somehow he had always known that one day something like this might happen. Rachel was so young, so full of life – while he was dull, settled in comparison, old enough to be her father. All along he had known that that was one of her reasons for marrying him. She had needed the security only a father figure could give yet by pledging herself to him she had had to crush down a lot of youthful desires and impulses. He had given her the security she needed, but he had never been able to return the passion of such a girl – and this was the result of all that – when faced with a temperament as youthful and as hungry as her own she hadn't been able to resist the temptation – and with a McKenzie too – always it had been with a McKenzie. He had expected it with Lewis, that carefree, vigorous young McKenzie who always won the hearts of women – but he hadn't expected it to happen with Lorn – who was married to Ruth, the child with the sweet face and golden hair. But perhaps she was like him, not passionate enough, too gentle and uncertain to be able to fully satisfy vital, strong people like Lorn and Rachel.

He turned his face towards the sea. The cool air of night seeped into him, making him shiver. A mist blurred his vision. He put out his tongue and tasted salt – salt from the sea or from his own tears? A shudder went through him. He stumbled down a sheep track and came to the wide white stretch of Aosdana Bay, Bay of the Poet. His feet whispered over the sand, the wind from the sea ruffled his hair. He didn't know how long he walked, it could have been minutes, hours, he was too confused to know or care. Finally he sat down on a rock to huddle into his jacket and clasp his hands together. He sat like that for a long time. Idly he picked up pebbles and threw them into the waves. The sea lapped his feet, he watched it, stared fascinated at the tangle of seaweed swaying in the silken water. The ocean sighed, the great empty reaches of it stretching far into the infinite loneliness of night. Time drifted rather than passed. He felt small, insignificant. It was a good place to get things into their proper perspective. Perhaps, now, Rachel might have got rid of some of her restlessness. He had sensed it for years, that unrest which filled her eyes with a turbulence he had felt could never be stilled. This was perhaps a phase in her life which she'd had to pass through – which they had to pass through before she was finally and completely – his.

Torment and indecision pulled at him till finally an unutterable sense of peace flooded his being. He didn't know if it came from within himself or from the haunting serenity of wild lonely places but it was powerful enough to make him get stiffly to his feet and make his way back to the croft, utterly spent in mind and body . . . He would go and see Rachel tomorrow, try to pretend that nothing had happened – it was up to her now to prove to him that she had put Lorn McKenzie out of her life for good.

But to his surprise Rachel was waiting for him in the warm kitchen of Croft na Ard. Apprehensively she looked at his white, tired face and self-loathing flooded her being. Dear, kind, gentle Jon, he had given her his life and this was how she had repaid him. In an agony of shame she went to him and put her arms around him. He held her at arm's length and looked deep into her eyes. In a calm, steady voice he explained that he had come home unexpectedly and not finding her at Fàilte had gone for a long walk, intending to see her in the morning. 'And instead I find you here to welcome me back, liebling.' His voice became husky with emotion. 'Did you use these strange powers of yours to tell you where to find me?'

She was stunned. Nervously she played with the buttons of her dress. She had expected accusations, an outpouring of anger, yet she might have guessed there would be none of that. This was Jon after all, and he was pretending not to know, protecting her as he had always protected her – only this time she didn't want his protection – would have welcomed anger, recriminations. She wanted to beat her fists against his chest, to scream the truth at him, make him face the fact that she was imperfect, human, weak. But she couldn't scream. The silent protestations beat inside her head and she knew that would be her punishment, to keep up the pretence for his sake, to go on as if nothing had happened. And he thought he was being kind, behaving as if everything was as it had been; he wasn't to know that she had witnessed his departure from the woods by Sliach so he was letting her think that her so-called secret was known only to her and Lorn.

Anton came into the room, tying his dressing gown round him. 'Where have you been all this time, Jon?' His keen blue gaze took in the two white faces. 'You look done in and in need of your bed – Rachel has been waiting for hours—' He halted, wondering suddenly why Rachel had put in such an unexpected appearance in the first place. What had made her decide to leave the cottage and come here – and the children? Who was looking after them? He put the question to her and was quick to note the colour staining her cheeks.

'Lorn came by – I – left him to see to them,' she spelled out with her fingers, and Anton, who understood a good deal of the sign language, nodded slowly. The atmosphere was charged with tension and Anton knew something drastic had happened to put that look of strain on Jon's face, guilt on Rachel's. He took a deep breath. So he had been wrong to dismiss that chance sighting of Rachel in Lorn's arms. He could only guess at the outcome. One day perhaps Jon might tell him about it; yet in his own way Jon was deep, and where Rachel was concerned he was fathomless! If the haunted expression in Jon's eyes had been brought about by something she had done then it was quite likely it would remain a secret between the two forever.

Without another word he went to measure milk into a pan which he heated on the stove. 'A hot drink for you, my friend, then a good night's sleep.' He looked kindly at Jon. 'You can lie in as long as you like but no such luxury exists for me – I have to be up to see to things and also to make sure that my little sleepyhead rises in time – if it wasn't for me all her patients would be dead from neglect and that is the truth!'

Jon forced a smile and took the steaming mug of brandy-laced cocoa which Anton held out.

'Will you be around tomorrow?' Anton looked from one to the other. 'I know the arrangement was that you were both to stay here, but until Ruth comes home the children will have to be looked after.'

Jon passed a hand over his eyes. 'I'm sorry, I'm not thinking straight. Of course Rachel must fulfil her promise to her friend. I will go and stay with her at the cottage till Ruth comes home and then we will come back here – if that is all right.'

'Babbie would be most annoyed if you didn't. I had planned to take a day or two off so that we could all explore the island together – I have lived on it for many years and never seen half of it. So, it is arranged, you go and be driven mad with the children for a few days and then you come back here to relax.'

Rachel turned away, feeling that, hospitable as Anton was, it was for Jon's sake, not hers; yet she was sensible enough to realize that her view of the situation sprang from her feelings of guilt. She made her way up to the cosy little guest room that Babbie had prepared earlier. The corner of the fluffy quilt was thrown invitingly aside, the soft, pink glow from the bedlight, which in common with the rest of the house got its power from an outside generator, poured over the spotless white pillows. Rachel looked and she shivered. How could she lie in Jon's arms knowing what she did? He would take nothing that wasn't offered and at the moment she had nothing, absolutely nothing to offer him. She undressed and got into bed, gratefully hugging the hot bottle thoughtfully provided by Babbie. Her whole being was tense, listening, waiting to hear Jon's step on the stairs. But the hours of night crept slowly past and he didn't come.

At daybreak she awoke from an uneasy sleep to see him standing by the window. The bright light of dawn filtered over him. A dark stubble lay over his face, he looked haggard and utterly weary. Her heart went out to him. What had she done? Oh, what had she done to this dear, unselfish husband of hers? She wanted to reach out, to touch him, to let him know that she was sorry and would be every waking day for the rest of her life.

But somehow he was unapproachable that clear, bright spring dawn. He stood at the window, tall, thin and gentle looking, yet with a very strength about him that robed him in a mantle of dignity.

'I am sorry, liebling.' His voice was quiet, level, his gaze directed unseeingly over the deserted, dewy morning fields. 'I was weary from all my travels yesterday and fell asleep by the fire. Do not worry, it will never happen again – I am all right now.'

He turned his gaze back into the room and looked at her lying against the pillows. How eagerly he had looked forward to a night in her arms after so many endless nights away from her. She was watching him, her eyes big and troubled in the smooth cameo of her face. She had never looked more lovely, more desirable – and something else. For the first time he saw uncertainty in her expression, humility in her attitude.

With a little sense of wonder he realized that it was, after all, he that she looked up to, he above all whom she turned to for guidance and for the kind of steadfast devotion that he alone could give her. He also saw love in her look. Not the wild, passionate love that she must have given to Lorn McKenzie, but a deeper, steadier, more spiritual love – a special love that was for him alone. His heavy heart lifted a little and he smiled at her. 'It is early yet, liebling, I will go downstairs and make us a nice cup of tea. We will drink it together while we talk about all the nice things we are going to do when we come back to Anton and Babbie – though of course we must work out a schedule that leaves you time for your violin practice. No doubt you have been neglecting it without me here to keep you in order.'

Her trembling limbs relaxed. She nodded and lay back. She would like that, how very good it would be to lie here in this safe haven, drinking tea with Jon, listening to his quiet, steady voice outlining all the things they would do to fill the spring days that lay ahead of them – for he would be describing a dream that could never be fulfilled – she couldn't stay long on the island once Ruth came home – not now . . . But she would let him talk – it would keep her mind off Lorn – and – she shivered – would help her to turn her thoughts away from Ruth, from the terrible wrong she had done to the girl who had been her most enduring friend from childhood . . . Lorna and Douglas burst suddenly into her mind. She had enjoyed looking after those two adorable children – they had made her forget herself – her ambitions . . . Jon was at the door and she surprised him by sitting up and holding out her arms to him. With a sense of wonder he went to her, a little taken aback by the fierceness with which she kissed him. Her lips were very sweet, very insistent, her breasts in his hands were full and ripe and tantalizing. A flush spread over his thin face. The intoxicating magnetism of her nearness swept away all his reserve and as his mouth came down on hers he almost forgot the terrible doubts and fears of the last nightmare hours. She pulled back from him, her hands spelled out an urgent message, 'I would like to have your baby, Jon – so please – be as wild as you like with me.'

Trembling, he slipped the satin nightdress off her shoulders. Her lips were parted showing her teeth and the pink of her tongue. 'Liebling, oh, my liebling,' he murmured shakily, 'I love you and I know now that you love me, in spite of everything you love me.'

He pulled her in close to him, a new mastery in the arms that held her, a sureness in the hands that undressed her, a fierce possessiveness in the mouth that kissed her. She reached out and urged him to kiss her harder still. The gentle Jon that she knew was gone, replaced by a being whose passionate demands made her experience a new and beautiful thrill of wonder – and a love that reached down to pluck away any last romantic regrets she might feel for Lorn McKenzie – the ghost of Lewis hovered – but only briefly. In those exalted moments with the man who was her husband, the ghost of Lewis was allowed to go to its rest – firmly and for all time.

Chapter Eleven

Ruth came home, thinner but otherwise well and in high spirits. Her delight at being back with her children and husband made Lorn cringe with self-hatred. He had betrayed her trust and felt no satisfaction in knowing that he had cut off his relationship with Rachel. It would have complicated things too much if he had allowed it to carry on. His mouth twisted bitterly at this. What kind of fool was he? Things *were* complicated. What had been done could never be undone. He had spent sleepless nights and days in torment, wondering how he could face Ruth and behave normally. And now she was here, her sweet face breaking into smiles as she came over the threshold to cuddle the children to her breast.

Plunking herself down on a chair she said with a sigh, 'Oh, it's so good to be home. I just want to sit here forever and take it all in. I loved it before but now I really appreciate all the lovely things I have in my life.' She looked at her husband. He seemed thinner, anxious looking. She threw him a half-shy smile and held out her arms. 'Come here, Lorn, I've missed you, darling, more than you'll ever know.'

He went to her and buried his face in the warm hollow of her neck, his heart too full for words. Taking his head between her hands she kissed his mouth and laughed.

'What's wrong, Lorn? Don't tell me you're too shy to speak to your very own wife?'

He shook his head, his face serious. 'Not shy, just glad to see you back, Ruthie.'

The children were watching, so overcome with shyness they hadn't uttered a single word since their mother came through the door. She laughed gaily, a musical sound that tore Lorn's heart in two. 'What on earth is wrong with everyone? My husband is lost for words and my children have lost their tongues! What kind of welcome home is that?'

A slow smile spread over Lorna's face. Going to the hearth she retrieved the slippers warming there and kneeling by her mother she took off her shoes, replacing them with the slippers.

'That's better.' Ruth kissed her daughter's upturned face. 'Now I feel I'm really back – except—' she looked round – 'where are the animals? I thought I would be eaten alive the minute I came in.'

'That's why I put them in the parlour – I didn't want them hurting you. Lachlan says you'll be sore for a whily.'

'Och, to hell with my sore belly!' Ruth was in an abandoned mood. Her cheeks had turned pink, her eyes sparkled. 'Let them through. I don't care if they eat me alive.'

Lorn opened a door and a pile of hairy bodies descended, Ben to sweep a cup off the table with his tail, to howl with pleasure and place his paws on Ruth's shoulders and lick her ears resoundingly, the cats to purr and mince round her legs, thereafter to arrange themselves decoratively about her person. The children screamed in delight and clapped their hands. Ruth looked at Lorn, her hand closed over his. 'That's more like it. I'm really and truly home now – and I'll never go away again.'

Lorn could hardly bear to look at her, certain that his guilt must surely show in his eyes. He wanted to hold her, to stroke her hair, to tell her how good it was to have her home, but he couldn't bring himself to do any of those things. He had ruined everything by his foolishness and he wondered if he could ever feel natural with Ruth again.

She was watching him, a little strangely he thought, and though he wasn't exactly glad that Rachel appeared at that moment at least she created the diversion he needed. Ruth was profuse in her thanks to her friend, taking her hands and holding them tightly. Rachel looked at the honest sincerity in the lovely big eyes and died inside with shame. She was unable to put on any kind of act and after she had seen the family settled at the tea table she took herself off to Croft na Ard, indicating that she would come back next day to help out.

Ruth said nothing, taking Rachel's strangeness as a sign that Lorn had given her a bad time with his moody tempers. Yet she had thought that they had come to terms with one another, though perhaps, she reflected, he had been worried about her and had taken his feelings out on Rachel.

Ruth sighed a little as she ate the delicious cheese soufflé Rachel had prepared specially for her. She decided that it hadn't after all been a good thing to ask her friend to stay at the cottage. Lorn had been right after all. None of them had enjoyed the visit greatly and her taking ill and having to go to hospital had complicated matters still further. Rachel certainly had not had the kind of relaxed holiday she had so badly needed and some of Ruth's happiness left her as she reflected it was all her fault – she had to go and take ill just when everything seemed to be working out.

That evening, when the children were in bed, she sat with her husband in the kitchen. She lay back in her chair, relaxed, annoyed at how weary she felt and how insistently the idea of bed drummed in her brain.

'You'll be tired for a good whily to come.' Lorn spoke softly, his face turned away from her, his features indistinct in the firelight, for gloaming was settled over the country-side and they had not yet lit the lamps.

'Ay, Lorn, I know that, but I have to get back to normal, there's the bairns to see to and . . .'

'Weesht, Shona's going to come over to help out. Also Rachel will be here every day till she and Jon leave.'

She examined her hands. 'She's been good, hasn't she, Lorn? I don't know what I would have done without her. The house is like a new pin and I'm thinking 'tis a good job I came home when I did or you might have decided you didn't need me here – even the bairns were shy of me, as if they couldn't decide whether to come to me or Rachel.'

An angry flush spread over his face. 'Don't say things like that, Ruthie. I'm glad you're back – you'll never know how glad.'

She studied him tenderly and giggled. 'All right, Lorn, you don't have to be so – so angry about it. No wonder poor Rachel isn't herself. No doubt you've been shouting your head off at her too – ordering her to do this and that.'

He moved restlessly, glanced down at his hands, seemed about to say something then thought better of it. For the next half hour he regaled her with all the latest village gossip, feeling himself relaxing as he talked of everyday things that were safely outside the family circle. He told her about Old Bob's win on the pools and she threw back her fair head and laughed in delight. 'Dear Old Bob, I'm so glad for him – but what will he do with all that money?'

'He doesny know yet, he still hasn't gotten over the shock – mind you, he did say something about looking for a wife. The cailleachs are already fighting each other for his attentions and Behag has marked him down as a bad lot. She says his fortune will only lead him to sin and that he will likely take himself off to Lochgilphead or Oban to go crazy with drink and wild women. Old Sorcha actually puffed her way up to his cottage to present him with a home-made cake and while she was there she offered to make his tea for him.' Lorn chuckled. 'According to Sorcha she was shown the door and given her marching orders. Bob's no fool and won't be taken in by the gold diggers – besides, he already has his eye on your Aunt Grace. He's paid two visits to her house in one week, all tooshed up and wearing his best kilt too.'

Ruth's eyes were sparkling. 'But Captain Mac already has his eye on her. He was paying her a lot of attention at Father's wedding.'

'Ay, and he was hopping mad because Old Joe sat beside her for most of the evening spinning her tales about fairies and mermaids till she was green about the gills.'

Ruth clasped her hands. 'Sparks will fly before the year is through. Fancy Aunt Grace with all these men chasing her. She'll be wondering if she's done the right thing coming to live on Rhanna.'

Lorn laughed, forgetting himself in the lightness of the moment. 'It would seem the island is full of old studs all after the same mare. But never you fear, Aunt Grace is enjoying every minute. I saw both Captain Mac and Joe at her door the other day and she was positively revelling in the dirty looks they were drawing one another, no' to mention the ogling glances they were giving her.'

The talk switched to Fiona and Grant, and to the determination of both Phebie and Kirsteen to have their respective offspring staying with them.

'Sparks will fly there too,' predicted Lorn. 'I've never

seen Mother so het up about anything for a long time and I'm hoping she and Phebie won't fall out over it.'

'Ach, surely not,' said Ruth decidedly. 'They've been friends too long and will come to some agreement that will suit them both. Talking about friends, I made a lovely one in hospital – an old lady who lives on a farm in Ayrshire. She invited me there for a holiday any time I feel like it.'

She went on talking about Jean Jackson, her enthusiasm growing as she described her newfound friend. Lorn listened, wishing in those intimate moments that he could turn back the clock, wipe the slate clean, arrange events so that things could be as they had always been and he could look at his wife and feel clean and good instead of feeling degraded and unhappy. He was reluctant for bedtime to come but by ten o'clock Ruth was tired and drawn and he knew that the cosy interlude had to end, that there was no way he could escape the intimacy of the bedroom. She drank her cocoa and went yawning through to bed while he saw to all the last-minute jobs both in and out of doors.

When he finally went through to the bedroom she appeared to be asleep. Her eyes were closed, her fair hair tumbled about on the pillow. But when he got in beside her she turned and snuggled against him though he couldn't bring himself to touch her. In some strange way he felt that he would tarnish her, soil her with hands that had so intimately explored the body of another woman.

'It's truly lovely to be with you again, Lorn.' Her voice

came, sleepy and contented as a child's. 'It was awful lying in that hospital bed without you. I kept thinking of you, how lonely you must have been too. I'm still a bit sore but I'll be fine in a day or two – meantime we'll just have to be content to coorie into each other.'

He kissed the top of her head, glad that she couldn't see the stark shame that lay over his face. 'That's all right, Ruthie, just you go to sleep and I'll hold you in my arms and keep you safe. Don't worry about anything, you'll be well and strong again in no time.'

She lay back and sighed, feeling lucky to have a husband who was so understanding. She was asleep in minutes but beside her Lorn lay awake, staring at the ceiling well into the small hours of morning.

Several days passed and Ruth began to suspect something was wrong with Lorn, either he was ill – or – she could hardly bear to think of it – something had happened between him and Rachel. But what? Perhaps there had been a terrible argument. She thought back – both of them had been strange on her return but she had been too glad to be home to give it much thought. Now she cast her mind back. Rachel – downcast, her black eyes hooded – hiding something – hiding what? And Lorn – what about Lorn? His anger against Rachel had gone. Yes, that was it – there had been no anger left in him for the girl he had so vehemently rejected since the days of Lewis.

In the place of anger there had been . . . She drew a deep breath, unable to put a name to the thing that smouldered deep in his eyes. He had worn that same look on another occasion – during the aftermath of that terrible row they had had over the question of Rachel coming to stay. He had made his peace by giving her a present and in his eyes she had seen misery and a stark look of guilt – guilt? Yes, the same look was on him this time but why should he feel guilty – unless – she drew in her breath, her whole being rebelling at the idea but it needled into her brain and refused to be ignored. She shook her head. It couldn't be – he didn't even like Rachel. But there had been little indication of that over the last few days. They had been formal to each other – like two people trying desperately to keep up appearances – there had been no anger in him – and all the defensiveness had left Rachel.

Yesterday Jon and Rachel had left the island. Ruth recalled Lorn's farewell to her. It had been short, brusque, tinged with a certain quality she hadn't been able to define at the time. Now she saw it as the goodbyes of a man to a woman he had had some liaison with. Oh God! She was imagining it! Or was she being a blind fool trying to ignore all the signs set out before her? Suddenly she remembered something else. Jon had been his usual, quiet courteous self but she had caught him looking at Lorn in a certain way – as if at that moment he disliked him intensely and was trying hard not to let it show. Did that mean that Jon knew that something had happened between his wife and her husband and that though he had forgiven Rachel he certainly didn't feel similarly disposed towards the man in the affair?

Unable to bear her own wild suppositions she put on her raincoat and set off towards Glen Fallan, looking in briefly on Shona who had taken the children off her hands every afternoon since her return. Lorna and Douglas were happily surrounded by recuperating dogs, cats, a talking budgie, and the bold Sporran revelling joyfully in the centre of the activities.

'They're having a grand time.' Shona shooed Ruth to the door. 'Away you go and enjoy your freedom while you can. You'll be back soon enough to dull routine.'

The spell of good weather had broken. A soft drizzling rain was falling, blotting out the hills, adding to her sense of depression as she made her way to the Post Office to fulfil her promise to her father about keeping an eye on Behag.

The shop was empty but for Behag clacking away at her knitting behind the counter. She looked down her nose as Ruth's slight figure came into the premises. 'It is yourself, Ruth,' she acknowledged, her beady eyes roving over Ruth's face. 'I didny think to see you out and about so soon.'

'Ay, it is me right enough,' nodded Ruth with a gentle hint of sarcasm for Behag's patronizing manner never failed to bring out the worst in her.

'You are lookin' well – considering,' Behag said solicitously.

'I am well enough, thanking you. I just looked in to see how you are managing.'

Behag's lips folded sourly. So, the lass hadn't come to purchase anything but to 'spy' on her as Behag put it to herself. 'You will find everything in order.' Her palsied head swivelled round as she took in her surroundings with proud approval. 'I have cleaned the place up a bitty and put things back the way I aye liked them. Totie has some queer ideas in her head about management, but of course she was aye a one for putting everything into cubbyholes where other folks canny find them.' She studied Ruth's face more thoroughly. 'You're still lookin' a bitty pale. 'Tis no wonder of course, an inflamed appendix is no laughing matter – a bad enough thing for anybody to cope with on its own – but of course – you had Lorn and Rachel to put up wi' as well. It's as well you are home – a terrible thing to come back to a thing like that and you as weak as a kitten – poor sowel,' she ended with a solicitous sniff.

Ruth had been prepared to be friendly and polite to Behag but, as others had found to their cost, intentions like these quickly dissipated after just a few minutes in the old woman's company. The smile froze on Ruth's face and she said stiffly, 'Just what are you implying, Behag?'

'Nothing, nothing at all, lassie,' Behag said evasively, her beady eyes glistening at the memory of seeing Rachel and Lorn walking together hand in hand over by Sliach. She had not been slow to spread the news and as a result several people had been eyeing Lorn askance of late, one or two going so far as to shun him in the street. 'It's what I see and hear I'm talking about. I canny help hearin' what other folks are saying. You know what people are like.'

Ruth's small frame tensed. 'Ay, you always were innocent, Behag.' Her voice was dangerously calm. 'It's always other folks who are at fault, never yourself.'

Behag's eyes glittered. Viciously she clamped a bulldog clip on to a sheaf of forms and said through tightly folded lips, 'Sarcasm doesny suit you, Ruth. I expected it from your mither of course, but never from her daughter. Oh no, I aye liked you, Ruth, you were aye a sweet-tempered lass – though lately I've seen a change coming over you and that's a pure fact. Of course, being married to a McKenzie would be enough to try the patience o' a saint. I wouldny blame you if he's maybe the reason you are no' as good-natured as you used to be.' She slid Ruth a sidelong glance. 'It was just a pity you took ill when you did – when the cat's away the mice will play. It's as well you are home, I've said it once and I'll say it again. That Rachel is no' the sort o' lass to content herself lookin' after simple bairns. That poor wee man o' hers found that out when he came home from his mither's sickbed unexpected. On the night he came back he was seen wandering like a soul demented, yonder by Aosdana Bay – and he was alone mind – yet he came running off that boat as if he couldny get to see his wife fast enough. I just wonder what he saw over by Sliach to make him behave like that – ay – I just wonder.'

Ruth stood rigid, staring at Behag's creped hands on

the counter, but she wouldn't give the old witch the satisfaction of seeing how painfully her words had hit home. Holding her head high, she said firmly and politely, 'If you'll be excusing me, I have better things to do with my time than stay here listening to vindictive gossip. I will write and let my father know how you are managing – he and Totie will be home in a fortnight and then we will have the place back to normal again.'

Turning on her heel she stumbled to the door to wrench it open. Closing it behind her she stood leaning against it, the discordant jangling of the bells plucking at every nerve in her body. She stared at the grey clouds drifting above. It was a warm humid day but she felt icy cold. Behag was a vicious, troublemaking old gossip but never did she fail to hit on some spark of truth in the things she said. She wandered home, her mind in a turmoil. Not even bothering to remove her outdoor things she sat at the fire, staring into space, coming slowly and reluctantly to a very painful decision.

That evening when the house was quiet, she confronted Lorn with her suspicions. 'Lorn, I have something I want to ask you,' she began reluctantly, 'only I – I don't know where to begin.'

She sat, staring down at her hands working nervously on her lap and he stood looking down at the top of her bowed head, a flush spreading across his face, as if he knew what was coming.

'Well?' His voice was tense. 'What have you got on your mind, Ruthie?'

A shudder went through her. The words she had to say sprang to her lips, yet the effort to get them out was almost beyond her. A long silence sprang between them, a silence laden with fearful suspense. The hearts of husband and wife beat swiftly. The sound of Lorn's tightly controlled breathing surged through the room, adding to the unbearable tension which oozed between the two young people, growing tighter and tighter with each passing second – like an invisible noose binding them into a situation from which there was no escape . . .

'Lorn – there have been certain rumours.' At last Ruth got the words to come out. She didn't dare look at him, a tiny dew of sweat gleamed on her upper lip, her hands felt cold and clammy.

Lorn's brows drew together. 'Rumours? What about?'

Ruth's hands trembled. 'About you and Rachel.' She looked up at him then, her eyes big in her pale face. 'Lorn, listen to me! I don't care about the gossips and what they think they saw. I was never one to listen to rumour. You are my husband and I'll no' believe ill about you. Just you tell me from your own lips that there is no truth in what folks are saying.'

He gasped and stared at her, the irises of his eyes the colour of ripe blaeberries. No quick denials sprang to h lips. He seemed unable to do anything, but just looked at her, wearing such an expression of stunned shock that she knew her deepest fears were true. Sinking down on to the nearest chair he buried his head in his hands and whispered, 'Oh God, Ruthie! What can I say? I never wanted you to be hurt – I would never have burdened you with it. It's true, God forgive me, it's true! I wish – oh how I wish I could turn the clock back! I'm not blaming Rachel – I'm blaming myself. I can make no excuse for what I did – oh God – I wish I was dead.'

Bitterness boiled in Ruth's breast. She felt sick and icy cold. She stared at the top of his bowed head and her voice came out hard and brittle. 'And well you might, Lorn McKenzie – well you might.'

She spun round and limped to the door, hardly aware of what she was doing. There was a mist in front of her eyes, a buzzing in her ears. Going through to the parlour she sank into a chair and put a trembling hand to her eyes, so stunned her mind refused to work. She felt empty, drained of all emotion, and sat looking into space for a long time. No fire burned in the parlour grate, the room was cold, but nothing penetrated Ruth's consciousness. She sat, as frozen and as pale as a marble statue, feeling nothing, seeing nothing. Lorn didn't follow her. In the dim mists of her conscious mind she was aware that he had left the house but she sat on, immobile. The house was very quiet, as if nobody lived there, as if the walls had never known laughter – tears. There was no sound from the children's room, no murmur from the animals. Outside the rain drummed on the window panes, mist blotted out the trees, the hills, seemed to creep into the room to embrace Ruth in its cloying damp clutches, enclosing her in a claustrophobic world from which there was no escape. Darkness came down, creeping over the countryside like a sombre portent of doom and still Ruth sat on, her eyes big and dry in her white face.

The tears overwhelmed her so suddenly she was unprepared for them. A great sob broke in her throat and bowing her golden head she cried as if she would never stop. Her entire body was seized by uncontrollable shuddering. She had never felt more alone, more lonely. Thoughts of her father crept into her mind. 'Oh, Father,' she whispered brokenly, 'I wish you were here. You're the only one I would have wanted at a time like this.'

But she pushed such thoughts away. How stupid, how weak, to want her father at a time when he had just found happiness. Far better that he was away. If he had been here it would just have complicated matters further. A ghost of an idea was slowly forming in her confused mind, but the more she concentrated the stronger it grew. She sat back, lost in thought, absorbed with the new and stupendous thing which was beginning to root in her brain.

She would go away, leave Lorn, she could never bear to stay on in the house with him, not after tonight. Ay, it was a good thing her father wasn't here. Her strong attachment to him might have swayed her thinking and he would never have allowed her to leave the island, not without a struggle.

Her thoughts were racing feverishly now, making and rejecting plans, going round and round in circles till she felt she would go mad. She forced herself to start at the beginning, deciding that first she must pack the necessities she would need to start her off. Stiffly she uncurled her frozen limbs and got to her feet. Going through to the bedroom she gazed round distractedly, not knowing where to begin. Lorn still wasn't back and she made an effort to hurry, not wanting to face him – to explain. Rapidly she stuffed clothes into a small suitcase which she carried through to the little room off the parlour, the room so recently occupied by Rachel. A sweet, light fragrance still hung in the air, making Ruth shudder in revulsion. Until then all her bitterness had been against Lorn, but now it switched to the girl who had been her childhood friend. But she didn't waste time in useless recriminations – these would come later, when she had more time to think. Just now there was too much to do if her plans were to be carried out successfully.

Going through to the children's room she stood looking down at Lorna. Douglas wasn't here. He and Ellie Dawn, being so near in age, were extremely attached to one another, and he often spent the night at Mo Dhachaidh. Shona had mentioned that she was going with Niall on his rounds in the morning taking the children with her and Douglas in particular had been over the moon about this, as he loved animals of all kinds and delighted in any opportunity that took him amongst them. Ruth was glad that the little boy wasn't there that night. She could never have taken the decision to leave him behind yet she knew she could never cope with two children on her own. Douglas was too much of a baby yet – too helpless . . .

She put her cold fingers to her lips. 'Oh, God, help me,' she whispered. 'Help me, help me . . .'

The full import of the step she was about to take struck her with full force. Looking at Lorna lying so peacefully asleep in her bed made things appear normal, as if the life she had had with her children could never change – but it had changed, changed dramatically and so suddenly she felt herself being sucked into an unknown chasm of dread. But she had made up her mind – there was no turning back now. Tears filled her eyes as she studied Lorna's sleep-flushed face. She lay completely relaxed, her arms spread over the pillows, her earth-brown curls rumpled over her high brow. Her face in repose was beautiful. The small straight nose was sprinkled with freckles, a chaste smile lifted the corners of her mouth. Some people had nicknamed her Lorna the Smile because the upturned corners of her mouth gave the impression of a perpetual smile. It was so small a face, yet it contained a lot of character for such a wee lass. Ruth sighed deeply. How Lorn loved this child – yet she wasn't his daughter when all was said and done. He had no real right to her really, and if it broke his heart to lose the little girl he adored then so be it – it would serve him right if he suffered for all his treachery.

Without more hesitation, Ruth went to pack a small case for her daughter, taking it through to put it beside her own under the bed where they would be hidden should Lorn look in. But he didn't. She lay in the unfamiliar bed, her eyes swollen and hot, an anger in her so raw and bitter she felt only a contemptuous hatred for her husband when finally she heard him come in well after midnight, his unsteady footsteps telling her that he had been drinking. He went straight to his room, clicking the door softly shut and some time later she heard sounds like those of a soul tortured by nightmares. She didn't sleep at all that night. The hours ticked slowly by while she lay on her back, staring at the window, calm now as she plotted out the course she must take as soon as Lorn left the house.

Dawn filtered in, grey and desolate. Haar lay in pockets over the fields; swathed the trees by Sliach; erased the loch and the distant moors. Lorn rose earlier than usual. She heard him going to the kitchen, a short while later letting himself out of the house. Her lip curled. Too ashamed to dare to face her, to make any attempt at a reconciliation. She went to the window and watched him walking away, tall and straight in the morning light, his face turned away from her so that she couldn't see it. Ben had decided to go with him and walked obediently at his heels, his greying muzzle to the ground, sniffing happily at all the fresh smells. Lorn didn't look back at the house. She noticed that his steps were slow, faltering, so unlike his usual sure, springy stride. She would most likely never see him again. The realization filled her head with a pain so deep she felt all her resolutions tumbling about her. She would never see Ben too – he was old – he couldn't live many more years – she would have to leave behind all the animals, the house, everything that had been so good, so sweet in life.

The enormity of what she had planned struck her with renewed force – she couldn't do it – she wasn't strong enough, courageous enough to run away from the only life she had ever known. Then a fresh surge of anger gave her the strength she needed – and mixing with it all was a determination to make Lorn suffer for what he had done – she never wanted to see him again – never.

Splashing her face with cold water from the big flowery jug she dressed hurriedly then went through to dress Lorna. She was in the highest of spirits and wanted to linger to play with the animals but Ruth hurried her through breakfast. She knew if she didn't do everything swiftly she would have time to think and thinking was dangerous at a time like this.

She fed the hens, put bowls of milk out for the cats, settled the fire and put the guard over it. Lastly she seized her pen and scribbled a hasty note to Lorn which she propped against the sugar bowl on the table.

Lorna was ready, asking no questions, accepting the fact that her mother was taking her out early. Ruth checked through her bag. Money, enough of it to see her through for a while, all the bits and pieces she always carried, a comb for Lorna's hair on the boat, one or two addresses she would need. Lifting up the cases she bade Lorna follow her and they went outside, shutting the door for the last time.

She stood for a moment, breathing deeply of the hill air. The mist was rolling away from the fields, trees loomed like ghosts among the swirling wraiths, the clouds were breaking apart, patches of blue appeared. It was very still and peaceful. The hens crooned from the knoll; the cows grazed placidly; the scent of peat smoke drifted from the chimneys of Fàilte mingling with that blowing lazily from Laigmhor. Lorna was splashing in the pools of water lying in the hollows of the drying green, her face alight with mischief. Ruth took one last, lingering look at the little house in which she had known bliss beyond compare. Sadness lay over her face, her vision grew blurred. Abruptly she pulled her gaze away and set off over the fields, not wanting to take the glen road in case she might meet someone who would start asking awkward questions about her luggage. Even so, she anxiously scanned the landscape just in case Lorn might be working nearby. He had been busy in the top fields for the last week so she couldn't be too careful. She stumbled as she walked, blinded by tears that suddenly swamped her and Lorna's fingers curled consolingly into her hand.

'Don't cry, Mam, it's all better.' The words were meant to be reassuring but the child's voice trembled on a note of uncertainty.

Ruth straightened her shoulders resolutely. For Lorna's sake she had to be strong, had to behave normally. Squeezing the little hand she forced a smile. 'Ay, it's all better, my wee lamb, and it will be better still going for a nice sail in the boat. You'll like that, won't you?'

Lorna's face was solemn, the kind of solemnity she wore when she sensed unhappiness in those around her. 'Will Douglas be coming wiv us?'

'No, he has to stay with your grannie. Come on, we have to hurry, the boat will be leaving in a wee while.'

Taking her daughter's hand she led her firmly along the road to the harbour. Except for Merry Mary knitting on a chair outside the shop, the place was deserted and thankfully Ruth led Lorna up the gangplank. From one of the harbour cottages music from a wireless drifted and Ruth stiffened as she recognized the strains of the *Song of Rhanna*. To her, in those unhappy, fraught moments, it seemed like a mockery, tormenting her, reminding her of people she had loved and who had repaid her trust by being unfaithful behind her back, who had drained her when she was least strong. Her legs shook as she stood at the rail, her purpled gaze sweeping over the hills and the glens she so loved.

Merry Mary looked up, shading her eyes from the glare, and she wondered why Ruth hadn't mentioned yesterday in the shop that she was taking a trip away from the island. Little Lorna was raising her hand, waving, and Merry Mary's heart swelled with affection for Ruth's daughter. Bustling into the shop she emerged with a box of sweets and puffed up to the quay just as the gangplank was being raised.

'Here.' She thrust the package at a bearded boathand. 'Give these to wee Lorna McKenzie. She has just got on the boat wi' her mother. I didny know Ruth was taking a trip away from the island. I saw her yesterday and she never mentioned it.'

The boathand grinned. 'Ay, Mary, you know a lot but no' enough! Ask Kate, she knows everybody's business and will likely tell you that Ruth is away to meet a secret lover she's hidden away for years in Oban or the like.' He snorted with glee at the look of disapproval on Merry Mary's face. 'Ach, it was a joke. I'll see the bairn gets the sweeties – now get out o' my way before the ropes ca' you off your feets. You wouldny like a dip this mornin', the water's too cold.'

Merry Mary shaded her eyes again and waved up to Lorna standing at the rails with her mother, her face composed, her finger in her mouth as if she wasn't too keen on the idea of this unexpected trip.

Ruth didn't want to know the pain of watching her beloved island slipping away but against her will she stood as if rooted to the spot, seeing everything in a blur. Impatiently she wiped her eyes. The sun was slanting through the clouds, bathing the mountain tops in gold. The fresh greenery of spring clothed the fields and trees; tiny white specks that were lambs dotted the meadows round Laigmhor – and – she tried to drag her gaze away but stared as one transfixed – beyond Laigmhor she could just make out the chimneys of Fàilte. A drift of blue smoke hazed the hollow; a tiny matchstick figure walked in the fields. Her heart filled with a bittersweet yearning. Was it Lorn? Striding homewards, perhaps because he had forgotten something or else coming back to see her – he would find the house empty – see the note . . .

Far, far in the hidden glens of Rhanna the cuckoo had arrived and was calling, its notes echoing and re-echoing against the hills, drifting down to the harbour. Of all the triumphant sounds of spring this was the one which appealed most to Ruth's poetic soul. Always she had waited with a kind of breathless expectancy for the cuckoo to herald the approach of summer. Somehow it seemed to her that in its simple notes lay the portent of golden Hebridean days, when all the world was blue, when exotic butterflies danced upon the flowers and lovers cried and laughed in each other's arms in fragrant fields of ripening hay . . .

She stared at the scene till her eyes grew hot and her legs felt weak beneath her. Unable to bear the sadness any longer, she seized Lorna's hand and guided her away from the rails. But she couldn't resist taking one last lingering look over her shoulder. Already a good stretch of water separated them from the island. Pearly clouds ringed the hills, everything was merging, changing shape as the boat swung round. She couldn't distinguish one field, one glen from the next; the sea lapped the dazzling white beaches, then even that too changed. In a few short minutes the hills were just an ethereal shape against the sky, the island a blue blur floating on the ocean. She was no longer a part of it, no longer a part of anything that had been her life for more than twenty-two years.

Chapter Twelve

Lorn stood in the kitchen and faced his father, bracing himself for the storm he knew must surely follow the news he had to impart. He was drawn and pallid, with a dark stubble lying over his hollowed face. He had spent a harrowing, sleepless night sitting in a stunned stupor with Ruth's letter crushed in his hand. In it she had told him she was leaving and taking Lorna with her. 'You aren't her father after all,' the note read. 'You can tell your parents what you like, I don't care. I warn you not to come looking for me, you would be wasting your time. If you push me too hard it could come to a divorce. I would get both children in view of your faithlessness – this way at least you have your son, so for your own sake it would be best to leave things as they are till I have had more time to think. At the moment I can't see things too clearly. I only know I have to get away from you. I will get a job and Lorna will be well looked after. When my father gets back I want you to tell him what's happened – tell him not to worry – I will be in touch with him when I'm feeling more settled. Ruth.'

Lorn had been too shocked to immediately take in the

full import of the letter's contents. In a daze he had gone over to Mo Dhachaidh to collect his son and then he had sat in the kitchen for the rest of the night while little by little the full realization of what had happened sank into his disbelieving mind. Now he had to tell his parents and he didn't know how he was going to be able to deliver such a blow coherently. His mother wasn't in the room, only his father, black eyes burning into him questioningly, the lines of his face set – as if he was preparing himself for some sort of shock.

'Would you – I think I could talk to you better outside.' Lorn didn't recognize his own voice, it was high and ragged.

'Right, we'll go up to the south pasture.' Fergus was already at the door, striding away in front, stopping only when he reached the high, windblown field that curved gently to meet the lower slopes of Ben Machrie. Lorn had followed slowly, dreading the awful moment of truth. He was breathing heavily, not from exertion but from the burden of his seething emotions. Fergus stood waiting, saying nothing. Lorn wished he would speak, say something, anything to ease the steely tension that had arisen between them ever since he had told his father he had something important to tell him.

He took a deep breath. 'Ruthie's left me,' he imparted shortly.

Fergus' eyes raked his son's face. 'Left you! What the hell do you mean?'

'What I say.' Lorn's voice was soft with despair. 'She – she's taken Lorna – but not Douglas—'

'Why?' Fergus snapped the query out.

'Because – because of – things she heard about me and Rachel.'

'And were they true?' Fergus spat the words, his face deathly white.

'Ay – ay, they were.' Lorn's voice broke, he sagged, as if the effort to hold himself upright was suddenly too much. He was totally unprepared for what happened next. His father's fist shot out, crashing like a steel ball into the side of his face with such force he staggered and fell. Dazedly he lay on the grass, shaking his head, blood spurting from a gash on his lip.

Fergus was breathing hard, nostrils dilated, eyes glittering like coals in the pallor of his face. 'I ought to thrash the living daylights out of you! You bloody young fool – why did you do it?'

Lorn staggered to his feet. His father's face swam in his blurred vision. He had an almost irresistible urge to hit back; his breath rasped in his throat; his fists curled into balls at his sides, but with a supreme effort he stayed himself.

'I lost my head!' he hurled the words out. 'For once in my life I lost my bloody head! Do you think I don't hate myself for what I've done? Why are you such a God Almighty judge anyway! Haven't you ever done anything in your life of which you can look back and be so

273

ashamed you feel sick to the guts every time you think about it?'

Fergus' jaw clenched. 'We're not discussing my life – we're talking about the buggering mess you've made of yours . . .' He stopped dead and stared at his son. It seemed that in some strange way history was repeating itself. Lorn was right. Oh God! How right he was. There had been a time when he had hated himself for things he had done. Time had dulled his memories but this confrontation with Lorn brought it all flooding back – Kirsteen leaving him to bring up his child in some strange place – far away from everything that was dear and familiar. The circumstances had been different from those of his son but in the end it all amounted to much the same thing.

He looked at the young face in front of him, saw the stark misery lying like a grey shadow over it. The thought struck him – perhaps he had always expected too much of this youngest son of his – and – instead of beating him he should be doing everything in his power to help. Drawing his fingers across his mouth he studied Lorn contemplatively, giving himself time to think, time to decide on the right approach. With a quick, decisive gesture he threw out his arm and placed it firmly about the boy's shoulders. Lorn had instinctively jerked his head back, as if he had been prepared for another blow, and Fergus laughed dryly. 'Don't fret, I'm not going to spend precious time thrashing you, though if I'd been ten years younger I might have done for it's no more than you deserve. Here.'

He thrust his hanky into the other's hand. 'Clean your face then we'll sit here on the bank and talk this over like two sensible adults.'

Lorn sank down gratefully on the mossy ground. He hadn't eaten since dinner time the day before and felt as weak as a kitten. Before his father could speak he burst out impetuously, 'I'm going to look for her! She said not to but I'm damned if I'll sit back and let her take Lorna away from me. I have as much right to her as Ruthie – oh God! Poor wee lassie – she's the one who's going to suffer most from all this.'

Burying his head in his hands he gave vent to his feelings, the dry harsh sobs shaking his shoulders with their depth. Fergus let him cry. He had seen strong men weep before, he himself had done it in despair and sorrow many a time. In those moments he felt closer than ever to his son and had to swallow a lump in his own throat at the sight of the manly shoulders shuddering like those of a small boy.

Lorn raised a tearstained ashamed face. 'You must think me a weak fool.' He wiped frantically at his eyes. 'Weeping as easily as any woman.'

'Ach, I've done it myself often enough.'

'You?' Lorn's tones were disbelieving.

'Ay, me, don't look so surprised. I might be your father but that doesn't mean I'm not human. Now – first things first. We're going back to let your mother know what's happened. You and Douglas will both stay at Laigmhor till all this is settled. I wouldny worry too much about

Ruth. She'll come back; given time, she'll come back. At the moment she'll be feeling too angry and hurt to know what she's doing but she's a mother as well as a wife and she won't stay away from her son any longer than she needs to. Give her a week or two to calm down and if she's not back by then go and look for her – though I warn you, that might no' be as easy as it sounds.'

Lorn looked at his hands. 'She – she might want to leave me – for good I mean – in her place I might feel the same.'

'Ach, c'mon, man, don't cross bridges. Just now she'll feel anything but liking for you but that will pass.'

'Will it?' Lorn's voice was flat. 'I'm not so sure, Ruthie's very – unworldly. Everything was cut and dried in her life till this happened and she might no' be able to face the reality of it. I see a good lot of Morag in her, it's getting plainer as the years pass. Och, nothing like Morag's fanatical ways, but to Morag the world was a harsh place, she couldn't take too much of it and buried herself in religion in an effort to escape. In a way Ruthie's the same only she didn't bury herself in religion, she buried herself in me – and now that I've proved I'm not a saint, just another human being, everything in her rosy world has crumbled and she might no' be able to forgive me for it.'

Fergus stood up. 'Come on, Lorn, that kind of talk won't get you anywhere. You have a son who needs you. He will be wondering where his mother is and it's up to you as his father to make sure that he doesn't become more bewildered than he already is.'

That night Lorn lay in his old room at Laigmhor, the room he had shared with his brother for so many years and with Ruth during the first months of their marriage. In this room, in this bed, she had given birth to Lorna, Lewis' daughter, but so much a part of him he had almost forgotten that another man had fathered her. Ruth's note had cruelly reminded him of the fact and with that excuse she had seen fit to remove his darling little girl from his life.

A feeling of unreality washed over him. Only two nights ago he had lain with his wife, had caressed the softness of her body – now she was gone from him – but more than miles separated them, they were apart in every sense and he felt lost in a void of useless longing.

He thought briefly of Rachel but she seemed to belong to another time, a time of which only the more prominent details made any impression in his restless thinking. He didn't blame her for anything that had happened, he blamed only himself and it was a heavy weight which lay like a cold lump of lead in the pit of his belly. From along the passage he heard Douglas gurgling and laughing with Kirsteen. Thinking about her reaction to the news made him squirm afresh with guilt. She had merely looked at him strangely, those keen blue eyes of hers hurt and sad.

She had known a great deal of tragedy in recent years, but lately life had been kinder to her. Grant was coming home; she was going to be a grandmother again. She had learned to laugh more, but today he had taken it all away with just a few words. The familiar look of pain was back in eyes which had stared at him in disbelief and, finally, unwilling acceptance.

'I had thought better of you, Lorn.' That was all she said. It had been a brief judgement but one which made him feel more sorrow than any bitter outpouring. Shona hadn't said much either but there had been an odd expression on her face, as if in some strange way she hadn't been greatly surprised by the news. He had been glad of Niall's support. He had taken him into his study and made him swallow a good dram of whisky.

'These things happen to the best of us.' His brown eyes had been full of compassion and had reminded Lorn of Lachlan. 'You're no worse or no better than many, so stop going around as if you and you alone were the perpetrator of this particular situation.'

Despite his kind words Lorn *did* feel that he was worse than anyone else. Lying there in his lonely bed he felt small and mean, and his heart hurt so much for the wrong he had done he wanted only to curl up into a tight ball and die.

Down below in the cobbled yard, Ben lifted his nose to the night sky and howled. It was as if he knew what had happened and was commiserating in his own particular way as if he was aware that the secure routine of his life was in jeopardy and he sensed that he might not live long enough to see the return of people and things which had been part of his life for so long.

Lorn stood in the cluttered homely kitchen of Dungowrie Farm and faced Jean Jackson with pleading in his eyes. 'Please, can I see my wife?' His voice was soft, frayed with the anxiety he had endured on his long journey to Ayrshire.

His father's optimistic predictions about Ruth coming back to him had not come to fruition. A month had elapsed. In that time he had waited every other day for Erchy the Post to bring some news that would let him know that his wife was safe, that Lorna was well, but nothing, not even a note, came. He had gone from moods of despair and sorrow to anger, bitterness, self-pity. He argued with himself continually, convinced himself that Ruth had never loved him, if she had she wouldn't have done this to him, couldn't let him suffer so heartlessly. He loved her one minute, hated her the next, longed for her, rejected her fiercely.

But through all his various emotional swings, the knowledge was always there at the back of his mind that he was the cause of all that had happened and he grew weary to the point of exhaustion from endless nights of broken sleep. And the gossips were starting to get suspicious about

Ruth's absence even though it had been put about that she had gone off to recuperate from her illness, taking Lorna with her for company.

Whenever he had reason to go to the Post Office, Behag eyed him in knowing disdain while everyone else asked after Ruth's health till he was driven to distraction. To make matters worse, Merry Mary had witnessed Ruth's early morning departure from the island and, more from genuine concern than maliciousness, had broadcast the fact far and wide.

'The poor lassie looked so peakit and ill and that bonny wee bairnie was so quiet and miserable looking. I could have run after her and hugged her to my bosom – and never a soul to see them off – and she only had two wee cases, a if she had packed them in quite a hurry and couldny wai to take more.'

And then Dugald and Totie had come home, the forme bright-eyed, with a spring in his step. Lorn had tried t break the news gently but had instead blurted it out, an the stunned look on Dugald's face had brought all his gui and self-hatred flooding back. He had hoped that Ruth ha written to her father, but there was nothing, not even postcard. It had been a fine welcome home for a coupl just starting a new life together, yet Dugald had wasted n time in useless accusations. Instead he had regarded Lor for long thoughtful moments then finally said, 'You we feart something like it would happen – that day Ruthie to me you and she had argued about Rachel coming to st

I knew you had a good reason for not wanting the lass in your home.'

'That doesn't make any of this easier,' Lorn had said bitterly.

'No, no, lad, it doesn't, but we mustny waste time arguing, we'll have to see this thing through together for we're the only two people in the world who really love our Ruthie. What you did was shocking and shameful and if I was a younger man I might have given you a good hiding for it, but I'm old enough to know that you love my lassie despite what you did. I also know you're going to do everything in your power to make her forgive you and come back to you.'

The three of them had discussed the matter well into the small hours, exploring all the possibilities of Ruth's whereabouts, but there had been so few of them they had been in despair. Outside her family Ruth had few contacts. Lorn mentioned the possibility of reporting her missing to the authorities but both Dugald and Totie rejected the suggestion. This was a family affair – God knows what Ruth might do if she learned the police were after her. In the end Lorn remembered Jean Jackson whom his wife had spoken of with such enthusiasm and the very next morning he left Rhanna to find Dungowrie Farm.

His heart beat fast as he spoke to the tiny, grey-haired woman with her kindly face, rotund figure, and eyes the colour of cornflowers. They had twinkled when she had come round the corner of the byre and saw him standing at the front door of the big, untidy farmhouse looking sheepish and unsure but they weren't twinkling now on hearing why he had come.

'Sit ye doon, laddie,' she directed kindly. 'You're big and I'm wee and I'll get a sair neck squintin' up at ye.'

Lorn sat himself on the edge of a well-patched sofa and she sat down near him. 'I'm glad ye've come,' she nodded. 'I ken what happened between the pair o' ye. I'm no' one to judge so I'll no' bother tellin' ye what a silly laddie ye've been for by the look o' ye, ye ken that already.'

'Is Ruthie here?' he broke in roughly, unable to bear the suspense any longer.

Jean nodded slowly. 'Ay, she's here right enough, but a very different lassie from the one I knew in hospital. Oh, she's a grand help about the place though I don't let her tackle anything too heavy. Davie – that's my man – likes her fine for she knows a lot aboot runnin' a farm and was able to help him wi' a calving the other night. But och, she's no' a happy lass. I hear her greetin' in her room at night – and the wee one, my, but she's a quiet wee thing – nary a word to say for herself.'

Lorn's heart plummeted. Lorna, quiet? That happy child who gave him such joy with her singing and her whimsical ways. From the corner of his eye he saw Ruth and Lorna coming across the yard towards the house. He stood up, his big frame tense, a coil of nerves in his belly as he waited for the door to open. She came in slowly, as if somehow she had expected him. She was thin and pale, her face expressionless as she saw him standing beside Jean's diminutive form.

'Ruthie.' Her name was a mere breath on his lips. Lorna's eyes had grown big at sight of him, an expression of disbelief flitting over her face.

'*Favver!*' She sang out the name, joyfully, lovingly, then she was flying across the room, a tiny blur of delight. He caught her and gathered her to his heart, awash with love for this little mite with her soft brown hair and her huge violet-blue eyes. Her arms went round his neck and then she held his dark head between her two small hands and said again softly, shyly, 'Favver,' as if she couldn't believe he was real and might disappear at any moment. A rush of love overwhelmed him. Kissing her petal-soft cheek he murmured, 'My babby, my babby,' and all the while he was aware that Ruth's expression had barely changed though there was such burning resentment in her eyes he could almost hear her saying, 'Why are you here? I warned you not to come looking for me.'

'Could we – talk, Ruthie?'

The lilting voice fell on her ears like the purling of the burn that ran through Fàilte's green fields. She looked at him, at his strong, handsome face pale with misery and guilt, at the deep cleft in his chin that had entranced her from the start, at his big powerful male body, so tall his head almost touched the low-beamed ceiling, and her heart twisted with a renewal of the pain she had endured since her departure from Rhanna's shores. She had almost convinced herself that she hated him and now here he was, so big and real she was overwhelmed by him, by his blue eyes piercing her soul with their expression of pleading.

She saw the change in him a few short weeks had wrought, he was thinner, his young face was strangely gaunt.

She despised herself for being weak enough to want to take him in her arms, to tell him that she still loved him, that all she needed was time to get over the hurt and humiliation he had caused her . . .

'I told you not to come, Lorn.' Her voice was so brittle it was a surprise even to herself and she knew she could never forgive him for what he had done. In coming here he had just made matters worse – he should have stayed away. Suddenly she had a mental picture of Rachel touching the bronzed exciting body that she had thought was hers alone – of him touching Rachel . . .

Jean Jackson murmured something about tea and made to withdraw from the room, taking an unwilling Lorna with her, but Ruth stayed her by saying, 'No, Jean, don't go, what my husband has to say isn't important.'

She ignored the pleading in his eyes, the message that said plainer than words, 'Don't do this to me, Ruthie – to us.'

Her face was set and hard, so unlike the girl he knew he felt she was a stranger, someone he had never known – never loved.

Jean's plump face showed her embarrassment. Shaking

her head sorrowfully, she went from the room, closing the door softly behind her. The last thing Lorn saw of his daughter was her beseeching gaze turned towards him, making him more determined than ever to try to persuade Ruth to come back to him.

The door had hardly shut when she faced him angrily and said through gritted teeth, 'Get away from here, Lorn, I warn you, if you don't, I'll do something far worse than just leave you with Douglas – I'll make it so you'll be left with nothing and you'll wish you had never been born a McKenzie! You're all the same, every one of you, lustful, deceitful – weak . . .' She halted. That wasn't true. From the beginning Lorn's strength had been the quality that had struck her most. In the early days when he had fought one battle after another with ill health, his strength had come to him from within. Later, when he had overcome his physical weaknesses she had admired every aspect of his strength – yet all that had been swept away in one weak moment of his life – but it was that moment that mattered most, it scattered everything that went before as easily as gossamer threads before the wind.

He spread his hands. 'Ruthie, if you ever loved me, forgive me – if not for my sake then for the children. Douglas is only a baby. He needs you, Ruthie.'

Her head went up. 'In that case I'll come back and get him. It will no' be easy coping with two bairns but . . .'

'That's not what I meant and fine you know it!'

She heard the break in his voice, his effort to imbue

firmness into his tones. She thought of her little son, asking for her, wondering when she was coming back and she couldn't stop the tears welling into her eyes. She longed for him, his bonny baby face, his hearty, pot-bellied laughter. She forced the tears back – she couldn't – she must not weaken.

'Your father is back, Ruthie – he was happy till he found out that you were gone.' It was his final weapon, a last desperate effort to get her to come home. But it was his undoing. Her fist flew to her mouth, she took a step backwards, an awkward heavy step that emphasized her limp.

'If my father's unhappy it's because of you,' she accused bitterly. 'Don't use him against me. Tell him I'll write – I didn't before because I couldn't thole the idea of a letter like that waiting for him – and because I was so ashamed of what had happened. I hate you, Lorn,' she continued, her voice flat, lifeless. 'Go away from here now. I never want to see you again. You've taken everything from me I ever loved – my family – my home. I'll suffer more than you will because you still have all that. The only thing I can wish on you is a humiliation as deep and as sore as mine. It will serve you right if the cailleachs rant on about you till you feel you can never hold up your head again, for whatever excuses you have made up about my leaving will soon go like a puff of wind.'

She laughed, a high hysterical laugh that cut him to the bone. 'As for Rachel – if ever she has reason to come back to Rhanna without Jon – just think, you and she can lust together all you like and no one there to deceive or lie to—'

'For God's sake, Ruthie, you make it sound as if I had made a habit of going with other women! Rachel was the only one . . .'

'Once is once too often,' she spat at him maliciously. 'Go home and dream about your one and only mistress! If you play your cards right you and Rachel can have a really good time to yourselves in future – and just think – the poor dumb cratur' will never be able to nag you or ask you who you are with when you're no' with her!'

Her eyes were wild, staring. Lorn looked at her in disbelief. Had he done this to her or had it always been there just waiting to come out? She wrenched the door open, almost bumping into Jean with her tray of tea things. At sight of the two heated faces Jean's kindly face fell. She had hoped for a reconciliation between the two young people, had hoped to see smiles instead of fury.

'My husband is just going, Jean.' Ruth looked at him, challenging him to say otherwise. He straightened, lifted his head, squared his shoulders. 'Write and let me know how Lorna is.' His tones were clipped.

'I'll write to my father – ask him if there's anything you want to know.'

He brushed past her, murmuring his thanks to Jean

who put out her hand and touched him sympathetically on the shoulder. He stumbled outside, unable to see for tears. The golden fields of Ayrshire rolled into the blue distance; a tractor purred; a blackbird sang from a nearby tree – and far far away the cuckoo was calling, as if it had followed him here and was letting him know that his place wasn't in the flatlands of Ayrshire but among the hills and glens of Rhanna.

He didn't look back once at the rambling farmhouse, didn't see Lorna gazing forlornly from the window. He couldn't think straight, wasn't even certain where he would stay that night, he had visualized a reconciliation with Ruth, a night at the farm, a journey back to Rhanna with Lorna and Ruth at his side.

He went to the nearest hotel to drink himself insensible before falling into a strange bed, too anaesthetized with liquor to be able to care about anything or anyone.

When he got back to Rhanna he went straight to Dugald to tell him the news then he went home to put money in an envelope which he addressed to Dungowrie Farm. If Ruthie wouldn't allow him to have his little girl back at least he could send money to ensure that she was properly clothed and fed. He paused with his pen in his hand and remembered the joy in her face when she had beheld him standing in Jean Jackson's kitchen. A tremor went through him. He could send as much money as he liked but that could never buy the security that an intelligent, sensitive child like Lorna needed – and for the first time fear gripped him – fear that he might never know the joy of watching his daughter grow up – and all because he had allowed a moment of weakness to overrule the sagacity that had been with him all his life.

Part Three

Summer 1964

Chapter Thirteen

'She is a woman! A young one at that!' Todd cried aghast, staring in disbelief at the slender figure walking on the road below Kate's cottage. 'I will no' have a woman lookin' at my private parts!'

'She will be a foreigner likely,' expostulated Jim Jim in dismay. 'She will no' be able to understand our ways!'

'Ach, she is not foreign, she is Welsh – Doctor Jenkins to you seeing you'll just be her patients. She told me to call her Megan wi' me being part o' the family so to speak.' Elspeth puffed out her scrawny bosom importantly, a pride in her because she had been introduced to the new doctor in common with the rest of the family. It made her feel that she was one of them, not just the housekeeper, an outsider who had to be kept in her proper place. They were all having a blether outside Kate's cottage. A few of them had met to keep each other company on the walk over to the doctor's surgery where they were heading in just a few moments. The sight of the new doctor, also making her way to Lachlan's house, had induced a temporary unanimity among them, for Behag was in their midst, her usual grumbles having caused a few spicy remarks to fly before the diversion created by Doctor Jenkins.

'From what I can see o' her at this distance she looks a bonny young woman,' Kate observed.

Tam, still dwelling on Todd's remarks, rubbed his hands together with anticipatory fervour. 'She can look at my private parts all she likes – she is a bonny one and no mistake.'

'Ach, she's too skinny,' said Ranald in disgust, while Kate damped Tam's ardour with a well-aimed swipe at his face with the soapy cloth she had been using to clean her windows.

'Skinny or no',' nodded Kate, 'it will be a change for us womenfolk to have a lady doctor to look to our ails. Lachlan is a bonny doctor, but there were times when I didny like showin' him the kind o' things I'd rather show a woman.'

'That's all very well but what about the rest o' us?' grumbled Jim Jim. 'I have been havin' a wee bitty bother wi' my bladder this whily back but I'm damty sure I'll no' be showin' it to that slip o' a lassie.'

'You will have no need to worry yourself for a whily yet,' Elspeth imparted sourly, her manner most unsympathetic towards Jim Jim and his bladder ever since she had caught him emptying it behind a bush. Instead of showing embarrassment he had waved at her most offensively 'and it wasny wi' his hands', she had stressed meaningfully. 'Doctor Lachlan will no' be giving up the practice right away.

He will be showing the new doctor the way things are done here and they will be working together for quite a few months before she is on her own.'

Jim Jim breathed a sigh of relief. 'Ach, that is indeed good news. I will get along to Lachlan's wi' an easy mind and see what he is going to do about it. I am getting to the stage where I want to stop at every bush I see.'

'Only dogs do that, you dirty bodach,' Elspeth sniffed haughtily.

Tam winked at Jim Jim and shook his head sadly. 'That is no' a good sign right enough, Jim Jim, you will be gettin' a sore leg if you keep that going.'

Behag examined his face to assess whether he was being serious but seeing his doleful expression she dared to ask, 'And what on earth has a sore leg got to do wi' a weak bladder, Tam McKinnon?'

Kate turned away quickly, her hand to her mouth to stifle the anticipated mirth as Tam said earnestly, 'Well, Behag, seeing you are a woman you will never have the misery of such a complaint but every man knows that no matter how much he shakes his peg the last wee drip runs down his leg.'

The men burst into guffaws which were not quenched by Behag's enraged glowers and Elspeth's disgusted 'Hmph' before she stalked away, her nose stuck firmly in the air. Her scurrying gait took her quickly to the side of Megan Jenkins who turned at the sound of footsteps on the stony ground.

She was a tall, willowy young woman of about twenty-eight with soft shining brown hair that curled inward just below the curve of her ears. Her eyes were a light hazel in the pale transparency of her face and held a certain amount of trepidation as she beheld Elspeth for she had already assessed the gaunt-faced housekeeper of Slochmhor as a personage of strict moral code and a relentless ear for gossip.

'It is yourself, Doctor Megan,' greeted Elspeth, her inherent reserve not allowing for a more informal approach despite her boasting.

'Elspeth.' The new doctor tried to instil enthusiasm into the soft tones of her voice which held faint but pleasing traces of her native Welsh accents. Years of working and living in England had robbed it of much of its singing quality but it was still there, under the surface, and the more she talked the more evident it became.

'I am just going to Slochmhor (this she pronounced as it should be, 'Sloch – vor') for evening surgery.'

'I will get you along the way.' Elspeth fell into step, enjoying the glances of curiosity from the group she had just left. 'You will be havin' a full surgery tonight and no mistake,' she predicted with a certain amount of satisfaction, revelling in the advantage she had of knowing the ways of the islanders.

'I won't be taking surgery for a while yet,' Megan explained politely. 'Doctor McLachlan thought it would be better if I got to know his patients gradually, so to begin with I will be more or less a bystander.'

'That is a pity; they are all anxious to meet you and for you to see to their ails for them.' Elspeth forgave herself the ready lie with the excuse she was saving the new doctor the embarrassment of finding out too harshly that the islanders were not in the least looking forward to her taking over the practice. She eyed the young woman's somewhat reserved countenance. 'Will you be liking it here, do you think?'

Megan's eyes shone so much they appeared amber in a burst of sunlight spilling over the grey clouds above. 'It's early days but already I love my house down by the shore. Last night I lay awake for hours just listening to the seabirds and the ocean sighing.'

Elspeth merely grunted. Hers was a purely practical nature and she had little time to spare for the more poetical aspects of life. They were passing Laigmhor just then and in the short space of a few minutes she had given the new doctor an almost chronological history of the McKenzies and their affairs.

'McKenzie o' the Glen is a proud one and no mistake,' she said tightly. 'Though he should be hangin' his head in shame for the things he and his family have done. Always there is some scandal in that family and now of course it's the turn of Lorn, McKenzie's youngest son. We all thought he was going to be different from the rest – he was always such a good, kind laddie, but of course, blood will out and as he's got older he is just his father all over again. They are womanizers, you know, canny seem to help themselves. His wife has left him takin' one o' the bairns wi' her and folks are saying it's because he went and had some sort of entanglement wi' her best friend. Mind you, thon Rachel is no' better herself, aye was as wild as a gypsy and now she flaunts herself in a way that would make any decent man lose his head . . .'

'You mean Rachel Jodl, don't you?' Megan cut in, glad to change the subject. 'I had heard that she came from Rhanna. She's a wonderful musician – I was at one of her concerts in London and never heard a finer violinist.'

'Och, ay, she's a clever enough lass,' Elspeth had to agree, 'and unlike the McKenzies she has given the island a good name, but it doesny give her the right to behave as she does. Lorn and Ruth were quite happy till she came back and broke them up. It has caused quite a scandal I can tell you. Lorn is going about wi' his head down – and well he might – for the rascal deserves all he gets. His sister is married to the doctor's son. A fine laddie is Niall.' Elspeth's tones grew warm as she liked nothing better than to boast about a member of the family she considered herself part of. 'He had his sorrows to seek wi' that madam, Shona, oh ay, she led him into mischief from the start. What man doesny fall for a pretty face? Nobody could blame Niall for the things that happened . . .'

The monologue went on and by the time Slochmhor was reached Megan's head was whirling and she was only too thankful to reach the safe haven of the parlour where Phebie and Lachlan were having their usual late-afternoon tea. Elspeth disappeared to the kitchen regions and Lachlan laughed when he saw Megan's bewildered face.

'I see Elspeth has been regaling you with local gossip. You mustny mind her too much; her good points outweigh the bad – only just. In the beginning we were all scared stiff of her rantings, but the years have mellowed us all and she is a damned good housekeeper.'

'That is Elspeth mellowed?' said Megan faintly. 'I don't think I would have fancied knowing her when she was in full vigour.'

'You will have a cuppy?' Phebie asked, the teapot poised ready.

Megan pushed back her hair and sat down thankfully. 'I'd love one. I can see that cuppies and cracks are quite a feature of island life. I've only been here since yesterday and already I've been invited into several homes for a wee strupak.'

Lachlan grinned. 'At the moment they're dying to have a look at you and their invitations are a combination of friendliness and curiosity. Later on, when you're part of the scenery, you'll find a strupak is just an excuse to combine hospitality with an exchange of gossip.'

Megan sighed. 'I wonder if I will ever feel part of the scenery. Life here is so different from what I've been used to, although I started off life in the country I've spent a lot of it in cities.'

Lachlan said softly, 'I know you'll fit in here, that's wh[y]
I had my eye on you from the start.'

She coloured and as she turned to talk to Phebie h[e]
studied her, struck by the grace of her slender figure, [by]
her fine hands with their small bones and astonishing[ly]
long fingers. A casual observer might have dismisse[d]
her as having no particular beauty, but a more leisure[ly]
study revealed certain delightful features: the honesty i[n]
her strikingly lovely eyes; the sensitive, well-shaped mou[th]
and straight white teeth which only revealed themselve[s]
when she spoke because, as Lachlan had already noted, sh[e]
rarely smiled. But it wasn't her physical attributes which ha[d]
attracted his attention at the Executive Council Intervie[w]
Board which he had attended in Inverness. Quietly he ha[d]
sized up the shortlisted GPs and though each had the[ir]
merits, there had been something about the young fema[le]
doctor which he had liked. Although quiet and gentle, the[re]
was a decisiveness in her attitude to doctoring tempere[d]
by a true caring for her profession. She had put forward [a]
good case for wanting the position on Rhanna. The oth[er]
candidates had had varied reasons for wanting the job to[o]
but, as far as Lachlan was concerned, Megan Jenkins ha[d]
tendered the most pertinent. She had spent many holida[ys]
in the Hebrides and had fallen in love, not only wi[th]
the islands, but with the people and would welcome t[he]
opportunity to live and work among them.

There had been another important point in her favou[r.]
Being Welsh she spoke Welsh Gaelic and also had a f[a-]

smattering of Scottish Gaelic. One or two of the other applicants had shown contempt for the Gaelic language, another rather officious type had told the Council, 'I'd soon get those people into the twentieth century, need stirring up a bit – lazy from what I hear.' Lachlan had shuddered at that, he had also shuddered when he learned that a tall man with a mop of grey hair and a bearing and manner more suited to Harley Street, had given away the fact that he was something of a Holy Wullie and was a lay preacher in his spare time.

Lachlan's experience had helped in the final decision, and he had been delighted when Megan was chosen. He and Phebie had asked her to stay at Slochmhor but she had opted to take a house over by Burg Bay with the wild Atlantic beating the shore just a few yards away and breathtaking views over the Sound of Rhanna.

'Your nearest neighbour will be Mark James, the minister,' Lachlan had told her. 'If you need anything I know he'll be only too pleased to help.'

At that point in time Megan had not met the minister and she had no intention of calling on him for assistance, nor anyone else for that matter. She was perfectly content to be by herself and to manage her own affairs, no matter how difficult that might be in a house with no electricity, running water, or any of the other basic amenities she had been used to. She saw her new way of life as a challenge and was quite excited at the prospect of stretching her initiative. Besides, she wanted as different a life as possible from the one she had previously led. She needed time to be by herself in order to try and get over a recent, traumatic love affair. She had felt guilty at not mentioning to Lachlan that that had been another of her reasons for wanting the post but decided it was a personal matter and one she wished to keep firmly to herself.

'I was hearing something of the affairs of a family named McKenzie,' she hazarded tentatively, not wishing to let the McLachlans mistake polite conversation for gossip.

'They have had their share of troubles like everyone else.' Lachlan cursed Elspeth for her loose tongue and for giving a newcomer an instantly wrong impression about people who were so close to his heart. 'Elspeth will have told you about Lorn – and a lot more besides. What he needs now is help – not hindrance – but you'll find out for yourself what kind of people the McKenzies are and can form your own opinion of them.'

As it happened the new doctor was about to find out a bit more of the family under discussion, a whole lot sooner than she expected, because Kirsteen arrived at that moment, her fair skin flushed, her blue eyes sparkling in her face. Lachlan introduced her to Megan whom she acknowledged warmly, welcoming her to the island and hoping that she would like it, then she turned to the others and said breathlessly, 'I have just had a phone call from Grant.'

Without any preliminaries she plunged into an account of her conversation with her eldest son, in her exuberance seeming not to mind the new doctor hearing everything she had to say. Phebie poured another cup of tea and listened, her own face growing rosy with anticipation as Kirsteen talked on.

When she revealed that the young people had finally decided to settle down on the island both Lachlan and Phebie gave a shout of delight. 'Och, it will be just grand to have them back,' Phebie beamed. 'And lovely to have a baby about the place again.' She glanced at Lachlan's happy face. 'And here you were thinking you would have too much time on your hands when you retired – Fiona will see to it that your days are well filled.'

'Bang goes all the lovely long mornings in bed – and those fishing trips I planned with Fergus.' Lachlan tried to look woeful, but was secretly looking forward to having young people in his life again. He had made quite a few plans for the future. For the first time in all their married years on the island he and Phebie would know the luxury of having the entire run of the house. The surgery and dispensary could now be integrated. He planned to make one of the rooms into a den, somewhere he could go to relax, perhaps start writing a book about his experiences as an island GP. He hadn't told Phebie this yet, the idea had only recently taken root in his mind, but the more it fermented the more enthusiastic he became . . .

'Of course, they'll be staying at Laigmhor till they get a place of their own. I'm busy getting the rooms ready now,' Kirsteen's voice recalled Lachlan to the present. 'They won't be home till August at least, but I want Fergus to do some decorating. He's never been exactly enthusiastic about such things so he'll need time to get used to the idea.'

Lachlan's eyes went at once to Phebie's face. The words might have come from her, he had heard them almost every day since the news of the expected baby. He braced himself for what was to come, glancing rather nervously at Megan who was sitting quietly in the background looking slightly embarrassed. He saw Phebie's struggle to remain calm, saw the dangerous gleam in her normally placid eyes which told him that she was entirely unable to control the outburst that followed.

'Oh but, Kirsteen, I'm all set for them to come here, I thought you knew that. I made it perfectly plain that I want my daughter to have her baby in the very house she herself was born in. You can come over whenever you like of course but . . .'

Kirsteen's face went from pink to red, her eyes sparkled blue fire. 'Havers, Phebie! We have much more room at Laigmhor. We can give them their own set of rooms and a nursery for the bairn . . .'

'You forget you have Lorn back staying with you.' Phebie's voice rose. 'How can you be so selfish, Kirsteen? I never thought it of you of all people. You already have one son at home so why grudge us the right to have our daughter? Besides, with the surgery and dispensary no longer in use we will have more space than we need – not to mention the empty bedrooms upstairs!'

Inwardly Lachlan groaned as he saw all his carefully laid plans go up in smoke and he said as patiently as he could, 'Hey, c'mon you two. It's far too early to make any such plans. No doubt Fiona and Grant will have their own ideas on where they want to stay.'

Kirsteen tossed her head. 'Grant as much as hinted he would be wanting to come back to Laigmhor and I will certainly go ahead and get the decorating done.'

Phebie lifted her plump chin. 'And so will I, Kirsteen – as a matter of fact I have already started to paint the bedrooms.'

Kirsteen stood up, a determination on her face that both Phebie and Lachlan knew so well, for she had had so much trouble thrust upon her in recent years she had developed a resilience that was as tough as leather. 'I think I've said enough on the subject.' Her voice was tight and firm. 'And I'm not going to stay here and listen to another word. You had better get used to the idea of the young ones coming to Laigmhor, for if you don't you will only bring unnecessary hurt upon yourselves.'

With that, she flounced away, ignoring Elspeth's sharp face hovering curiously in the hall. The door banged shut behind her with such energy the plates on the dresser rattled and the windows shook in their frames.

A rather shamefaced Lachlan grinned at Megan, 'No doubt you will already be forming your own opinions about the McKenzies. Kirsteen inherited the title only through marriage of course, but I'd say she gave as good a show of temper as any true blue McKenzie any day.'

Megan's face was sober and anyone simply glancing at her would have thought that she had taken the whole affair seriously. But her hazel eyes were twinkling beneath her fringe of dark lashes which she had hastily and discreetly lowered. In the face of Phebie's ire she daren't show anything else but sympathy for the occasion. Nevertheless she decided to play safe and steer a middle course by saying thoughtfully, 'I saw her on the road yesterday evening and she gave the impression of being as calm and sweet as a sunny summer's day.'

'Oh she is – normally,' Lachlan hastened to assure. He spread his hands resignedly. 'Today was a very rare exception, a good example of how families fight over their offspring.'

Phebie gave him a cold look. 'I am *not* fighting, and I will expect you, Lachlan McLachlan, to support me in this matter.'

Lachlan sighed and stood up. 'Time we went to take surgery, Megan. Elspeth usually has everything ready though she's spent so much time in the hall listening I doubt the patients will find everything at sixes and sevens when they arrive.'

The patients had already arrived. Together with Elspeth they had eavesdropped on the argument with avid enjoyment. They had also witnessed Kirsteen's hasty exit from the premises and Kate shook her head in dismay. 'Ach my, I would never have believed it if I hadny heard it wi' my very own lugs. That pair have been friends for years. I never thought I'd see the day they would be bawling at each other like a couple o' schoolchildren.'

Behag folded her hands on her lap, sniffed, and said with quiet satisfaction, 'There is a first time for everything – and of course, what can you expect from a body so entrenched in the McKenzie ways? She has developed the same wicked temper though mind you, I for one canny blame her – even though she knew what she was doing when she came back to McKenzie complete wi' his son born out of wedlock. She has had to thole a lot from that family and now she has Lorn to contend wi' it's little wonder she is turning into a sour cailleach.'

Kate chuckled. 'She is maybe modelling herself on you, Behag, though I doubt it. It would take a normal body a hundred and more years to accomplish what you have done in just sixty-seven. She will never have your greetin' auld face, that's for sure, she is far too nice lookin' for that.'

Behag glared and turned her back on Kate just as Megan came out of the parlour to cross the hall into the surgery. In face of the new diversion all else paled and men and women alike gaped at her without reserve. She took one look at the gimlet-eyed gathering, swallowed hard, and passed hastily into the surgery, her neat, high-heeled shoes making a rhythmical tapping on the linoleum, her glossy brown head held as high as it would go.

'My my,' Fingal McLeod, a lanky, tousle-haired crofter with a peg leg, watched her disappearance through the door with admiration. 'So that is the new doctor? Have you ever seen such a bonny pair o' legs? They just go on and on for miles.' He sniggered. 'I wonder if I show her old Peggy will she maybe return the compliment and let me see one o' hers – though two would be better.'

'Hmph,' Behag's jowls were hanging in disapproving layers. 'Fancy a doctor wearin' they ridiculous spiky shoes. She will be leaving wee pits all over the floors and breaking her ankles into the bargain.'

'And she was wearin' a white coat.' Jim Jim looked uneasy. 'I never could be natural speakin' to a body in a white coat.'

Everyone looked at everyone else uncomfortably. To them a doctor in a white coat meant officiousness and was a most effective barrier against friendly overtures.

'Lachlan's never worn a white coat in all the time he's been here,' said Merry Mary nervously. 'I mind once he was away and a locum in his place wore a coat so thick wi' starch it stood up on its own according to Elspeth. She had to launder the damty things and got excreta on her hands. They were all dry and scaly like a fish.'

'Eczema,' corrected Mollie automatically. 'You are gettin' mixed up wi' dung, Merry Mary.'

'Indeed I am not,' asserted Merry Mary witheringly. 'Elspeth had her own cure for dry hands. Every night before bedtime she coated her hands in dung from my very own byre and went to bed wi' cotton gloves over them.'

Todd's round face positively beamed. 'It is no wonder she could never get another man after Hector died. I wouldny like to go to bed wi' her at the best o' times but the idea o' her pawin' me wi' shitty fingers would be the last straw.'

'It worked too,' put in Kate who had been quietly wondering how she was going to tell a doctor in a white coat that she was having bother with her piles again. 'I mind Elspeth showed me her hands, lily white they were and as smooth as a baby's bum. "My, Elspeth," I says, "it just shows what a good dollop o' dung will do to a body's parts." I suggested she should try it on her face and she never spoke to me for a month after.'

Phebie's exit from the parlour very effectively quelled further gossip. Her eyes were red as if she had just been crying and her usual cheery smile of greeting was conspicuous by its absence.

Behag clicked her tongue and said solicitously, 'And how are you this evening, Mistress McLachlan? No' too happy from the look of you, but never mind, you will soon have the family round you again and will have no time to feel anything for no doubt they will keep you busier than you have ever been before.'

It was an inflammatory remark and everyone there, not the least Phebie, knew that it was a deliberate attempt to draw her into speaking about the argument with Kirsteen.

Phebie's ample bosom heaved, the look she cast at Behag would have withered a forest. 'And I suppose you know all about young families, Behag? Maybe you have been keeping one hidden up your sleeve to surprise us with – or maybe you just throw a few ingredients into a witch's pot, shout "Abracadabra" and a ready-made set o' bairns come tripping out to throw their arms about you and shout "Mother"!'

Behag spluttered and turned purple, everyone else stared at Phebie in open-mouthed astonishment, while Kate threw up her hands and gave vent to peals of such infectious laughter she soon had everyone else joining in. Even Phebie saw the funny side and broke first into a giggle then into a full-bellied laugh which soon dispelled her previous gloom. Only Behag failed to see humour in the situation and as soon as Elspeth appeared to announce that the doctors were ready, she got up and flounced into the surgery, ignoring Jim Jim's protests that he was first.

'The buggering old cheat,' he fumed, then appealing to the rest, 'I hope that the new doctor tries pokin' butter up her erse wi' a red hot needle – ay, and down her throat as well!'

'Ach God!' Kate was off again, Phebie collapsed on chair and clutched her stomach, Jim Jim shot a perfectl aimed spit into a flower pot in his exuberance, everyon else wobbled and snorted.

The mirthful sounds wafted through the solid oak doc of the surgery. Lachlan's lips twitched, Megan looked :

Behag's wizened red countenance, heard her stuttered request for something to cure her constipation and valiantly squashed down an irrepressible urge to shout with mirth. Hastily she rushed into the little dispensary where she collapsed against the shelves and allowed herself the luxury of a good laugh.

Her eyes roved over the various bottles containing cures for constipation and seizing one she measured out an amount which would ensure that Behag would be back in a few days complaining of diarrhoea. Already she had judged the ex-postmistress as a source of mischief-making and had no qualms in giving her the medicine. Another wave of mirth wafted from the hall. Pushing the hair from her neck she smiled, a soft, quiet, radiant smile which completely transformed her hitherto pensive face into one of vibrant attractiveness. She knew she was going to enjoy living on Rhanna with people like the McLachlans and the McKenzies, whom she didn't yet know, but who sounded interesting. And of course she had already fallen in love with the villagers with their open honest faces and what was obviously a hilarious sense of fun. Even old Behag, for all her faults and sly tongue was very much a character in her own right. She was part of the scheme of things and in every community there had to be a Behag to make you appreciate the more good-hearted in your midst.

Chapter Fourteen

Kirsteen burst into the kitchen, threw herself on a chair and cried passionately, 'I will never speak to Phebie McLachlan again! I never thought she could be so pig-headed and stubborn!'

Fergus looked up from his paper and eyed his wife in some surprise. Tears of frustration were dancing in her eyes, her cheeks were flushed, the hand she pushed through her hair was not quite steady. Patiently he folded up the paper, laid it on the coalbox, and waited for an explanation of the outburst. In a choked voice she related all that had transpired between herself and Phebie, finishing with the somewhat petty exclamation, 'And to think I believed she was my friend!'

Fergus put his pipe between his teeth and, with slow deliberation, lit it from a paper spill held to the fire. He cleared his throat, realizing that this was a delicate situation which needed careful handling.

'You must see her side of the picture as well as your own,' he said, choosing each word carefully. 'If you think Phebie's being unreasonable, she must be thinking exactly the same thing as yourself, for isn't it a fact that you both want the selfsame thing?'

It was the wrong thing to say. Kirsteen's reaction told him that immediately. With disbelieving eyes she glared at him. 'Oh, so you are taking her side in all this? I thought *you* at least would see reason.'

He sighed. 'I am just trying to see both sides and you're the one who isn't seeing reason . . .'

Lorn came in at that point. An apathy had settled over him in the last few weeks that nothing seemed to penetrate. He was thin and tired looking, the hollows in his face alarming Kirsteen so much she was afraid that he might relapse back into the delicate state of health of his early years. He had written to Ruth, sent her money for Lorna, but just a week ago the letters had been sent back unopened. Humiliated beyond bearing, he had in desperation phoned Dungowrie Farm. Jean Jackson had answered and her voice had been full of sympathy when she explained that Ruth had left the farm taking Lorna with her, and she didn't know where they'd gone. Ruth had been strange and uncommunicative for a long time. All she would say was that she was going to get a job, and that Jean wasn't to worry as she would be in touch as soon as she was settled.

Putting the phone down, Lorn had gone up to his room, buried his face in his hands and sunk into an abyss of lonely despair. All he could think of was Lorna, his darling child, her little face bewildered as she was taken to one strange place after another. Because of him she was suffering, an innocent baby who had never done a wrong thing in the short years she had lived on earth. Anger against Ruth had swamped him. He had asked himself over and over how she could be so heartless as to use their daughter to get back at him. He wasn't so worried about the effect on his son, who was too young to know what was happening and had settled happily at Laigmhor – but Lorna – she knew all right. Wise beyond her years, she would know only too well that she was being kept apart from her father because of something he had done – and – the thought curdled his blood – in time she might grow to blame him as much as Ruth was blaming him – to even perhaps – hate him.

'But no,' he had whispered in torment to the empty room, 'I won't allow that to happen, my babby. I'll get you back, somehow I'll get you back.'

He had gone to Glasgow to scour the streets with no success. He had ignored Dugald's earlier advice and had gone to several police stations to ask them to keep a lookout for his missing wife and child for they *were* missing, as surely as if they had just disappeared off the face of the earth. He had phoned the police almost every day since but they had nothing to report. No young woman by the name of Ruth McKenzie had come to their notice. Lorn's misery and dejection grew till his parents were driven to distraction and a heartfelt desire for Ruth to come to her senses and at least let everyone know she was well and managing.

Dugald too had lost his earlier contentment and was steadily reverting back to his former state of unhappiness.

He had received only one or two sketchy postcards from his daughter and in them she hoped he was well and not worrying about her, hardly a word about how she or Lorna were coping. Totie, furious at how things were turning out, coaxed him to take an interest in the things he loved, and for her sake he made the effort though if hers hadn't been such a strong personality he might well have succumbed to perpetual depression.

At sight of Lorn by the window, his gaze fixed blindly on the rain-smirred distance, Kirsteen, in her present mood, instead of feeling sympathy, experienced instead an almost overwhelming desire to go and shake him, tell him if he had to moon around, would he mind doing it where no one else could see him. With an effort she controlled herself, contenting herself by saying more sharply than she meant, 'For heaven's sake, Lorn, if you go on like this you'll make yourself ill – and the rest of us with you. Can you not find something to do other than mope? Och, it will be good to have Grant back again – of all my sons he's the one who's been the least bother . . .'

She had gone too far and she knew it. Fergus glowered at her from lowered brows, Lorn stared, thunderstruck.

She passed her hand distractedly over her eyes and said pleadingly, 'Lorn, Lorn, I'm sorry, I didn't mean any of it – it's just, well, we all have our worries and I've just had a row with Phebie—'

'And that's all you have to bother about, eh?' Lorn's voice was harsh with hurt. 'You had a petty argument with

Phebie over Grant and that's so important you canny see what's under your very nose! I'm seeing a new side o' you, Mother, one that I don't like very much.'

'We all have sides to our nature that aren't very pleasant, Lorn,' she cried in appeal, her cheeks burning with shame. 'I was angry – I took it out on you, we all do that in our lives – you must have done it . . .'

'Where's Douglas?' he demanded roughly.

Bewildered she had to think for a moment. 'Outside – playing with the cats in the wee shed.'

'Fine. I'm going out with the tractor and I want to take him with me, it's time he started to learn . . .'

'But he's only a baby!' protested Kirsteen, rather afraid of the stark wildness staring out of her son's eyes.

'I was a baby when Father took me out to the fields. My love of the soil grew from babyhood and I want Douglas to be the same.'

Without another word he went to the door, pushed his feet into his wellingtons, and strode away round to the little garden at the back of the house. The rain, which had been falling steadily for almost a week, had stopped, and a watery sun was breaking through the grey mantle of cloud. In the distance the little white houses of Portcull stood out against the grey heaving mass of the Atlantic; the smell of grass and wet earth was sweet and heavy in the air; the perfume of roses wafted from the flower bed set against the mossy stones of a small rambling shed where garden tools and all sorts of bits and pieces were stored. The roses had been

Mirabelle's doing, planted in a burst of optimism and a craving for something of beauty amidst the weeds which flourished in the sandy soil of the area. With love and care, the bushes had flourished to give pleasure to many and now Lorn stood for a long moment, breathing the scent of them, seeing the perfection of one single pink rosebud amidst the green foliage. A vision came to him, of Ruth on the night of the Burnbreddie dance, a figure of feminine sweetness in a white dress, a single pink rosebud pinned over her breast.

'Oh God, Ruthie!' He ran his fingers through his hair, blinked his eyes to get rid of the tears. His bout of anger against her had passed once more, in its place was a craving to see her, touch her, hear that dear musical voice of hers saying his name . . .

His heart felt as heavy as lead as he went to get his son. The little boy toddled towards him, his face upturned so that he could look up at the giant of a man who was his father. He was flushed and grubby, his lint-white hair full of straw and cat's hairs, but he was smiling and happy and Lorn scooped him up to sit him on his shoulders. The little boy crooned with delight which turned to a gurgle of joy when he saw that they were making for the tractor, for he liked nothing better than to ride in the big machine beside his father.

The fields were sodden, seagulls and oystercatchers swam happily in the pools lying in the hollows. The tractor climbed upwards, towards the better drained high ground which was in the process of being ploughed. Wet weather had forestalled progress and Lorn knew that he should wait for it to dry out before proceeding with the work. But he had wanted an excuse to get away from the house, away from eyes that he felt contained accusations, away from his mother who was normally so understanding but who had proved with just a few thoughtless words that she blamed him as much as anyone. The fragrance of the wet fields filled his senses, the freedom of high lonely places washed over him . . . but there was no freedom in his life anymore, it was all around him yet failed to touch him. He was ensnared by loneliness and his own bleak thoughts. Douglas prattled and chuckled by his side; he pointed a chubby finger making Lorn look into the distance. Away to the east a rainbow appeared, its perfect curve spanning the grey reaches of the sea, imbuing it with colour, life . . . In days gone by Lorn had always looked upon the rainbow as a symbol of hope, a sign that where there was rain also there was sunshine, but now he saw it with the dull eyes of a man without hope, a man who had had everything and had foolishly exchanged it for the swift passing pleasure of forbidden love . . . Lewis came to him, quite suddenly, so near and real he might have been sitting in the cab beside him. Fresh rage spurted through Lorn's veins. In his present state of mind he saw Lewis as a spectre at the feast, come to gloat at the ruins of his brother's life. He wanted to shout out, to tell Lewis to go away, leave him, but he choked the words down so that he wouldn't frighten his son. He drove the tractor faster, as if by doing so he could somehow leave behind the spirit of his dead brother – but the faster he went, the stronger Lewis' presence became and he could almost hear the well-known voice saying, 'Careful, Lorn, my lad, careful.'

The tractor careered towards a steep slope, the great wheels chewing up clods of grass, a beam of sunlight slanted down, glinting on the millions of raindrops which misted the grass . . . Lorn put up his hand to shield his eyes from the glare. The ground was racing to meet him and he realized he was going too fast. He braked but his reflex actions were slow and in the mists of his mind he knew he had left it too late. He was sideways on at the crest of the slope, without any warning the big lumbering machine began slowly to tilt over . . . adrenalin pumped through his veins, goading his heart to a frightening gallop. The sky reeled, spun, as if in slow motion the tractor went over.

'Lewis! Lewis!' He screamed his brother's name and in that split moment in time he realized that the spirit of Lewis only came to him in time of danger, to warn him when it was imminent, not to goad him into doing wrongful things as he had imagined that hot sun-filled day in the fields when he had come upon Rachel lying half-naked in the hollow of the knoll . . . A scream that was not his own pierced his eardrums, filled his head. Letting the wheel go his arms shot out to pull his son to him, then he twisted round in his seat so that the child would have some protection from the inevitable crash to follow. The tractor seemed to hang suspended for infinite moments before it spun down the wet slope, rolling over twice before it plunged sickeningly into an outcrop of rock at the bottom. Bits of it peeled away like cardboard, the shattering of the windscreen was a hellish explosion inside Lorn's head.

He felt himself being lifted as if by a giant's hand, had the sensation of flying through the air before being tossed mercilessly to the ground like a helpless doll. In the split second before the impact he twisted round violently so that his son, who was held to his breast, would be protected from the full horror of that which was to come. Flesh and bone thudded into the earth, all the breath was squeezed from his lungs, a blinding flash of pain went through his head, he heard a dull crack and in the mists of his consciousness imagined it to come from the tractor and not from his own body. From somewhere nearby Douglas was screaming, a terrified sound that beat into Lorn's head in fuzzy waves – relief swamped him – the screams meant the little boy was alive. He was aware of the sky, the clouds rolling, the dampness of the sodden grass soaking into his clothes – and he was amazed to know that he could still see – feel.

'Douglas!' The name tore from his throat yet seemed to come from another being outwith himself, one that could open his lips yet had no voice. Raising his head he saw the little boy crawling over the grass towards him and in his relief words bubbled over one another, 'Thank God! Oh, thank God!' Yet, although he seemed to have shouted the words no sound came. A veil of frustrated tears filled his eyes and he lay back as waves of pain bit into him like red hot knives ... His eyelids were heavy, pulled down by leaden weights – he wanted nothing more than to close them but he had to stay awake, had to make sure his son was all right.

Ruth sank exhausted into a chair by the empty fireplace and gazed round with dull eyes at the tiny, single-end apartment she had been staying in since her departure from Dungowrie Farm. She shuddered in a mixture of cold and distaste. It was all so different from what she had been used to, but it was all she had been able to find after trudging the length and breadth of Glasgow. At least the rent was low and she had made friends with a young woman in the flat above. Annie had three children of her own and it was no bother to her to look after Lorna while Ruth went out looking for a job. Physically and mentally exhausted, she had halfheartedly scanned the jobs columns in the papers, despair overwhelming her because she had had no training for anything and was coming to the conclusion that she would have to be satisfied with the most menial of positions – if she was lucky enough to be accepted for one. She had gone from one place to the next only to find the jobs taken or were beyond her physical capabilities. Then two days ago a visit to the employment exchange had resulted in her being sent to one of the big newspaper offices in the city. As a result of her interview she got the job and though she was little more than an office girl, making tea and generally cleaning and tidying up, at least she could now support herself and Lorna and she had a roof over her head.

The door opened and Annie came in with Lorna, who immediately went over to her mother and scrambled on to her knee. 'Has she behaved herself?' Ruth asked, ruffling her daughter's hair.

'Oh ay,' said Annie cheerfully. 'She's a quiet wee soul mind. She just hangs about and keeps asking when she's going to see her father and her wee brother.'

Ruth coloured and got up quickly. 'I'll have to see about getting her something to eat. I had to wait ages for a tram and thought I would never get home—' She paused and looked at the dingy walls surrounding her. How could she ever think of this as home? Home was far away, everything that she had known and loved was on Rhanna and she wondered if she would ever see it again. She thought suddenly of Lorn and an odd little shiver of dread went through her. She went to put the kettle on while Annie prattled on about her children – but Ruth wasn't listening. An unease had gripped her and no matter how hard she tried to shake it off it refused to go away. She wasn't to know that at that very minute Lorn lay in the fields above Laigmhor badly injured and that her little son, bewildered and terrified, needed her more than he had ever needed her before . . .

*　　*　　*

At the sound of a child screaming, Anton and Babbie, walking hand in hand along the cliffs above the wild rocky outcrops of Caillich Point, the Witches' Place, stiffened and looked up startled.

'Where did that come from?' Babbie said, shading her eyes against the evening sun cascading over the country-side.

Anton pulled her in close to him and smiled. 'Do not worry your head, liebling, it will just be some children from the village having a skylark.'

She shook her red head. 'No, I've heard enough babies in my time to know it came from one – and it sounded terrified – come on, lazy, we'd better go and look.'

Anton followed her unwillingly, loth to relinquish the rare interlude of an evening stroll with his wife. But as they climbed up the slopes of Laigmhor's fields the sight that met his eyes made him forget all else. Babbie's feet were pounding the turf ahead of him. Catching her up he reached down to pluck up a sobbing, petrified Douglas, in time to stop him reaching the blood-stained figure of his father. Swiftly Babbie checked the child over, relieved to see that he only had superficial cuts and bruises. Anton tore off his jacket to wrap it round the little boy's trembling body while Babbie fell on her knees by Lorn's prone figure. Her keen professional gaze roved over his body which was lying at an unnaturally twisted angle. What he had imagined to be dampness from the earth was in fact blood spurting from a gash in his leg, soaking into his clothing as if it was blotting paper. His face and head were a mass of cuts, like crimson chalk marks on the deathly pallor of his face. His lips were moving and Babbie told him urgently, 'Douglas is fine, Lorn, don't try to move – can you feel your legs at all?'

As she spoke she was removing her nylon stockings, using one to tie a tourniquet above the wound in his leg. Feebly he moved his head and she spoke to Anton quickly. 'Go up to Laigmhor and call Lachlan – tell him to come as quickly as he can. Surgery should still be on so you should get him all right.'

Cuddling the now quiet Douglas to his chest, Anton rushed off, his athletic stride taking him easily over the top of the fields which was the shortest route to Laigmhor. Left alone Babbie folded her jacket and placed it under Lorn's head. He was only just hanging on to consciousness and she bit her lip, looking again and again at his face while she worked with the tourniquet, alternately loosening and tightening it. She hardly dared look at his legs . . .

'Of course, they could just be fractured,' she consoled herself and didn't think beyond that. It was very quiet up here on the windblown field. In the woods below, the trees rustled, bluebells covered the leafy earth in a dense carpet. A corncrake was calling nearby, its bare, harsh sound boring into her head. Yet she was glad of it, for somehow it lessened the harshness of Lorn's breathing. He was beginning to moan softly and she wished with all her heart that she had her bag with her so that she could have given him something to lessen the pain he was obviously suffering.

His lips moved again and this time he managed to croak out a few exhausted words. 'Lewis – tried to warn me – he tried. My punishment for – what I did – to Ruthie.'

Babbie took his big hand in hers. It was cold and clammy. She spoke to him, softly, comfortingly, lifted her free hand to look at her watch. Anton had just been gone fifteen minutes yet it seemed as if she had been kneeling there for the same amount of hours . . . Voices floated down the slopes, figures appeared over a rise – the tense running figures of Kirsteen and Fergus. As they came nearer, Lorn heard them too. He opened his eyes but everything was veiled in a red mist and he couldn't distinguish the features on the two pale blobs which hovered suddenly above him.

Kirsteen took one look at her youngest son and her hand flew to her mouth. 'It's my fault,' she whispered in fear. 'I said things—'

Fergus reached out to her, pulled her against him. 'Weesht, weesht,' he soothed. 'You mustny blame yourself. For his sake pull yourself together.'

Comforting though his words were, they were entirely automatic. Every time his eyes strayed to his son lying so helplessly on the wet grass of the field his stomach heaved in fear and trepidation. Kirsteen straightened up, wiped her eyes and appeared to pull herself together, for she was able to fall on her knees beside her son and gently stroke the hair from his brow.

The purring of a tractor came to their ears, shortly it appeared with Anton at the wheel, Lachlan beside him. Anton had taken the smaller machine from the shed at Laigmhor simply because it was far quicker than walking. He had gone in it to Slochmhor, leaving Douglas with Elspeth, the new doctor to deal with the remaining patients while Lachlan grabbed his bag and came at once.

He bent over Lorn, made a swift, sure examination. His brown eyes were worried when he finally straightened up to speak quietly to the others. 'He's come down on his back with a Godawful thump – it's difficult to say how bad it is but he doesn't seem able to feel his legs. The rest isn't as bad as it looks but that gash on his leg will need stitches. We must get him over to Slochmhor at once. He's banged his head too and has maybe got a bit of concussion – I'm going to give him an injection for the pain – it will put him out for a while.'

The needle pierced Lorn's flesh, he murmured something about Ruth, relaxed, was glad to feel the drug rushing over his brain and he could sink into oblivion.

Lachlan pushed the hair back from his eyes, a frown creasing his brow. He was loth to move the boy though of course it was inevitable. He would do all he could for him at Slochmhor but they would have to get him to hospital for X-rays, find out the extent of damage to his back – also there could be internal injuries . . . He shook his head, better to take one thing at a time, first move was to Slochmhor – not such an easy task as it sounded, he mustn't suffer any unnecessary movement. As if reading his thoughts Anton spoke to him quietly. Lachlan nodded and without ado began to peel off his jacket, directing everyone else to do likewise. In minutes the garments had been fashioned into a soft, pliable makeshift stretcher into which Lorn was placed. On the slow, careful plod over the fields, Babbie kept working with the tourniquet and Lachlan, watching, thanked the Gods for a nurse as devoted and as brilliant as she. Whenever he praised her she merely smiled her radiant smile and told him she had learned from Biddy how to cope with people's feelings and from him how to deal with broken bodies.

Lachlan mused on how speedily and safely Ruth had been transported to hospital when she had taken ill and he wished the laird's flying friend could be here now to relieve them in the present crisis. As if in answer to his prayers the drone of a small aircraft sounded above. Automatically everyone looked upwards, Anton pausing to rest and crane his neck heavenwards. His handsome face lit. 'It's Charlie, or I'm a Dutchman! All fresh and sober and dropping in on Burnbreddie for the weekend. I'll phone him as soon as we get to Slochmhor! Lorn should be in hospital in the bat of an eyebrow.'

'Lid,' corrected Babbie, giggling in her relief.

Fergus' arm tightened round Kirsteen's waist. 'God is

on our side, mo cridhe,' he murmured into her ear and she snuggled against him, glad of his hard strength.

An hour later Lorn was on his way to hospital, cleaned and stitched, a blood transfusion dripping into his arm, Fergus in the front seat beside a sober and slightly bemused Charlie, ideas running through his head about starting an air ambulance service on Rhanna. Kirsteen stood with Douglas in her arms, watching the plane disappear into the clouds wishing with all her heart that she was in the aircraft with her son. But Douglas needed her more than he had ever needed anyone in his young life. He clung to her, terrified to let her out of his sight, his small face harrowed and tear-stained, his warm mouth moving against her neck, alternately crying for his mother and father.

'My poor wee babby.' Her arms tightened around him even as a tight band of dread closed round her heart. Lachlan had tried to reassure her about Lorn but she knew he was only being kind. She couldn't stop the bleak thoughts from crowding in on her. Lorn was badly injured – he might never walk again . . . A sob rose in her throat. Anton put his arm round her and guided her over the fields. In the distance a plump figure was approaching and soon Phebie's sweet, concerned features became discernible. She had been out when the news had come about Lorn. Having just learned of the accident she had left Slochmhor at once and now she came running, panting from her exertions, without hesitation coming straight up to her friend and throwing her arms about her. For a long moment, her comforting embrace lingered on Kirsteen's slender shoulders before she stood back to dab her eyes with a corner of her cardigan.

'Oh, Kirsteen, I'm so sorry about everything,' she said brokenly. 'I was a selfish besom to say I wanted Grant and Fiona to stay with me – and now this has happened and I feel so petty and mean.'

Kirsteen laid her hand on the other's arm. 'Don't, Phebie, please don't, I was sillier than anyone. When that two come home they can decide for themselves where they want to stay.' Her lip trembled. 'We're just a couple of old grannies fighting over nothing.'

A smile of relief chased away Phebie's tears and she said huskily, 'So – are we friends again?'

'We were never anything else. Now I'd better get home and put this wee lad to bed. He's had a terrible fright.'

'I'll come with you,' Phebie decided. 'I – I would like to wait with you till you hear word about Lorn – if you don't mind that is.'

Kirsteen could not think of anyone else she would rather have with her during what she knew would be a suspenseful period of waiting. She nodded gratefully at the suggestion and walked with her friend through the quiet gloaming to the strangely empty atmosphere that all at once pervaded the rooms of Laigmhor.

Part Four

Autumn 1964

Chapter Fifteen

It was a warm, golden September with the rays of the mellow sun pouring over the heather on the hills, slanting through the dying bracken, turning it to amber. The smoke from the chimneys of Portcull spiralled lazily into a deep blue sky, its azure depths echoed in the tiny lochans that dotted the moors. Every morning the villagers took their carts and peat creels up to the peat hags to collect the stacks of turf which had lain all summer drying in the wind and sun. Tam had acquired an ancient ramshackle of a lorry. In the days it didn't break down he hired it out, with himself as the driver thrown in for free, to bring down loads of peat from the various hags. But a lot of folk grumbled at the prices he charged, especially as he declined to help in the backbreaking work of lifting and loading, and quite a few refused to take advantage of his services, preferring the more traditional and less costly methods.

Old Bob, throwing innate caution to the winds, treated himself to a brand new van in which to collect his peat, though the track up to his house was so unsuitable for a vehicle he was forced to leave it at the bottom and plod up the hill with barrowloads of winter fuel, helped in the venture by a few of the villagers hoping he would perhaps lend out his van.

'You could have bought yourself a fine new house on the level wi' all that money o' yours,' a sweating Ranald told him in envious tones, but Bob merely spat his disapproval of the suggestion and intoned that his house would do him well enough till he thought about retiring.

'Retiring!' Ranald was incredulous. 'You should have retired years ago, you mean auld bodach.'

'Ay, maybe I should but I didny,' Old Bob said placidly. 'And I'm no' going to either till I have a good reason.'

Ranald's eyes gleamed. 'Ach, you're meaning Grace Donaldson. She'll be your reason, Bob, we've seen you goin' to her house wi' presents o' grouse and pheasant. You can court her all you like and give her fish and game till they are comin' out her ears but it will no' work. Old Joe has his foot in her door – I even saw him kissing her one day – though only on the cheek mind.'

Old Bob grew red, but retaliated with dignity, 'My affairs are my own, I will no' be discussing them wi' you or anybody else and that's an end o' the matter.'

From the window of Laigmhor's parlour, Lorn lay on the couch and every day watched the comings and goings on the road. He had spent a lot of his boyhood hours on the selfsame couch by the parlour window and often, in the course of the last three months, a sense of unreality swamped him. He was hardly able to take in the fact that here he was again – an invalid who couldn't get up – walk – go outside. The time of the accident was a vague blur in his mind. He could only recall certain parts of it but in the days that followed he was made cruelly aware of what the incident had cost him.

The time in hospital hadn't been so bad. You expected things like stitches and bandages after a serious accident. It was afterwards that the full import of his injuries had struck him like a physical blow. His cuts and grazes had healed quickly enough but it was what the doctors had discovered about his back which wouldn't be so easy to heal – if ever. He moved restlessly, as if trying to escape the dark thoughts which overwhelmed him, but he couldn't escape the stark reality of legs that wouldn't move – the doctors had said some nerves had been damaged by the fall – it could be a temporary paralysis – or it could be . . . oh, God, no! He shook his head and forced his eyes back to the window – to the rugged grandeur of the hills, to the people he knew and loved going about their daily business, waving to him as they passed by. It was they who kept him going when his thoughts were bleak and dark, they who made him feel a part of that glorious outside world – even though he might never be in it again . . .

'Stop it!' he told himself fiercely. 'Of course you'll bloody well walk again, it will just take time, that's all . . .' In the distance a girl with golden hair was coming down the track from Nigg. His thoughts flew unbidden to Ruth. Lying here, day after day, he had plenty of time to think, but he tried to stifle thoughts of Ruth, to push them down to the pit of his being where they couldn't hurt. To a certain degree he had succeeded, yet he couldn't deny she was more in his mind than out of it – and his little girl. She filled his thoughts almost continually.

Where was she? How was she? What was she doing? Had she forgotten him? Did she still look upon him as the big strong man she had respected and loved or did she see him as an ogre? One who had somehow made her mother unhappy? Yet much as he longed to see her he dreaded her seeing him as he was. His father had suggested that he use a wheelchair but he had rejected this with the fierce declaration that he would go out under his own steam and not before. Fergus had looked at him strangely and had said seriously, 'Don't let pride stand in your way, Lorn. You were always better balanced than me in that respect, for pity's sake don't let yourself down now.'

'It isn't pride,' Lorn had told him through gritted teeth. 'I lost what I had of that months ago.'

Fergus' black eyes had glittered. 'No, then what is it that makes a man too ashamed to let the world see that his body is as capable of being broken as that of any other man?'

'Because I've already been through all that,' Lorn had answered flatly. 'I've had the pity and about as much compassion as I can damned well take in a lifetime. I don't want anyone to feel sorry for me again and I won't go out of that door till I am bloody well ready.'

Yet in his heart, he knew that his father was right – but only up to a point. It wasn't pride that made him feel as he did, but sheer lack of fighting spirit, though he didn't dare tell his father that, he would be too ashamed to admit it aloud for he hardly dared admit it to himself. Far better to let everyone believe what they would – just so long as they didn't think he was a cowardly defeatist.

His hands went down to fondle Ben's soft ears and he whispered, 'Thank God for you, Ben, you don't ask questions, you just accept me – as I am.'

The old dog had taken to lying, either on the couch at his master's feet, or on the floor beside him. Day after day he lay with his muzzle on his paws, his brown, intelligent gaze fixed on the young man he loved, accepting his state of immobility with a resigned patience that Lorn wished could be transferred to the human beings around him; for though they didn't say as much he sensed their anxiety and at times, in his frustration, resented it . . .

The savoury aroma of stewing steak wafted from the kitchen. He could visualize the scene, his mother at the shining, blackleaded range, his father stripped to the waist at the sink, washing off the morning grime. It had been a routine that Lorn had accepted in his life but now that it was out of his reach he longed for the commonplace certainty of it, pined for old, familiar ways. He had worried because his father had had to shoulder the brunt of the work, but if it was a strain on him it didn't show. He was as ruggedly strong and vital as ever and seemed positively to revel in

hard physical work. Only Kirsteen knew that he was often
more weary than he would ever admit. Only she saw the
hollows in his face when he came in at night and flopped
exhausted into a chair to sleep for perhaps half an hour
before his meal, something he had seldom done before.
And only she saw him in repose after he had fallen into
bed to sleep as soon as his head touched the pillow and
she knew the dread of realizing that though he looked ten
years younger he was after all in his sixty-fifth year and no
longer a young man.

But canny Old Bob noticed more than he ever let on and
just a month ago he had complained to Fergus that he was
finding things hard going even with Donald and Matthew
to help. He had asked Fergus to consider taking on another
man for general farm labouring and Fergus had scrutinized
his walnut-brown face keenly and had said suspiciously,
'I've never known you complain before, maybe the time
has come for you to give up farming.'

'Na, na, lad, I'll no' do that,' Bob had forcibly replied.
'Besides, deny it how you will, you need all the hands
you can get wi' Lorn laid up and that means auld yins
too.' Nonchalantly he had examined his grimy nails. 'I
was thinkin' o' askin' Mairi's lad to help out. He's keen
on farming but hasny managed to get much since he left
the smacks and remember he was aye good on the croft
before he went to sea. I'd make the young bugger pull his
weight if you thought to take him on here.'

And so Davie McKinnon, a tall lanky youth with a

continual drip at his nose which folk said had been inherited from Wullie, his father, came to work at Laigmhor, throwing himself into his job with such a will Fergus almost forgot his early reputation for drinking himself sober. Kirsteen was able to breathe a sigh of relief as gradually the spring came back to Fergus' step and he had enough energy to coorie in beside her at night to talk and frequently to make love.

Doctor Megan was taking over more and more of Lachlan's duties and it was she who had attended Lorn most frequently since his accident. At first she had been quiet and shy with none of the ready repartee that everyone enjoyed in Lachlan.

With Lorn though, she gradually blossomed out till she was able to sit on the couch beside him and in her clear, attractive voice recount some of the problems she had encountered in her dealings with some of the older islanders. When she laughed a sprite lit her hazel eyes, a bloom came to her cheeks and she was so different from the young woman that everyone was appraising in a suspicious fashion that Lorn knew it was only a matter of time before her charm became apparent to everyone.

On the day however that a visit from Mark James coincided with hers she immediately reverted back to her more reserved self. A spot of colour had burned in her cheeks as the minister's smoky gaze swept over her and she had been so confused she had dropped her bag and its contents on to the floor. Gallantly, Mark James got down on the floor to help her gather up the things. Lorn had expected a bit of banter from him over the incident but none was forthcoming. Instead he seemed as confused as the doctor. Her thanks to him were noticeably succinct; his reply equally brief. They had seemed embarrassed and awkward in one another's company and Doctor Megan's visit had been very short indeed, her departure so laden with relief Lorn had stared out of the window at her receding figure in some bemusement.

After her departure Mark James had been detached and inattentive, his gaze going again and again to the window as if mentally he had followed Doctor Megan down the road to her cottage at Burg. Lorn had mentioned all this to Shona, and an odd look had come into her blue eyes. She had clasped her fingers to her lips and had said almost to herself, 'I wonder – oh – if only it could be.'

Lorn had asked her what she meant and with a laugh she had looked him straight in the eye and said simply, 'Don't you think they are well suited? Our Mark James and the new doctor?'

In view of the scene that he had just witnessed Lorn had expressed some doubts over this and Shona, eyes sparkling, had scolded him. 'Ach, Lorn, use your head! Have you no romance in you at all! Think about it.'

And think about it Lorn did, in the end coming to the conclusion that his sister was right and that there existed between the minister and the doctor the beginnings of what could only be described as romance.

As always Bob came every day to take his midday meal at Laigmhor. Lorn looked forward to his visits, enjoying them even more than those of younger acquaintances. There was a serenity about Bob, a quality about his manner that could only come with the dignity of old age. He was also possessed of a dry wit and piquant tongue that could be wonderfully stimulating. In the evenings he toiled down the steep brae from his cottage, bringing his fiddle. He and Lorn would play together happily for hours or they would simply get out the cards and have a few games and a dram. Bob also had a fund of stories to relate about his shepherding days as a boy and Lorn would listen enthralled, realizing that he was honoured to hear them as the old man was normally as reserved as the hills about the days of his past.

Quite often Fergus and Kirsteen came to join in the cards or the singing. If Shona and Niall, or Phebie and Lachlan came over, a ceilidh would often develop and these were Lorn's happiest times, surrounded by family and friends, no time to mope, to think. He had the wireless set to listen to if he so desired but almost every time he switched on the *Song of Rhanna* seemed to be playing. The words which had been composed by Mark James had been bought by a recording company and it was one of the most popular tunes of that summer. Lorn switched off whenever he heard it. It was too evocative, bringing back so many painful memories he wished only to forget. His time with Rachel seemed so unreal to him he couldn't believe it had actually happened, had cost so much pain and suffering to so many. Yet he couldn't ignore Rachel's existence, a feeling that she had a right to know everything that had happened since her departure, so he had written to her, explaining. A letter came back, full of the same kind of remorse he was going through. But she had known something momentous had happened. She had written letters to Ruth addressed to Fàilte with never an answering note and Lorn realized that his father, who went regularly to the cottage to collect the mail Erchy in his absent-mindedness popped through the door, had kept back Rachel's letters with the intention of sparing his son such painful reminders of the past . . .

The door opened, interrupting Lorn's musings. Old Bob came through, bearing his dinner on a tray, Kirsteen at his heels to set Lorn's down on a chair while she plumped his pillows. 'I want it all eaten,' she said as lightly as she could, sadness swamping her as she looked at the hollows in her son's face, saw a delicacy in him she had thought had disappeared with boyhood. He was rarely hungry, taking only as much as he thought would ward off the comments about his lack of appetite. She didn't fuss, she had never fussed, it was one of the things he loved most about her but she couldn't stop the concern showing on her face and he hated himself for being the cause of it. Douglas tottered in at her back, fretfully declaring that he wanted to eat his dinner with his father, but Kirsteen, knowing from experience how tiring his boisterous company could be even to the most fit, shooed him back into the kitchen. He went unwillingly, tearing his bib off as a gesture of defiance, and Kirsteen sighed, knowing that for the rest of the meal he would be in a bad temper, for he had inherited that trait very strongly and was too young to know how to control it. He had been difficult since his father's accident, often keeping her awake till the small hours with his tantrums and his refusal to sleep. At other times he was a sunny lovable scamp, his highly developed sense of humour so infectious it never failed to raise a laugh even in the sourest of company.

Stolidly Bob ate his dinner, never one to indulge in idle chatter while the serious business of eating was in progress, remaining silent till every scrap was eaten and the plate scraped clean by means of a hunk of crusty bread. Satisfied he at last sat back, tapped out his pipe on his boot, lit it, and sat puffing for a few thoughtful minutes. Normally when he spoke it was with the slow, easy deliberation of the Hebridean, but on this occasion there was a certain suppressed excitement in his voice as he said carefully, 'I was just after seein' Grant and Fiona makin' their way over the fields to Slochmhor – I didny say anything to your folks for I had a mind they might like to know the surprise o' it for themselves . . .

'Grant and Fiona!' A flush of colour touched Lorn's face.

'You old de'il! How could you know a thing like that and still eat your dinner as if Ben was going to steal it!'

'Ach well, I like to take my time wi' my food – at my age you have to be careful wi' the chewing.'

Lorn's eyes were sparkling. 'How the hell *can* they be on the island? The steamer came last night and nary a sign of them.'

'I'm thinkin' they came on a fishing boat. You mind Grant was aye a lad for that kind of thing and of course the lads at Oban have long memories. Grant would have no trouble hitching a lift. The boat likely docked at Portvoynachan.'

'Did they see you? How did they look – was Fiona able to walk that far! She must be about ready to have her baby.'

Bob drew on his pipe. It made a sucking bubbling sound and he removed it from his mouth to take it apart, blow down it, peer through it. Satisfied that all was well he put it together again and placed the mouthpiece in a little shallow trench on his lower lip which had either been there all along or had conveniently worn away with continual use.

'Ay, she must,' he agreed reflectively. 'Her belly is no' as big as some I've seen mind, she was holding herself well and Grant bein' all gentlemanly and holding her by the waist. They didny see me for I was down in the barley field which is near as high as myself just now. I have a fancy the door will be opening in a wee whily and you will hear your mother screechin' wi' pleasure and your father makin' noises like a bull wi' the wind.'

Almost before he finished speaking there came from the kitchen a skirling of shouts and laughter such as had never been heard in the house since the days of Lewis' tornado-like homecomings. Fergus' deep laugh boomed out, above it rose Kirsteen's high, delighted voice, Lachlan's pleasant tones, Phebie's girlish giggle.

Bob sucked placidly at his pipe, his eyes on Lorn's face, smiling to himself at the anticipation stamped across it. The next moment the door burst open, the silence in the room shattered as it filled with people. Out of the sea of faces leapt one that Lorn had ached to see, Grant, bronzed, dark eyes alive with laughter, his strapping brawny figure dwarfing that of his neatly made wife. For a split second he remained still, his eyes alighting on Lorn's face, then he was leaping forward, taking Lorn's hands, gripping them tightly. His laughter-bright face did not change with the shock that registered within him at sight of a Lorn he had once known many years ago, the Lorn of old, too thin, too pale.

His deep voice boomed out. 'Lorn, you young bugger! I thought you might have been at the door to welcome us back – and don't give me your Lorn look, all stubborn and annoyed. It's as well I'm home, I can see things have been allowed to slide around here. I'll have you up on your feet in no time. We canny have lazy buggers like you cluttering up the house – it's untidy enough as it is.'

'Of all the cheek,' Kirsteen's face was alight. 'Just for that I'll make you do some of the housework to teach you a lesson.'

Old Bob, silent while the family exchanged their excited greetings, tucked his pipe away into an inner pocket and stood up. 'If you'll be excusing me I have to get back to my work – it's no' everybody has the time to stand around gossiping.' His blue eyes twinkled as he spoke and Grant laughed.

'Oh no you don't, Bob my lad, we have still to hear all your news. A wee bird told me you had won the pools and something else even more astounding.'

Bob rubbed his grizzled chin. 'Oh, and what would that be I'd like to know?'

'You are courting that's what, you cunning old devil!' Fiona burst out in delight. 'It's the talk of the town! Jock Simpson of Rumhor gave us a lift over and he was full of you and your romantic affairs.'

'Ach, it is just a lot o' palaver over nothing,' Bob sniffed disdainfully. Nevertheless he thoroughly enjoyed holding court for the next few minutes though in his canny way giving little away about his business.

'Other folks are good at tellin' me what I am supposed to be gettin' up to,' was his parting shot at the door, 'so I will just let you all talk yourselves blue in the face. At the end o' the day we will see who has been right and who has been wrong. That is one thing about gossip, it is all just like a wee puzzle wi' everybody addin' a bit then when the truth comes out all the damty pieces are scattered to the wind for they are about as much good as a castrated ram to a breeding yowe.'

Lorn looked at Fiona, standing with an arm round each of her parents. Though in the last stages of her pregnancy it was difficult to believe. Because she was normally so slender and fairly tall, she carried herself well yet looked inordinately proud of her little lump of a belly. Her sun-kissed face was glowing, her bright brown eyes sparkling under the heavy fringe of her shining hair. Lorn grinned at her. 'Bob saw this brother of mine hauling you over the fields. Don't tell me he made you walk all the way from Portvoynachan?'

'I'm not that daft and fine Dimples McKenzie knows it!' She threw her husband a laughing glance. 'We hitched a lift as far as Caillich Point then walked the rest of the way over the fields to surprise everyone.'

'You certainly did *that*,' said Lachlan decidedly. 'There I was, enjoying a nap as befits a gentleman of my years, when all at once the peace of the house was invaded by two young heathens.'

Grant was unperturbed. 'Ach, you'll get to sleep all you like in the next week or two. Fiona is going to put her feet up and drive you crazy with her chatter while I divide my time between young Lorn here and the lobster fishing. I'm longing to do a bit of that.'

Kirsteen and Phebie exchanged rather shamefaced glances. After all the arguments Grant had decided in just a few short words what he and Fiona planned to do with their time.

Fiona snuggled further against her father. 'I came home for two very special reasons, one to have my baby on

Rhanna and two, to have it delivered by my very own doctor daddy.' Lachlan touched her hair. To him she was still the little girl he had nursed on his knee, attended to the many bumps and bruises of childhood, chased through the sunlit woods in games of hide and seek with her bubbling laughter echoing from tree to tree. She was thirty-one now, a grown woman, yet he knew he would always look at her and see a little bit of the child that she had been. 'Your doctor daddy will be so proud he might never get his head inside another door again. After all, it isn't every man who has the honour of bringing his very own grandchild into the world.'

Lorn lay back and listened to the banter around him and a feeling of happiness such as he hadn't experienced in months, crept into his heart like a tiny ray of warm sunshine.

Grant was as good as his word. Babbie had set out a programme of exercises and every day he came to Laigmhor to make sure Lorn carried them out. Sometimes he brought Fiona, who seemed quite content to sit in the cool parlour watching proceedings. But unobtrusive as her presence was Lorn preferred when Grant came alone as he was embarrassed at the idea of a woman being present while his brother put him through a programme of exercises. He was ashamed of how much the muscles in his legs had wasted in such a short space of time, but as the days wore on he ceased to worry about such trivialities. Grant was a hard taskmaster and wouldn't let up for a moment, not even on the days when frustration goaded Lorn into unreasoning temper which he took out on anyone who crossed his path. He was minded of the days his brother, very often against their father's wishes, had taught him how to swim, to play football, to do a lot of the things Fergus had forbidden. In the end Grant's teachings had proved invaluable, he had had a big hand in fashioning Lorn into the kind of young man he was to become, tough, fearless, afraid of no obstacle. Now Grant was again a man with a purpose. It saddened him to see his proud young brother going under, lacking the will to get up and go, the way he had done with such brave determination all these years ago. Kirsteen, afraid that her eldest son was driving his brother too hard, asked him to ease up.

'Would you have him an invalid for the rest of his days?' he asked bluntly. 'Because he will be if he's allowed to lie and rot on that couch feeling sorry for himself.' At Lorn, one trying, uncooperative day, he flared into a temper and ordered, 'Get up yourself today, man! Do you think Lewis would have knuckled down! Christ Almighty! He was a rogue, but never a coward. He hated illness, ay, ran from it all his days while you fought a good fight, but in the end illness caught up with him and he turned to face it squarely in its black, terrifying face!'

'Don't talk to me about Lewis and what he did!' Lorn retaliated furiously. 'He only had it at the end. I've had it all my buggering life and I'm too tired to fight it anymore!'

Grant's jaw jutted. Lorn felt he was looking at his father. 'Too buggering right you are. Somewhere along the way you mislaid that beautiful fighting spirit I used to admire in you till I was drunk with pride in my wee brother.' His black eyes flashed. 'Of course, I might have been wrong about you all along. It just needed a woman to leave you in the lurch to make you behave like one yourself. I haveny a doubt Ruth *isn't* lying back feeling sorry for herself. She's got too much bloody gumption! She's stronger than you, Lorn, you'll go under while she comes out on top – you'll see!'

Rage bubbled in Lorn's breast, his pupils dilated, his fists balled. 'Watch your mouth, McKenzie!' he almost sobbed, fury blinding him to the fact that his brother's harsh words were uttered in a desperate bid to goad him on to his feet.

And not only did Grant berate Lorn unmercifully, he employed half the village to do the same. Laigmhor had never been busier. Hour after hour, day after day, there was always someone at Lorn's side, encouraging him, haranguing him. Babbie came in her spare time to massage his feet and legs, Shona also took her turn, as did Kate, Barra, any of the womenfolk who felt themselves to be capable of the task. Only Kirsteen remained dubious while Fergus became as hard and as determined as Grant, turning a deaf ear to Lorn's pleas for mercy. It became a grim, resolute battle but everyone had the same goal in mind: 'to see young McKenzie up on his feet'. Lorn was swept along on a tide of enthusiasm but during rare quiet moments when he had the parlour to himself, he was glad to sink into the abyss of his innermost thoughts and it was during these times that he knew he could never get truly well till he found out Ruth's whereabouts and discovered for himself if she loved him enough ever to forgive him.

The arrival of Grant and Fiona's son caused a temporary and welcome lull in what had become to Lorn an almost unbearable ordeal. Ian Lachlan McKenzie made his forceful entry into the world at 7 a.m. on a still, misty morning in mid-October.

Lachlan held his tiny grandson in his arms and experienced a rush of such emotion he felt a mist of tears before his vision. He had delivered many babies in his day. Every one had brought him a sense of wonder at the miracle of new creation, but never had he known the humbling and incredible thrill of bringing the flesh of his flesh into the world. It had been a long and exhausting night, weariness had sat heavy on his shoulders, he had felt the age of every bone in his body and a little voice from within told him it was as well he would be retiring soon. Now, as he laughed down into the small new face lying contentedly in the crook of his arm he felt a vigour as of youth flowing in his veins and in his exuberance he gave a little yelp of delight and chuckled, a low musical cadence of sheer pride.

Babbie, busy at Fiona's bedside, glanced up and smiled despite a pang of poignancy in the knowing that this would

be one of the last times she might work with him in h
official capacity as GP on Rhanna – it would certainly
the last baby they would deliver together. Doctor Jenki
was taking over more and more of the running of t
practice and while Babbie was gradually coming to li
her and they both worked together amicably, she kne
that things would never be quite the same again witho
Lachlan at the helm. Theirs had been a long associatio
more than twenty years in fact; she had grown used
his ways, to the warm, caring compassion he had alwa
displayed towards his patients no matter how he mig
be feeling himself. Yet she knew she had to relinqui
him with a show of nonchalance. He and Phebie we
so looking forward to their days of freedom and so ric
deserved them it would have seemed selfish, if not childis
of her to harp on about what his leaving would mean to h
and his patients. He was anxious too for Doctor Jenkins
be liked, and well he might be for, though the islanders h
surmounted their initial suspicion of a newcomer and we
now extending the cautious hand of friendship, there we
still many obstacles to overcome and Doctor Jenkins fac
a long uphill climb before she would ever be accepted
good enough to take his place. But Lachlan himself h
had to overcome the selfsame barriers when he had cor
to Rhanna as a fresh-faced young GP and just as 'Au
McLure' had been held up to him so he in turn would
held in comparison to Doctor Megan.

But she had several advantages to her credit. The island

had quickly gotten over the surprise of 'a leddy doctor' in Lachlan's place, to the women she was a godsend in that they could discuss personal ailments without embarrassment; to the menfolk she was 'beautiful just' though they weren't so willing to bring matters of a personal nature to her attention. Her other saving grace was her knowledge of the Gaelic language which though not extensive was enough to allow her to understand and converse reasonably well with the older Gaels. She had taken a gentle hint from Lachlan and had stopped wearing her white coat for everyday consultations and little by little the islanders were breathing easier in her presence and creeping out of their shells of reserve.

'At least, she's good wi' the needle,' Kate had approved with some satisfaction after being subjected to a course of injections for an inflamed bunion. 'I had to bare my bum for the jags and there I was wi' my breeks at my ankles and waiting. Before you could say "wheech" she had the job done and me never knowing a thing till it was all over.'

Everyone agreed with Kate that the new doctor was indeed a wizard in this respect and when Jim Jim made a further observation to the effect that 'she has good hands for a leddy doctor, no' too gentle and no' too coarse wi' a touch to them that is just sublime', heads nodded in sage agreement while everyone vied with each other to bring Doctor Megan's other good points into the open. News of her progress filtered through to Megan's ear making her breathe a sigh of heartfelt relief as she had reached the stage of feeling that she would never be accepted by the canny islanders. With this in mind, Babbie had been careful to make her own attitude to the new doctor as agreeable as possible though inwardly she rebelled at the inevitable changes taking place in her own working routine, so the look she threw at Lachlan had more than a touch of tenderness in it as she asked teasingly, 'Are you going to fawn over him all day or do you think the new mother might have a shot at holding her firstborn?'

Lachlan looked at his daughter lying against the pillows, her face hollowed with the fatigue of childbirth. Yet she was radiant. She had always been attractive rather than beautiful but now she glowed with an inner light and in the brightness of her eyes he saw mirrored the mischievous sprite of yesteryear while an echo of her child's voice came to him, declaring vehemently to the world at large that she would never, never have children. His own eyes twinkled at the memory. 'Ach, she doesn't mind her old man getting a whily with the bairn – after all she was always so adamant about not having any, she might not even want a peep at the wee cratur' who has just put her through a night of hell.'

But Fiona had already gotten over the pain of childbirth. She took the child in her arms and gazed down at him, then what Lachlan called her 'Fiona smile' dimpled roguishly over her face. 'Decidedly ugly,' she giggled, 'but he'll grow bonny and big and he'll proudly bear his grandfather's name . . .' She looked up at her father and reaching out squeezed his hand. 'And what could be a nobler thing?'

Her voice was husky. 'If he's lucky enough to grow in the least like you then he will indeed be blessed – it's just a pity the family surname won't get to continue – the McKenzies are doing fine in that respect but we McLachlans are lagging behind.'

'Don't be so sure of that,' he said decidedly. 'Shona and Niall are always coming up with surprises, I know Shona at least would like another, anything's possible with that lassie.'

'Ay, but she isn't such a lassie now,' Fiona said bluntly. 'And she'll have to ca' canny if she's thinking about adding to her family.'

At that point the door opened and in came Phebie, Elspeth, and Grant, the latter having just arrived back from a night's fishing with the smacks. Elspeth had been shocked by his departure the evening before, everyone else relieved. He had brought them all to the point of screaming, with his floor-pacing and his nail-biting and in the end it was Lachlan who had suggested he go fishing as it was going to be a long night of waiting. And so the big, sturdy McKenzie had thankfully taken himself off after getting full approval from his wife. A night with the smacks had done a lot to ease his anxiety. Seizing the excuse of drinking the baby into the world his cronies and he had become slowly and merrily intoxicated. On his arrival back at Slochmhor he had earned Elspeth's further disapproval by giggling his head off at nothing and swinging both she and Phebie round and round in his arms till they were red-faced and dizzy. His delight at seeing his newborn son was infectious. He showered his wife with praise and kisses, black eyes snapping in an excess of pride and mischief. He kissed the younger women, shook hands with Lachlan, advanced on Elspeth who backed away, something like a smile beginning to dawn on her gaunt, immobile face. 'Hearken to me,' she warned severely. 'Just you get a grip on yourself, laddie. I was never one for all that kind o' palaver.'

Grant grinned wickedly and stretched out his strong muscular arms. 'Elspeth, Elspeth,' he implored in delight. 'Would you deny a new father a congratulatory kiss from your very own bonny lips?'

From the bed Fiona snorted with laughter. The scene presented by the wizened old woman fighting off the attentions of the brawny young man was utterly hilarious. Catching her Grant pinioned her arms briefly and bending his head kissed her soundly on the lips.

Elspeth was stunned, inwardly thrilled. Two spots of red flared high on her cheeks. 'Never, never have I been so insulted,' she said, too adamantly. 'The McKenzies are all the same – mad, the lot o' them.'

She scurried to the bedside, giving Grant a wide berth. Her eyes were oddly bright as she gazed down at the new addition to the household. 'My, my, he is bonny just – but his wee hands feel cold. Let me take him and warm his feets by the fire. I've got his wee goonies all ready – flannelette they are – I made them myself, nice and soft for his tender skin.'

Over her wispy grey head Fiona caught her parents' eyes and she threw them a slow, deliberate wink. It was plain that Elspeth was overjoyed to have a baby about the house again; it was also plain that Fiona and the old housekeeper were bound to have some spicy disagreements over the child's upbringing. Elspeth was entirely old-fashioned in her outlook and had already expressed shock at some of Fiona's ideas. She was very much the independent modern young woman and had very decided ideas of her own on childrearing. But for the moment she let the old woman have her own way, an unexpected sadness enveloping her at sight of Elspeth's creped hands next to the baby's flawless skin. Elspeth was crooning to him, taking him to the fire to let the heat wash over him. The toes of his tiny pink feet spread, then curled in bliss; his toothless mouth stretched into a lopsided yawn, his eyes went out of focus and he squinted at the flames in the grate. The dear, tender little head, with its mop of jet black hair, nestled trustingly against Elspeth's scrawny bosom and the wonder of it brought tears to her eyes.

Everyone in the room was touched by the tenderness of the moment, by the deep and sincere attachment of a childless old woman to a helpless scrap who had so recently taken his first breath of life.

Grant collapsed on the bed beside Fiona to cuddle her and kiss the tip of her nose, all at once sobered by the thought that he was at last really and truly a father. Lachlan put his arm around Phebie's waist and drew her in close.

Silently they looked back and remembered the wondrous moments of their own children's births. Now these children were grown, producing children of their own, gradually the older people, the grandparents were taking a back seat. Soon Lachlan would be retiring – they were approaching the evening of their life – yet how near – how sweet were the memories of youth . . .

Babbie gave a self-conscious little laugh and confessed, 'I don't often feel left out during such times but somehow, watching all your pensive faces, I'm almost convinced that I've missed out on something pretty earthshattering – and now I'm too old to do anything about it. Perhaps I should have given up nursing and had an absolute wheen of bairns.'

Lachlan laughed. 'Each to his own, Babbie; you chose the right course for you. And you picked the right word to describe having and rearing children – earthshattering it certainly is . . .' Just then the baby opened its mouth and gave its lungs full throttle.

'And earsplitting into the bargain,' Lachlan added putting his hands over his ears and making haste to go downstairs to a well-earned breakfast.

Later that day Fiona and Grant had a visitor in the shape of Dodie bearing a very sophisticated gift tray containing a well-known brand of baby powder, soap and shampoo. For a long time he had had his eye on it reposing on a shelf in Merry Mary's shop and as soon as he heard that his favourite male McKenzie was the proud father of a son he galloped to the shop to purchase the gift, complete with blue wrappings, closing his big ears to the teasing of the village men, feeling inordinately proud that he was able to buy such a fine present instead of having to resort to his usual home-made offerings.

Fiona tore off the wrapping and her face fell, as did that of her husband.

'You dinna like it!' Dodie wailed. 'It was the nicest thing in the shop too wi' all they fancy blue ribbons and bitties o' paper tied round it.'

'Of course we like it,' Grant chose his words carefully. 'It's just – well – we've seen the lovely painted stones you gave to Shona and wee Ellie. I had hoped – thought, you would have maybe given us one for our firstborn. Your stones are unique you see, Dodie, this, well, anyone can have the likes o' that but not everyone can have your bonny stones.'

Dodie was speechless with delight. He blushed and stammered, backed out of the room, knocked over a small table in the process, then turned and loped off home where he picked out his very best painted stone. Sitting down by a ramshackle table he painstakingly scratched the name 'Ian Lachlan McKenzie' across the bottom then turning it over he added his own unique mark, the initial 'D' shakily and unobtrusively scrawled in a corner.

When he at last presented the stone to the new parents, the look on their faces was a reward that would keep his spirits buoyed for many days to come. Rather disdainfully he flicked a calloused finger over the contents of the little blue tray. 'You can be giving these to the jumble sale in the hall next week, an ordinary bairnie might be glad o' them.'

Fiona and Grant exchanged laughing glances. Dodie could be quite a snob on occasion and from the prim pursing of his lips they guessed that this was one time he had every intention of boasting to all and sundry: 'Only the best is good enough for the best – if you ask Grant and Fiona they will tell you the truth o' that.'

Part Five

Winter 1964/65

Chapter Sixteen

It had been a wet windy winter with the rain sweeping horizontally over the hills and gale force winds boiling the Sound of Rhanna to fury. It was on such a day, three weeks before Christmas, that Grant came breezing into Laigmhor's parlour, his dark head glistening with raindrops, the shoulders of his blue fisherknit fuzzed with rain, for he often scorned wearing a raincoat, risking a severe reprisal from his mother for being 'a daft gowk of a laddie'. Much to everyone's joy, he and Fiona had decided to make their permanent home on Rhanna, a decision hastened by the fact that his application for the job as skipper on the new Western Islands ferry had been successful. He and his wife were presently making a languid attempt to look for a house, though at the moment Fiona seemed perfectly content to stay with her parents at Slochmhor, despite a continual battle with Elspeth over the baby's upbringing.

The arrangement suited Grant. He got on well with his in-laws and enjoyed the easy-going atmosphere of the house, also he was near enough his old home to be able to go there every day, at least until he started his new job in a few weeks' time. He was putting Lorn through a routine that had become all too familiar to them both.

Lorn was growing weary of it. After an initial hopeful start he seemed to have reached his full potential and now there existed a state of deadlock which Grant stubbornly refused to believe, but which must have been apparent to everyone else. It was brought home to him very forcibly by Captain Mac who was these days spending much of his time on Hanaay with his sister but who came over to Rhanna whenever he could.

'Look you, son,' he said to Grant, prodding his pipe at the other's chest. 'That brother o' yours is never going to get off his damty backside unless something drastic happens to make him. You see, son,' Captain Mac's bewhiskered face grew as serious as his jolly, bulbous nose would allow, 'he hasny the heart to fight. He lost it when that bonny wee wife o' his walked out on him. I have known the laddie all his days and as brave and bonny a fighter I have yet to meet. But in the old days he was grapplin' wi' physical ill health – now it's his mind and his heart that are needin' healed. There is only one person in the whole world can do that. We can coax and persuade him till we're blue in the face but at the end o' the day it is the miracle o' Ruth that he needs – ay – and the wee one too for he loved her sorely and will no' be happy till he claps eyes on her again.'

Frustration boiled in Grant. Punching his fists together he vowed that he would never give in even while he knew in his heart that Captain Mac was right. 'It's the miracle o' Ruth that he needs.' The old man's words rang inside his head till he thought he would go mad listening to them. For long he had suspected that Dugald knew more about his daughter's whereabouts than he would ever let on. He had been very quiet about her of late, hardly, if ever, referring to her at all, and so Grant had gone to see Dugald, only to be so shocked by his aged appearance that he hadn't mentioned Ruth at all but instead had turned to Totie, who, her strong, handsome face set into grim lines, told him, 'He's as wise as you are about Ruth. It hurts him to think that his very own lassie, whom he trusted and adored, doesny trust him enough to write tellin' him how she is. He just canny bring himself to talk about her anymore.' Her eyes had grown hard. 'And to think that lassie lectured me about her father's happiness. I tell you this, Grant my lad, if I could get a hold o' her right now I would shake some sense into that prim wee head o' hers — ay, that I would.'

Grant had left the house in a worse state of frustration than ever but there was a new light in his eyes that day he burst into the parlour and a firmness in his voice when he announced, 'Rachel's back! She and Jon have bought a house over near Croft na Ard. It seems Anton's been keeping a lookout for a suitable house for ages. It's only a cottage — a sort of hideaway when things get on top of them. I've seen Rachel and I've asked her to come over here as soon as she can.'

Lorn had turned a livid white. He was up sitting in a chair

by the fire, the glow of it tanning his pale skin to a rich copper. He exploded into a stream of wrath, shouting at his brother that he couldn't, he mustn't see Rachel ever again. If such a thing got to Ruth's ears it would jeopardize any slim chance there was of her coming back to the island.

A muscle worked in Grant's jaw, but he strove to remain calm. 'Rachel has a gift, Lorn, the gift of healing. You need all you can get of that, so shut up for once in your life and do as you're damned well told. I've just about had it with you. I've tried to help you, Christ Almighty how I've tried!' His patience finally snapped. 'And so has everyone else in case you haven't noticed. Mother and Father don't know what to do for the best and the only way you repay them for tending you hand and foot is by scowling and sulking and shutting yourself in this room. Look at you now! Sitting on your lazy arse at the fireside like a buggering old man! God, when I think what you were like as a wee laddie, game for anything, letting me teach you things that everyone said was beyond your capabilities. Now you haven't the gumption left in you to even fart in case it lets you know you're alive and kicking.'

Grant was white-faced, his breathing loud and heavy, his fists clenching at his sides. Lorn opened his mouth to speak but the other gave him no opportunity. Banging his fist down on the table he roared, 'Open your lugs and hear this! I've had enough – for the moment – but I'm damned if I'll ever give up on you even if you've given up on yourself! I have a wife and new baby who need me, but I'll be back, as sure as my name's McKenzie I'll be back. Meanwhile, Rachel is coming to take over and don't you dare turn her away or I'll come round and personally thrash the shit out of you!'

He stamped away, banging the door shut, leaving Lorn open-mouthed and utterly bereft of words. In the hall Kirsteen apprehended him. Her blue eyes were sparkling fire as she demanded, 'What on earth was all that about? You're driving him too hard, Grant, I warned you it would do no good . . .'

Taking her by the arm he propelled her into the kitchen, banged shut the door with his foot, led her over to a chair by the fireplace, and, twisting her round, pushed her into it where, despite an indignant protest, she remained seated. Taken aback she stared up at this brawny eldest son of hers, surprised to see so much anger in the one member of the family normally so placid and easy going.

'Now listen to me, Mother,' he began in tones that brooked no interruption. 'Ever since I came home I've put everything I had into the effort of getting that young bugger up on his feet . . .' She opened her mouth but he held up his hand and glared at her. 'Hear me out, Mother, I'm not a stupid wee laddie at your apron strings any longer. I'm free, I'm independent, I can go anywhere in the world I buggering well choose and if you don't want to listen to what I have to say I am quite capable of taking Fiona and my son and clearing off out of it all. I don't need any of this, Mother, but because I love my family and because

I have a heartfelt desire to see my brother behaving like a man again I've taken it on. I can't go it alone though, I need all the help I can get and that includes yours.'

A faint smile touched Kirsteen's lips. If she didn't know better she might have thought it was Fergus who stood before her now, black eyes full of fight, jaw muscles working. Grant had very seldom displayed the McKenzie temper and she realized that he had taken the affair of Lorn very much to his heart. 'Grant, Grant, calm down and sit down,' she said resignedly. 'You're towering over me like a glowering big mountain and I'm getting a crick in my neck.'

Rather ashamed of his outburst, he seated himself in the inglenook opposite the chair and stared down at his thumbs twisting together. 'Ach, I'm sorry I shouted at you – it's just – well – I need someone to see my point of view and you haven't been exactly bubbling over with enthusiasm for anything I've so far attempted.' He raised his head and looked her straight in the eye. 'Mother, I'm going to tell you something that might make you angry – a few things in fact. First of all Lorn is as paralysed as I am. On his last visit to the hospital you said yourself that the doctors told you they couldn't understand why he wasn't yet up on his feet. I could have told them the reason for that. He's not trying. Oh, he pretends that we are all making his life a hell by forcing him to do something the can't, but the truth is he can and damned well won't – a lot of it has to do with his pining for Ruth – but a great deal of it is because of you, Mother.'

She was incredulous. 'Me! What on earth are you saying, Grant?'

'This. Cast your mind back to when he was a frail wee laddie. Father was aye afraid for him but you – you turned a blind eye to the things I used to teach him simply because you longed for him to be less dependent, to be strong while he was at his most weak – you encouraged him to do all the things he shouldn't because you had faith, Mother, faith that one day he would be as strong as your other sons and in the end – you were right and Father was wrong.'

Kirsteen sat back and stared at her son. It was true, every word, she and Fergus had had many a bitter argument over their divided opinions on the matter. Her vision had been clearer and because of her continued resistance to Fergus, her son had grown up to become a strong young man, the farmer that Fergus had thought he could never be . . .

'You're pampering him, Mother,' Grant's voice came almost apologetically. 'You're making the same mistakes Father made all these years ago because you think Lorn isn't strong enough to take me and my browbeating.'

Her fingers curled on the arm of the chair and she gave a funny little laugh. 'It must be old age, Grant, I can't see things as clear as I used to . . .'

He squeezed his hands together till the knuckles were white. 'It isn't old age, Mother, and bloody fine you know it – it's – well – I don't know how to say this without hurting you, so you'll just have to be hurt.' He glanced away from her. 'I think you're enjoying having Lorn at home – looking after him – knowing that at least one of your sons is depending on you – like – like when we were all children and you were the only woman in any of our lives.'

He kept his face averted, not daring to look at her. She was staring at him aghast, a furious outpouring of denials springing up to her lips. But somehow she held it all back, swallowed the bitter words – for she saw in a flash that he was right – that from the moment she had gotten over the shock of Ruth's leaving she had started to enjoy having him back at Laigmhor, all safe and cosy in a little nest where she could spoil him, see to it somehow that nothing, no one, could ever hurt him again . . . She put her fingers to her lips.

'God forgive me, Grant, it's true,' she whispered, shocked by her own confession. 'So much has happened – I wanted to hold one of my sons to my bosom and keep him safe.'

He raised his eyes to her then and said softly, 'But that's not possible, is it, Mother? Lorn's more hurt, more unhappy than he's ever been. You could keep him locked up forever and he will never be truly yours again – now that his heart belongs to another woman.'

A mist of tears drowned the blue brilliance of her eyes. She bit her lip and said huskily, 'It's hard – to give up your sons. I never realized till now how painful it really is for all along I had thought that all of you had kept a corner of your hearts especially for me.'

Laughing he took her in his arms and rocked her like a little girl. 'Daft, bonny Mother. You know how we feel about you. Lewis worshipped the ground you walked on – so too does Lorn – as for me, I've always been a big lump of dough in your hands. Of course we fall in love and give ourselves to other women – but in the end it's Mother we run to when we're afraid or unhappy.'

She gave a watery, laughing sniff and pushed him away. 'No wonder women fell for you – that tongue drips pure honey – you even know how to sweeten up Elspeth.' Her chin went up. 'Right then, my lad, what is it you want me to do for Lorn?'

Briefly he told her about Rachel. At first she was aghast at the very idea of letting the girl over her doorstep because deep in her maternal mind she blamed Rachel for having led her son astray, for the subsequent unhappy events that had clouded all their lives. But in a few short sharp words Grant had rid her of her illusions.

'Make no mistake, Mother, Lorn was as much to blame as Rachel for everything that happened. He chose the wrong time to sow his wild oats – most of us manage that before we pledge ourselves to one girl. In his case he never got the chance – that's the only excuse I can make for him, though there's probably others. But it's over between him and Rachel, infatuation like that rarely lasts.'

'But if, as you seem to think, there's nothing wrong with Lorn's legs, what good can Rachel possibly do?'

'Lorn's illness is all of the mind, Mother. He knows –

we all know that Rachel does possess the power of healing. Whether it's a matter of pure psychology that works on receptive minds, or whether it's something else beyond our understanding doesn't really matter. What matters is that Rachel just might be the means we need of getting through to Lorn, one way or another. At least give it a try.'

He was so earnest in his desire to see his brother fit again that Kirsteen experienced a renewed surge of respect for this eldest son who had been born of the pure love and passion she and Fergus had shared in those wondrous, far-off days. With a sense of wonder she reached out and touched Grant's hair – so like his father's when he was young – and then she saw the tiny white hairs gleaming like silver among the jet black. It seemed impossible that any son of hers should be old enough, but then Grant was almost thirty, no longer the boy she had always thought him, but a mature young man perfectly capable of talking to her in the same determined manner as his father.

'Let Rachel come,' she said softly. 'They're bound to have crossed paths sooner or later so better get it over with now.'

Grant nodded and gripped her hand. 'I knew you would see sense. I'll leave it to you to tell Father so that he doesn't go up in smoke when he sees Rachel here at Laigmhor.'

Rachel was shocked to see how much Lorn had changed. She stood in the doorway of the parlour, eyeing him with some trepidation. It had taken a lot of courage for her to come here like this – to face Lorn – to face his family – in fact all the people who had been affected in some way by that brief passionate affair which seemed to have happened in a far distant dream which had no part in reality. She had marvelled at Jon for letting her come here – but he had looked at her with those steady brown eyes of his and told her, 'I trust you, liebling, more than ever I trust you.'

She took a step further into the room and gazed long at the man who had so easily and swiftly carried her to heights of euphoric rapture, and she was surprised at how calm she felt – at the lack of excitement which she had thought the sight of him would surely bring her. But it was over, whatever she had felt for him, and whatever fantasies of Lewis his brother had satisfied in her were gone, as dead and as pale as the ashes of the past. Jon was right to trust her now. Lorn McKenzie was as attractive as any of the young men she might be likely to encounter on her travels, but that was all and her heart flipped over with relief that she could look at him and no longer be afraid of the emotions he could arouse in her.

Her one great emotion now was sorrow, sorrow that it had happened at all. She recognized that Lorn was the loser in it all. Except for Ruth, she still had everything that she had had before – and more. Her mother had unexpectedly and miraculously welcomed her home with open arms and for the past few days had challenged anyone to dare to speak about her daughter. In a way Rachel understood why. Annie had been unfaithful to her own husband in his lifetime. In defending her daughter she was defending her own reputation and in the process getting back at all those who had talked behind her back – yet Rachel could never forgive her mother for so easily casting aside the memory of the big, black-bearded giant Rachel had adored, to take in his place Torquill Andrew, a good man but one she could never accept in her father's place . . . She cast such thoughts from her mind and concentrated on Lorn, on how much he had changed since her last vision of him at the gate of Fàilte when she had said her goodbyes to him and to Ruth . . .

Lorn had wondered how he would feel seeing again the girl who had so completely changed his life that sunny spring day not so many months ago – God, as short a time ago as that! It seemed like years. He had heard all about her of course. Rachel was news these days, young, lovely, successful, she was a newspaper reporter's dream. The *Song of Rhanna* had been played continually on the wireless, and because of it more tourists than ever had come to the island, many to stand gaping at Rachel's birthplace till Annie could stand it no more. In a fit of exasperated inspiration she had erected a notice outside her house which read, 'BEWARE OF TICKS. The grass is hotching with them, the sheep are hotching, the dogs and cats are hotching and YOU will be too if you don't KEEP OFF.'

The items concerning Rachel in the newspapers had been many and varied and the islanders, despite gossiping their heads off about the 'Lorn and Rachel affair', glowed with pride in her achievements and were quick to defend her name should a stranger dare to say one word that might be construed against her.

Lorn studied her intently as she came through the door. She was still as beautiful, still as vibrantly alive as she had always been, but he felt no more for her than the same sort of affection he might feel for any attractive woman of his acquaintance. Relief washed over him. He had lain awake for several nights dreading this meeting but it was going to be all right after all – yet even so, the sight of her opened up all the deep raw wounds of guilt he had tried so hard to keep buried.

'Rachel.' Lorn's acknowledgement in his lilting tongue seemed to startle her out of a reverie. Slowly she came forward and putting her arms around him embraced him and kissed the top of his dark head. It was a warm, brief, impulsive gesture but it said all that was in their hearts. A mist blurred his vision, the flames in the hearth wavered. She drew away to seat herself in the chair opposite and he saw that she too had been moved to tears. Her huge dark eyes were glazed with them. She stared into the fire and didn't look at him for a long time.

The door opened. He was surprised at the sense of relief he felt at the intrusion of his mother bringing in a piled tray, never a word or a glance giving away the doubts she had harboured since Grant's suggestion. She spoke warmly to Rachel, making her feel welcome and at home. 'Be firm with him, Rachel,' she instructed. 'He'll make all sorts of excuses for not letting you see those bonny hairy legs of his, but men are like that – all vanity and no sense.'

It broke the ice. A smile broke the solemnity of Rachel's face, visibly she relaxed and when Kirsteen left the room she poured tea and they drank it in companionable awareness of one another's feelings.

After that she came almost every day to massage his legs, to encourage him to try and move about the room. To his amazement he found a strength returning, life flooding back to muscles he had imagined would never work properly again. Whether it was purely psychological or whether it was because Rachel truly did have the gift of healing he neither knew or cared. All that mattered was the wonder of experiencing returning movement. Two weeks after Rachel's first visit he was moving about the room with the aid of walking sticks which had hitherto been mere family heirlooms sitting in the stand in the hall. Every day there was some improvement. He progressed from his room to other parts of the house, soon he was taking his first steps outside. On that day he stood at the gate, letting the air from the hills fill his lungs. It was a damp raw day but to him the island had never looked more beautiful. The stark tracery of winter branches clawed at the wet grey rainclouds, a steady drizzle bathed his upturned face. Putting out his tongue he tasted the coolness of it. Life had never seemed more precious, more desirable in those wondrous moments of longed-for freedom.

At the window Fergus put his arm round Kirsteen and said huskily in her ear, 'Thank God.'

'Not forgetting Grant and Rachel,' Kirsteen reminded him, delighting in the little bubble of joy that burst suddenly within her heart.

On Christmas morning Lorn watched his son tearing open his gifts. He had had his flaxen curls recently cropped and overnight it seemed he had grown from a baby into a sturdy little boy. A parcel had arrived for him the day before. It had contained gifts from Ruth, but though Lorn had searched frantically for some sort of sign that might tell him her whereabouts there was none, only the postmark gave him a clue for it had come from Ayrshire. With hope choking him he had phoned Dungowrie Farm only to learn that Ruth had been there, leaving the parcel for Jean to post. She hadn't given away where she was staying.

'Are you sure she didn't say anything?' he had asked almost pleadingly.

Jean's voice had been warm with sympathy. 'I'm sorry, lad, she wouldn't say.'

'How was she? Did she look well – is Lorna all right?'

'Ay, they're both right enough – peakit mind – but that's to be expected when you live in the city.'

'So, they're in the city – does that mean Glasgow?'

'Ye ken as much as me. I'd like to help. I tried to talk some sense into the lass but she's changed from the time I knew her in hospital – guarded is the word – ay, and she's lost that bonny soft sweet nature o' hers too – hard is what she is now. She only came to leave a wee thing for Davie and me for Christmas and to ask me to post the parcel to the bairnie – nary a word about where she's staying, what she's doing. I fancy she's pining for her wee boy or she would never have bothered to come here wi' gifts for him. She knew you would phone me when you saw the postmark and she told me to tell you – she doesny want to see you again – if she ever comes back it will be for the wee one. I gathered she's working hard to get some sort o' home together for her bairnies.'

He had put the phone down, saddened and defeated. Douglas had enjoyed exploring the contents of the parcel but in a thoughtful moment he had looked up to ask, 'Where's Muvver?'

He had asked that question frequently in the beginning, but gradually he had ceased to ask and had immersed himself in the delights of the farm. Now Lorn realized that the little boy had not forgotten, that somewhere at the back of his young mind lay the mystery of his mother's sudden disappearance. The arrival of the parcel had brought the ghost of Ruth into Christmas, blighting it for everyone. A ceilidh had been arranged to celebrate the return of Grant and Fiona to the island and to welcome Ian Lachlan McKenzie into the world. Everyone sang, the strains of the pipes and the fiddles filled the room, the seanachaidhs spun their magical tales by the fire's glow, laughter and joy filled the house, and Grant watched his young brother's attempts at jollity and knew he would never get truly well till the 'miracle o' Ruth' made it possible.

Chapter Seventeen

The Rev. Mark James was sitting in the back of a taxi driving through Glasgow's east end. He had spent a few days in the city, visiting some of his old parishioners who had hailed him with delight and had been anxious to hear about the new life he had made for himself in the Hebrides. He sat back, feeling pleased at the success of his trip, but glad to be heading for the station and the train that would take him to Oban. Yet all through his contentment of spirit there ran a strangely restless anticipation at the thought of going home. He always felt like that after a spell in the city but this time there was something more, an exhilaration mingling with a sweet longing which lay deep at the core of his heart. No matter how much he tried to ignore it, it wouldn't go away and so he decided the best way to be rid of it was to face up to the fruitlessness of such useless hankerings. Immediately the sweet, serene face of Megan Jenkins darted into his mind, so clear he could see the pale milkiness of her skin – her soft brown hair gleaming in the sun . . .

He was totally unprepared for the sight of Ruth McKenzie limping dispiritedly along on the opposite side of the street, little Lorna holding tightly to her hand. Startled out of his

reverie with such suddenness he was confused, his train of
thought leapt from Megan to Ruth and his mind began to
race. Leaning forward he opened the glass partition to the
driver's cab and requested him to stop.

'No' here, mister, I'd get done if the police caught me
on a yellow line.'

The man's tones were very decided and the minister
glanced desperately outside. He couldn't let Ruth escape
now. 'Dear God, not now,' he prayed quickly. Just then
Ruth halted and appeared to scan the busy thoroughfare
as if she was looking for someone or else – the thought
came swiftly to the minister's mind – she was checking to
make sure that no one she knew was watching her.

Mark James turned his dark head away. The taxi driver
had slowed but was definitely not stopping. Mark James
looked again. Ruth and Lorna were disappearing into
the mouth of a close, and he had to know if this was
where she was staying. Raking in his pocket he found
his wallet and, extracting two pound notes, waved them
enticingly through the partition. The driver scratched his
head, muttered something, then drew the vehicle to a halt
at the pavement.

'Don't you be long now,' he said grumblingly. 'If you're
no' back in five minutes I'm for the off.'

'Two ticks.' The minister was already swinging his long
legs outside. A few quick strides took him over the road.
He paused at the close mouth and looked cautiously up the
narrow dark cavern. It was deserted and he went quickly

to scan the nameplates on the doors. R. Donaldson. The name on the scratched metal plate leapt out at him. She was here all right and she was using her maiden name – little wonder she had been so difficult to locate. He hesitated, wondering if he should knock the door, but no, he decided against it, he might only succeed in frightening her away. Much more sensible to go back to Rhanna and let her family know where they could find her.

In his wisdom, the minister did not approach any of the people directly connected with Ruth. They were all too emotionally involved to be able to see things objectively and so he went to Grant, Shona and Totie, people who were only too aware of the problems but who were far enough back from them to be able to view them in a clearer light. Shona was in the kitchen when the tall, handsome figure she knew so well came in, the black cap of his hair glistening with raindrops, his skin fresh and clean looking after the walk over the glen road.

She too had just come in from feeding the hens. Her rain-studded cheeks were glowing, her thick mass of auburn hair tossed into disarray by the bullying January winds.

He glanced at her appreciatively, his white teeth showing as he said softly, 'Your hair is as bonny as a wet autumn leaf – yet there was a time you took it into your head to lop the whole lot off with a pair of kitchen shears.'

The flush on her cheeks deepened. 'Fancy you remem‐
bering that. Niall never lets me forget it but I didn't thin
that you—'

His smoky gaze held hers. 'There's a lot I remember
about you, Shona, some things can never be forgotten.'

She took a deep breath. 'I know – yet they must b
hidden or they could shock and hurt other people, ever
though we didn't sin in the true sense of the word. Rut
was shocked when I let it slip about us . . .'

His head jerked up. 'You told her about – what hap
pened?'

'Oh, not in so many words,' she was angry at hersel
for the slip. 'I was just going on about things and
came out. Ruth was – well you know Ruth, she's s
naïve about certain things – at least she was until thi
affair over Lorn and Rachel. I think that's why she find
it so hard to forgive Lorn: she seems to have forgotter
how readily he forgave her and accepted Lewis' baby . .
She stopped short, horrified at herself. 'Forget I said that
she pleaded, flustered and red-faced. 'I don't usually g
around giving away family secrets – I think – well – yo
caught me unawares and one thing seemed to lead t
another.'

'So,' he murmured almost to himself. 'Lorna is Lewi
child and Lorn took Ruth and married her when perhap
he wasn't ready to bear such responsibilities.'

'I always felt that,' she said miserably. 'Lorn was alway
so steady and levelheaded but I think in every one of u

there's a wildness that has to be unleashed – sooner or later – there has to be an outlet.'

He regarded her steadily. 'I know what you're trying to say, Shona, and believe me, what you have just told me will be safe with me – you know you can trust me.'

'Ay, I can trust you, Mark,' she said softly. 'Always I could trust you.'

He studied her intently. 'There is something I want to ask you. I've already spoken to Grant and to Totie Donaldson and they have agreed to do as I ask – I'm hoping you will too.'

She heard him out in silence and when he had finished it was to give him the answer that he had expected. 'Ay, I'll go with Totie and try to talk to Ruth.' She sighed deeply. 'It won't be easy, mind; Ruth might be quiet but there's another side to her that I know well. She can be as stubborn as a mule's arse when she wants.' Her dimples showed. 'There I go again – swearing in front of a minister.'

'I'll always be more than that to you, Shona.' His voice was soft, serious.

'Ay, I know, but I'm hoping you'll be more than that also to a certain young woman whose path you have crossed but briefly but who might already be destined to walk the same road with you eventually.' She looked at him from under her lashes and they both burst out laughing.

'You're a romantic, Shona McLachlan, but I warn you now, this isn't the time to start playing Cupid. At the moment we're concerned not with me but with Ruth and

Lorn. Despite what has happened those two were meant for each other and the sooner we get them back together again the better.'

That evening Shona confided her doubts about the venture to Niall. Taking her hand he kissed it and looked laughingly into her face. 'Shona, mo ghaoil, if anybody can talk to Ruth you can. She's always trusted you and will surely listen to reason . . .'

'As long as I don't lose my temper,' she wailed. 'Ruth can be infuriating at times and she hasn't stood firm all this time to be taken in by me and my sermons.'

'Grant will keep the whole business on a steady level,' he said with conviction. 'Of all the McKenzies he's the one blessed with the most cool-headed sense.'

'Cheeky brute,' she laughed. 'Just for that I won't massage your tired old back tonight.'

His brown eyes twinkled. 'My back is neither tired nor old – but maybe I ought to stop talking about it and prove it to you.'

'First things first, my lad. This trip to Glasgow for a start, the minister thinks we ought to go as soon as possible and I for one would like to get it over with.'

He glanced through the window to the rain sweeping across the hills. 'Gales are forecast for the next week. I'd feel happier if you left it till the weather has settled.'

But she shook her head. 'Blethers! If I don't go on the next boat I'll never make the effort. I'll ask Kirsteen to look after Ellie, though I won't say why I have to go to Glasgow.

Grant and myself will cook up something between us, and no doubt Totie can do the same though Doug's lost so much interest in everything I doubt he wouldn't hear if she said she was going to the moon.' She frowned. 'I wonder how Totie will handle Ruth. She isn't exactly renowned for tact and can be a bit of a bully if something gets up her hump – she's angry at what Ruth's stubbornness has done to her marriage and she might not be able to hold her tongue.'

Niall shook his head. 'Ay, Totie's all that and more but she can be gey canny when she likes. Don't forget, she was never a bosom friend of Morag's yet for years she managed to hold her tongue so that neither he nor Ruth would be hurt.'

'I wonder why the minister asked three of us to go? Surely it would be better for just one of us to talk to Ruth?'

Niall's answer came readily. 'Our Mark James has his head screwed on. He knows how much Ruth has trusted you in the past, and if anyone can persuade her to see sense you can. Totie was chosen because of her direct connection with Doug. Totie's the person to make Ruth squirm for hurting her father – Grant's the levelheaded one of you all. If Totie goes too far, or if you look like losing that witch's temper of yours he'll be there to wave the olive branches.'

She giggled and threw a cushion at his head and in the scuffle that followed she forgot for the moment the mission that lay ahead of her.

*   *   *

Ruth opened the door and stared speechless at the three people standing on her doorstep, but in seconds she seemed to compose herself, her expression altering to one of deep suspicion.

'Quite a deputation,' she said flatly. 'Three against one.'

'Can we come in, Ruth?' Grant was the first to speak. 'We've come a long way and could be doing with a cuppy.'

Ruth didn't answer at once. The draught blew in from the close mouth, swirling round Totie's legs, making her shiver. Unlike Shona she wasn't wearing 'the trouser' and though her lisle stockings were sturdily thick they weren't adequate enough to combat the chill of the draughty Glasgow streets. Sleety rain was swirling along the pavements, billowing into the narrow aperture in which they stood and Totie stamped her feet in some impatience. Several weeks had passed since the minister's discovery of Ruth's whereabouts. Continual storm force winds had made travel difficult and January had moved into February before the storms had abated sufficiently for the journey to Glasgow to be undertaken.

At Grant's words, Ruth moved reluctantly back into the dark, cavernous lobby. With a mere flick of her head she invited them inside and all three thankfully left the chill-ridden close, though each looked at the other in some trepidation as they walked through the lobby and into the only apartment contained therein. The house was a single end, a recess in the wall contained a double bed, the sink and cooker were situated under the half-barred, grubby-looking window in which a pane of glass had been replaced by a piece of plywood. The room contained little furniture, two chairs, a table, some odds and ends. But it was clean and polished, a bright fire burned in the grate. On the floor, on top of the only rug, sat a little girl, hands folded passively in her lap, her big eyes staring solemnly as the visitors came into the room. At first Shona didn't recognize her as the happy, intelligent child who had roamed in carefree acceptance of the glens of her birth. Her face was thin, her once rosy skin blotched and pale.

'Lorna!' The name was torn from Shona, more a cry of protest than a recognition.

'She's had the measles – but she's over the worst of it now.' The words spoken by Ruth were succinct and held undercurrents of defiance. Lorna didn't move from the rug and rushing forward, Shona lifted her up to cuddle her to her breast.

'Lorna, Lorna,' she crooned gently. 'Don't you know me? Don't you remember your Aunt Shona? I used to tickle you – like this.'

The child lifted one shoulder shyly, the ghostly dawning of a smile hovered at her mouth. 'Aunt Shona.' She whispered the name as if she couldn't believe it then slowly her arms crept round Shona's neck and tiredly she laid her head against the comforting shoulder. Shona was too overcome to speak again. Ruth didn't invite them to sit down and they all stood, awkward, embarrassed, Grant's brawny figure looking ridiculously out of place in the tiny room, Totie's solid, big-bosomed form equally so. She was wearing her fur jacket and one of her big floppy fur hats to match and though they had seen better days they endowed her with an air of affluence in the shabby surroundings.

Meaningfully Shona glanced at the others and flounced rather than walked over to one of the chairs to sit herself down and put Lorna on her knee. Taking her cue, Totie marched over to sit on the remaining chair leaving Grant awkward and red in the face till Shona patted the arm of her chair and bade him sit beside her.

Ruth glanced round the room. 'It isn't much – no' yet – but at least it's a roof and by the time I'm done it will be like a wee palace.'

Shona lowered her face and nuzzled Lorna's hair. Never had she felt so depressed in any surroundings, not even in old Meggie's blackhouse with its atmosphere of ageless dignity and cosy welcoming warmth. How could Ruth bear it after the charm of Fàilte, the clean open spaces of Rhanna? And this was where Ruth hoped eventually to bring Douglas – that sprite of the countryside who had all his babyhood days known only the freedom of being surrounded by light and space. She shook off her depression and felt some of her spirit returning. She would have to talk Ruth out of remaining here, try to get her to come back to Rhanna, if not to Lorn at least to some place where her children could have the kind of life that was their birthright.

'I'll make tea.' The shock of events had brought colour to Ruth's face but now it was receding leaving her pale and drawn with dark circles under her eyes. She was also much thinner than she had been; her clothes hung shapelessly on her body, her limp was very pronounced as she went to the sink to fill the kettle.

'How did you know where I was?' She tossed the question resentfully over her shoulder.

'Mr James was in Glasgow a whily back and saw you coming in here,' Totie explained.

Ruth turned, her face set. 'Mr James, eh? I might have known he would come snooping about – he seems to be very good at finding women who have left their husbands.' She looked meaningfully at Shona as she spoke and immediately Shona's cheeks flamed and sparks flew from her eyes. But no! She wouldn't let her temper get the better of her – not after coming all this way.

Tea was drunk in an awkward silence then everyone seemed to speak at once though it was Grant's deep voice that won in the end. He told Ruth about Lorn, about the accident that had rendered him a near invalid for months.

'Douglas – what about him? He – wasn't hurt, was he?' It was a cry of anguish, torn from Ruth in concern for her child.

'Douglas is fine,' Grant assured her. 'He's a resilient wee chap – not so his father. He's made progress but there is a deep unhappiness inside him which is impeding his full return to health. You know what that is, Ruth.'

Her cheeks reddened angrily. 'Ay, too well I know!' Her face was set and hard. 'He allowed the lusts of the flesh to rule his head – and now he is being punished for it.' Everyone stared at her with disbelieving eyes. If it hadn't been Ruth standing there they might have thought Morag Ruadh had uttered the words, and Shona couldn't stop herself conveying this to Ruth.

The heated colour left Ruth's face, she turned white and reached for a chair for support. 'How dare you speak ill of my mother!' she blazed. She gave a short, bitter laugh. 'Maybe she was right all along, she spoke through madness, ay, but she wasn't always that way.'

Shona's lips folded grimly. 'Ay, she was like what you've become, Ruth, a woman with no forgiveness in her heart and because of that she died a lonely, bitter soul whom nobody loved.'

'I think you had all better leave my house,' Ruth's tones were frighteningly calm. 'I never invited you here and you are not welcome in this home.'

'What home?' Shona threw at her scornfully, angry at herself for the turn of events but unable to take a single word back. She looked around her disdainfully. 'How can you live here, Ruth? How can you let Lorna live here? Lorn sent you money – you could at least have swallowed your pride and used it to make things better for the wee one. Look at her, she's not the same bonny bairn I knew, she looks ill. What kind of a life is that to give a child — you're just using her to get back at Lorn and that in itself is the worst crime any mother can commit against her own child.'

'Things will get better,' Ruth said stubbornly, her breath coming quickly. 'I was ill when first I came to Glasgow and couldn't work, now I have a job and Lorna is well looked after by a neighbour. Besides, none of it is any of your business — any of you — what I do with my life and the life of my daughter is my affair.'

Grant looked at his hands and spoke quietly. 'Lorna is my brother's affair too, Ruth. He worships her and you're using her to punish him.'

'Oh, he has to be punished,' Ruth said coldly. 'He made me suffer enough. Do you honestly think I enjoy any of this? There have been times when I have been tempted to run back to Rhanna and leave it all behind — then I remember the humiliation — the pointing fingers, everyone talking about the innocent little fool who lost her husband to her best friend.'

Shona took a deep breath, determined to hold on to her temper. 'Wasn't some of that your own fault? I think Lorn tried to warn you right at the beginning . . .'

Ruth was incredulous. 'Warn me! Warn me that he knew, given the chance, he was going to be unfaithful! What kind of a man is he?'

'A very human man,' Shona groped for the right things to say. 'He's not the sort to be swayed by the attentions of women – but I think he must have recognized the danger with Rachel and opposed her coming to stay with you. Didn't the pair of you have a row about it right at the start?'

Ruth remembered that first really serious row with her husband. 'Ay,' she said slowly then bitterly, 'But at the time I thought it was because he couldny stand Rachel – little did I know it was because he knew he couldn't trust himself to be alone with someone I thought was my friend.'

'Och, c'mon, Ruth; he could hardly tell you how he felt, could he?' hazarded Grant.

'It might have been better if he had,' Ruth cried passionately. 'Then none of this might ever have happened – anyway – you can say what you like, I'm not coming back and that's final!'

Up till then, Totie hadn't uttered a single word. She had been staring into the fire, listening to the arguments bouncing back and forth. She lifted her head and turned her strong face to Ruth.

'Have you ever stopped to think how many people, other than you and Lorn, have been made to suffer by all this? When I was going to marry your father you made it plain how concerned you were about his happiness – well as it turned out, we were sublimely happy till we came home and found out you had left, taking the wee one with you. Where was your concern for your father there, Ruth? You were so wrapped up in your own misery you gave no thought to the misery he might feel – no, nor the hell he has gone through since you left. He worships you and looked every day for a word that would let him know how you were. If you thought he was unhappy during his time wi' your mother you should see him now. He is suddenly an old man with no interest in any of the things he once loved. I am his wife and I have to stand helplessly by watching him growing unhappier wi' each passing day – and you have the cheek to think I was the one who was going to make him unhappy! I haveny had a damt chance to prove what kind o' a wife I am yet and I'm getting sick o' the ghost o' his daughter coming between he and me.' Totie's voice shook slightly as she finished speaking but she had made her point well. Something of the old Ruth shone through, her mask of hardness fell away and a flash of her former vulnerability showed through the pain in her eyes.

'I was too ashamed to write,' she whispered. 'Every waking day of my life I took up my pen to write to my father but always I was so sick with misery – I – I just couldny do it. I – I think it would be better if he just forgot all about me. He has you – I'm thinking he will no' need me so much—'

'He's always needed you,' Totie interposed harshly, her green eyes flashing. 'And how in the name o' heaven could he forget his own lassie! You have a lot o' growing up to do yet, my girl, and it's high time you started or Shona will be right – you will become as bitter and as unforgiving as your poor mother and that is something I wouldny wish on anybody.'

Ruth was ashen and trembling so much that Shona went to put a comforting arm round her shoulders and to ask if she had any brandy or whisky in the house.

'In the wee cupboard under the sink.' Ruth pointed a shaking finger and Shona went to pour out a generous dram of whisky which she made Ruth swallow.

'I feel better now.' Ruth set the glass down on the hearth and folded her hands in her lap, her flaxen hair falling over her face, hiding it. 'Please go now,' her voice was so low it was barely audible. 'I know you came here with the best of intentions but I – I wasny ready for you – for any of you. I'm tired, I need time to think; so please go.'

'You will write to your father, Ruth?' It wasn't a question but a demand. Ruth looked at her stepmother's strong, determined face and nodded.

'Ay, I'll write – just let me have a bitty more time to think everything over – tell him – I think of him every day – I love him.' Her voice broke.

The visitors began to take their leave but as Shona turned away Ruth blindly sought her hand. 'It's been – wonderful to see all your bonny faces.' She raised her face and Shona saw the tears drowning the purple orbs. 'You've brought a breath of fresh air into this dingy room.' She glanced round at her surroundings and her lips twisted. 'I hate it, Shona, I want more than anything to get away from it – but if I do – it won't be to come back to Rhanna. I haveny the courage to face anyone there again – please try to understand.'

Shona gazed at little Lorna peeping at her through her fingers. 'There was a time, Ruth, when I thought you were made of sterner stuff – that you could be as tough as any McKenzie any day and able to stand in front of the wind to dare it to stop blowing. Now I see how mistaken I was.'

It was a harsh and hurtful thing to say. Shona hated herself for it but it was a shot in the dark, a last hope that she could shock Ruth into coming to her senses.

Ruth's eyes had grown dark with hurt. 'I learned, Shona, that to stand in front of the wind is only asking to be broken by it – as I was when for once in my life I defied Lorn and asked Rachel to stay.'

Shona shook her head. 'The shoots of a broken tree very often grow taller, stronger, than they were originally. If you gave yourself the chance, Ruth, you wouldn't allow anything to stunt the growth of your spirit. You're not so frightened of life as you would have yourself believe – I think underneath you are still the same girl who half-killed a boy in school because he called you names – and you were just a shy wee lassie when that happened, how much of that spirit has developed with time only you know – and only you can do anything about it.'

Unable to bear the pathos in Lorna's face a moment longer she went hurriedly through the dark lobby to where the others were waiting in the close. Reaching out she made to pull the door to but before it clicked shut she heard the unmistakable sound of Lorna crying, her heartbroken sobs smiting the hearts of those who stood outside Ruth's door, looking at each other and knowing that their mission had been in vain.

Chapter Eighteen

Lorn tossed and turned, adrift in an uneasy world of dreams that gave him no rest. So it had been for the past three nights, ever since Grant and Shona had told him they had been to see Ruth and of the outcome. He awoke with a start, the sweat moist and warm on his brow, his heart beating uncomfortably fast. Dawn was just a promise in the sky to the east, the house slept, only he, it seemed, was unable to find solace in the merciful world of real sleep.

He had dreamed again, dreamed of Ruth and his children, but unlike the nightmares of past nights when he had watched them floating further and further out of his reach, this dream had been eerily real, as if someone was inside his head talking to him, telling him what he had to do. He stared wide-eyed into the darkness, knowing that it had been Lewis who had come to him, to guide his subconscious mind to make a decision which though drastic, became more feasible the more he thought about it.

'All right, Lewis,' he thought, 'this time I'll listen, this time I'll heed what you are trying to tell me.'

The luminous hands on the clock on the mantelpiece

were at five o'clock and he would have to get up immediately if he was to accomplish what was in his mind. Raising himself up he reached out to pull the heavy curtains across the window before swinging his legs out of the bed. The fire in the hearth had long ago faded into ashes and he shivered as the keen air of morning seeped into him. Fumbling for his sticks he hauled himself upright and made his way over to the bureau to light the lamp, his heart in his mouth lest he should make a noise, giving a hint to those upstairs that he was up and about. He got dressed, cursing his awkwardness, willing his limbs to move with more speed. It took him half an hour to reach the top of the stairs, another ten minutes to get to the door of his son's room. It was his first trip to the upper part of the house in months and by the time he had accomplished it he was trembling, a combination of suspense in case his mother's door should open and a tiring of muscles that were awkward and tensed. He knew every stair that squeaked, every floorboard that creaked, nevertheless he imagined that every fumbling step made enough noise to waken the dead. For fully five minutes he stood in the dark passageway to gather himself together then carefully he turned the handle of the door and with his heartbeat drumming in his ears moved stealthily inside to thankfully shut the door behind him. A nightlight flickered in a safety container atop the chest of drawers, left there by Kirsteen to still the fears that had beset the little boy since his father's accident. Lorn reached the bed and sat down, very aware of his shaking legs.

His son lay spreadeagled, his sleeping face cherubic in the faint light. Lorn stared at him and licked his dry lips, wondering if he could possibly go through with what seemed an impossible venture. Then he thought of his empty life, the longings, the frustrations, and before he could change his mind he reached out to gently shake his son awake. The child immediately began to whimper. Lorn enclosed the small body in his arms and spoke calmly. 'Weesht, weesht, babby, it's your father, don't cry.'

Douglas rubbed his eyes to stare in disbelief at his father. A smile broke over his face, his pearly teeth showed.

'How would you like to go with me on a big boat?' Lorn whispered persuasively. The child nodded eagerly. 'You can only come if you promise to be very, very quiet and do exactly as I tell you.'

Seeing the whole episode as a new and exciting game, the child allowed his father to dress him. 'Stay close by my side,' Lorn instructed. 'We canny put on any lights so you'll walk behind me and hang on to my jacket. You must not make a murmur when you pass your Granpa's room. After that, creep downstairs like a mouse and wait for me in the kitchen.'

More than thirty minutes later all Lorn wanted to do was to sit in the warmth of the kitchen and relax by the slumbering fire but he daren't allow himself to ease up for a moment. Somehow he got Douglas a warm breakfast but he himself was unable to eat and smiling inwardly at what his mother would say, he heated up the remains of the tea from the night before, and sat drinking it with one eye on the clock. The animals had barely stirred at the unusually early intrusion into their world. Ben lay on the hearthrug, his nose in his paws, his tail flicking the whiskers of Bramble who always slept curled into the flanks of the old sheepdog. A yawning Douglas was inclined to coorie down beside the animals and go to sleep too and for a while Lorn let him have his way while he wrote a note for his mother which read: 'I have taken Douglas and we are away on the early boat to see Ruth. I knew you might have worried about me going on my own and that is why I didn't disturb you or Father. Don't worry, I can manage. This is something I have to do and Douglas is being a wee man about it all. I am hoping to come back with Ruth and the children — if it doesn't work out that way I'll be coming back on my own. Lorn.'

Propping the note against the clock on the mantelpiece he sat down and rubbed the back of his neck. He was tense, unable to relax for a second, worried in case his father should rise and catch him out before he had even started off on his journey.

He aroused Douglas and got him into his outdoor clothes then he checked to make sure that he had enough money in his pocket. 'C'mon, son,' he ushered the little boy to the door. 'You walk beside me and don't make a sound going down the path. The boat is waiting in the harbour and we will have to go now if we want to get on it.' The glen road was reached without mishap. Lorn stood for a minute, gazing down the winding grey ribbon that led to Portcull. In days gone by he could have covered the distance in no time but now the village seemed a formidably long way off. Taking a deep breath he set off, the pads on the end of his sticks making little squelching sounds with each step. Although it was only seven o'clock there were signs of stirring in the houses he passed, smoke was spiralling from the chimneys of the village houses, one or two people were going about their business. Tam was coming out of his gate a little way off and he stopped short at sight of Lorn and his son making their way towards him.

'My, my, I never thought I'd see the day,' Tam greeted Lorn with a beaming smile. 'It would seem that my granddaughter has the power in her hands right enough. Where are you heading and I'll give you an arm?'

'The harbour.' Lorn's explanation was brief and inwardly he blessed Tam for his tact on this occasion as not once did he ask the purpose of Lorn's early morning journey. Lorn leaned gratefully on his arm and they arrived at the harbour much sooner than he had ever expected. He looked at Tam's honest, happy face and impulsively confided, 'I'm going to see Ruth, Tam, to have everything out once and for all.'

'Good luck to you, son.' Tam shook his hand heartily. 'I'll expect to see the lot o' you back on the next boat for I'll be keeping my fingers crossed for you.'

He helped Lorn up the gangplank and saw him settled in the saloon before going off, a gay little whistle between his teeth. Half an hour later the boat sailed away from Portcull Harbour to the excited chatter of Douglas who was enthralled with everything he saw. Lorn stared out of the porthole, saw Rhanna slipping away. Now that he was on his way the coil of nerves in his belly began to unwind and he was aware of a strong sensation of confidence stealing through his being. 'You're there, Lewis, you bugger,' he whispered, and smiled. The boat hooted, swung round to head out to sea, taking a father and son away from the island as it had taken mother and daughter on a spring morning many many months before.

Ruth stared at Lorn as if she was looking at a ghost. 'How – how did you get here?' she gasped, her eyes big with shock.

'Same way as you, no doubt. I took a taxi from the station, it brought me right to the door.'

Roughly he pushed past her, somehow managing to hold Douglas' hand in a firm grip despite the encumbrance of his walking sticks. Ruth came quickly in at his back, her eyes feasting on the little boy who stood in the middle of the room as if transfixed.

'Douglas,' she whispered, holding out her arms. 'You've grown, my wee laddie, you're no longer the baby you were.'

But Douglas sidled away from her to stand behind his father's back and almost simultaneously Lorna went to hide behind her mother's skirts; her thumb jammed firmly in her mouth.

Lorn's mouth twisted. 'Do you see what we've done to them, Ruthie? We're all strangers to one another – in just a few short months.' He twisted round and grabbing his son's hand pulled him forward. 'Here he is, Ruthie, your son, I've saved you the bother of coming to collect him. He's all yours.'

His voice was hard, but only to hide the dreadful feeling of insecurity that had beset him the minute he stepped over the threshold. The venture was one of the biggest gambles he had ever taken in his life and he was already beginning to regret it – if Ruth called his bluff he was finished – and he would be left with nothing.

Ruth's heart was pounding so fast she felt she would faint. For the last few nights she had dreamed continually of Lorn, now here he was, living, real; standing in the shabby little room of which she was so ashamed. He was as tall as ever but that was all. The aura of strength that emanated from him came only from within, he was frail looking, his shoulders drooped, the sticks that held him up were not so much a surprise to her but a silent accusation which aimed directly at her heart. The truth was she had given little thought to what the accident must have done to him. In her mind he was almost indestructible, she had imagined that he would still be the powerful, upright McKenzie of her last memories of him and the reality of seeing that he was just as frail and susceptible as any other human being struck her like a physical blow.

'Lorn, sit down,' she said and her voice was soft with shame.

He kept his back to her and remained where he was, in the middle of the room with his son's hand held in a firm grip. 'I haven't come to socialize.' He could hardly get the words out. 'I have brought your son to you and I want you to give me your answer right now as to what you intend to do . . .' His eye fell on two cases lying on the bed, packed neatly ready to be shut.

'I was coming home anyway,' Ruth's voice came softly at his back. 'But – I'm so very very glad that you – thought enough of me and the children – to come and fetch us.'

Slowly he turned, a look of disbelief smouldering in the depths of his eyes. 'Ruthie,' her name was a mere breath on his lips. 'Do you really mean that?'

She nodded. 'Ay, Lorn, what's the use of pretending, I canny live my life without you, I tried and I failed. That's what made it so difficult for me – to know that I needed you, that I couldn't go on without you . . .'

He was staring at her, his eyes so luminously blue she was mesmerized by the intensity in them. 'Then you felt as I did, Ruthie, I've been – nothing without you – we'll have to face the truth – we were meant to be together. I at any rate – am useless without my Ruthie at my side—' His voice broke.

She held her breath. 'Oh, Lorn, I've missed you so. I

was coming back because I knew I had to have the courage to face the McKenzies again, to give myself a chance to prove that I'm as good as any of them – any day. Shona said something to me. I thought and thought about it – I am going to be the broken tree that grows taller and stronger—'

She laughed at the expression of bemusement on his face and fingered a letter in her pocket, one that she had carried about with her for two days.

It was from the Rev. Mark James and in it he had written, 'Ruth, I have talked to Shona and she has told me that you haven't yet found it in you to forgive Lorn. Don't you think it's time you swallowed your pride? You've proved your point, that's obvious to everyone. I know about Lorna, what happened with you and Lewis. Lorn loved you enough to forgive you that affair with his brother. He was but a mere boy at the time but he was man enough to marry you and give your child a name. Have you ever thought that he was perhaps plunged into marriage before he was ready for it? I am not trying to excuse what he did, I am only looking at the reasons why. Lorn must have loved you very much to do what he did. He entered into marriage with forgiveness in his heart and he was mature enough spiritually to be able to do it successfully – up to a point. It's time now for you both to grow up, to give as well as take. You will be thinking that I have a cheek to lecture you on the rights and wrongs. And you would be right. Shona told you certain things about me. In my mind I have sinned as Lorn has sinned. I am human, I am as weak as the next man. Only from God do I get my strength and only from Him do I receive forgiveness. Always remember, Ruth, let he who is without sin cast the first stone. By the same token, she who agrees with this will take this letter to the fire and burn it; if not, then you are at liberty to show it to whoever you like: Mark James, your minister.'

Ruth had read and re-read the letter till she knew it off by heart and in absorbing the wisdom of the words the last layers of her pride and bitterness had peeled away leaving her feeling new and good and full of an eagerness to be reunited with her husband. With a smile she went over to the fire and taking the letter from her pocket threw it into the flames and watched it burning. Shona had planted the seeds of resolve in her heart, Mark James had nurtured them and allowed them to grow strong and upright. The children were watching each other, shyly smiling from lowered brows. Lorna's hand went out to her little brother. With a gurgle of laughter he left his father's side and allowed his sister to lead him over to the hearthrug where an assortment of toys were scattered. Soon both children were immersed in their own little world. Lorn looked at Ruth. 'I wish it could be that simple for us.'

Ruth had felt a weakness invading her ever since the moment she saw Lorn standing on her doorstep. Now a new kind of trembling weakness pervaded her limbs and in a strangely calm acceptance she realized it was a feeling brought about by an emotion of pure love for her husband, a stronger love than ever before, a love that she knew would allow her to reach out to him, take him in her arms, hold him to her breast.

'It can be that simple, Lorn, we'll make it so.' She held out her arms and he went into them to bury his dark head against her breasts. 'I want to hold you forever,' he whispered into her hair, hair that was like fine threads of spun gold and which never failed to touch him with its beauty. 'It's been so long, Ruthie, I can't believe I'm here – at last, in your arms.'

Love sprang between them like a living thing. Both were aware of the strength of it, the power of its healing, taking away all the misery and uncertainty they had both endured. Tears were flowing unchecked down Ruth's face, cleansing her, washing away all the hatred and bitterness that had lain like poison in her heart since her departure from Rhanna. The arms that held her were gentle but there was a strength in them that reminded her of how it had been in the beginning.

'I never stopped loving you, Ruthie,' he said fiercely. 'I don't know what possessed me to do what I did with——' He straightened and looked away from her, a terrible shadow of shame lying starkly over his face.

Gently she put a finger on his lips. 'Weesht, Lorn, I am just as guilty as you. There's a lot we have to talk about, but it will keep for a whily. I just want you to know that what we had was something so beautiful I couldn't bear to know another had shared it. But you must have felt like that when you found out about me and Lewis, and yet you cared enough for me to forgive me. It's all over now and I want you to promise me that never again will you look as ashamed as you did a moment ago. It doesn't sit well on McKenzie shoulders – pride, yes – shame, no.'

Lorn kissed her then, a kiss born of sheer exuberance and joy. 'We're going home,' he almost sang the words. 'C'mon bairnies, put your toys away, we're going home – to Rhanna.'

Home! The word sang in Ruth's heart. Quite unbidden the *Song of Rhanna* came to her, the words, composed by the minister, beat inside her head: 'Take me back where I belong, where the skylark sings his song . . .' Ruth shook her hair and laughed. Soon, soon she would hear again the sea's tumultuous roar, see the mist upon the corries on the bens. She reached out her hand to her little son – and he took it, shyly, his head lowered coyly on to his chest. 'Muvver.' He spoke the word hesitantly.

Lorna gazed at him thoughtfully. 'Mother,' she corrected. 'She is Mother.'

Lorn grabbed Ruth's hand and chuckled. 'Come on, Muvver, I canny wait to get you back. I crept out of the house like a thief at the crack of dawn this morning and my muvver and favver will be anxiously waiting to know what's been happening.'

Ruth wandered through all the rooms of Fàilte, touching things, hearing the echo of laughter that had once rung through the house. It was her first time in the house since her return to the island a week ago. In spite of all her apprehensions at coming back it had been a wonderful week, filled with the excitement of seeing again dear familiar faces and places. The pointing fingers that she had so dreaded had been conspicuous by their absence. Everyone was genuinely glad to have her back, her father overjoyed. She would never forget the look on his face at sight of her, he had been incredulous, laughing; tears had shone in his eyes then he had folded her into his arms to stroke her hair and murmur words of thankfulness that smote her heart with their tenderness. There had been a large bundle of mail waiting for her at Laigmhor, among them a fairly recent letter telling her that the BBC wished to adapt one of her short stories into a play for radio. It was then she confessed to Lorn that she had written a book during her exile, one so full of self-pity and loathing that she destroyed it without ever showing it to anyone.

'But do you remember the one I was writing before any of this happened? I'm going to finish it now that I'm back – and when it's done I want you to read it and let me know what you think.'

One day Old Bob had spoken seriously to both her and Lorn, telling them that he had just bought a house on the outskirts of the village. 'I will no' be needing it for a whily yet,' the old man had said with an odd little smile. 'It is yours to live in for as long as you need.' They both knew what he meant. He was telling them that he understood that they might not want to go back to living at Fàilte, and Ruth loved the old shepherd for his thoughtfulness and tact. She had harboured serious doubts about living in a house that might invoke jealous thoughts of Lorn and Rachel together there. After hearing Old Bob's offer Lorn, in a confusion of embarrassment, had told Ruth that he would never have dreamed of doing anything with another woman in a house that was so intimately connected with her. But she had to know for herself, had to go back and absorb the atmosphere of the dear little cottage sitting so serenely beneath the knoll.

Now as she stood in the bedroom she knew Lorn was telling the truth, there was no sense of shame in any of the rooms, the walls had nothing to hide. Only peace, serenity and love lay still in the house, as if waiting for its owners to come back and breathe life into it once more. A tear made her catch her breath as she stood with her hand on the back of the old tapestry couch upon which she and Lorn had made so many plans, shared so much love. 'I love you, dear little house,' she whispered then laughed aloud at the absurdity of talking in such a way to four empty walls. 'But you're not just walls and a roof to me,' she said, gazing round with affection. 'You're everything I ever wanted in my life and I canny leave you for a place that has nothing of Lorn in it or the bairns. I'm coming back to you, never you fear.'

'Can I come too?' Lorn's voice from the doorway made her jump.

'Lorn, Lorn,' she gasped. 'I didn't hear you come in.'

'No wonder, talking to empty rooms as if they could hear.'

'But they're not empty and they *can* hear,' she protested vehemently.

'Ruthie,' he laughed tenderly. 'You're profound for such a wee lass. Maybe we're both daft – but I feel the same way about the old house.'

He had come nearer, she could see the laughing depths in his blue blue eyes, saw his gaze sweeping over her face to come to rest on her mouth.

'They can not only hear,' she said firmly, 'they can speak too – and they have told me everything I wanted to know.'

'It's all right then to tell Bob that we're staying here?'

'Ay, Grant and Fiona are looking for a place, maybe Bob will let them have . . .'

The rest of her words were smothered as his lips came down to claim hers in a kiss that robbed them both of all resistance. It was the first time he had kissed her since coming back to the island. All week she had stayed with her father and Totie, feeling that she needed time to readjust after months of upheaval. After all, almost a year had passed since she had left and everything that had once been familiar to her now seemed strange. But the moment Lorn kissed her, everything fell back into place.

'Ruthie,' he whispered, 'I love you and I'll never give you cause to leave me again.' His face was wet with tears.

She took his head between her hands and gently kissed his face. He took her hand and touched it with his lips and then in a growing tide of passion they kissed over and over before breaking away to gaze at one another in a daze of longing.

'Sweet Ruth, and will you go with me, my helpmate in the woods to be?'

Her heart stood still. It was an echo of Lewis' voice, speaking to her from the past. He had quoted these selfsame verses when he had turned to her for the comfort he had so desperately needed. An unbearable sense of sadness washed over her, for time wasted, for a love she had thought was lost to her but which was here before her now, tender, real. She glanced up at the tall young man who was her husband. He had forgiven her so readily for her weaknesses and she was now able to cast away any last doubts she had harboured in her heart about him. She put her hand in his.

'Ay, Lorn, I will go with you – to the end of life itself, never never will I leave your side again.'

'Ruthie – if I tell you something will you promise not to think me – daft?'

She smiled a little. 'I promise I won't think you daft.'

'Ever since Lewis died I've had the feeling that he was by my side. Only recently did I realize he only came to me in times of danger – to warn me when something bad was about to happen. Since the accident he's been back to sort of guide me. He came to me in a dream the night before

I came to you – and it was Lewis who helped me make that decision.' He looked at her anxiously. '*Do* you think I'm daft – or do you believe me?'

'I believe you, Lorn,' she said softly. 'You were so close in life – death canny break a bond like that.'

He stumbled against her and looked ruefully down at his sticks. 'I won't feel I am truly fit till I can throw these away, I hope soon it will be possible.'

She laughed; a happy, carefree sound that was music to his ears. 'We will make a vow, Lorn – when the bluebells are on the hill we will walk together up to Brodie's Burn and paddle our feet in the trout pool – you won't need your sticks by then and I'll be there to help you.'

Gently he stroked the silken strands of hair from her brow. 'Ay, Ruthie,' he said, 'we'll do that together you and I – when the bluebells are on the hill.'

Part Six

Summer 1965

Chapter Nineteen

'Fancy the ungrateful bodach gettin' married at his age!' Kate's yell of outrage burst upon Tam's ears as he came through the door of his house.

'Ay, so you've heard the news, Kate?' Tam spoke placatingly, his eye roving over the table to see if by any chance it was set for the midday meal. But only the bare tablecloth met his gaze and he sighed resignedly, knowing it would be one of those days when he would be sent over to his daughter-in-law's house for a bite to eat.

'Ay, I've heard the news,' Kate glared at her husband accusingly. 'And second hand too! Here I am, his very own kin, and the bodach too much o' a coward to tell me himself!' Kate's nostrils flared. 'And what right have you to come in here smilin' all over your damt face? The old bugger will have made us the laughing stock o' the place. After all I've done for him too! There were times when I could have seen him far enough. He was never out from under my feets. Lookin' for privacy wi' Joe about was like lookin' for a fart on the moon! I couldny even wash my breeks but he was peerin' over my shoulder to see what I was doing.'

Tam strove to look thoughtfully nonchalant. He had often felt sorry for Joe having to be at home all day on the receiving end of Kate's none too tender tongue and he had had a quiet chortle to himself at the idea of the old man's daring, latest venture.

'Ach well,' he said indulgently. 'He has had more than enough years o' freedom and if you feel that way about him then he has done you a favour. There's no' many gets an innings like that. It is high time he settled down wi' a good woman to look to him in his auld age.'

'And was I just twiddlin' my thumbs and lettin' the old rogue fall into ruin?' demanded Kate indignantly. 'At his age it's no' as if it's Grace's charms he'll be after. Miracles is miracles but even the auldest fiddles go out o' tune wi' age. Just what can she give him that I couldny?'

Tam's eyes twinkled. 'Her bum to warm his hands against on a cold winter's night and a hoosie wi' a view o' the harbour.'

And Tam sprachled away before Kate could raise further argument. In the days preceding the wedding Kate continued to be outraged over the whole affair but when, three weeks later, Joe and Grace were married in the kirk on the Hillock, the ceremony presided over by a delighted Mark James, she could not help but be moved by the beauty and dignity of the ceremony. Old Joe was dressed in his Sunday best, a tweedy charcoal-grey suit with an enormous pink carnation decorating the old-fashioned lapels. His boots had been polished till they shone like mirrors, his whiskers brushed and smoothed, his snowy hair sparkling and neat after an enforced session at Mairi's hairdressing salon, even the little bald patch on his crown looked as if it had been newly polished.

Beside him Grace looked diminutive, her sweet face composed into serious lines but a very definite hint of a triumphant smile hovering at the corners of her mouth. The kirk was packed to capacity on a day which was very special in more ways than one to the islanders, for Lachlan had chosen the day of Grace and Joe's wedding to hold his official retirement party. It had been a deliberate move on his part. Wishing to make the day as memorable as possible for the old couple, and knowing how proud they were as regards taking gifts of money, he had arranged for all the trimmings of a true Highland wedding to be paid for by himself with the excuse that most of it was entirely for his own benefit. Only his immediate family knew of the lengths he had gone to ensure that Grace and Joe would never lose face over the matter and during the prayers Phebie looked tenderly at his bowed head, her breath catching a little with her undying love for him.

It was a blue sunlit day with tiny puffball clouds floating serenely above. The bright light of the summer's day filtered in through the stained glass window, splashing rubies on to the silvery heads of the couple at the altar. Rachel and Jon had arrived unexpectedly on last evening's boat and they were now in kirk, sitting looking very composed in one of the back pews, pointedly ignoring the craning necks and the curious glances thrown at them from all quarters. Everyone was agog to see the reaction of Lorn and Ruth to such an interesting situation but like Rachel and Jon they kept their eyes firmly to the front, seemingly engrossed in the proceedings. A kilted and extremely dignified Bob the Shepherd was acting as best man, supported by a combed and polished Captain Mac, his kilt swinging proudly round his hairy knees.

Surreptitiously Kate wiped her eyes with her hanky at sight of Old Joe's rheumaticky fingers fumbling with the ring. For the umpteenth time she wondered how Grace had managed to steer her various suitors' intentions into such amicable channels. She was peeved to think she hadn't yet managed to find out how it had all been achieved, for Grace could be as reserved as Bob when it came to personal affairs and not even the happy-go-lucky Mac had given away anything but the barest of details on the subject. Old Bob appeared sublimely happy as he kissed Grace on the cheek and planted his horny hand in Old Joe's in a congratulatory gesture. Yet the old shepherd had bought a fine cottage outside the village, and rumour had it that the investment had been a carrot to dangle in front of Grace's nose. Just recently however, Grant and Fiona McKenzie had been installed happily into the house and everyone was asking everyone else just what Bob was playing at. Captain Mac hadn't gone as far as buying a house though it was said that he had been making speculative inquiries about a houseboat that had come up for sale.

Kate poked her elbow into Tam's ribs. 'Why are the bodachs no' angry wi' Grace? Look at them all skirlin' and laughing together as if they were bosom pals.'

'Ach, go and ask them,' Tam told her in aggrieved tones, rubbing his rib cage and going to join the crowd filing out of kirk.

Kate took herself off to wait for Grace but sighed as she saw the crowd that surrounded the old couple. The newspapers had somehow got to know about the wedding and in loud voices they were asking Old Joe what it felt like to be married for the first time at the ripe old age of one hundred and four.

Joe's sea-green eyes twinkled. 'Ach well, it is too early yet to tell but I'm thinkin' it will be just sublime. I should have taken the plunge years ago but I was never findin' the right woman to suit me.' To everyone's delight he placed his hand suggestively on Grace's well-rounded bottom. 'She is just right for me, I will never have cold feets wi' Grace in bed to warm me up and she is no' likely to give me the kind o' chilblains I got from using a hot water bottle.'

Kissing Grace's blushing cheek he winked at the crowd and intoned sorrowfully, 'It is just a pity we are no' likely to have children – she would have made a bonny wee mother and that's a fact.'

The crowd skirled, the reporters jotted furiously. Some time later Grace tottered away from the ranks to sit herself on a bench outside the railings and fan herself with the corner of her dress. Seizing her chance, Kate marched over to sit beside her and say respectfully, 'If you'll be sparin' me a minute, Grace, I would like to have a wee talk wi' you.'

Aunt Grace was wearing her best hat that day, a wide-brimmed straw lavishly adorned with felt rosebuds and slightly faded pansies. Pushing it back on her silvery hair which had been elegantly coiffured by Mairi, she smiled sweetly at Kate and bade her to ask what she liked so long as it wasn't too personal.

'Well, in the first place, I'd like fine to know what made you pick Joe in favour of Mac or Bob.'

'Ach well,' began Grace placidly, 'Mac is young enough to get any lassie he fancies. He already has one in mind. Nellie is after tellin' me he is courtin' a Hanaay widow, a young woman of sixty or so. He is hopin' to persuade her to come over here to live in a houseboat wi' him. He saw a whily ago that I wasny payin' any heed to his attentions so he just went and found a younger woman.' Her eyes twinkled at Kate's astonished expression. 'As for Bob, well I must admit to havin' a hankering after him. He is such a gentleman and like Joe he's a mite too auld to want more from me than a full belly and a warm bed.' Coyly she straightened the hem of her violet-sprigged skirt. 'Joe only has one or two years left to him if he's lucky and I want to make them happy ones – besides,' she blushed girlishly, 'I aye liked the old sea dog and that's a fact. I only wish I had asked him to wed me sooner.'

'You asked him!' expostulated Kate.

'I did that,' Grace's eyes had grown dreamy. 'I knew

fine what he was after, more my house than myself but I didny care. He was dithering about that much I was feart he would die on me before he got the blessed words out so I said them for him and he accepted wi' more than a mite gratitude I can tell you.' She drew Kate a sidelong glance. 'Bob is willing to wait for me – he has bought me a bonny house and I'm no' missing the chance o' that if I can help it. The young ones will keep it fired till they get a place o' their own, but after that it will be mine and Bob's. The harbour is a fine enough place to stay if you like bustle and noise but I was used to my croft in Coll where there was that much silence you could hear the mice farting in the grass. The harbour will do me the now, my bonny new mannie just loves it there and I'll no' do anything wi' him that might put Bob off the notion of me.'

Kate threw her head back and gave vent to peals of laughter. 'By God, you old Jezebel, that you are!' she spluttered when she had regained her breath. 'Marrying one and keepin' another on a string.' She thrust her big, capable hand into Grace's dainty little one. ''Tis glad I am to welcome you into the family, Grace, and grateful to you for taking the bodach off my hands. He can be a thrawn bugger betimes and you will have an awful job gettin' the dirty drawers off his backside when you want to wash them. Mind you, he might do things for you he would never do for me and I wish you luck wi' him. I'll come over every month to shear his hair and bring him some o' my nice wee cakes but other than that I will no' interfere wi' your lives – you can take that on the word o' a McKinnon.'

She went off chuckling and Old Joe, who had come up in time to hear the tail end of the conversation, winked at Grace and they both burst into gales of merriment.

'Nice wee cakes indeed.' Old Joe wiped his eyes. 'They are one o' the reasons I wanted out the house. Every time I chewed one it stuck in my gullet and a fine way that would be to go to the Lord – choking on rock cake and no' able to tell Him I was no' yet ready to die.'

Rachel and Jon had stayed behind to talk to the minister and were only now coming out of kirk. In the excitement nobody paid them much attention, but Ruth, at the fringe of the crowd beside the door, was unable to avoid looking directly into the face of the girl who had once been her friend. Lorn had told Ruth how Rachel's patient ministrations had helped him on the road to recovery and she wasn't prepared for the upsurge of bitterness she felt in those fraught moments. Rachel's eyes were big and dark with emotion as she gazed at Ruth, her hand came out as if to touch the other's shoulder but seeing the stark expression of rejection lying like a shadow across Ruth's face she allowed her hand to fall to her side and turned quickly to Jon. He nodded and she went off in the direction of the cliffs. Ruth stood, nonplussed, feeling no triumph at having rebuffed Rachel with such ease. Jon came over and took her by the arm. 'Ruth, can we talk, I have a few things I would like to say to you.'

Ruth hesitated, looked round for Lorn. But he was engrossed along with everyone else in examining Dodie's wedding present to Joe and Grace, a great old iron telescope that weighed a ton, but which delighted Joe so much he was doing a little jig of joy round the object lying on the grass. Dodie had brought it along on a wheelbarrow and despite much prodding from everyone he simply would not give away the fact that he had found the telescope half buried in the sands of Burg Bay. Ruth looked at Jon and nodded. 'All right, Jon, though I mustny be too long. I promised to help with some last-minute decorations to the hall.'

'We will go down by the shore,' Jon said quietly. 'It is peaceful there.'

Reluctantly Ruth followed him to the quiet stretches of shore that skirted the harbour. Jon was looking sad, she thought, and her heart went out to him. He, like she, had suffered pain and heartache in the past year and she laid her hand on his arm. 'It's all right, Jon, I'm no' going to eat you. You can talk to me.'

He turned to face her squarely. 'It took a great deal of courage for Rachel to come to church today. She only did it for two reasons, one, to see her dear Old Joe married, two, to perhaps get a chance to talk things over with you.' He smiled ruefully. 'The look she saw on your face just now very effectively put an end to that, so I thought I would try to tell you some of the things that are in her heart.'

'Och, please, I don't think I am ready yet to understand the sort of things Rachel has hidden in her heart!' Ruth made to walk away but Jon's hand on her arm stayed her.

'Ruth, you and I have certain things in common. I of all people understand how you feel but I love Rachel and I think it is time you tried to understand her a bit more. You see, she has always been a very lonely girl. She lost her adored father when she was very young, ambition made her give up the only man she really ever loved – yes – I admit to that, Ruth. The only way I have been able to face the truth of it is by knowing that for me she has a special love and that no matter what happens she will in the end come back to me. I have to protect her you see, her mother has never taken a great deal of interest in her affairs so, in a way, I am the only one she can turn to in the end. Her affair with – your husband – brought her no consolation, instead she has suffered more loneliness and heartache for she cannot forgive herself for what she did to you. I live with her, I see her striving to be happy, but always there is a shadow, the shadow of Ruth, the friend whom she loved and whom she feels will never look kindly at her again. The only thing in the world she wants is to be an ordinary young woman, but her talent won't allow her to rest. She is obsessed – possessed if you like. It takes a rare type of person to understand a genius like Rachel – in me she found one – in you another . . .'

'She should have thought of that before it was too late!' Ruth cried in angry protest but Jon went on as if she hadn't spoken, telling her that Rachel could never be like other young women of her age.

'She used not to care about children – now—' he spread his hands, 'she would do anything to have beautiful babies like you, Ruth.'

'She of all people should know how to go about getting them,' said Ruth coldly.

A new kind of sadness showed in Jon's eyes. 'Rachel might not be able to have babies, Ruth. We have tried but so far we have had no luck. You are the lucky one of the two, you have been blessed with a talent for writing, but it didn't stand in the way of motherhood – your two adorable children are gifts far greater than anything Rachel might ever have.'

Ruth's kindly heart turned over. Jon had made his point well. She looked at him steadily.

'Where can I find her?'

'Over by the cliffs of Burg.'

She walked away from Jon and took the winding cliff road above the great crags of Port Rum Point. In the distance she saw Rachel walking with her head bent and in an instant knew that Jon was right. Rachel was lonely. She was beautiful, talented, widely admired, fame had brought her material gain but little else. She had no children to love, or to love her. She walked through her life, shut into a lonely existence, never to be able to express her hopes, her fears, never able to communicate with another living soul except through the medium of her hands and those wonderfully expressive eyes which bared so much of her tragically isolated soul. All at once Ruth felt herself to be the luckiest person in the whole world. She had her adored father, she had children who were her world and a husband whose love was doubly precious to her after knowing what it was like to live without it, and she had just finished a book which Lorn had read. Entranced by its warmth and power he had hugged her and made her send it off to a publisher right away.

Rachel turned then and saw her, her steps slowed, stopped, her whole attitude was one of tensed longing, of waiting.

'Rachel!' Ruth's voice was light and clear. 'Are you coming down now? The ceilidhing will be starting soon.'

Rachel came slowly, as if she couldn't quite believe what was happening. Reaching Ruth she stopped short, her eyes searching the other's face for a sign that would tell her it was all a pretence, that there could never be a reconciliation with the girl she had so wronged. But she saw only the sweet, warm expression of honesty on Ruth's face – and something else – a new strength and determination that gave the young face a rare and special kind of beauty. Rachel's lips moved, forming the name 'Ruth', a hesitant smile touched her mouth and there on the lonely windswept cliff they embraced briefly before walking side by side over the flower-strewn turf to the village nestling below.

*   *   *

Mark James stood at the kirk door smiling at the banter flying back and forth on the Hillock, then he turned inside and going to the vestry removed his robes and laid them neatly over a chair. Going out of the side door, he made his way up to the Manse where he shut himself in his study and sat for a long time at the window, staring out over the garden to the Sound of Rhanna lying beyond the cliffs of Burg. He saw the figures of two girls on the machair above Burg Bay and a little smile of triumph lit his face. His little talk with Jon and Rachel in kirk looked as if it had worked after all. Rachel had wanted to go to Ruth right away, to try to explain to her how badly she felt about everything, but he had advised Jon to talk first with Ruth. It was a situation that required more than an eloquent pair of hands to get everything into its proper perspective.

Getting up, he paced for a while then going back to the window he trained his vision on the sturdily built house down by the shore, where on a stormy day the wild Atlantic tossed its spray over the walled garden and helpings of seaweed draped themselves over bushes and gateposts. The front of the house looked out on a green oasis of machair cropped short by the cows who roamed this part of the island at will. For months now the sight of the house had evoked in him a strange sweet yearning that grew more insistent with each passing day.

The very idea of Megan Jenkins living so near filled him with a restlessness that wouldn't be stilled. She was so near and yet so far out of his reach as all his approaches had been met with politely but with decided coolness. When first she had come to the island and was finding life in the old house anything but easy, she had, after the initial polite refusals, been obliged to accept his neighbourly offers of help. He had carried coal for her, arranged for a stack of peats to be delivered to her shed, had fixed a temporary water supply to the house after first shoring up the burn that tumbled from the moors on its way to the sea.

As work progressed on the ancient building, as plumbing and other amenities became fixtures, she had required his assistance less and less so that finally there had been no excuse to go and visit her. But the more time he spent away from her the more intrigued he was by her and was actually glad one day to have Tina, his housekeeper, call her out to minister to him during a bad bout of 'flu. But the visit had been a disaster. She had been clumsy and confused, had spilled pills all over his bed and in helping her to scoop them up their heads had come together with a clatter. In a fit of humiliation she had gone to seek out Tina in order to leave medication and instructions before departing the house as hastily as she could.

Placing the palms of his hands on the windowseat he hunched his powerful frame nearer the window and saw that smoke was spiralling from her chimney. His mouth set resolutely and before he could change his mind he threw on his old tweed jacket and was soon making his way down through the Manse garden and out on to the machair atop the cliffs. The wind buffeted him, ruffling his cap of thick dark hair, stinging his ears, making him dig his hands deeper into his pockets, for although it was a warm day it was always colder up here on the crags.

Megan watched the approach of the loose-limbed, athletic figure and she tried vainly to stay the fluttering response that the sight of him never failed to invoke. In the beginning she had resented his warmhearted, well-meaning attempts to be friendly but the passage of time had changed her attitude entirely. Now she burned for a glimpse of his tall, straight figure, did everything she could to ensure that their paths crossed – and yet when they did she was so disturbed by him she always made a complete and utter fool of herself. In trying to hide her feelings, she had adopted a front that wasn't just cool, it was icy. She hated herself for it but there was no way she could behave rationally in his presence without the protection of such a façade.

All her defences were up as she intercepted him at the door, though inwardly her heart melted at the sight of his big handsome frame dressed in casual jacket and slacks, the collar of his shirt lying open at the neck, exposing a little gold wedding ring hanging on a chain. She had heard about the tragic death of his wife and child and knew that the ring must have belonged to his wife. Nevertheless it did nothing to instil the confidence into her that she so badly needed. She didn't dare look at his face, having had previous experience of the things his penetrating smoky gaze did to her reason and so she lowered her eyes as she told him rather shortly that she was just on her way out.

'This won't take a moment.' His deep, pleasant tones were clipped, and miserably she wished that he would speak to her as he had done at the start, in that lovely, warm, caring way that had so entranced her. She led the way into the sitting room. It was a small room, pleasantly furnished with chintzy sofas and brimming bookcases. Outside the window the ocean heaved and sighed, rattled the pebbles over the smooth white sands. Her eyes were very bright that day, sprinkled, he noticed, with warm gold flecks. Her shining brown hair had been cut just recently and curled inwards just below the curve of her dainty ears. Her face was sun-flushed, the skin on her arms tanned to a deep golden brown. His eyes lingered on the well-shaped contours of her mouth then he saw her watching him and with an effort he tore his gaze away. She was looking at the clock on the mantelpiece and again he spoke brusquely. 'I have something to ask you. Do you think you could spare a few moments of your time to hear me out?'

Crimson stained her cheekbones. Motioning him to sit down she placed herself on a chair some distance from his. He spoke haltingly at first but as he warmed to his subject his voice glowed with enthusiasm, his hands moved expressively. They were nice hands, she mused, strong and masculine, yet the fingers tapering – hands that could easily extract pleasing sounds from a piano – hands that could do anything they wanted – with anybody.

'Do you – would you come with me, Megan? Everybody else will have a partner of some sort and it would be far nicer than sitting on our own hoping that someone will be kind enough to dance with us. It was when I saw Old Joe and Grace today, looking so contented and happy together, that the irony of the whole thing struck me. He's well into his second century and still extracting as much as he can from life and here we are, a quarter of his age and both of us scurrying about our daily business, trying to pretend that the other doesn't exist. I think, Megan, the time has come for us to face facts.'

Her Christian name, spoken in his slow, deep voice, brought a sensation of wonder to her being. She looked at him in a daze, only comprehending part of what he was saying, the part that mattered most to her and which she could hardly take in.

'Yes, yes, Mr James. That would be fine.' She was furious with herself for sounding so stilted and prudish. She wanted to get up, behave foolishly, do a dance of joy round the room, yet all she could do was stammer out a few words and call him by his surname. Even to her own ears she sounded unbelievably stuffy and she hardly dared look at him to see what his reaction had been.

He stood up, filling her vision, overwhelming her. 'That's settled then, I'll come down for you in about an hour – and please – just call me Mark – only beings like Elspeth call me by my surname.'

She too got up and went with him to the door. He was

so close she could see the pulse beating under the bronzed skin of his neck. 'I'll – I'd better go and get ready.' She was doing it again, stammering, behaving like an awkward schoolgirl, and she glanced at him quickly to see what he was thinking. The full battery of his fascinating gaze was on her, she saw plainly the dark curve of his eyelashes – and – her heart began to pound so hard she couldn't suppress a small protesting cry – he was reaching out to her – the touch of his fingers on her bare arm so electrifying, she shivered. Without a word, he took her face in his hands to kiss her gently on the lips. She drew back as if she had been scalded, colour invaded her face, making her all at once vibrantly alive and lovely.

'How dare you do that!' she demanded angrily, though she wasn't sure if her anger was directed against him or at herself for having savoured the feel of his lips on hers.

A smile lifted the corners of his well-shaped mouth. 'I dared because I sensed you wanted it as much as I did – I told you it would only take a moment but I think you will agree with me it was a moment that was very well spent – for the two of us.'

Before she could say more he was off, his long stride taking him easily and swiftly to the sheep track leading to the cliff top. Some time elapsed before her heart returned to its normal beat and the hour that followed passed in a strangely unreal daze as she recalled over and over the warm, sweet joy of his mouth on hers.

*   *   *

A marquee had been erected on the grassy stretch between the hall and the shore. It was crammed with people helping themselves to the variety of delicacies spread out on the buffet tables while the men were already taking full advantage of the bar set up in a far corner. An enormous wedding cake reposed on a table inside the marquee, provided by a mainland bakery who had been so intrigued by the news of Old Joe's marriage they had also sent over an army of caterers for the event. The gesture was not without its ulterior motives however, as the size of the cake caused such a stir among the newspaper photographers they spent a full ten minutes and much of their film snapping it from every angle. Eventually the bridegroom was moved to a violent protest. Brandishing a large carving knife he waved it at the photographers and yelled, 'Is it blind you are? It is no' the cake who got wed today and I'll thank you to pay a bitty more attention to me and my good lady.'

The subsequent shower of flashbulbs was adequate enough to satisfy the old man's sudden thirst for fame. Beside the cake he posed with Grace and in days to come he was to cause quite a sensation over the nation's breakfast tables. The uisge beatha was flowing, the skirl of the pipes reeling through the air. It seemed everyone on the island had gathered in Portcull for the combined celebration of Joe's wedding and Lachlan's retirement. Not that everyone viewed the retirement as a reason to celebrate. It made Lachlan's farewell to his patients too heartrendingly final, and by the end of the afternoon the tears were flowing as freely as the whisky, though everyone pulled themselves together when a move was made from the marquee into the hall where the dance and ceilidh were to take place.

Here an even greater effort than usual had been made to cover up the hall's rather sombre and sadly neglected decor. Huge bunches of brightly coloured balloons hung from the rafters, the platform where the presentations were to take place was gay with streamers and banners of every description. Barra had loaned some of her picturesque little watercolours to hang on the walls along with several of Dugald's humorous sketches of wildlife of the area. As these included caricatures of Tam and his cronies, caught in various stages of inebriation crawling through the heather, the hall was soon in an uproar of laughter which reached a crescendo as the real thing came staggering through the door in ones and twos. The night that followed was to be one of the most memorable in the minds of everyone present. Joe and his new wife led the dancing, followed by Lachlan and Phebie. During the course of the evening Lorn found himself dancing with his mother.

'You'll have to hold me up,' he grinned, 'I'm still unsteady without my sticks.'

'Hold you up indeed,' she said firmly. 'You don't need them anymore, Lorn, soon you'll be throwing them away.'

He looked at her thoughtfully. 'Ay, you might be right at that, Mother, I think they've become more a habit than anything.' He glanced round the room, looking for Ruth and saw her in the arms of Grant who was making her do a reel while everyone else was dancing a waltz. In the middle of the floor Fiona was hooching and skirling, completely past the stage of knowing which leg was supposed to be doing which. Lorn threw back his head and laughed. 'Our new parents are letting their hair down tonight, Fiona is fleeing in more ways than one.'

'It's so good to see you laughing again, Lorn,' Kirsteen observed and in a mood of abandonment he grabbed her and kissed the tip of her nose. She felt good and happy, everything had fallen back into place, Ruth and Lorn and the children were all back together again, Grant and Fiona were settling in happily to island life. She would never tell Lorn that both she and Fergus had heard him moving about the house on that fateful morning of his taking Douglas to Ruth. Her first instinct had been to rise and go and find out if anything was wrong, but Fergus had pushed her back and told her to let their son go his own way. If Lorn didn't do it then he never would and he would blame them for standing in his way.

Lorn went off to join his younger companions and Kirsteen floated into Fergus' embrace. He nuzzled her hair. 'Mmm, you smell lovely tonight, and you look lovely too.'

She studied his handsome strong face and her breath caught in her throat. 'I love you, McKenzie o' the Glen. We've had an eventful married life but it's been so rich and fulfilling because you've always been at my side.'

His arm tightened round her, his black eyes looked deep

into hers. 'Mo cridhe,' he said huskily, 'do I detect a wee bitty sadness in your voice on this night of nights?'

She nodded. 'Ay, just a wee bit. We've come a long way, you and I, and each day seems to go faster and faster, there's no holding back time any longer. Phebie and Lachlan too, it's so strange to think that he's retired now, yet when first we knew them both they were young, just starting off really – like us.'

His eyes had grown strangely shiny. 'I know fine what you mean, mo cridhe, but just remember: "grow old along with me, the best is yet to be, the last of life for which the first was made".'

She buried her face in his shoulder. 'Oh, Fergie, you're being a poet again, I love it when you drop all that tough façade you show to the world and say beautiful things.'

He looked around at the familiar faces that surrounded them. 'It's a night for poetry, it's a night for many things – but most of all – it's a night for love.'

Phebie and Lachlan too were in a pensive mood. He put his arms tightly round her warm soft waist and whispered 'Phebie, can I tell you how much you've always meant to me, all through our years together you've stood by me, helped in every way you could. I would never have reached this stage in life if it hadn't been for you.'

'Lachy,' she touched the unruly lock of hair on his brow 'we could never have reached this stage if we hadn't helped each other. I look back and I remember all the love we've had and I feel so lucky. Do you remember that day

Sauchiehall Street? I was rushing along, not even aware that a man called Lachlan McLachlan existed . . .'

'Ay, it was fate or something of the kind that made us bump into each other,' he said, his eyes misty with reminiscence. He stumbled against her and laughed. 'And we're still bumping into each other, come closer, so that I can hold you tighter and keep you safe.'

Shona and Niall watched their respective parents locked away in worlds of their own. 'They're re-living things they've shared,' Shona said with a soft little smile. 'How I love those four people. They have always been there when we needed them. Now they are as alone as they were in the beginning, all their families married with lives of their own.'

Niall's brown eyes were tender. 'It's time they all had a bit of a rest from us – and yet, we'll go on needing them in the future, parents are parents for the rest of their lives.'

'Ay, Niall, like us. I hope our wee Ellie will always feel she can turn to us when she needs help – and—' she looked at him through her lashes, 'I hope too that our son will feel the same in years to come.'

He frowned. 'But we haven't got a . . .' He stared at her incredulously. 'You're not – don't tell me . . .'

She pulled him to her and laughed. 'Ay, Niall, I am, around Christmas I think. If we're lucky it might be a son – Santa might bring him down the lum in his sack.'

Niall was so stunned he sat down suddenly pulling her with him. 'Mrs McLachlan, I want you to repeat all that very very slowly and then I would be grateful if you could go and fetch me a large whisky to steady my nerves!'

Robbie and Barra, walking arm in arm along the harbour on their way to the hall, came upon Dodie having the wits scared out of him by a leering Canty Tam, recounting gory tales of murder and magic most foul. Dodie was looking even more mournful than usual and Robbie, after sending Canty Tam on his way with a few sharp words, said kindly, 'What ails you, Dodie? Are you no' goin' in for the ceilidhing? I would have thought you would have wanted to see Lachlan bein' handed all his bonny retiral presents.'

'I canny go in like this!' Dodie wailed, scrubbing his nose with the back of a grimy hand. 'I had to tramp miles to give Ealasaid her potach and now there will no' be time to go back to my hoosie and change. I have a wee something I wanted to give Lachlan too.'

Robbie looked at his wife and they both nodded in unison. 'You're comin' back to our house,' Robbie said decidedly, leading a protesting Dodie by the arm. 'Och, c'mon now, man, just do as you are told for once in your life. I have a bonny jacket and trousers that you can borrow if you feel you canny bring yourself to keep them.'

Once inside the cosy harbour house, Robbie speedily divested the old eccentric of his smelly outer layers, took him to the scullery where he made him scrub the dirt from his face and hands before bundling him into fresh clothing.

Barra came bustling through from the bedroom with a pair of stout shoes in her hands.

'Take off your wellingtons and put these on,' she ordered kindly.

Dodie turned a bright crimson. 'I canny!' he wailed. 'I have holes in my socks and I haveny had a chance to wash my feets for a whily.'

Patiently Barra went to fetch clean socks and after gulping in a few deep breaths of wholesome air she joined her husband in the battle to get the big knobbly boots from Dodie's feet. They heaved and groaned while Dodie sat in helpless red-faced embarrassment. Just as they were thinking they would have to give up, the great wellingtons came away with a loud sucking sound and both Barra and Robbie went flying backwards to land with some surprise on the rug. The released smells from the boots drifted into all the lavender-smelling corners of the clean little house and without more ado Robbie pushed socks and shoes at Dodie and bade him put them on as quickly as he knew how.

His body enclosed in the size too small clothes, with his cap removed and his baby fine hair slicked down with water, Dodie looked as presentable as he ever would and, each taking one of his long arms, Barra and Robbie hustled him outside and along to the hall without further ado.

Leading him straight over to Lachlan and Phebie sitting together on a bench, they nudged him and in some confusion he produced an untidily wrapped package from somewhere in the regions of his vest. 'It's no' much,' he explained with his usual reticence. 'I found it on the shore just after Grant's bairnie was born – but – I thought it would be just the thing to be remindin' you of all the babies you have delivered into the world. I polished it up a wee bitty to preserve it for it was dead as an old bone the way it was.'

Lachlan pulled back the paper to reveal a piece of driftwood shaped exactly like a baby lying in the foetal position in a little nest of polished wood. The features of the child held all the wondrous innocence of new creation, its little arms were crossed over its chest, its fists curled under its chin. It was the most exquisitely natural piece of sculpture that Lachlan had ever seen. Dodie's 'wee bitty polish' had been lavished on it with a love and care that must have taken many painstaking nights of work to bring the white wood to its present delicate sheen. On the base of it Dodie had lovingly scratched, 'To Doctor Lachlan – a grandson. from D.' It sounded exactly like a notice from a birth column, one so full of unworldly nuances that Lachlan felt an unexpected lump rising in his throat. Getting up he threw his arm across Dodie's bent back.

'Biddy was right about you, Dodie, you seem to know instinctively just what to give to a body. You were blessed with a precious gift of insight that few people have and because of that you are indeed a man blessed by God.' His voice was husky. The expression of gratitude on the old man's face was utterly touching. 'Don't look so grateful, man, it is me who is feeling that in full measure. Your bonny gift will have pride o' place in my den. I will look at it and I'll remember all the innocent wee cratur's I helped into the world and I will also remember you, Dodie, and bless you.'

Dodie was overwhelmed. Tears fell out of his strange grey-green eyes and dripped down his chin. 'I'll miss ye, ay, I will that, you were aye that good to me when I wasny feelin' like myself.'

Lachlan fumbled in his pocket and produced a length of tobacco. 'Here, you take this baccy and enjoy it and if you'll be coming over to the bar wi' me I will be honoured if you'll have a good stiff dram with a man who has just been given the gift of a grandson who will never grow old.'

A short time later the laird arrived to preside over the presentation. There were gifts galore from the villagers to Old Joe and Grace, a long, humorous, affectionate speech to Lachlan along with a beautiful, ornate mantelclock, fishing rods and basket and, because news had leaked out that he was writing a book about his experiences as an island GP, a portable typewriter complete with carrying case. Phebie was showered with flowers and gifts of a feminine nature and just when it seemed the pair were about to erupt into tears the laird handed Lachlan a new battery for his car. Tears changed to laughter, echoed by everyone in the hall.

Lachlan's temperamental old car was a standing joke among the islanders and whenever he was late anywhere everyone shook their heads and told each other, 'It will be thon mad wee car o' his playing up again. It only starts if it is in a good mood.'

Lachlan looked around at the sea of well-kent faces before him. Tears of laughter and pain shone in his brown gentle eyes, the eyes into which countless of his patients had gazed in their dying moments to see mirrored in them love, compassion and a reassurance so full of faith they were able to go on their last, final journey without fear.

He shook his head. 'I – don't know what to say. I've made many speeches in my time but never before have I felt so – overwhelmed – not only in the things you've given to me and to Phebie – but by the love and caring behind each gift. I know you all so well—' A smile lit his thin face. 'Ay, every last part of you . . .' He paused to allow the laughter and banter to die down. 'You can be a gey thrawn lot when the mood takes you but I know that behind every dour, bonny face, there lies a heart as big as a house and if I was to change the name of this island I think I would have to call it Hospitality Island. I will miss you, but I'll be thinking of you whenever I look at my mantelpiece and see this truly grand clock and when I'm out on the water with my rods. But I warn you now, if my book ever gets finished and even more to the point, if it ever gets published, you needny think I'm going to share the proceeds with you.'

He drew Phebie forward. 'Here's the bonny lass who will be sharing with me anything I have. She more than me deserves a long long holiday. I call her my bonny plump rose. There was a time when she would have hit me over the head with a spurtle for calling her any such thing.' He smiled at his blushing wife. 'But I know you will agree with me that, not only has she been my right hand man all these years, she has been a comfort to every patient who ever walked through my door for no matter how she was feeling herself she never failed to have a smile for everyone.'

There were cheers and whistles, many of the womenfolk held hankies to their eyes.

'Mercy, mercy me,' Kate blew her nose loudly. 'Is he no' a bonny mannie just? I'd like fine to run up there and throw my arms about his dear, kind shoulders.'

Elspeth was crying hardest of all, quite unable to help herself she burst into loud sobs and spluttered out, 'Never the likes o' him will we see on this island again, never, never. 'Tis glad I am that he and Phebie are allowing me to carry on working to them. Wi' me being one o' the family they just couldny bring themselves to let me go.'

'Here, look,' Mollie nudged Kate. 'He is asking Doctor Megan up to the platform.'

Lachlan had gone down into the crowd, from it extracting a red-faced, protesting Megan, leading her up to the platform and holding up his hand. She was looking exceedingly attractive that evening in a softly flowing blue dress that showed her slender figure and shapely legs to advantage. The men looked at one another and commented favourably on her appearance but it was Mark James, the minister, who was most appreciative of all. He stood tall above the crowd, his eyes seeking Megan's, throwing glances of reassurance that helped in some measure to steady her shaky legs.

Lachlan took Megan's hand and smiled at her affectionately, then he looked all round the hall, taking in all the faces so that they felt personally included in what he was about to say. 'I give you your new doctor – Megan Jenkins. I know from personal experience how hard it is to come to an insular community like this and to try to be accepted.' His brows came down and he glared with mock severity at the gathering. 'You all gave me a buggering hard time of it and Phebie an even worse one because she didn't have a word of the Gaelic. You've done the same with Megan . . .' A murmur went round and Lachlan grinned. 'Oh yes you have and you needny try to deny it but I also know that in the short time she's been here she's made more progress than I did in several years, and I for one think that is an achievement which deserves three hearty cheers.'

The hall cheered willingly, swept along on a tide of delighted enthusiasm. Lachlan called Babbie up beside him and the cheers became deafening roars. Grace and Joe were recalled to the scene and stood holding hands and blushing much to the delight of everyone.

'Charge your glasses everyone,' Lachlan cried and there was a rush as everyone willingly obeyed. He held up his glass. 'Here's to our newly married couple, may they have a long and happy life, here's to you all and may all your ails be little ones so that Megan will have a long and happy life.' There were smiles and nudges. 'And here's to all our departed friends – in particular one who sat on this very same platform not so many years ago to receive her MBE, a reward she so richly deserved for her services to this community – will you join me in a toast – to Biddy.'

'To Biddy!' echoed the laird and the beloved and well-remembered name rang and bounced round the hall. The hankies were out again, tears and laughter mingled.

Seizing her chance to escape, Megan retreated from the platform, helped gallantly by a waiting Mark James.

'Here, do you see that?' Behag's beady eyes were riveted on the two, trying to melt unobtrusively into the background.

'I have thought as much this whily back,' supplemented Kate eagerly. 'They were just a mite too cool to each other for it to be natural.'

'Well, my my,' nodded a round-eyed Todd. 'Who will be marryin' the minister? He canny very well marry himself.'

Further speculation was drowned in a burst of singing that suddenly soared to the rafters. All faces were turned to the platform as the strains of 'Keep Right On to the End of the Road' rang forth. It was a moving and never-to-be-forgotten moment. Phebie's eyes were wet, Lachlan's shiny with gratitude.

Lorn took Ruth's hand. 'I think the time has come for us to make that trip up to Brodie's Burn.'

She watched him propping his sticks in a corner and

nodded her flaxen hair. 'Ay, I think you're right,' she agreed softly and held out her arm to him.

As they left the hall the well-known notes of 'Will Ye No' Come Back Again' soared up from within.

'We're no' goin' anywhere,' hiccuped Tam who, with a few of his contemporaries, was lounging lopsidedly on the steps at the door.

It was a warm, fragrant evening, with cottonwool clouds sailing in a blue, endless sky. Lorn looked up and smiled. Lewis would have called it a fluffy cloud night. He seemed very close as Lorn walked with Ruth up to the green slopes that led to Brodie's Burn. Lorn took a deep breath and straightened his shoulders. His face, now bronzed and healthy as it had been before his accident, was lit with a glow that came from deep within his soul. He felt strong and happy, Ruthie was by his side, her hair a sheaf of gold against the great ball of the sinking sun. The hills and woods were carpeted with so many bluebells they looked like blue grass from a distance. Ranks of them flanked the banks of the burn tumbling down from the bens, onwards they marched, blue scented, beautiful. Lorn climbed steadily, feeling that he could never tire.

When they reached the Seanachaidh's Stone they sat on its sun-warmed surface and holding hands gazed down at the panorama spread below. The dear green land that was their home lay stretched out in undulations of purest greens and misted blues; the Sound of Rhanna sparkled like a sapphire; little puffs of peat smoke spiralled from the chimneys of the white sugar lump cottages around the bay; the purling of the burn was music that blended with the tumbling song of the skylark; fish jumped in the umber-coloured trout pool beneath the stones; the dew-fresh fingers of young ferns were slowly unfurling among the massed white flowerets of wild carrot which fought the bluebells for supremacy.

'Ruthie, Ruthie,' Lorn put his arm round her and drew her in close. 'I feel truly blessed to have all this – and above all – you.'

Ruth put her head on his shoulder and hugged her knees. Lorn was warm and hard beside her, the hills of her home were at her feet. Far, far in distant glens a cuckoo was calling, the evocative sound of it mingling with the bubbling song of the curlew from the meadows down below. A bubble of pure happiness burst out of her heart, and it seemed to her, as she sat on the Seanachaidh's Stone with the man she loved, that a haunting melody pulsed against the hills. A little cry of joy escaped her for she knew, as surely as she knew night from day, that the song which was borne to her on the summer breezes whispering down from the hilltops could only be the poignant, unforgettable strains of the *Song of Rhanna*.